MY·NEW
CURATE

MY
NEW CURATE

By The Very Rev.
P. A. Canon SHEEHAN, D.D.

THE MERCIER PRESS
CORK AND DUBLIN

The Mercier Press, 4 Bridge Street, Cork.
24 Lower Abbey Street, Dublin 1.

This edition 1989

ISBN 0 85342 877 8

Printed by Leinster Leader Ltd., Naas, Co. Kildare.

*N*OTE

" My New Curate " originally appeared as a serial in the " American Ecclesiastical Review."

Contents

viii.   CONTENTS

MY NEW CURATE

CHAPTER I

THE CHANGE

It is all my own fault. I was too free with my tongue.
I said in a moment of bitterness: " What can a Bishop
do with a parish priest? He's independent of him." It
was not grammatical, and it was not respectful. But the
bad grammar and the impertinence were carried to his
Lordship, and he answered: " What can I *do*? I can
send him a curate who will break his heart in six weeks."

I was not too much surprised, then, when one evening my dear old friend and curate, Father Tom Laverty,
came to me, with tears in his eyes, and an open letter in
his hand:—

" I am off, Father Dan. Look at this! "

It was a succinct, laconic order to present himself to
a parish priest twenty miles distant, and to be in time to
discharge his duties in that parish the following Saturday
and Sunday, for his jurisdiction was transferred, etc.

It was a hard stroke. I was genuinely attached to
Father Tom. We had the same tastes and habits—easy,
contented, conservative, with a cordial dislike of innovations of any kind. We held the same political opinions,
preached the same sermons, administered the Sacraments
in the old way, and had a reverence for antiquities in
general. It was a sad break in my life to part with him;
and it is a harmless vanity on my part to say that he
was sorry to part from me.

" I suppose there's no help for it? " said he.

" No," said I; " but if you care—— "

" No use," said he; " when *he* has made up his mind
you might as well be talking to a milestone."

" And you must be off to-morrow? " said I, consulting the bishop's letter.

" Yes," said he, " short shrift."

" And who am I getting? " I wondered.

" Hard to guess," said he.   He was in no humour for
conversation.

The following week, that most melancholy of proces-
sions, a curate's furniture *en route*, filed slowly through
the village, and out along the highroad, that led through
bog and fen, and by lake borders to the town of N——.
First came three loads of black turf, carefully piled and
roped; then two loads of hay; a cow with a yearling calf;
and lastly, the house furniture, mostly of rough deal.
The articles, that would be hardly good enough for one
of our new labourers' cottages, were crowned by a kitchen
table, its four legs pointing steadily to the firmament,
like an untrussed fowl's, and between them, carefully
roped, was the plague and the pet of the village, Nanny
the goat, with her little kid beside her.   What Nanny
could not do in the way of mischief was so insignificant
that it need not be told.   But the Celtic vocabulary, particularly rich in expletives, failed to meet the ever-growing
vituperative wants of the villagers.   They had to fall
back on the Saxon, and call her " a rep," " a rip," " de
ribble," etc., etc.   I walked side by side with Father
Laverty, who, with head bent on his breast, scarcely
noticed the lamentations of the women, who came to
their cross-doors, and poured out a Jeremiad of lamentations that made me think my own well-meant ministrations were but scantily appreciated.

" Wisha, God be wid you, Father, wherever you go! "

" Wisha, may your journey thry wid you.   Sure 'tis
we'll miss you! "

" Yerra, what'll the poor do now, whin he's gone? "

" Bishop, inagh, 'tis aisy for him wid his ring and his
mitre, and his grand carriage.   Couldn't he let him
alone? "

"Father," said a young girl, earnestly, her black hair blinding her eyes, "may God be with you." She ran after him. "Pray for me," she whispered. "You don't know all the good you done me." She hadn't been very sensible.

He turned towards her.

"Yes! Nance, I'll remember you. And don't forget all that I told you."

He held out his hand. It was such an honour, such a condescension, that she blushed scarlet: and hastily rubbing her hand in her apron, she grasped his.

"May God Almighty bless you," she said.

But the great trial came when we were passing the school-house. It was after three o'clock, the time for breaking up: and there at the wall were all the little boys and the *sheilas* with their wide eyes full of sorrow. He passed by hastily, never looking up. His heart was with these children. I believe the only real pleasure he ever allowed himself was to go amongst them. teach them. amuse them, and listen to their little songs. And now——

"Good-bye, Father—— "

"Good-bye, Father—— "

Then, Alice Moylan gave a big "boo-hoo!" and in a moment they were all in tears; and I, too, began to wink, in a queer way, at the landscape.

At last, we came to the little bridge that humps itself over the trout stream. Many a summer evening we had made this the terminus of our. evening's walk; for I was feeble enough on my limbs, though my head is as clear as a boy's of seventeen. And here we used to lean over the parapet, and talk of all things, politics, literature (the little we knew of it), the old classics, college stories, tales of the mission, etc.; and now we were to part.

"Good-bye, Father Tom," I said. "You know, there's always a bite and a sup and a bed, whenever you come hither. Good-bye. God knows, I'm sorry to part with you."

"Good-bye," he said. Not another word. I watched
and waited, till I saw the melancholy procession fade
away, and until he became a speck on the horizon. Then,
with a heavy heart I turned homewards.

If I had the least doubt about the wonderful elasticity.
of the Irish mind, or its talent for adaptation, it would
have been dispelled as I passed again through the village. I had no idea I was so popular, or that my little
labours were so warmly appreciated.

"Well, thank God, we have *himself* whatever."

Gentle reader, " himself " and " herself " are two pro-
nouns, that in our village idioms mean the master and
mistress of the situation, beyond whom there is no appeal.

"Wisha, the Lord spare him to us. God help us, if
he wint."

"The heads of our Church, God spare them long!
Wisha, your reverence might have a copper about you
to help a poor lone widow? "

I must say this subtle flattery did not raise my drooped
spirits. I went home, sat down by my little table, and
gave myself up to gloomy reflections.

It must have been eight o'clock, or more, for the twilight had come down, and my books and little pictures
were looking misty, when a rat-tat-tat rang at the door.
I didn't hear the car, for the road was muddy, I suppose; but I straightened myself up in my arm-chair, and
drew my breviary towards me. I had read my Matins
and Lauds for the following day, before dinner; I always
do, to keep up the old tradition amongst the Irish priests,
but I read somewhere that it is always a good thing to
edify people who come to see you. And I didn't want
anyone to suspect that I had been for a few minutes
asleep. In a moment, Hannah, my old housekeeper,
came in.   She held a tiny piece of card between her
fingers, which were carefully covered with her check
apron, lest she should soil it. I took it—while I asked—

"Who is it? "

"I don't know, your reverence."

" Is't a priest? "

" No, but I think he's a gintleman," she whispered.
" He talks like the people up at the great house."

She got a candle, and I read:—

Rev. Edward Letheby, B.A., C.C.

" 'Tis the new curate," I said.

" Oyeh," said Hannah, whose dread and admiration for
the " strange gintleman " evaporated when she found
he was a mere curate.

I went out and welcomed with what warmth I could
my new co-operator. It was too dark for me to see what
manner of man he was; but I came to some rapid conclusions from the way he spoke. He bit off his words, as
riflemen bite their cartridges, he chiselled every conso-
nant, and gave full free scope to every vowel. This was
all the accent he had, an accent of prevision and determination and formalism, that struck like a knell, clear
and piercing on my heart.

" I took the liberty of calling, sir," he said, " and I
hope you will excuse my troubling you at such an un-
seasonable hour; but I am utterly unacquainted with the
locality, and I should be thankful to you if you would
refer me to a hotel."

" There's but one hotel in the village," I replied
slowly. " It has also the advantage of being the post-
office, and the additional advantage of being an emporium
for all sorts of merchandise, from a packet of pins to
Reckitt's blue, and from pigs' crubeens to the best Limerick flitches. There's a conglomeration of smells," I
continued, " that would shame the City on the Bos-
phorus; and there are some nice visitors there now in
the shape of two Amazons who are going to give selec-
tions from ' Maritana ' in the school-house this evening;
and a drunken acrobat, the leavings of the last circus."

" Good heavens," he said, under his breath.

I think I astonished him, as I was determined to do.
Then I relented, as I had the victory.

" If, however," said I, " you could be content with

the humble accommodation and poor fare that this poor presbytery affords, I shall be delighted to have you as my guest, until you can secure your own little domicile."

" I thank you very much, Sir," said he, " you are extremely kind. Would you pardon me a moment, whilst I dismiss the driver and bring in my portmanteau? "

He was a little humbled and I was softened. But I was determined to maintain my dignity.

He followed me into the parlour, where the lamp was now lighting, and I had a good opportunity of observing him. I always sit with my back to the light, which has the double advantage of obscuring my own features and lighting up the features of those whom I am addressing. He sat opposite me, straight as an arrow. One hand was gloved; he was toying gently with the other glove. But he was a fine fellow. Fairly tall, square-shouldered, not a bit stout, but clean cut from head to spur, I thought I should not like to meet him in a wrestling bout, or try a collision over a football. He had a mass of black hair, glossy and curled, and parted at the left side. Large, blue-black luminous eyes, that looked you squarely in the face, were hardly as expressive as a clear mouth that now in repose seemed too quiet even for breathing. He was dressed *ad*——. Pardon me, dear reader, I have had to brush up my classics, and Horace is like a spring eruption. There was not a line of white visible above his black collar; but a square of white in front, where the edges parted. A heavy chain hung from his vest; and his boots glistened and winked in the lamplight.

" You'll take something? " I said. " You have had a long drive."

" If not too much trouble," he said, " I'll have a cup of tea."

I rang the bell.

" Get a cup of tea, Hannah," I said.

" A cup of wha—at? " queried Hannah. She had the usual feminine contempt for men that drink tea.

" A cup of tea," I said decisively, "and don't be long."

" Oyeh! " said Hannah. But she brought in a few minutes later the tea and hot cakes that would make an alderman hungry, and two poached eggs on toast. I was awfully proud of my domestic arrangements. But I was puzzled. Hannah was not always so courteous. She explained next day.

" I didn't like him at all, at all," she said, " but whin I came out and saw his portmanty all brass knobs, and took up his rug, whew! it was that soft and fine it would do to wrap up the Queen, I said to myself, ' This is a gintleman, Hannah; who knows but he's the Bishop on his tower.' "

" I hope you like your tea? " I said.

" It's simply delicious," he answered.

He ate heartily. Poor fellow, he was hungry after a long drive; but he chewed every morsel as a cow would chew the cud on a lazy summer afternoon, without noise or haste, and he lifted my poor old china cup as daintily as if it were Sèvres. Then we fell to talking.

" I am afraid," I said tentatively, " that you'll find this place dull after your last mission. But have you been on the mission before? "

" Oh yes, Father," he said, " I thought the Bishop might have written to you."

" Well," I said, " I had reason to know you were coming; but the Bishop is rather laconic in his epistles. He prides himself on his virtue of reticence."

I said this, because it would never do to let him suppose that the Bishop would send me a curate without letting me know of it. And I thought I was using select language, an opinion which, after the nine years and more of Horace, I have no reason to alter.

" My only mission hitherto," he said, " has been in Manchester, at St. Chad's. It was a populous mission, and quite full of those daily trials and contingencies that make life wearisome to a priest. I confess I was not sorry to have been called home."

" But you had society," I interjected, " and unless you

wish to spend an hour at the constabulary barracks, you
must seek your society here in an occasional *conversazione*
with some old woman over her cross-door, or a chat with
the boys at the forge—— "

" But I have got my books, Father," he said, " and I
assure you I want some time to brush up the little I have
ever read. I haven't opened a serious book for seven
years."

This was candid; and it made me warm towards him.

" Then," I said, " there's no use in preaching fine
English sermons, they won't be understood. And you
must be prepared for many a night call to mountain
cabins, the only access to which is through a bog or the
bed of a mountain stream; and your income will reach
the princely sum of sixty pounds per annum. But," I
added hastily, " you'll have plenty of turf, and oats and
hay for your horse, an occasional pound of butter, and
you'll have to export all the turkeys you'll get at Christmas."

" You have painted the lights and shadows, Father,"
he said cheerily, " and I am prepared to take them together. I am sure I'll like the poor people. It won't be
my fault."

Then my heart rose up to this bright, cheery, handsome fellow, who had no more pride in him than a bare-
legged gossoon; and who was prepared to find his pleasure amongst such untoward surroundings. But I didn't
like to let myself out as yet. I had to keep up some show
of dignity.

My education commenced next morning. He had
served my Mass, and said his own in my little oratory;
and he came down to breakfast, clean, alert, happy. I
asked him how he had slept.

" Right well," he said, " I never woke till I heard
some far-off bell in the morning."

" The six o'clock bell at the great house," I replied.
" But where are you going? "

" Nowhere, Sir," said he, " I understood I was to re-main over Sunday."

" But you're shaved? " said I.

" Oh yes," he said, with the faintest ripple of a smile. " I couldn't think of sitting down to breakfast, much less of celebrating the Holy Sacrifice, without shaving."

" And you have a clean collar. Do you mean to say you change your collar every morning? "

" Certainly, Sir," he said.

" Poor Father Tom! " I exclaimed mentally, " this is a change." But I said nothing; but sent out my razors in the afternoon to be set.

There was a letter from the Bishop. It ran thus:—

My Dear Father Dan:—I have thought it necessary to make a change of curates in your parish. I have removed Father Laverty on promotion; and I am sending you one of the most promising young priests in my diocese. He has just returned from England, where he won golden opinions from the people and the priests. I may mention that he was an exhibitioner under the Intermediate System; and took a gold medal for Greek. Perhaps you will stimulate him to renew his studies in that department, as he says he has got quite rusty from want of time to study. Between you both, there will be quite an Academia at Kilronan.

Yours in Christ.

" Clever, my Lord," I soliloquized, " clever! " Then, as the " gold medal in Greek " caught my eye again, I almost let the letter fall to the ground; and I thought of his Lordship's words: " I can send him a curate who will break his heart in six weeks." But as I looked over my cup at Father Letheby, I couldn't believe that there was any lurking *diablerie* there. He looked in the morning a frank, bright, cheery, handsome fellow. But, will he do?

CHAPTER II

A RETROSPECT

Long ago, when I used to read an occasional novel, if the author dared to say: " But I am anticipating; we must go back here twenty years to understand the thread of this history," I invariably flung down the book in disgust. The idea of taking you back to ancient history when you were dying to know what was to become of the yellow-haired Blumine, or the grand chivalrous Roland. Well, I am just going to commit the very same sin; and, dear reader, be patient just a little while.

It is many years since I was appointed to the parish of Kilronan. It happened in this wise. The Bishop, the old man, sent for me; and said, with what I would call a tone of pity or contempt, but he was incapable of either, for he was the essence of charity and sincerity:—

" Father Dan, you are a bit of a littérateur, I understand. Kilronan is vacant. You'll have plenty of time for poetizing and dreaming there. What do you say to it?"

I put on a little dignity, and, though my heart was beating with delight, I quietly thanked his Lordship. But, when I had passed beyond the reach of episcopal vision, which is far stretching enough, I spun my hat in the air, and shouted like a schoolboy: " Hurrah!"

You wonder at my ecstasies! Listen. I was a dreamer, and the dream of my life, when shut up in musty towns, where the atmosphere was redolent of drink, and you heard nothing but scandal, and saw nothing but sin—the dream of my life was a home by the sea, with its purity

and freedom, and its infinite expanse, telling me of God.
For, from the time when as a child the roar of the surges
set my pulse beating, and the scents of the weed and the
brine would make me turn pale with pleasure, I used to
pray that some day, when my life's work would be nearly
done, and I had put in my years of honest labour in the
dusty streets, I might spend my declining years in the
peace of a seaside village, and go down to my grave,
washed free from the contaminations of life in the daily
watching and loving of those

> " Moving waters at their priestlike task
> Of pure ablution round earth's human shores."

My wish was realized, and I was jubilant.

Returning home by train, when my emotion had
calmed down, my mind could not help recurring to the
expression used by the Bishop; and it suggested the following reflections: How has it come to pass in Ireland
that " poet " and " saint " are terms which denote some
weakness or irregularity in their possessors? At one time
in our history we know that the bard was second only to
the King in power and influence; and are we not vaguely
proud of that title the world gives us—Island of Saints?
Yet, nowadays, through some fatal degeneracy, a poet is
looked upon as an idealist, an unpractical builder of airy
castles, to whom no one would go for advice in an important matter, or intrust with the investment of a five-
pound note. And to speak of a man or woman as a
" saint " is to hint at some secret imbecility, which it
would be charitable to pass over in silence. I was quite
well aware, therefore, on that day, when I had the secret
pleasure and the sublime misfortune of seeing my name
in print over some wretched verses, that I was ruining
my prospects in life. The fact of being a littérateur,
although in the most modest and hidden manner, stamped
me as a volatile, flighty creature, who was no more to be
depended upon than a feather in the wind; or, as the

Italians say, *qu' al piume al vento*. It is a curious prejudice, and a purely insular one. And sometimes I think, or rather I used to think, that there was something infinitely grotesque in these narrow ideas, that shut us out from sympathy with the quick moving, subtle world as completely as if we were fakirs by the banks of the sacred Ganges. For what does modern literature deal with? Exactly those questions of philosophy, ethics, and morality which form the staple material of theological studies and discussion in our own colleges and academies. Novels, poetry, essays, lectures, treatises on the natural sciences —all deal with the great central questions of man's being, his origin, and his conduct. And surely it is folly to ignore these discussions in the market places of the world, because they are literature, and not couched in scholastic syllogisms. Dear me! I am philosophizing—I, old Daddy Dan, with the children plucking at my coat-tails and the brown snuff staining my waist-coat, and, ah, yes! the place already marked in my little chapel, where I shall sleep at last. I must have been angry, or gloomy, that day, thirty years ago, when I stepped on the platform at M—— after my interview with the Bishop, and met my friends, who had already become aware that I was elevated out of the junior ranks, and had become an independent officer of the Church Militant.

" You don't mean to say that you have accepted that awful place? " said one.

" You'll have nothing but fish to eat," said another. " The butcher's van goes there but once a week."

" And no society but fishermen," said a third. " And they speak nothing but Irish, and you know you cannot bless yourself in Irish."

" Well," I replied, " my Job's comforters, I have accepted Kilronan, and am going there. If all things go well, and you are good boys, I may ask for some of you as curate—— "

" You'll be glad to get a curacy yourself in six months," they shouted in chorus.

And so I came to Kilronan, and here have I been since.
The years have rolled by swiftly. Life is a coach, whose
wheels move slowly and painfully at the start; but, once
set moving, particularly when going down the deep decline of life, the years move so swiftly you cannot see the
spokes in the wheels, which are the days we number so
sadly. What glorious resolutions I made the first months
of my residence here! How I would read and write and
burn the midnight oil, and astonish the world, and grow
from dignity to dignity into an honoured old age! Alas!
circumstances are too much for us all, and here I am, in
my seventieth year, poor old Daddy Dan, with no great
earthly trouble, indeed, and some few consolations—my
breviary and the grand psalms of 'hope—my daily Mass
and its hidden and unutterable sweetness—the love of
little children and their daily smiles—the prayers of my
old women, and, I think, the reverence of the men. But
there comes a little sting sometimes, when I see young
priests, who served my Masses long ago, standing in cathedral stalls in all the glory of purple and ermine, and when
I see great parishes passing into the hands of mere boys,
and poor old Daddy Dan passed over in silence. I know,
if I were really good and resigned, I would bless God for
it all, and I do.   But human nature will revolt sometimes, and people will say, " What a shame, Father Dan;
why haven't you the red buttons as well as so and so? "
or, " What ails the Bishop, passing over one of the most
learned men in the diocese for a parcel of gossoons! " I
suppose it was my own fault. I remember what magnificent ideas I had. I would build factories, I would pave
the streets, I would establish a fishing station and make
Kilronan the favourite bathing resort on the western coast;
I would write books and be, all round, a model of push,
energy, and enterprise. And I did try. I might as well
have tried to remove yonder mountain with a pitchfork,
or stop the roll of the Atlantic with a rope of sand. Nothing on earth can cure the inertia of Ireland. It weighs
down like the weeping clouds on the damp heavy earth,

and there's no lifting it, nor disburthening of the souls of
men of this intolerable weight. I was met on every side
with a stare of curiosity, as if I were propounding something immoral or heretical. People looked at me, put
their hands in their pockets, whistled dubiously, and went
slowly away. Oh, it was weary, weary work! The blood
was stagnant in the veins of the people and their feet were
shod with lead. They walked slowly, spoke with difficulty, stared all day at leaden clouds or pale sunlight,
stood at the corners of the village for hours looking into
vacuity, and the dear little children became old the moment they left school, and lost the smiles and the sunlight of childhood. It was a land of the lotos. The
people were narcotized. Was it the sea air? I think I
read somewhere in an old philosopher, called Berkeley,
that the damp salt air of the sea has a curious phlegmatic
effect on the blood, and will coagulate it and produce
gout and sundry disorders. However that be, there was a
weary weight on everything around Kilronan. The cattle
slept in the fields, the fishermen slept in their coracles.
It was a land of sleep and dreams.

I approached the agent about a foreshore for the pier,
for you cannot, in Ireland, take the most preliminary and
initial step in anything without going, cap in hand, to the
agent. I explained my intentions. He smiled, but was
polite.

" Lord L——, you know, is either in Monte Carlo or
yachting in the Levant. He must be consulted. I can
do nothing."

" And when will his Lordship return? "

" Probably in two years."

" You have no power to grant a lease of the foreshore,
or even give temporary permission to erect a pier? "

" None whatever."

I went to the Presentment Sessions about a grant for
paving or flagging the wretched street. I woke a nest of
hornets.

" What! More taxation! Aren't the people crushed

enough already? Where can we get money to meet rates and taxes? Flagging Kilronan! Oh, of course! Wouldn't you reverence go in for gas or the electric light? Begor, ye'll be wanting a water supply next," etc., etc.

I applied to a factory a few miles distant to establish a local industry by cottage labour, which is cheap and remunerative.

" They would be delighted, but—— " And so all my castles came tumbling down from the clouds, and left them black and lowering and leaden as before. Once or twice, later on, I made a few spasmodic efforts to galvanize the place into life; they, too, failed, and I accepted the inevitable. When Father Laverty came he helped me to bear the situation with philosophical calmness. He had seen the world, and had been rubbed badly in contact with it. He had adopted as his motto and watchword the fatal *Cui bono*? And he had printed in large Gothic letters over his mantelpiece the legend:

'TWILL BE ALL THE SAME IN A HUNDRED YEARS.

And so I drifted, drifted down from high empyreans of great ideals and lofty speculations into a humdrum life, that was only saved from sordidness by the sacred duties of my office. After all, I find that we are not independent of our circumstances. We are fashioned and moulded by them as plaster of Paris is fashioned and moulded into angels or gargoyles by the deft hand of the sculptor. " Thou shalt lower to his level, ' true of the wife in Locksley Hall, is true of all who are thrown by fate or fortune into unhappy environments. In my leisure moments, when I took up my pen to write, some evil spirit whispered, *Cui bono*? and I laid down my pen and hid my manuscript. Once or twice I took up some old Greek poets and essayed to translate them. I have kept the paper still, frayed and yellow with age; but the fatal *Cui bono*? disheartened me, and I flung it aside. Even my love for the sea had vanished, and I had begun to hate it. During the first few years of my ministry I spent hours by the cliffs and shores. or out on the heaving waters. Then the loneliness of the desert and barren wastes repelled me, and I had begun to loathe it. Altogether I was soured and discontented, and I had a dread consciousness that my life was a failure. All its possibilities had passed without being seized and utilized. I was the barren fig tree, fit only to be cut down. May I escape the fire! Such were my surroundings and disposition when Father Letheby came.

CHAPTER III

A NIGHT CALL

It must have been about two o'clock on Sunday morning, when the house bell was pulled violently and a rapid series of fierce, sharp knocks woke up the house. What priest does not know the tocsin of the night, and the start from peaceful slumbers? I heard the housekeeper wake up Father Letheby; and in a short time I heard him go down stairs. Then there was the usual hurried colloquy at the hall door, then the retreating noises of galloping feet. I pulled the blankets around my shoulders, lifted the pillow, and said, " Poor fellow! " He had to say last Mass next day, and this was some consolation, as he could sleep a few hours in the morning. I met him at breakfast about half past one o'clock. There he was, clean, cool, cheerful, as if nothing had happened.

" I was sorry you had that night call," I said; " how far had you to go? "

" To some place called Knocktorisha," he replied, opening his egg; " 'twas a little remote, but I was well repaid."

" Indeed," said I; " the poor people are very grateful. And they generally pay for whatever trouble they give."

He flushed up.

" Oh, I didn't mean any pecuniary recompense," he said, a little nettled. " I meant that I was repaid by the extraordinary faith and fervour of the people."

I waited.

" Why, Father," said he, turning around and flicking a few invisible crumbs with his napkin, " I never saw

17

anything like it. I had quite an escort of cavalry, two horsemen, who rode side by side with me the whole way to the mountain, and then, when we had to dismount and climb up through the boulders of some dry torrent course, I had two linkmen or torchbearers, leaping on the crest of the ditch on either side, and lighting me right up to the door of the cabin. It was a picture that Rembrandt might have painted."

He paused and blushed a little, as if he had been pedantic.

" But tell me, Father," said he, " is this the custom in the country? "

" Oh, yes," said I; " we look upon it as a matter of course. Your predecessors didn't make much of it."

" It seems to me," he said, " infinitely picturesque and beautiful. It must have been some tradition of the Church when she was free to practise her ceremonies. But where do they get these torches? "

" Bog-oak, steeped in petroleum," I said. " It is, now that you recall it, very beautiful and picturesque. Our people will never allow a priest, with the Blessed Sacrament with him, to go unescorted."

" Now that you have mentioned it," he said, " I distinctly recall the custom that existed among the poor of Salford. They would insist always on accompanying me home from a night sick-call. I thought it was superfluous politeness, and often insisted on being alone, particularly as the streets were always well lighted. But no. If the men hesitated, the women insisted; and I had always an escort to my door. But this little mountain ceremony here is very touching."

" Who was sick? "

" Old Conroy—a mountain ranger, I believe. He is very poorly; and I anointed him." " By Jove," said he, after a pause, " how he did pray—and all in Irish. I could imagine the old Hebrew prophets talking to God from their mountains just in that manner. But why do they expected to be anointed on the breast? "

" I do not know," I replied, " I think it is a Gallican
custom introduced by the French refugee priests at the
beginning of the century. The people invariably expect
it."

" But you don't? " he asked in surprise.

" Oh dear, no. It would be hardly orthodox. Come,
and if you are not too tired, we'll have a walk."

I took him through the village, where he met salaams
and genuflections enough; and was stared at by the men,
and blessed by the women, and received the mute adoration of the children. We passed along the bog road,
where on either side were heaps of black turf drying, and
off the road were deep pools of black water, filling the
holes whence the turf was cut. It was lonely; for to-day
we had not even the pale sunshine to light up the gloomy
landscape, and to the east the bleak mountains stood,
clear-cut and uniform in shagginess and savagery, against
the cold, gray sky. The white balls of the bog cotton
waved dismally in the light breeze, which curled the surface of a few pools, and drew a curlew or plover from his
retreat, and sent him whistling dolefully, and beating
the heavy air, as he swept towards mountain or lake. After
half an hour's walking, painful to me, the ground gently
rose, and down in the hollow a nest of poplars hid from
the western gales. I took Father Letheby through a
secret path in the plantation. We rested a little while,
and talked of many things. Then we followed a tiny
path, strewn with withered pine needles, and which cut
upward through the hill. We passed from the shelter
of the trees, and stood on the brow of a high declivity. I
never saw such surprise in a human face before, and such
delight. Like summer clouds sweeping over, and dappling a meadow, sensations of wonder and ecstasy rolled
visibly across his fine mobile features. Then, he turned,
and said, as if not quite sure of himself: —

" *Why! 'tis the sea!* "

So it was. God's own sea, and his retreat, where men
come but seldom, and then at their peril. There the

great ball-room of the winds and spirits stretched before
us, to-day as smooth as if waxed and polished, and it was
tessellated with bands of blue and green and purple, at
the far horizon line, where, down through a deep mine
shaft in the clouds, the hidden sun was making a silent
glory. It was a dead sea, if you will. No gleam of sail
near or afar, lit up its loneliness. No flash of sea-bird,
poised for its prey, or beating slowly over the desolate
waste, broke the heavy dulness that lay upon the breast
of the deep. The sky stooped down and blackened the
still waters; and anear, beneath the cliff on which we
were standing, a faint fringe of foam alone was proof that
the sea still lived, though its face was rigid and its voice
was stilled, as of the dead.

Father Letheby continued gazing in silence over the
solemn scene for some time. Then lifting his hat he said
aloud:—

> " Mirabiles elationes maris;
> Mirabilis in altis Dominus! "

" Not very many ' upliftings ' to-day," I replied.
" You see our great friend at a disadvantage. But you
know she has moods: and you will like her."

" Like her! " he replied.   " It is not liking. It is
worship. Some kind of pantheism which I cannot explain. Nowhere are the loneliness and grandeur of. God
so manifested. Mind, I don't quite sympathize with
that comparison of St. Augustine's where he detects a
resemblance between yon spectra of purple and green
and the plumage of a dove. What has a dove to do with
such magnificence and grandeur? It was an anti-climax,
a bathos, of which St. Augustine is seldom guilty. ' And
the Spirit of God moved upon the face of the waters.'
There's the sublime!."

" It is desolate," said I. " Not even a seamew or a
gull."

" Quite so," he replied. · " It is limitless and uncon-
ditioned. There is its grandeur. If that sea were

ploughed by navies, or disfigured by the hideous black
hulks of men-of-war, it would lose its magnificence. It
would become a poor limited thing, with pygmies sport-
ing on its bosom. It is now unlimited, free, uncondi-
tioned, as space. It is the infinite and the eternal in it
that appeals to us. When we were children, the infinite
lay beyond the next mountain, because it was the unknown. We grew up and we got knowledge; and knowledge destroyed our dreams, and left us only the commonplace. It is the unknown and unlimited that still appeals
to us—the *something* behind the dawn, and beyond the
sunset, and far away athwart the black line of that horizon, that is forever calling, calling, and beckoning to us
to go thither. Now, there is something in that sombre
glory that speaks to you and me. It will disappear
immediately; and we will feel sad. What is it? Voice-
less echoes of light from the light that streams from the
Lamb?"

"I hope," I said demurely, for I began to fear this
young enthusiast, "that you don't preach in that tone to
the people!"

"Oh dear, no," he said, with a little laugh, "but you
must forgive my nonsense. You gave me such a shock of
surprise."

"But," he said, after a pause, "how happy your life
must have been here! I always felt in Manchester that
I was living at the bottom of a black chimney, in smoke
and noise and fetor, material and spiritual. Here, you
have your holy people, and the silence and quiet of God.
How happy you must have been!"

"What would you think if we returned," I said. "It's
almost our dinner hour."

It was not so late, however, but that I was able to take
a ten minutes' stroll through the village, and bid "good
day" to some of my parishioners.

I suppose there was a note of interrogation hidden

away somewhere under my greeting, for I was told in
different tones and degrees of enthusiasm:—

" Yerra, your reverence, he's a nate man."

" Yerra, we never saw his likes before."

" He spakes almost as plain and common as yourself."

" They say, your reverence, that he's the son of a
jook."

Some old cronies, who retained a lingering gratitude for
Father Laverty's snuff, diluted their enthusiasm a little.

" He is, indeed, a rale nice man. But God be with
poor Father Tom wherever he is. Sure 'twas he was
kind to the poor."

There was a deputation of young men waiting at my
house. I have been pestered from deputations and
speeches since the Land League. A shaggy giant stepped
forward and said:—

" We have preshumed, your reverence, to call upon you
to ascertain whether you'd be agreeable to our what I
may call unanimous intinsion of asking the new cojutor
to be prisident of the Gaelic association of Kilronan,
called the ' Holy Terrors.' "

I said I was agreeable to anything they wished: and
Father Letheby became president of the " Holy Terrors."

After dinner something put me into better humour. I
suppose it was the mountain mutton, for there's nothing
like it in Ireland—mutton raised on limestone land, where
the grass is as tender to the lips of the sheep, as the
sheep to the lips of men. I thought I had an excellent
opportunity of eliciting my curate's proficiency in his
classics. With a certain amount of timidity, for you
never know when you are treading on a volcano with these
young men, I drew the subject around. I have a way of
talking enigmatically, which never fails, however, to re-
veal my meaning. And after a few clever passes, I said,
demurely, drawing out my faded and yellow translation,
made nearly thirty years ago:—

" I was once interested in other things. Here is a

little weak translation I once made of a piece of Greek poetry, with which you are quite familiar. Ah me! I had great notions at the time, ideas of corresponding with classical journals, and perhaps, sooner or later, of editing a classic myself. But *Cui bono?* paralyzed everything. That fatal *Cui bono?* that is the motto and watchword of every thinking and unthinking man in Ireland. However, now that you have come, perhaps—who knows? What do you think of this? "

I read solemnly :—

> " I have argued and asked in my sorrow
>   What shall please me? what manner of life?
> At home am I burdened with cares that borrow
>   Their colour from a world of strife.
> The fields are burdened with toil,
>   The seas are sown with the dead,
> With never a hand of a priest to assoil
>   A soul that in sin hath fled.
> I have gold: I dread the danger by night;
>   I have none: I repine and fret;
> I have children: they darken the pale sunlight;
>   I have none: I'm in nature's debt.
> The young lack wisdom; the old lack life;
>   I have brains; but I shake at the knees;
> Alas! who could covet a scene of strife?
>   Give me peace in this life's surcease! "

" What do you think of this? It is a loose translation from Posidippus."

" It swings well," said Father Letheby. " But who was he? "

" One of the gnomic, or sententious poets," I replied.

" Greek or Latin? " he asked.

Then I succumbed.

" You never heard his name before? " I said.

" Never," said he, emphatically.

I paused and reflected.

" The Bishop told me," said I, " that you were a great Greek scholar, and took a medal in Greek composition? "

" The Bishop told me," said he, " that you were the

best Greek scholar in Ireland, with the exception, perhaps, of a Jesuit Father in Dublin.''

We looked at each other. Then burst simultaneously into a fit of laughter, the likes of which had not been heard in that room for many a day.

'' I am not sure,'' said I, '' about his Lordship's classical attainments; but he knows human nature well.''

Father Letheby left next morning to see after his furniture. He had taken a slated, one-storied cottage in the heart of the village. It was humble enough; but it looked quite aristocratic amongst its ragged neighbours.

CHAPTER IV

THE PANTECHNICON

THE usual deadly silence of a country village in Ireland, which is never broken but by the squeal of a pig, or the clucking of chickens, or a high voice, heard occasionally in anger, was rudely shocked on the following Thursday evening. The unusual commotion commenced with a stampede of sans-culottish boys, and red-legged, wild-eyed girls, who burst into the village streets with shouts of

" Rah! rah! the circus! the circus! the wild baste show! Rah! rah! "

In an instant every door frame was filled with a living picture. Women of all shapes, and in all manners of *habille* and *dishabille*, leaned over the cross-doors and gazed curiously at the coming show. The men, too phlegmatic even in their curiosity, simply shifted the pipe from one side of the mouth to the other; and, as the object of all this curiosity lumbered into the street, three loafers, who supported a blank wall opposite my door, steered round as slowly as a vessel swings with the tide, and leaned the right shoulder, instead of the left, against the gable. It was a tremendous expenditure of energy; and I am quite sure it demanded a drink. And I, feeling from these indications that something unusual was at hand, drew back my window curtains, and stared decorously at the passing wonder. It was a long van, drawn by two horses, which sweated and panted under the whip of their driver. It was painted a dark green; and in gold letters that glittered on the green, I read the magic legend:—

PANTECHNICON.

25

" Pan " is Greek for " all," thought I; and " tech-
nicon " is appertaining to art.   It means an exhibition
of all the arts; that is, a Gypsy wagon with bric-à-brac,
or one of these peep-shows, which exhibits to admiring
youngsters Napoleon crossing the Alps, or Marius sitting on the ruins of Carthage.   I let the curtain fall, and
went back to my books; but in a moment I heard the cara-
van stopping just a few doors below, and I heard my
bedroom window raised; and I knew that Hannah was
half way between heaven and earth.   I have not a par-
ticle of curiosity in my composition, but I drew back the
curtain again, and looked down the street.   The van had
stopped at Father Letheby's new house, and a vast crowd
surged around it.   The girls kept at a respectful distance,
whilst the men unyoked their horses; but the boys stood
near, in the attitude of runners at a tournament, ready
to make off the moment the first ominous growl was heard.
The adults were less excited, though quite as curious, and
I could hear the questionings over the silence of expectation that had fallen on the village.

" Yerra, what is it? "

" How do I know?   It's the place where the circus
people live."

" O—yeh! what a quare place to live in!   And where
do they sleep? "

" In the waggon."

" An' ate? "

" In the waggon."

" Yerra, they're not Christians at all, at all."

Then the men slowly opened the door of the waggon,
and took out, from a mass of canvas and straw, a dainty
satin-covered chair.   A tidy, well-dressed servant, with
a lace cap perched on the top of her head, and what the
village folk called " sthramers " flying behind, came out
of Father Letheby's cottage, and helped to take the furniture within.   As each pretty article appeared, there
was a chorus of " oh-h-hs " from the children.   But the

climax of delight was reached when a gilt mirror appeared. Then for the first time sundry boys and girls saw their own dear smutty faces; and huge was their delight. But I am wrong. The climax came when the heaviest article appeared. Great was the curiosity.

"What is it? what is it? " " A bed? " " No." " A dresser? " " No." " A thing for books? " " No."

But one enlightened individual, who had been up to the great house at a spring cleaning, astonished the natives by declaring that it was a piano.

"A pianney? Yeh, for what? A priest with a pianney! Yerra, his niece is going to live wid him. Yerra, no! He'll play it himself."

Which last interpretation was received with shouts of incredulous laughter. What a versatile people we are! And how adoration and laughter, and reverence and sarcasm, move side by side in our character, apparently on good terms with each other. Will the time come when the laughter and the wit, grown rampant, will rudely jostle aside all the reverential elements in our nature, and mount upwards to those fatal heights which other nations have scaled like Satan—and thence have been flung into the abyss?

I was curious to know what Hannah thought of it all. Hannah too is versatile; and leaps from adoration to envy with wonderful facility.

"Father Letheby's furniture, I suppose? " I said, when she brought in the dinner.

"I believe so," she replied, in a tone of ineffable scorn —" a parcel of gimcracks and kimmeens."

"I thought they looked nice from here," I said.

"Don't sit on his chairs, unless you have your will made," she said.

"Did I see a looking-glass? " I asked.

"Oh yes! to curl his hair, I suppose. And a pianney to play polkas."

" It isn't as solid as ours, Hannah," I said. This
opened the flood-gates of wrath.

" No," she said, in that accent of sarcasm in which
an Irish peasant is past master, " nor purtier. Look at
that sophy now. Isn't it fit for any lady in the land?
And these chairs? Only for the smith, they'd be gone
to pieces long ago. And that lovely carpet? 'Twould
do for a flag for the ' lague.' You haven't one cup and
saucer that isn't cracked, nor a plate that isn't burnt,
nor a napkin, nor a tablecloth, nor a salt-cellar, nor—
nor a—nor a—— "

" I'll tell you what, Hannah," I said. " Father
Letheby is going to show us what's what. I'll furnish
the whole house from top to bottom. Was that his housekeeper? "

" I suppose so," she said contemptuously. " Some
poor girl from an orphanage. If she wasn't, she wouldn't
wear them curifixes."

I admit that Hannah's scorn for my scanty belongings
was well bestowed. The sofa, which appeared to affect
her æsthetic sense most keenly, was certainly a dilapi-
dated article. Having but three legs, it leaned in a
loafing way against the wall, and its rags of horsehair and
protruding springs gave it a most trampish and disreputable appearance. The chairs were solid, for the smith
had bound them in iron clamps. And the carpet?—Well,
I pitied it. It was threadbare and transparent. Yet,
when I looked around, I felt no feminine scorn. They
all appealed to me and said :—

" We have been forty years in your service. We
have seen good things and evil things. Our faces are
familiar to you. We have spent ourselves in your
service."

And I vowed that, even under the coming exigencies,
when I should have to put on an appearance of grace and
dignity—exigencies which I clearly foresaw the moment
my curate made his appearance, these old veterans should

never be set aside or cast as lumber, when their aristocratic friends would make their appearance. And my
books looked at me as much as to say :—

" You're not ashamed of us? "

No, dear silent friends, I should be the meanest, most
ungrateful of mortals if I could be ashamed of you. For
forty years you have been my companions in solitude;
to you I owe whatever inspirations I have ever felt; from
you have descended in copious streams the ideas that
raised my poor life above the commonplace, and the sen-
timents that have animated every good thing and every
holy purpose that I have accomplished. Friends that
never obtruded on my loneliness by idle chatter and gos-
sip, but always spoke wise, inspiriting things when most
I needed them; friends that never replied in irritation to
my own disturbed imaginings, but always uttered your
calm wisdom like voices from eternity, to soothe, to control, or to elevate; friends that never tired and never complained; that went back to your recesses without a murmur; and never resented by stubborn silence my neglect
—treasures of thought and fountains of inspiration, you
are the last things on earth on which my eyes shall rest
in love, and like the orphans of my flock your future shall
be my care. True, like your authors, you look sometimes disreputable enough. Your clothes, more to my
shame, hang loose and tattered around you, and some of
your faces are ink-stained or thumb-worn from contact
with the years and my own carelessness. I would dress
you in purple and fine linen if I may, yet you would
reproach me and I think I was weary of your homely
faces. Like the beggar-maid you would entreat to be
allowed to go back from queenly glory and pomp to the
tatters and contentment of your years. So shall it be!
but between you and me there must be no divorce, so
long as time shall last for me. Other friends will come
and go, but nothing shall dissolve our union based upon
gratitude and such love as man's heart may have for the
ideal and insensible.

When there had been time for perfecting all his arrangements, I strolled down to pay a formal visit to Father Letheby. The atmosphere of absolute primness and neatness struck my senses when I entered. Waxed floors, dainty rugs, shining brasses, coquettish little mirrors here and there, a choice selection of daintily bound volumes, and on a writing desk a large pile of virgin manuscript, spoke the scholar and the gentleman. My heart sank, as I thought how sick of all this he will be in a few weeks, when the days draw in, and the skies scowl, and the windows are washed, and the house rocked under the fierce sou'westers that sweep up the floor of the Atlantic, and throw all its dripping deluges on the little hamlet of Kilronan. But I said:—

"You have made a cosy little nest for yourself, Father Letheby; may you long enjoy it."

"Yes," he said, as if answering my horrible scepticism, "God has been very good to send me here."

Now what can you do with an optimist like that?

"There is just one drawback," I said, with a faint attempt at humour, "to all this æstheticism." I pointed to a window against which four very dirty noses were flattened, and four pairs of delighted eyes were wandering over this fairy-land, and a dirty finger occasionally pointed out some particularly attractive object.

"Poor little things," he said, "it gives them pleasure, and does me no harm."

"Then, why not bring them in?" I said.

"Oh, no," he replied, with a little laugh, "I draw the line there." He pointed to the shining waxed floors. "Besides, it would destroy their heaven. To touch and handle the ideal, brings it toppling down about our ears."

We spoke long and earnestly about a lot of things. Then, looking a little nervously at me, he made a great leap of thought.

"Would you mind my saying a serious word to you, sir?" said he.

"Certainly not," I replied, "go ahead."

"It seems to me, then," he said, deliberately, "that we are not making all that we might out of the magnificent possibilities that lie at our disposal. There is no doubt things are pretty backward in Ireland. Yet, we have an intelligent people, splendid natural advantages— an infernally bad government it is true—but can we not share the blame with the government in allowing things to remain as they are? Now, I am not an advocate for great political designs: I go in for decentralization, by which I mean that each of us should do his very best exactly in that place where Providence has placed him. To be precise, what is there to prevent us from improving the material condition of these poor people? There is a pier to be built. I am told shoals of fish whiten the sea in the summer, and there are no appliances to help our fishermen to catch them and sell them at a vast profit. There is an old mill lying idle down near the creek. Why not furnish it up, and get work for our young girls there? We have but a poor water supply; and, I am told, there is a periodical recurrence of fever. Pardon me, sir," he continued, "if I seem to be finding fault with the ministry of the priests here, but I am sure you do not misunderstand me?"

"Certainly not," said I, "go on."

And he went on with his airy optimism, drawing wonderful castles with the light pencils of his young fancy, and I seemed to hear my own voice echoing back from thirty years long passed by, when the very same words were on my lips and the same ideas throbbed through my brain. But would it be kind to leave him undeceived? I decided not.

"Your first step," I said, "is to see the landlord, who owns the sloping fields and the foreshore."

"Certainly," he said, "that's quite easy. What's his address?" He took up his notebook.

"I am not quite sure," I replied. "He is probably this moment staking half his property on the red at

Monte Carlo, or trying to peep into a harem at Stamboul or dining off bison steak in some cañon in the Sierras."

He looked shocked.

" But his agent—his representative? "

" Oh! he's quite available. He will be very polite, and tell you in well chosen words that he can do—nothing."

" But the Governmental Office—the Board of Works?"

" Quite so. You'll write a polite letter. It will be answered in four weeks to the day : ' We beg to acknow-ledge receipt of your communication, which shall have our earliest attention.' You'll write again. Reply in four weeks : ' We beg to acknowledge receipt of your communication, which we have placed before the Board.' You'll hear no more on the matter. But don't let me de-press you! "

" But is there no redress? What about Parliament? "

" Oh, to be sure! A question will be asked in the House of Commons. The Chief Secretary will reply: ' The matter is under the deliberation of the Board of Works, with whose counsels we do not wish to inter-fere.' "

He was silent.

" About the factory," I continued. " You know there is a large shirt factory in Loughboro, six miles away. If you apply to have a branch factory established here, the manager will come down, look at the store, turn up his nose, ask you where are you to find funds to put the building in proper order, and do you propose to make the store also a fish-curing establishment; and then he will probably write what a high-born lady said of the first Napoleon : ' Il salissait tout ce qu'il touchait.' "

" It's a damned lie," said Father Letheby, springing up, and, I regret to say, demolishing sundry little Japan-ese gimcracks, " our people are the cleanest, purest, sweetest people in the world in their own personal habits, whatever be said of their wretched cabins. But you are not serious, sir? "

He bent his glowing eyes upon me. I liked his anger.
And I liked very much that explosive expletive. How
often, during my ministry, did I yearn to be able to
utter the emphatic word! Mind, it is not a cuss-word.
It is only an innocent adjective—condemned. But what
eloquence and emphasis there is in it! How often I
could have flung it at the head of a confirmed toper, as
he knelt at my feet to take the pledge. How often I
could have shot it at the virago, who was disturbing the
peace of the village; and on whom my vituperation,
which fell like a shot without powder, made no impression! It sounded honest. I like a good fit of anger,
honest anger, and such a gleam of lightning through it.
" I am," I said, " quite serious. You want to create
a Utopia. You forget your Greek."
He smiled.
" I am reserving the worst," I said.
" What is it? " he cried. " Let me know the worst."
" Well," I said slowly, " the people won't thank you
even in the impossible hypothesis that you succeed."
He looked incredulous.
" What! that they won't be glad to lift themselves
from all this squalor and misery, and be raised into a
newer and sweeter life? "
" Precisely. They are happy. Leave them so. They
have not the higher pleasures. Neither have they the
higher perils. ' They sow not, neither do they spin.'
But neither do they envy Solomon in all his glory. Jack
Haslem and Dave Olden sleep all day in their coracles.
They put down their lobster pots at night. Next day,
they have caught enough of these ugly brutes to pay for
a glorious drunk. Then sleep again. How can you add
to such happiness? By building a schooner, and sending them out on the high seas, exposed to all the dangers
of the deep; and they have to face hunger and cold and
death, for what? A little more money and a little more
drink; and your sentence: Why didn't he leave us alone?
Weren't we just as well off as we were? which is the

everlasting song of your respected predecessor, only he put it in Latin : *Cui bono?* "

He pondered deeply for a long time. Then he said : " It sounds sensible; but there is some vile fallacy at the bottom of it. Anyhow, I'll try. Father, give me your blessing ! "

" There again," I said, " see how innocent you are. You don't know the vernacular."

He looked surprised.

" When you know us better," I answered, in reply to his looks, " you will understand that by that formula you ask for a drink. And as I don't happen to be under my own roof just now—— "

His glorious laugh stopped me. It was like the ringing of a peal of bells.

" No matter," he said. " I may go on? "

" Certainly," I replied. " You'll have a few gray hairs in your raven locks in twelve months time—that's all."

" What a hare," I thought, as I went home, " is madness, the youth, to leap over the meshes of good counsel, the cripple." Which is not mine, but that philosopher, Will Shakespeare; or is it Francis Bacon?

CHAPTER V

A SLIGHT MISUNDERSTANDING

FATHER LETHEBY commenced sooner than I had expected. I think it was about nine or ten days after his formal instalment in his new house, just as I was reading after breakfast the *Freeman's Journal* of two days past, the door of my parlour was suddenly flung open, a bunch of keys was thrown angrily on the table, and a voice (which I recognized as that of Mrs. Darcy, the chapel woman), strained to the highest tension of indignation, shouted:—

"There! and may there be no child to pray over my grave if ever I touch them again! Wisha! where in the world did you get him? or where did he come from, at all, at all? The son of a jook! the son of a draper over there at Kilkeel. Didn't Mrs. Morarty tell me how she sowld socks to his ould father? An' he comes here complaining of dacent people! ' Dirt,' sez he. ' Where? ' sez I. ' There,' sez he. ' Where? ' sez I. I came of as dacent people as him. Wondher *you* never complained. But you're too aisy. You always allow these galivanters of curates to crow over you. But I tell you I won't stand it. If I had to beg my bread from house to house, I won't stand being told I'm dirty. Why, the ladies of the Great House said they could see their faces in the candlesticks; and didn't the Bishop say 'twas the natest vestry in the diocese? And this new cojutor with his gran' accent, which no one can understand, and his gran' furniture, and his whipster of a servant, begor, no one can stand him. We must all clear out. And, after me eighteen years, scrubbing, and washing, and ironing,

35

wid me two little orphans, which that blackguard, Jem Darcy (the Lord have mercy on his sowl!) left me, must go to foreign countries to airn me bread, because I'm not good enough for his reverence. Well, 'tis you'll be sorry. But, if you wint down on your two binded knees and said : ' Mrs. Darcy, I deplore you to take up them kays and go back to your juties,' I wouldn't! No! Get some whipster that will suit his reverence. Mary Darcy isn't good enough."

She left the room, only to return. She spoke with forced calmness.

" De thrifle of money you owe me, yer reverence, ye can sind it down to the house before I start for America. And dere's two glasses of althar wine in the bottle, and half a pound of candles."

She went out again, but returned immediately.

" The surplus is over at Nell O'Brien's washing, and the black vestment is over at Tom Carmody's since the last station. The kay of the safe is under the door of the linny¹ to de left, and the chalice is in the basket, wrapped in the handkercher. And, if you don't mind giving me a charackter, perhaps, Hannah will take it down in the evening."

She went out again; but kept her hand on the door.

" Good-bye, your reverence, and God bless you! Sure, thin, you never said a hard word to a poor woman." Then there was the sound of falling tears.

To all this tremendous philippic I never replied. I never do reply to a woman until I have my hand on the door handle and my finger on the key. I looked steadily at the column of stocks and shares on the paper, though I never read a word.

" This is rather a bad mess," said I. " He is coming out too strong."

The minute particulars I had from Hannah soon after.

¹Saxon, linhay.

Hannah and Mrs. Darcy are not friends. Two such village potentates could not be friends any more than two poets, or two critics, or two philosophers. As a rule, Hannah rather looked down on the chapel woman, and generally addressed her with studied politeness. " How are you *to-day*, Mrs. Darcy? " or more frequently, " Good *morning*, Mrs. Darcy." On the other hand, Mary Darcy, as arbitress at stations, wakes, and weddings, had a wide influence in the parish, and I fear used to speak contemptuously sometimes of my housekeeper. But now there was what the newspapers call a Dual Alliance against the newcomers, and a stern determination that any attempt at superiority should be repressed with a firm hand, and to Mrs. Darcy's lot it fell to bear the martyrdom of high principle and to fire the first shot, that should be also the final one. And so it was, but not in the way Mrs. Darcy anticipated.

It would appear, then, that Father Letheby had visited the sacristy, and taken a most minute inventory of its treasures, and had, with all the zeal of a new reformer, found matters in a very bad state. Now, he was not one to smile benignantly at such irregularities and then throw the burden of correcting them on his pastor. He was outspoken and honest. He tore open drawers, and drew out their slimy, mildewed contents, sniffed ominously at the stuffy atmosphere, flung aside with gestures of contempt some of Mrs. Darcy's dearest treasures, such as a magnificent reredos of blue paper with gold stars; held up gingerly, and with curled lip, corporals and purificators, and wound up the awful inspection with the sentence : —

" I never saw such abominable filth in my life."

Now, you may accuse us in Ireland of anything you please from coining to parricide, but if you don't want to see blazing eyes and hear vigorous language don't say Dirt. Mrs. Darcy bore the fierce scrutiny of her ménage without shrinking, but when he mentioned the ugly word, all her fury shot forth, and it was all the more terrible, because veiled under a show of studied politeness.

" Dirt! " she said.   " I'd be plazed to see your reverence show one speck of dirt in the place."

" Good heavens, woman! " he said, " what do you mean?   There is dirt everywhere, in the air, under my feet, in the grate, on the altar.   It would take the Atlantic to purify the place."

" You're the first gentleman that ever complained of the place," said Mrs. Darcy.   " Of coorse, there aren't carpets, and bearskins, and cowhides, which are now the fashion, I believe.   An' dere isn't a looking-glass, nor a pianney; but would your reverence again show me the dirt.   A poor woman's charackter is all she has."

" I didn't mean to impute anything to your character," he said, mildly, " but if you can't see that this place is frightfully dirty, I suppose I can't prove it.   Look at that! "

He pointed to a gruesome heap of cinders, half-burnt papers, brown ashes, etc., that choked up the grate.

" Yerra.   Glory be to God! " said Mrs. Darcy, appealing to an imaginary audience, " he calls the sweepings of the altar, and the clane ashes, dirt.   Yerra, what next? "

" This next," he said, determinedly; " come here." He took her out and pointed to the altar cloth.   It was wrinkled and grimy, God forgive me! and there were stars of all sizes and colours darkening it.

" Isn't that a disgrace to the Church? " he said, sternly.

" I see no disgrace in it," said Mrs. Darcy.   " It was washed and made up last Christmas, and is as clane to-day as the day it came from the mangle."

" Do you call that clean? " he shouted, pointing to the drippings of the candles.

" Yerra, what harm is that," said she, " a bit of blessed wax that fell from the candles?   Sure, 'tis of that they make the Agnus Deis."

" You're perfectly incorrigible," he said. " I'll report the whole wretched business to the parish priest, and let him deal with you."

" Begor you may," said she, " but I'll have my story first."

And so she had. Father Letheby gave me his version afterwards. He did so with the utmost delicacy, for it was all an indirect indictment of my own slovenliness and sinful carelessness. I listened with shamed face and bent head, and determined to let him have his way. I knew that Mrs. Darcy would not leave for America just yet.

But what was my surprise on the following Sunday, when, on entering the sacristy to prepare for Mass, I slid along a polished floor, and but for the wall would probably have left a vacancy at Kilronan to some expectant curate. The floor glinted and shone with wax; and there were dainty bits of fibre matting here and there. The grate was black-leaded, and there was a wonderful fire-screen with an Alpine landscape. The clock was clicking steadily, as if Time had not stood still for us all for many years : and there were my little altar boys in snowy surplices as neat as the acolytes that proffered soap and water to the Archbishop of Rheims, when he called for bell and book in the famous legend.

But oh! my anguish when I drew a stiff white amice over my head, instead of the dear old limp and wrinkled one I was used to; and when I feebly tried to push my hands through the lace meshes of an alb, that would stand with stiffness and pride, if I placed it on the floor. I would gladly have called for my old garment; but I knew that I too had to undergo the process of the new reformation; and, with much agony, I desisted. But I drew the line at a biretta which cut my temples with its angles, and I called out:—

" Mrs. Darcy."

A young woman, with her hair all tidied up, and with a white apron, laced at the edges, and pinned to her

breast, came out from a recess. She was smiling bashfully, and appeared as if she would like to run away and
hide somewhere.

" Mrs. Darcy," I called again.

The young woman smiled more deeply, and said with
a kind of smirk :—

" Here I am, your reverence! "

It is fortunate for me that I have acquired, after long
practice, the virtue of silence; for when I recognized the
voice of my old friend, I was thunderstruck. I'm sure
I would have said something very emphatic, but my
habits restrained me. But I regret to say it was all a
source of distraction to me in the celebration of the
Divine Mysteries, and during the day. What had occurred? I was dying to know; but it would not be con-
sistent with the dignity of my position to ask. To this
day, I congratulate myself on my reticence; for, who
could help asking how? when face to face with a miracle. It was some days before I discovered the secret
of the magical transformation.

It would appear, then, that the late lamented Jem
Darcy, when he departed to his reward, left his poor
widow two charges in the shape of children. What do
I say? Charges? No. She would scornfully repudiate
the word. For was not Patsey, the baby of eighteen
months, " the apple of her eye," and Jemmy, the little
hunchback of six summers, " the core of her heart "?
For them she laboured and toiled, and " moiled," as she
used to say; and worked herself into oil to get them
bread, and a pink ribbon for the baby's shoulder knot,
and a navy cap, with " Hero " in gold letters for Jemmy.
And across her troubled life, full of cares and apprehensions, poor soul! was there any gleam of sunshine, except that which was reflected in the iris of her baby's
eyes; or that which dappled the mud floor of her cabin,
when Jemmy lay there and played hide and seek with
the gossamer threads that shone through the chink in the

half-door? Ah me! it is easy to lecture the poor, and
complain of their horrid ways; but the love such as no
man hath gilds and enamels most of the crooked and
grimy things that disfigure their poor lives in the eyes
of the fastidious; and perhaps makes the angels of Him,
before whose Face the stars are not spotless, turn from
the cold perfection of the mansion and the castle to gaze
lovingly on the squalid lowliness of the hamlet and the
cabin. Well. On the morning that Mrs. Darcy gave
me formal notice of her relinquishment of the solemn
office she held, she bent her steps homeward with a
heavy heart. She had done her duty, like all the other
great people who have done disagreeable things; but it
brought no consolation. And she had flung behind her
her little cabin, and all the sweet associations connected
therewith, and the pomp and pride of power, when she
officiated at the public offices of the Church, and every
one knew her to be indispensable. For who could tell
the name of a defaulter at the station, but Mrs. Darcy?
And who arranged the screaming baby in the clumsy
arms of a young godmother, but Mrs. Darcy? And who
could lay out a corpse like Mrs. Darcy? And who but
Mrs. Darcy found the ring when the confused and blushing bridegroom fumbled in every pocket at the altar, and
the priest looked angry, and the bride ashamed?

And then her pride- in the Church! How wonderful
were her designs in holly and ivy at Christmas! What
fantasies she wove out of a rather limited imagination!
What art fancies, that would shame William Morris, poet
and socialist, did she conceive and execute in the month
of May for the Lady Altar! Didn't Miss Campion say
that she was a genius, but undeveloped? Didn't Miss
Campion's friend from Dublin declare that there was
nothing like it in Gardiner Street? And when her time
would be spent, and she was old and rheumatized, would
not little Jemmy, the hunchback, who was a born pre-
Raphaelite, take her place, and have a home, for he
could not face the rough world? Ah me! and it was all

gone; cast behind her through a righteous feeling of pride
and duty. She moved through the village with a heavy
heart; and her check apron went to her eyes.

She had an amiable habit of never entering her cabin
without playing " Peek-a-boo! " through the window
with the baby. For this purpose, the cradle was always
drawn so that the baby faced the window; and when it
saw the round face, which it knew so well, peeping over
the speck blossoms of the mignonette, well—there were
developments. On this particular morning, Mrs. Darcy
was in no humour for play acting; but the force of habit
is strong, and she peered through the little window with
reddened eyes. And these eyes, as she afterwards described it, " sprod in her head " at what she saw. For,
on the floor, in his favourite attitude, his head propped
between his hands, was the hunchback, Jemmy, studying
with all the intense appreciation of an Edison, how to
construct an airy castle out of certain painted wood-
blocks, which strewed the floor; and there, his back
turned towards the window, was her arch-enemy, Father
Letheby, his right hand raised aloft and dangling an
india-rubber baby; whilst Patsey, his eyes dilated with
excitement, made frantic attempts to seize the prize,
and crowed and chuckled in the exuberance of his delight. Mrs. Darcy drew back hastily, then peeped again.
No doubt of it. It was no phantasm of the imagination.
She looked again. Then whispered something softly to
herself, and, with a great lump in her throat, sped swiftly
through the village and up to the " Great House." The
result of her interview with Miss Campion we have seen.
Father Letheby has scored again. There were heavy
bets of fifteen to one in half-gallons of porter, laid by
desperate gamblers, that Father Letheby would make
Mrs. Darcy wash her face. It was supposed to be a
wild plunge in a hopeless speculation. I am told now,
that the betting has gone up at the forge, and is now
fifty to one that, before a month, she'll have a lace cap
and " sthramers " like the maids at the " Great House."

CHAPTER VI

AT THE STATION

CAPTAIN CAMPION was one of that singular race of Catholics, with which Ireland was familiar fifty years ago, but which is now dying rapidly away under the new conditions and environments of our age. A strong, rough lot they were, with whom a word meant a blow; gentlemen every inch of them, who would die for the faith whose dogmas they knew nothing of, and whose commands they ignored. Often in the town and country clubs of Ireland strange things happened, of which the outer world heard nothing; for stewards are discreet, and managers imbibe the spirit of respectability from their superiors. But the walls could tell of wine glasses shattered, and billiard cues broken, and hot blows exchanged for a word about the Pope, or against the priests; it was a leap of hot flame, which died out in a moment, and they were gentlemen again. And the perfervid imagination of the Celt had invented some such heroism about Captain Campion—particularly one brilliant achievement at a hunt, when he unhorsed with the butt of his riding whip, and then cut and lashed an unfortunate young officer in the Lancers, who had dared say something about Bittra— the " lovely Papist," who was toasted at the mess in distant Galway, and had set half the hunting men of the country wild with her beauty and her prowess. It may be supposed then that Captain Campion was not a practical Catholic. He came to Mass occasionally, where he fidgeted in his pew, and twisted and writhed under the sermon. He never went to Confession; not even to his

43

Easter duty—which prevented me from accepting the hos-
pitalities which he freely proffered.   There were other
little circumstances which made me wish not to be too
intimate.   Whatever political opinions I held, and they
were thin and colorless enough, were in direct antagon-
ism to his.   He was a three-bottle Tory, who regarded the
people as so many serfs, who provided labourers for his
comfort, and paid him for the privilege of living on stony
mountain or barren bog.   The idea of their having any
rights struck him as positively ludicrous.   There was
but one thing that had rights, and that was the fetish,
property.   Every attempt, therefore, to lift the people
from that condition of serfdom he regarded as absolutely
treasonable; and he was my chief opponent in any futile
attempts I made to introduce some improvements into
the wretched place.   And of course he was hated.   There
was hardly a family to whom he had not done an injury,
for he pushed the law to savage extremes.   He had
evicted, and burnt down the deserted cottages; he had
driven honest lads for some paltry act of poaching into
criminal and dishonest courses; he had harassed the
widow and unhoused the orphan; and every prayer that
went up for the sweet face of his child was weighted with
a curse for the savage and merciless father.   He knew
it, and didn't care.   For there were plenty to fawn upon
him and tell him he was quite right.   Ah me! how the
iron has sunk into our souls!   Seven centuries of slavery
have done their work well.

Bittra Campion sat in the large drawing-room, with
the high, broad windows, that looked over a dun, brown
moorland, to where the sea-line threw its clear curve
athwart the sky.   She was working quietly at some little
garment for a poor peasant girl or half-clad boy in the
mountains; but over her gentle and usually placid face
stole a look of apprehension, as if a shadow of coming
evil was thrown forward by the undefined future.   Yet
why should she fear, who hated no one, but poured her
love abroad upon all?   Ah, why? is it not upon the

gentle and the kind that the hailstones of destiny beat
oftenest, as if they felt that here, and not upon the
rugged and the stern, their pitiless strength should succeed? From time to time, Bittra looked to the door,
or paused in her work, to listen for a footstep. At last
it came—her father's heavy step, as he strode across the
corridor, and the doors slammed behind him.

" All alone, mignonne," he said. " A penny, nay, a
pound for your thoughts."

" Agreed, father," she said eagerly, " I want a pound
rather badly just now."

" Some new idiot discovered in the hills," he said,
" or some disreputable tramp with a good imagination.
You shall have it, Bittra," he said, coming over, and
gently stroking her hair. He looked down fondly upon
her, and said, suddenly changing his voice:—

" I am hungry as a hawk, Bittra; would you get me
some tea? "

She rose to meet his wishes, and as her tall, beautiful
figure passed from the room, he said to himself:—

" God, how like her mother! "

He threw himself on a sofa, and looked out over the
moor. But he saw——

A long, low island, with the plumes of palms crown-
ing the hill; and beneath, the white waves creeping up
the coral crests to mingle with the lazy waters of the
lagoon. A cottage, shaded with palms, close down by
the beach, with magnolias clustering round the windows,
and orchids far back in the moist shades, and creeping
vines tangled in and out amongst the palms, and a strong
sun, going down in an orange and crimson sky, and a
cool, welcome breeze from the sea, that just lifts up
the fans of the palms, and a stray curl on the forhead
of a girl—for she was hardly more than a girl—who sat
out on the tiny lawn, and at her feet the young naval
officer, who had carried off his bride at the last season at
the Castle and brought her here under southern skies,
and believed that this was the world—and heaven. His

ship lay at anchor on the eastern side; and here they were stationed for weeks, it may be for months, away from civilization and all its nuisances, and alone with Nature and the children of Nature, who came by degrees to love at least the gentle lady who was so kind to them and their brown babies. Alas for human happiness! One short year, and he was a widower, with the charge of a little babe.

"It was a bitter fate," he said to himself, "and I called her 'Bittra' in my rage. I must change that name."

He started, for the door opened and Bittra came in, immediately followed by the servant with tea.

"We've got a new neighbour, mignonne," he said, as he broke up his toast, "and must call immediately. Can you guess?"

"No, father," she said; but it fitted in with her apprehensions and made her shudder.

"Neither can I," he said, laughing. "But I have got mysterious hints that indicate a neighbour."

"Judith again," said Bittra. "She can never be explicit."

Then, after a long pause, she said, as if communing with herself:—

"I don't like new acquaintances. They are pretty certain to be troublesome. Can't we live for one another, father?"

"Gladly, my child," he said, darkly, "but what can you do? Life is warp and woof. It must be held together somehow. And the woof is what we call society."

"Father," she said, timidly, "there will be a station at the glen in the morning. Might I ask the priests to breakfast here?"

"By all means," he replied, "it will be better than a déjeuner in a room with two beds, and a squalling baby, with the bread taken from the blankets, and the butter from the top of the dresser."

" Ah, no, pap, 'tis never so bad as that. They do their best, poor things—— "

" All right," he cried. " Bring up their reverences. There are two or three sole brought up from the yacht."

It was a remarkable station, that at Glencarn, although we did not accept Miss Campion's invitation. I was rather apprehensive of the effect these country stations would have on my fastidious curate; and I narrowly watched him, as we left our car on the hills, and strode through soft yellow mud and dripping heather to some mountain cabin. And I think there was a little kindly malice in my thoughts when I allowed him enter first, and plunge into the night of smoke that generally filled these huts. Then the saying of Mass on a deal table, with a horse-collar overhead, and a huge collie dog beneath, and hens making frantic attempts to get on the altar-cloth—I smiled to myself, and was quite impatient to know what effect all these primitive surroundings would have on such refinement and daintiness. " He'll never stand it," I thought, " he'll pitch up the whole thing, and go back to England." As usual, I was quite wrong. Where I anticipated disgust, there were almost tears of delight and sympathy; where I expected indignation, I found enthusiasm.

" There's nothing like it in the world," he used say (this was a favourite expression of his); " such faith, such reverence, such kindly courtesy! Why, no empress could do the honours of the table like that poor woman! Did you notice her solicitude, her eagerness, her sensitiveness lest she should be intruding on our society. But those men in that smoky kitchen—it took me a long time to discern their faces in the gloom of the smoke. And then I'd have given half that I have ever learned to be able to paint them—strong, brave mountaineers, their faces ruddy from sun and wind; and such a reverential attitude! And then the idea of their coming over to me, a young lad like themselves, and kneeling down on the cobblestones, and whispering their little story—there in the presence of their comrades; and the little maidens with their sweet, pure faces hidden under the hoods of their shawls, and the eyes of wondering children, and the old men, bending over the fire—why you ought to be the happiest man on the face of the earth—they are a people to die for!"

Well, this morning at Glencarn we had a scene; and, as an easy, good-tempered old man, I hate scenes, and keep away from them. The morning was sullenly wet— not in fierce, autumnal gusts, but there was a steady persistent downpour of soft, sweet rain, that bathed your face like a sponge, and trickled under your coat collar, and soaked your frieze and waterproof, and made you feel flabby and warm and uncomfortable. We did not see the cabin until we were quite close to it; and when we entered, the first person we saw, kneeling on the mud floor, but the kindness of the people had placed a bag under her knees, was Bittra Campion. She was wrapped round about with a waterproof cloak, the hood of which, lined with blue, covered her head, and only left her face visible. There she knelt among the simple people; and if the saint of the day appeared in bodily form, I am not sure that he would have received more reverence than was poured around that gentle figure from the full hearts that beat silently near her. I was not much surprised, for I had seen Miss Campion at stations before; but Father Letheby started back in astonishment, and looked inquiringly at me. I took no notice, but passed in the little bedroom, and commenced hearing confessions.

The tinkling of the little bell was the only indication I had of the progress of the Holy Sacrifice; and when I knew it was ended, and was studying some faded photographs of American friends over the rude mantelpiece, I heard, amid the profound silence, Father Letheby's voice suddenly raised in anger.

" Kneel down at once! Have you no respect for Him whom you have just received, and who is before you on the altar? "

The people had arisen the moment the last prayer was said. It grated on the feelings of the young priest, who, as I afterwards found, had the most intense reverence and devotion towards the Most Holy Sacrament. I waited for some minutes; then came out, and read the Station List, and returned to the little bedroom off the kitchen. Miss Campion came in, and proffered the hospitality of her home. We gladly declined. It would have pained our humble hosts to have turned our backs upon them; and I confess I was infinitely more at my ease there in that little bedroom with its mud floor and painted chairs, than in Captain Campion's dining-room. It is quite true, that James Casey cut the bread very thick, and drank his tea with a good deal of expression from his saucer. But these were slight drawbacks. The eggs were fresh and milky, the cream delicious, the tea strong, the bread crispy, the butter sweet and golden; and the daughters of the house and the mother waited on us with a thoroughness and courtesy that would have done credit to a court; and we talked on all subjects— the weather, the harvest, the neighbours; and chaffed old Dan Downey—who was a great Biblical scholar—about the " Jeroakims," and asked him where a hare might be found on the mountains; but this was professional, so he stuffed his mouth with bread, and ensured his statutory silence. Then the little children crept in shyly for bits of sugar; and the neighbours waited patiently till the clergy were served; and we left the house with our blessing, and such gratitude as only an Irish priest can feel for his flock.

The same steady, persistent downpour of rain continued as we passed over the boulders of the torrent, and made our way through slushy mud and dripping heather to where our horse was waiting. Father Letheby was slightly moody.

At last, taking off his hat, and shaking down streams of water, he said:—

"That was a shocking thing this morning. You heard me speak angrily. Imagine those people standing up coolly, immediately after having received Holy Communion; and I have spoken to them so repeatedly about reverence."

"Did you notice where they were kneeling?" I said, not unkindly.

"Well, indeed it was not velvet."

"No," I said, "but rough cobblestones, rather pointed, like some allusions in our sermons. Do you know how long they were kneeling there?"

"During Mass," he said.

"No," I replied, "they knelt there during the confessions, and during Mass. I am not excusing them, but did you ever hear of the ancient penance of wearing peas in pilgrims' shoes? Some, I believe, and I think Erasmus is the authority, had the wisdom to boil those peas. But you cannot boil cobblestones. I never realized this part of our people's sufferings till a poor fellow one morning, whilst I sat comfortably by the fire, interrupted his confession to say:—

"For the love of God, your reverence, would you lave me put my cap under my knees?"

My curate laughed good-naturedly. We got out on the highroad at last; and as we jogged home in the soft, warm rain, I took the opportunity of giving a little advice. It is a little luxury I am rather fond of, like the kindred stimulant of a pinch of snuff; and as I have had but few luxuries in my life, no one ought grudge me this.

"My dear Father Letheby," I said, as we sat comfortably together, "the great principle of Irish life is *quieta non movere*. Because, when you lay a finger on the most harmless and impotent things they spring at once into hissing and spitting things, like the Lernæan hydra; and then, like that famous monster, you must cauterize the wound to heal, or prevent new hideous developments. You have, as yet, no idea of how many ways, all different and mutually antagonistic, there are, of looking at things in Ireland. To your mind there seems but one—one judgment, and therefore one course of action. There are a hundred mirrors concentrated on the same subject, and each catches its own shape and colour from passion and interest. And each is quite honest in its own portraiture, and each is prepared to fight for its own view to the bitter end."

" I beg your pardon, sir," my curate said, deferentially, " I am following you with great attention. Do I understand you to say that each mirror is prepared to fight for its own view to the bitter end? I have seen something like that in a comic picture—— "

" You know, you rascal, what I mean," I said, " I mean the hands that hold the mirrors."

" Of course," he said, " my stupidity. But I am a little bit of a purist in language."

Now, isn't this annoying? Poor Father Tom never interrupted me. He always used say: " Yes! yes! to be sure! to be sure! " or, " Ki bono? ki bono? " which grated horribly on my ears. I see I must be more careful; and I shall defer this lecture.

" Might I ask you to proceed, sir? " he said. " It is very interesting, indeed. You were talking about the pugnacity of mirrors."

There was a slight acidity here; but the poor fellow was put out.

" Never mind," I said, " you have a great deal to learn yet—with wrinkles and gray hairs. But if you want to keep these raven locks, now wet and dripping, intact, remember, *quieta non movere*! And if you want to keep your face, now smooth and ruddy, but, I regret to say, glistening with rain, free from wrinkles, remember, *quieta non movere*. Take now your frequent altar denunciations of local superstitions—the eggs found in the garden, and the consequent sterility of the milk, the

evil eye, and the cattle dying, etc., etc.—it will take more
than altar denunciations, believe me—it will take years
of vigorous education to relegate these ideas into the
limbo of exploded fantasies.   And the people won't be
comfortable without them.   You take away the poetry,
which is an essential element in the Gaelic character,
and you make the people prosaic and critical, which is
the worst thing possible for them.   Thiggin-thu?   But
I beg your pardon.   You are beyond all that."

    " It sounds plausible," he said, getting down from
the gig; " but it sounds also, pardon the expression,
cowardly.   However, we'll see ! "

CHAPTER VII

Captain Campion gave a large dinner party on All-Hallows-Eve. It is a ghostly time; and, in Ireland, every one, even the most advanced and materialistic, feels that the air is full of strange beings, who cannot be accounted for either by the microscope or the scalpel. Father Letheby was invited and went. I was rather glad he did go, for I felt that the village was rather dull for such a brilliant young fellow; and I had a kind of pardonable pride in thinking that he would be fully competent to meet on their own level any pretentious people that might stray hither from more civilized centres. There is hardly, indeed, any great risk of meeting too intellectual people in Ireland just now. The anatomy of a horse is about the term and end of the acquired knowledge of the stronger sex; and the latest ball—well, this won't do! I must suspend this criticism, otherwise I shall wound, and that does not suit an old priest, who is beginning to hear the murmurs of the eternal seas.

Father Letheby walked over across the moor to the "Great House." It was growing dark when he left home, and he allowed himself a full hour, as he had to make some calls by the way. One of these calls led him to a house where an old woman was bedridden. Her son, a strong man of thirty years or more, was doing something strange when the priest unexpectedly entered. He was suffering from a scrofulous ulcer in the neck, and it was a hideous disfigurement. He had just been standing before a broken piece of looking-glass, stuck in the

rough plaster of the wall; and he hastily hid something
as the priest entered. Father Letheby's suspicions were
instantly aroused. And he said hastily—for he detested
anything like concealment——

" What have you been doing? "

" Nothing, your reverence," said the peasant, nervously.

" Then, what are you hiding? " said Father Letheby.

" Nothing, your reverence," said the poor fellow.

" Tell the priest, Ned, alanna," said the old woman
from her bed. " Sure, 'tis only a charm which the good
'oman has set, Father. And it's cured him already."

The young man scowled at his aged mother; and in
response to an emphatic gesture from the priest, he
pulled out a little coil of rope, partly worn at the end into
a little wisp of flax.

" And are you such an utter fool," said the priest,
angrily, holding the rope gingerly between his fingers,
" as to believe that that wretched thing could cure you? "

" It *has* cured me," said the young man. " Look
here ! "

Father Letheby looked; and sure enough, there was
but a faint scar, as of a burn, on the place where he
knew well there had been a hideous running ulcer a few
days ago. He was struck dumb.

" I am not surprised," he said, recovering himself
rapidly; " I know Satan possesses supernatural power.
But you, unhappy man, do you not know that it is to the
devil you owe your cure? "

" I told him so, your reverence," whimpered the poor
mother. " I said, better be sick forever, Ned, than break
God's law. Sure, nothing good can come from it."

" Thin why did God allow it? " said the young man,
angrily.

" If you knew anything of your religion," said the
priest, " you might know that God permits evil things
to happen. So much the worse for evil doers. You have
committed grave sin."

"But, sure, this is good," said the poor fellow, feebly groping after theological lights, "and whatever is good comes from God."

"The effect may be good," said the priest, "the instrument is bad. What is that?" and he pointed to the rope that was dangling in his hand.

The young man was silent.

"You are afraid to tell? Now what is it? There's something uncanny about it?"

He fumbled with his vest, and looked sullenly into the darkening night.

"Then, as you won't answer, I'll take it with me," said the priest, folding the rope into a coil, and preparing to put it in his pocket.

There was a sullen smile around the young man's mouth.

"The owner will be looking for it," said he.

"Tell the owner that Father Letheby has it, and she can come to me for it," said the priest. He put the rope in his pocket and moved to the door.

"Don't! don't! Father dear," said the old woman. "It isn't good. Give it back, and Ned will give it to the good 'oman to-morrow."

"No! I shall give it myself," said the priest, "and a bit of my mind with it."

The young man moved to the door, and stood beside the priest.

"You would not touch it if you knew what it was," he whispered.

"What?" said Father Letheby.

"Do you remember old Simmons, the pinsioner, down at Lougheagle?"

"Who destroyed himself?"

"Yes! he hanged himself to a rafter in the barn."

"I remember having heard of it."

"He hanged himself with a rope."

"I presume so."

"Your reverence has the rope in your pocket."

The priest stepped back as if stung. The thing was so horrible that he lost his self-possession. Then a great flood of anger swept his soul; and taking the hideous instrument from his pocket, he passed over to the open hearth; with one or two turns of the wheel, that answers the purpose of a bellows in Ireland, he kindled the smouldering ashes into flame, buried the rope deep down in the glowing cinders, and watched it curl into a white ash, that bent and writhed like a serpent in pain. The old woman told her beads, and then blessed the priest, with, however, a tremor of nervous fear in her voice. The young man lifted his hat, as the priest, without a word, passed into the darkness.

" She'll be after asking for the rope, your reverence? " he said at length, when the priest had gone a few yards.

" Refer her to me," Father Letheby said. " And look here, young man," he cried, coming back and putting his face close to the peasant's, " I'd advise you to go to your confession as soon as you can, lest, in the words of Scripture, ' something worse happen to you.' "

It was a pleasant dinner party at the " Great House." Colonel Campion presided. Bittra sat opposite her father. Captain Ormsby, Inspector of Coast Guards, was near her. There were some bank officials from a neighboring town; Lord L——'s agent and his wife; a military surgeon; a widower, with two grown daughters; the new Protestant Rector and his wife. Father Letheby was very much pleased. He was again in the society that best suited his natural disposition. It was tolerably intelligent and refined. The lights, the flowers, the music, told on his senses, long numbed by the quietness and monotony of his daily life. He entered into the quiet pleasures of the evening with zest, made all around him happy, and even fascinated by the brilliancy with which he spoke, so much so that Bittra Campion said to him, as he was leaving about eleven o'clock:—

" Father, we are infinitely obliged to you."

He returned home, filled with a pleasant excitement,

that was now so unusual to him in his quiet, uneventful
life. The moonlight was streaming over sea and moorland, and he thought, as he passed over the little bridge
that spanned the fiord, and stepped out into the broad
road:—

" A delightful evening! But I must be careful. These
Sybaritic banquets unfit a man for sterner work! I shall
begin to hate my books and to loathe my little cabin.
God forbid! But how pleasant it was all. And how
Campion and Ormsby jumped at that idea of mine about
the fishing schooner, I look on the matter now as accomplished. After all, perhaps, these Irish gentry are
calumniated. Nothing could equal the ardour of these
men for the welfare of the poor fishermen. Who knows?
In six months' time, the ' Star of the Sea ' may be
ploughing the deep, and a fleet of sailing boats in her
wake; and then the fish-curing stores, and, at last, the
poor old village will look up and be known far and wide.
Dear me! I must get that lovely song out of my brain,
and the odour of those azaleas out of my senses. 'Twill
never do! A Kempis would shame me; would arraign
me as a rebel and a traitor. What a lovely night! and
how the waters sleep in the moonlight! Just there at
the bend we'll build the new pier. I see already the
' Star of the Sea ' putting out, and the waters whitening
in her wake."

He looked around, and saw the cottages of the pea-
sants and the labourers gleaming against the dark background of the moor and the mountain; and the thought
smote him: Perhaps there some little children went to
bed hungry to-night. He went home sadly, and, sitting
down, he said:—

" Let me see! Soup, entrées, joints, sweets, fruits,
wine, coffee. Let me see! White roses, azaleas, chry-
santhemums. Let me see! Waldteufel, Strauss, Wag-
ner! Let me see! "

He went over, and opened what appeared to be a rather

c

highly decorated cupboard. He drew back three shutters, and revealed a triptych, sunk deep in the wall of his
little parlour. It was the only thing of real value he
held. It was given to him by a Roman lady, who, for
one reason or another, chose to reside in England. It
nearly filled the entire space on the low wall. As he
drew back the shutters, the lamplight fell on the figure
that occupied the whole of the central panel. It was the
Christ. The tall shape was closely wrapped around in
the Jewish kethoneth—the first of the *vestes albæ* of the
priest, as St. John represents in the Apocalypse. The
capouche fell loosely over His head, and was embroidered
in many colours, as was also the hem of His long white
robe, which fell in folds over His sandalled feet. The
hood of the capouche shaded His eyes and threw a dark
shadow on the face as far as the lips. But the sacred
figure also held its right hand to shelter the eyes more
deeply from a strong glare of sunset. The left hand fell
loosely by His side, and the first of a large flock of sheep
had nestled its head comfortably in the open palm. The
large, gray eyes of Christ were filled with an anxious
light, as they gazed over the silent desert, questing for
some lost object; and the mouth, lightly fringed with
beard, was querulous with pain and solicitude. It was a
beautiful picture—one worthy to be screened from in-
devout eyes, or revealed only to those who loved and
worshipped.

The young priest gazed long and lovingly at this presentment of his Divine Master, whom he loved with the
strongest personal affection. Then he knelt down and
pressed his forehead against the dust-stained feet of
Christ, and moaned:—

" Master, if I have done wrong in aught this night,
let me know it! If I have betrayed Thy interests, or
brought Thy Name to shame, teach me in the sharpest
tones and flames of Thy anger, for I need a monitor; and
where shall I find so loving or so truthful a monitor as
Thou? Alas! how weak and pitiful I am, and how this

poor unsubdued nature of mine craves for things beyond
Thee! I know there is no truth but in Thee—no sincerity, no constancy. I know what men are; how de-
ceitful in their words; how unkind in their judgments.
Yet this lower being within my being forever stretches
out its longings to sensible things that deceive, and will
not rest in Thee, who art all Truth. But I must be
brought back to Thee through the sharp pangs of trial and
tears. Spare me not, O Master! only do not punish with
the deprivation of Thy Love! "

He rose up strengthened, yet with a premonition in his
heart of great trials awaiting him. Who would dream of
such tragic things under the heavy skies and the dull
environments of life in Ireland?

CHAPTER VIII

OUR CONCERT

The winter stole in quietly, heralded by the white frosts of late October; and nothing occurred to disturb the quiet of the village, except that Father Letheby's horse, a beautiful bay, ran suddenly lame one evening, as he topped a hill, and a long reach of mountain lay before him on his way to a sick-call. There were, of course, a hundred explanations from as many amateurs as to the cause of the accident. Then a quiet farmer, who suspected something, found a long needle driven deep into the hoof. It had gone deeper and deeper as the action of the horse forced it, until it touched the quick, and the horse ran dead lame. The wound festered, and the animal had to be strung up with leather bands to the roof of his stable for three months. Father Letheby felt the matter acutely; but it was only to myself he murmured the one significant word, Ahriman.

Late one evening in November a deputation waited on me. It consisted of the doctor, the schoolmaster, and one or two young fellows, generally distinguished by their vocal powers at the public house, when they were asked for " their fisht and their song." The doctor opened negotiations. I have a great regard for the doctor, and he knows it. He is a fine young fellow, a great student, and good and kind to the poor. I often spent a pleasant hour in his surgery over his microscope, where I saw wonderful things; but what has haunted me most is the recollection of a human brain, which the doctor had preserved in spirits, and on which he has given me several

60

lectures. I remember well my sensations when I first held the soft, dark, pulpy mass in my hand. All that I had ever read in psychology and metaphysics came back to me. This is the instrument of God's master-piece—the human soul. Over these nodes and fissures it floated, like the spirit of God over the face of the deep. Here, as on a beautiful instrument, the spirit touched the keys, and thought, like music, came forth; and here were impressed indelibly ideas of the vast universe without, of time and eternity; yea, even of the Infinite and Transcendent—of God. Hushed in the silence of prayer, here the soul brooded as a dove above its nest; and here in moments of temptation and repentance, it argued, reasoned, prayed, implored the inferior powers that rebelled or recanted beneath. With what sublime majesty it ruled and swayed the subjects that owned its imperial dominion; and how it touched heaven on the one hand for pity, and earth on the other in power! And when the turbulent passions raged and stormed, it soothed and quelled their rebellion; and then, in recompense to itself, it went out and up towards the celestials, and joined its emancipated sisters before the great white throne, and drank in peace and the blessedness of calm from the silences and worship of Heaven. Where is that soul now? Whither has it gone? Silent is the instrument, just crumbling to inevitable decay. But where in the boundless ocean of space is the deathless spirit that once ruled it in majesty, and drew from it music whose echoes roll through eternity? And how has science mapped and parcelled it, like a dead planet. Here is the " island of Reil," here the " pons Varolii "; here is the " arbor vitæ "; and here is the " subarachnoid space "; and here that wonderful contrivance of the great Designer that regulates the arterial supplies. I lift my hat reverentially and whisper, *Laudate*!

Well, the doctor knew how much I appreciated him. He was not nervous, therefore, in broaching the subject.

" We have come to see you, sir, about a concert."

" A what? " I said.

" A concert," he replied, in a little huff. " They have concerts every winter over at Labbawally, and at Balreddown, and even at Moydore; and why shouldn't we? "
I thought a little.

" I always was under the impression," I said, " that a concert meant singers."

" Of course," they replied.

" Well, and where are you to get singers here? Are you going to import again those delectable harridans that illustrated the genius of Verdi with rather raucous voices a few weeks ago? "

" Certainly not, sir," they replied in much indignation. " The boys here can do a little in that way; and we can get up a chorus amongst the school-children; and —and—— "

" And the doctor himself will do his share," said one of the deputation, coming to the aid of the modest doctor.

" And then," I said, " you must have a piano to accompany you, unless it is to be all in the style of ' come-all-yeen's.' "

" Oh, 'twill be something beyond that," said the doctor. " I think you'll be surprised, sir."

" And what might the object of the concert be? " I asked.

" Of course, the poor," they all shouted in chorus. " Wait, your reverence," said one diplomatist, " till you see all we'll give you for the poor at Christmas."

Visions of warm blankets for Nelly Purcell, and Mag Grady; visions of warm socks for my little children; visions of tons of coal and cartloads of timber; visions of vast chests of tea and mountains of currant-cake swam before my imagination; and I could only say:—

" Boys, ye have my blessing."

" Thank your reverence," said the doctor. " But what about a subscription? "

" For what? " I said. " If we all have to subscribe, what is the meaning of the concert? "

"Ah, but you know, sir, there are preliminary expenses—getting music, etc.—and we musk ask the respectable people to help us there."

This meant the usual guinea. Of course, they got it.

The evening of the concert came, and I was very reluctant to leave my arm-chair and the fire and the slippers. And now that my curate and I had set to work steadily at our Greek authors, to show the Bishop we could do something, I put aside my Homer with regret, and faced the frost of November. The concert was held in the old store down by the creek; and I shivered at the thought of two hours in that dreary room, with the windows open and a sea draught sweeping through. To my intense surprise, I gave up my ticket to a well-dressed young man with a basket of flowers in his button-hole; and I passed into a hall where the light blinded me, and I was dazed at the multitude of faces turned towards me. And there was a great shout of cheering; and I took off my great-coat, and was glad I had come.

There was a stage in front, covered with plants and carpeted; and a grand piano peeped out from a forest of shrubs and palms; and lamps twinkled everywhere; and I began to think it was all a dream, when Miss Campion came over, and said she was *so* glad I had come, etc., and I whispered:—

"I understand all now, when I see the little witch that has made the transformation."

Father Letheby sat by me, quiet and demure, as usual. He looked as if he had known nothing of all this wonderworking; and when I charged him solemnly with being chief organizer, builder, framer, and designer in all this magic, he put me off gently:—

"You know we must educate the people, sir. And you know our people are capable of anything."

I believed him.

Presently, there was a great stir at the end of the long room, and I looked around cautiously; for we were all so grand, I felt I should be dignified indeed.

" Who are these gentry, coming up the centre of the
hall? " I whispered; for a grand procession was streaming
in.

" Gentry? " he said.   " Why, these are the per-
formers." They were just passing—dainty little
maidens, in satin from the bows in their wavy and crisp
locks down to their white shoes; and they carried bou-
quets, and a subtle essence of a thousand odours filled the
air.

" Visitors at the Great House? " I whispered.

" Not at all," he cried impatiently. " They are our
own children. There's Mollie Lennon, the smith's daughter; and there's Annie Logan, whose father sells you the
mackerel; and there's Tessie Navin, and Maudie Ken-
nedy, and—— "

" Who's that grand young lady, with her hair done up
like the Greek girls of Tanagra? " I gasped.

" Why, that's Alice Moylan, the monitress."

" Good heavens," was all I could say. And the doctor
sailed in with his cohort, all in swallow-tails and white
fronts, their hair plastered down or curled, like the
fiddlers in an orchestra; and the doctor stooped down
and saw my amazement, and whispered:—

" Didn't I tell you we'd surprise you, Father Dan? "

Just then a young lad, dressed like a doll, and with
white kid gloves, handed me a perfumed programme.

" I charge a penny all around, but not to you, Father
Dan."

I thanked him politely and with reverence.

" Who's that young gentleman? " I whispered.

" Don't you know him? " said Father Letheby,
smothering a laugh.

" I never saw him before," I said.

" You cuffed him last Sunday for ringing the bell at
the *Agnus Dei.*"

" I cuffed that young ruffian, Carl Daly," I said.

" That's he," said Father Letheby. Then I thought
Father Letheby was making fun of me, and I was getting

cross, when I heard, " Hush! " and Miss Campion rose
up and passed on to the stage, and took her place at the
piano, and with one little wave of the hand, she mar-
shalled them into a crescent, and then there was a
pause, and then—a crash of music that sent every par-
ticle of blood in my old body dancing waltzes, and I began
to feel that I was no longer Daddy Dan, the old pastor of
Kilronan, but a young curate that thinks life all roses,
for his blood leaps up in ecstasy, and his eyes are straining afar.

One by one the singers came forward, timid, nervous,
but they went through their parts well.   At last, a young
lady, with bronze curls cut short, but running riot over
her head and forehead, came forward.   She must have
dressed in an awful hurry, for she forgot a lot of things.

" What's the meaning of this? " I whispered angrily.

" Sh', 'tis the fashion," said Father Letheby. " She's
not from our parish."

" Thank God," I said fervently.   I beckoned to Mrs.
Mullins, a fine motherly woman, who sat right across
the aisle.   She came over.

" Have you any particular use of that shawl lying on
your lap, Mrs. Mullins? " I said.

" No," she said, " I brought it against the night air."

" Then you'd do a great act of charity," I said, " if
you'd just step up on that stage and give it to that young
lady to cover her shoulders and arms.   She'll catch her
death of cold."

" For all the money you have in the National Bank,
Father Dan," said Mrs. Mullins, " and they say you
have a good little nest there, I wouldn't do it.   See how
she's looking at us.   She knows we are talking about
her.   And her mother is Julia Lonergan, who lives at
the Pike, in the parish of Moydore."

Sure enough, Phœbe Lonergan, for that was her name,
was looking at us; and her eyes were glinting and sparkling blue and green lights, like the dog-star on a frosty
night in January.   And I knew her mother well.   When

Julia Lonergan put her hands on her hips, and threw
back her head, the air became sulphurous and blue. I
determined not to mind the scantiness of the drapery,
though I should not like to see any of my own little children in such a state. Whilst I was meditating thus, she
came to the end of her song; and then let a yell out of
her that would startle a Red Indian.

" Why did she let that screech out of her? " said I to
Father Letheby. " Was it something stuck in her? "

" Oh, not at all," said he, " that's what they call a
bravura."

I began to feel very humble. And then a queer thing
happened. I thought I was a young curate, long before
the days of Maynooth statutes, and all these new regulations that bind us as tightly as Mrs. Darcy's new alb.
We were out at the hunt on a glorious November morning, the white frost on the grass, and the air crisp and
sunny. The smell of the fields, the heather, and the
withered bracken, came to us, and the bay coats and the
black coats of the horses shone like silk in the sunlight.
There were the usual courtesies, the morning salutes, and
the ladies' smiles; and then we moved to the cover, the
dogs quivering with excitement, and we not too com-
posed. And then far across the ploughed field we saw
the arch-enemy, Reynard, his brush straight out from his
back; and with one shout, Hoicks! and Harkaway! we
broke out into the open, and, with every nerve and
muscle strained, and the joy of the chase in our hearts,
we leaped onward to the contest. All the exhilaration
and intense joy of youth and freedom and the exercise
of life were in my veins, and I shouted Tally-ho! Harkaway, my boys! at the top of my voice.

A gentle hand was laid on mine, and I awoke from
my dream. The people were all smiling gravely, and
the chorus was just finishing the last bars of that best
of all finales: Tally-ho!   It was the witchery of the
music that called up the glorious past.

Then there was hunting for shawls and wraps, and such a din:—

" Wasn't it grand, Father Dan? "

" Aren't you proud of your people, Father Dan? "

" Where is Moydore now, Father Dan? "

" Didn't we do well, Father Dan? "

And then Miss Campion came over demurely and asked:—

" I hope you were pleased with our first performance, Father? "

And what could I say but that it was all beautiful and grand, and I hoped to hear it repeated, etc.

But then, when I had exhausted my enthusiasm, a band of these young fairies, their pretty faces flushed with excitement, and the stars in their curls bobbing and nodding at me, came around me.

" It's now our turn, Father Dan. We want one little dance before we go."

" What? " I cried, " children like you dancing! I'd be well in my way, indeed. Come now, sing ' Home, Sweet Home,' and away to Blanketland as fast as you can."

" Ah, do, Father Dan! "

" Ah, do, Father Dan! "

" One little dance! "

" We'll be home in half an hour! "

" Ah do, *Daddy* Dan! "

There was consternation. I knew that I was called by that affectionate, if very undignified title; but this was the first time it was spoken to my face; and there was horror on the faces of the young ones. But it carried the day. I looked around, and saw some white waistcoats peeping shyly behind a glass door.

" The boys are all gone home, I believe? " I said innocently.

" Oh, long and merry ago, Father. The lazy fellows wouldn't wait."

" And all the dancing will be amongst yourselves? "

Chorus: " Of course, Father!"

" And no waltzes or continental abominations?"

Chorus: " Oh dear, no!"

" And you'll all be in your beds at twelve o'clock?"

Chorus: " To the minute, Father."

" Well, God forgive me, but what can I do?   Go on,
you little heathens, and——"

" Thank you, Father——"

" Thank you, Father——"

" Thank you, Father——," etc., etc.

I went home with a troubled conscience, and I read
that blessed Maynooth statute about dances.   Then I had
no sleep that night.

The doctor and the deputation called on me about a
fortnight later to settle accounts.   I thought they were
not very enthusiastic.   They left the door open, and
sat near it.

" We came to settle about the concert, sir," said the
doctor; " we thought you would like to see our balance-
sheet."

" Yes," I said, demurely, " and, of course, if the
balance itself was convenient——"

" It isn't as much as we thought," said the doctor,
laying a small brown parcel on the table.   " The expenses were enormous.   Now, look at these," he said,
softly detaining my hand, as it moved towards the parcel.

I read the list of expenses.   It was appalling.   I cast
a corner of my eye farther down, and read, without pretending to see anything:—

" Total balance = 4s. 11½d."

" Boys," said I, as I saw them putting their hands
over their mouths with that unmistakable Hibernian
gesture, " you have done yourselves a great injustice."

" I assure you, sir," said the schoolmaster——

" You mistake my meaning," I interrupted.   " What
I was about to say was this—when young men give their
services gratuitously, and undertake great labour in the

cause of religion and charity, it would be most unfair to expect that they would also make a pecuniary sacrifice."

They looked relieved.

" Now, I have reason to know that you all have undergone great expense in connection with this concert."

There was a smirk of pharisaical satisfaction on their faces.

" But I cannot allow it. My conscience would not permit me. I see no record in this balance-sheet of the three dozen of Guinness that was ordered for the dressing-room. And there is not a word about the box of Havanas, which William Mescal ordered specially from Dublin; nor any mention of the soda-water and accompaniments that were hauled up in a basket through the back window. Really, I cannot allow it, gentlemen. Your generosity is overpowering—— "

The deep silence made me look around. They had vanished. I opened the brown parcel, and counted four shillings and eleven pence halfpenny in coppers.

CHAPTER IX

SEVERELY REPRIMANDED

IT was quite impossible that these changes or innovations could take place without a certain amount of reclamation, to us the theological expression, amongst the brethren. We are a conservative race, and our conservatism has been eminently successful in that matter of supreme moment—the preservation of the faith and the purity of our people. It is difficult, therefore, to see the necessity of change, to meet the exigencies of the times, and the higher demands of the nation and the race. Yet we have been forewarned a hundred times that we cannot put new wine into old bottles, and that a spirit is stirring amongst our people that must become unbridled and incontinent if not guided by new methods and new ideas. This is not intuitive wisdom on my part. It is gathered slowly and painfully amongst the thorns of experience.

But I cannot say I was too surprised when, one morning, an old and most valued friend called on me, and revealed his anxiety and perturbation of spirit by some very deep remarks about the weather. We agreed wonderfully on that most harmonious topic, and then I said :

" You have something on your mind? "

" To be candid with you, Father Dan," he replied, assuming a sudden warmth, " I have. But I don't like to be intrusive."

" Oh, never mind," I replied. " I am always open to fraternal correction."

" You know," he continued nervously, " we are old

friends, and I have always had the greatest interest in
you—— "

" For goodness' sake, Father James," I said, " spare
me all that. That is all *subintellectum*, as the theologians say when they take a good deal for granted."

" Well, then," said he—for this interruption rather
nettled him—" to be very plain with you, your parish
is going to the dogs. You are throwing up the sponge
and letting this young man do what he likes. Now, I
can tell you the people don't like it, the priests don't
like it, and when he hears it, as he is sure to hear it, the
Bishop won't like it either."

" Well, Father James," I said slowly, " passing by
the mixed metaphors about the dogs and the sponge,
what are exactly the specific charges made against this
young man? ".

" Everything," he replied vaguely. " We don't want
young English mashers coming around here to teach
old priests their business. We kept the faith—— "

" Spare me that," I said. " And don't say a word
about the famine years. That episode, and the grandeur
of the Irish priests, is written in Heaven. We want a
Manzoni to tell it—that is, if we would not prefer to
leave it unrecorded, except in the great book—which is
God's memory."

He softened a little at this.

" Now," said I, " you are a wise man. What do you
want me to do? "

" I want you to pitch into that young fellow," he said,
" to cuff him and make him keep his place."

" Very good. But be particular. Tell me, what am
I to say? "

" Say? Tell him you'll stand no innovations in your
parish. *Nil innovetur, nisi quod prius traditum est.* Tell
him that he must go along with all the other priests of the
diocese and conform to the general regulations—*Quod
semper, quod ubique, quod ab omnibus.* Tell him that

young men must know their place; and then take up the
Selva, or the Fathers, and prove it to him."

"God bless you!" said I, thankfully and humbly.
" You have taken a load off my heart. Now, let me see
would this do."

I took down from the dusty shelves a favourite little
volume—a kind of Anthology of the early Fathers, and I
opened it.

"We'll try the *sortes Virgilianæ*," I said, and read
slowly and with emphasis:—

"At nunc, etiam sacerdotes Dei, omissis Evangeliis
et Prophetis, vidimus comœdias legere, amatoria Buco-
licorum versuum verba cantare, tenere Virgilium, et id
quod in pueris necessitatis est, crimen in se facere volup-
tatis."

"That's not bad," said my hearer, critically, whilst
I held the book open with horror and amazement. " That
applies to him, I'm sure. But what's the matter, Father
Dan? You are not ill?"

"No," said I, "I'm not; but I'm slightly discon-
certed. That anathema strikes me between the two
eyes. What else have I been doing for fifty years but
thumbing Horace and Virgil?"

"Oh, never mind," he said, airily. "Who wrote
that? That's extreme, you know."

"An altogether wise and holy man, called St. Jerome,"
I said.

"Ah, well, he was a crank. I don't mean that. That
sounds disrespectful. But he was a reformer, you know."

"A kind of innovator, like this young man of mine?"
I said.

"Ah, well, try some sensible saint. Try now St.
Bernard. He was a wise, gentle adviser."

I turned to St. Bernard, and read:—

> "Lingua magniloqua—manus otiosa!
> Sermo multus—fructus nullus!
> Vultus gravis—actus levis!
> Ingens auctoritas—nutans stabilitas!"

That hit my friend between the eyes. The auguries were inauspicious. He took up his hat.

" You are not going? " said I, reaching for the bell. " I am just sending for Father Letheby to let you see how I can cuff him—— "

" I—I—must be going," he said; " I have a sick-call —that is—an engagement—I—er—expect a visitor—will call again. Good day."

" Stay and have a glass of wine! " I said.

" No, no, many thanks; the mare is young and rather restive. *Au revoir!* "

" *Au revoir!* " I replied, as I took up my hat and gold-headed cane and set out to interview and reprimand my curate. Clearly, something should be done, and done quickly. There was a good deal of talk abroad, and I was supposed to be sinking into a condition of senile incompetence. It is quite true that I could not challenge my curate's conduct in a single particular. He was in all things a perfect exemplar of a Christian priest, and everything he had done in the parish since his arrival contributed to the elevation of the people and the advancement of religion. But it wouldn't do. Every one said so; and, of course, every one in these cases is right. And yet there was some secret misgiving in my mind that I should do violence to my own conscience were I to check or forbid Father Letheby's splendid work; and there came a voice from my own dead past to warn me : " See that you are not opposing the work of the right hand of the Most High."

These were my doubts and apprehensions as I moved slowly along the road that led in a circuitous manner around the village and skirted the path up to the school-house. I woke from my unpleasant reverie to hear the gentle murmur of voices, moving rhythmically as in prayer; and in a short bend of the road I came face to face with the children leaving school. I had been accustomed to seeing these wild, bare-legged mountaineers breaking loose from school in a state of subdued frenzy, leaping up and down the side ditches, screaming, yelling, panting, with their elf-locks blinding their eyes, and their bare feet flashing amid the green of grasses or the brown of the ditch-mould. They might condescend to drop me a curtsy, and then—anarchy, as before. To-day they moved slowly, with eyes bent modestly on the ground, three by three, and all chanting in a sweet, low tone—the Rosary. The centre girl was the coryphæus with the " Our Fathers " and " Hail Marys "; the others, the chorus. I stood still in amazement and challenged them:—

" I am happy to see my little children so well employed. How long since you commenced to say the Rosary thus in common? "

In a twinkling the solemnity vanished and I was surrounded by a chattering group.

" Just a week, Fader; and Fader Letheby, Fader, he tould us of a place where they do be going to work in the morning, Fader, and dey all saying de Rosary togeder, Fader; and den, Fader, we do be saying to ourselves, why shouldn't we, Fader, say de Rosary coming to school, de same as dese Germans, Fader? "

" That's excellent," I said, running my eyes over the excited group; " and have you all got beads? "

" I have, Fader," said one of the coryphæi, " and de oders do be saying it on their fingers."

" I must get beads for every one of you," I said; " and to commence, here, Anstie, is my own."

I gave a little brown-eyed child my own mother-of-pearl beads, mounted in silver, and was glad I had it to give. The children moved away, murmuring the Rosary as before.

Now, here clearly was an innovation. Wasn't this intolerable? Who ever heard the like? Where would all this stop? Why, the parish is already going to the dogs! He has played right into my hands. Yes? Stop the Rosary? Prevent the little children from singing the praises of their Mother and Queen? I thought I saw the

face of the Queen Mother looking at me from the skies;
and I heard a voice saying, prophetically: "Ex ore in-
fantium et lactantium perfecisti laudem propter inimicos
tuos, ut destruas inimicum et ultorem." Clearly, the
fates are against me.

"Father Letheby was not at home, but would be back
presently. Would I take a chair and wait for a few
moments?"

I sat down in a comfortable arm-chair lined with the
soft rug that first elicited my housekeeper's admiration.
I looked around. Books were strewn here and there,
but there was no slovenliness or untidiness; and, ha!
there were the first signs of work on the white sheets of
manuscript paper. I wonder what is he writing about.
It is not quite honourable, but as I am on the war path,
perhaps I could get here a pretext for scalping him.
Notes!

"November 1. Dipped into several numbers of *Cornhill
Magazine*. Specially pleased with an article on ' Wordsworth's
ethics,' in the August number, 1876.
"November 2. Read over Sir H. Taylor's poems, principally
Philip van Artevelde,' ' Isaac Comnenus,' ' Edwin the Fair,'
The Eve of Conquest.'
            "*Comnenus*.—Not much the doubt
Comnenus would stand well with times to come,
Were there the hand to write his threnody,
Yet is he in sad truth a faulty man.

.   .   .   .   .   .
But be it said he had this honesty,
That, undesirous of a false renown,
He ever wished to pass for what he was,
One that swerved much, and oft, but being still
Deliberately bent upon the right,
Had kept it in the main; one that much loved
Whate'er in man is worthy high respect,
And in his soul devoutly did aspire
To be it all: yet felt from time to time
That littleness that clings to what is human,
And suffered from the shame of having felt it."

"Humph! This is advanced," I thought. "I wonder does he feel like Comnenus? It is a noble portrait,
and well worthy imitation."

Just then he came in. After the usual greetings he
exclaimed, in a tone of high delight :—

" Look here, Father, here's a delicious tit-bit. Confess you never read such a piece of sublime self-conceit
before."

He took up a review that was lying open on the desk,
and read this :—

"As for claims, these are my opinions. If Lord Liverpool
takes simply the claims of the scholar, Copleston's are fully
equal to mine. So, too, in general knowledge the world would
give it in favour of him. If Lord Liverpool looks to professional
merits, mine are to Copleston's as *the Andes to a molehill.*
There is no comparison between us ; Copleston is no theologue ;
I am. If, again, Lord Liverpool looks to weight and influence in the University, I will give Copleston a month's start
and beat him easily in any question that comes ·before us.
As to popularity in the appointment, mine will be popular
through the whole profession ; Copleston's the contrary. . . . .
I thought, as I tell you, honestly, I should be able to make
myself a bishop in due time. . . . I will conclude by telling
you my own real wishes about myself. My anxious desire is
to make myself a great divine, and to be accounted the best
in England. My second wish is to become the founder of a
school of theology at Oxford. Now, no bishopric will enable me
to do this but the See of Oxford. I have now told you my
most secret thoughts. What I desire is, after a few years, to
be sure of a retirement, with good provision in some easy
bishopric, or Van Mildert deanery. I want neither London
nor Canterbury : they will never suit me. But I want money,
because I am poor and have children ; and I desire character,
because I cannot live without it."

" Isn't that simply delicious? " said Father Letheby,
laying down the review, and challenging my admiration.

" Poor fellow," I could not help saying ; " the last little
bit of pathos about his children gilds the wretched picture. Who was he? "

" No less a person than Dr. Lloyd, Regius Professor
of Divinity in Oxford, and *the* originator of the Trac-
tarian Movement. But can you conceive a Catholic
priest writing such a letter? "

" No," I replied slowly, " I cannot. But I can conceive a Catholic priest thinking it. I am not so much
unlike the rest of mankind ; and I remember when I came

out on the mission, and had time to look around me, like a chicken just out of its shell, two things gave me a shock of intense surprise. First, I could not conceive how the Catholic Church had got on for eighteen hundred years without my coöperation and ability; and, secondly, I could not understand what fatuity possessed the Bishop to appoint as his vicar-general a feeble old man of seventy, who preached with hesitation, and, it was whispered, believed the world was flat, and that people were only joking when they spoke of it as a globe; and pass over such a paragon of perfection, an epitome of all the talents, like myself. It took me many years to recover from that surprise; and, alas! a little trace of it lingers yet. Believe me, my dear young friend, a good many of us are as alien in spirit to the Imitation as Dr. Lloyd, but we must not say it."

" By Jove! " he said, " I thought there was but one other Dr. Lloyd in the world, and that was Father James ——," mentioning the name of my morning visitor.

It was the first chink I had seen in the armour of my young Goliath, and I put in my rapier.

" You are not very busy? " I said.

" No, Father," he replied, surprised.

" Would you have time to listen to a little story? "

" Certainly," he said, settling back in his chair, his head on his hands.

" Well," I said slowly, " in the first years of my mission I had a fellow curate, a good many years younger than myself. I consequently looked down on him, especially as he was slightly pompous in his manner and too much addicted to Latin and French quotations. In fact, he looked quite a hollow fellow, and apparently a selfish and self-contented one. I changed my opinion later on. He was particularly fond of horses, though he never rode. He was a kind of specialist in horse-flesh. His opinion was regarded as infallible. He never kept any but the highest breed of animal. He had a particularly handsome little mare, which he called ' Winnie,' because he thought he saw in her some intelligence, like what he read of in the famous mare of a famous Robin Hood. She knew him, and followed him like a dog. He allowed no one to feed her, or even to groom her, but himself. He never touched her with a whip. He simply spoke to her, or whistled, and she did all he desired. He had refused one hundred and fifty pounds for her at a southern fair a few days before the occurrence which I am about to relate. One day he had been at conference, or rather we were both there, for he drove me to the conference and back. It was thirteen miles going and the same returning. The little mare came back somewhat fagged. He was no light-weight, nor was I.

" ' I shall not drive her there again,' he said; ' I'll get an old hack for these journeys.'

" Before he sat down to dinner he fed and groomed her, and threw her rug over her for the night. She whinnied with pleasure at reaching her own stable. Just as he sat down to dinner a sick-call was announced. It was declared ' urgent.' After a while you won't be too much alarmed at these ' urgent ' calls, for they generally mean but little; but on this occasion a short note was put into the priest's hand. It was from the doctor. It ran: ' Come as quickly as possible. It is a most critical case.'

" There was no choice there.

" ' Have you brought a horse? ' the priest cried.

" ' No, your reverence,' said the messenger. ' I crossed down the mountain by the goat-path. There was no time.'

" The priest went straight to the stable and unlocked it. The mare whinnied, for she knew his footstep. He flashed the light upon her as she turned her big eyes towards him.

" ' Come, little woman,' he said, ' we must be on the road again.'

" She understood him, and moaned.

" He led her out and put her to his trap. Then, without a word, he gave her the rein, and they pushed on in

the darkness. The road for five miles was as level as that
table, and she went rapidly forward. Then a steep hill
rose before them for about two miles, and he relaxed a
little, not wishing to drive her against the hill. Just
then, on the brow he saw lights flashing and waving to
and fro in the night. He knew the significance of it, and
shook out the reins. The poor little animal was so tired
she could not breast the hill. He urged her forward.
She refused. Then, for the first time in his life, he took
out his whip. He did not strike her, and to this day he
thanks God for it. But he merely shook it over her head.
Stung by the indignity, she drew herself together and
sprang against the hill. She went up and up, like a deer,
whilst the trap jolted and swung from side to side. Just
as they reached the crest of the hill and heard the shouts,
' Hurry, your reverence, you'll never overtake her,' the
little mare plunged forward and fell heavily. The priest
was flung against a boulder and struck insensible. When
he came to, the first word he heard was, ' She's dead, I
fear, your reverence.' ' Who? ' said the priest; ' the
woman? ' ' No, your reverence, but the mare ! ' ' Thank
God ! ' said the priest; and he meant it. Dazed, stupefied, bleeding, he stumbled across rocks of red sand-
stone, heather, gorse; he slipped over some rude stepping-
stones that crossed a mountain torrent; and, at last, made
his way to the rude cabin in the rough gorges of the
mountain. The doctor was washing his instruments as
the priest entered.

" ' It's all right, Father James,' he said, cheerily.
' The neatest case I ever had. But it was touch and go.
Hello ! you're bleeding on the temple. What's up? '

" ' Oh, nothing,' said the priest. ' The mare stumbled
and threw me. I may go in? '

" ' Certainly,' said the doctor; ' but just allow me to
wash that ugly wound.'

" ' Wound? 'Tis only a scratch.'

" The priest went in and went through his ordinary
ministrations. Then he came out, and still dazed and

not knowing what to think, he stumbled back to the crest of the mountain road. There were men grouped around the fallen animal and the broken trap. They made way for him. He knelt down by the poor beast and rubbed her ears, as he was in the habit of doing, and whispered, ' Winnie! ' The poor animal opened her eyes full upon him, then trembled convulsively, and died.

" ' You will bury her, boys,' said the priest, ' over there under that cairn of stones, and bring me down the trap and harness in the morning.'

" What his feelings were, as he walked home, I leave you to realize. We did not hear of it for some days; but that ' Thank God! ' changed all my opinions of him. I looked up to him ever since, and see under all his pomposity and dignity a good deal of the grit that makes a man a hero or a saint."

" I retract my remark unreservedly," said my curate; " it was unjust and unfair. It is curious that I have never yet made an unkind remark but I met with prompt punishment."

" You may not be a great theologian nor a deep thinker," said I, " but no man ever uttered a more profound saying. God may ignore our petty rebellions against Himself; but when we, little mites, sit in contemptuous judgment on one another, He cannot keep His hands from us! And so, *festina lente! festina lente!* It is wholesome advice, given in many languages."

" Is the accent on the *festina* or the *lente*, Father? " he said demurely.

I looked at him.

" Because," he said, " I have been doing things lately that sometimes seem inopportune—that concert for example, and—— "

" They are all right," I said, " but *lente! lente!!* "

" And that little interview with the chapel woman—felt I could have done better——? "

" It is all right," I repeated, " but *lente! lente!!* "

" And I think we must stop those little children from saying the Rosary—— "

This time I looked at him quite steadily. He was imperturbable and sphinx-like.

" Good evening," I said.   " Come up after dinner and let us have a chat about that line in the ' Odes ' we were speaking about."

I went homewards slowly, and, as I went, the thought would obtrude itself, how far I had recovered my lost authority, and succeeded in satisfying that insatiable monster called Public Opinion.   For my curate had been reading for me a story by some American author, in which the narrative ended in a problem whether a lady or a tiger would emerge from a cage under certain circumstances; and hence, a conundrum was puzzling the world—the tiger or the lady, which? And my conundrum was, Had I lectured my curate, or had my curate lectured me? I am trying to solve the problem to this day.

CHAPTER X

FATHER LETHEBY did come up, and we had one of those pleasant meetings on which my memory dwells with gratitude. I hope he thinks of them tenderly, too; for I believe he gave more pleasure and edification than he received. We old men are garrulous, and rather laudatory of the past than enthusiastic about the present. And this must needs chafe the nerves of those whose eyes are always turned toward the sanguine future. Well, this evening we had the famous epilogue of the Third Book of the Odes of Horace for discussion, and our thoughts turned on the poet's certainty of immortality—the immortality of fame, in which alone he believed. I remarked what a curious thing it was that men are forever craving for that which, when attained, they fling aside and despise.

" I remember a good old priest," I said, " who was very angry because he did not receive the ecclesiastical honours that sometimes accompany old age. And when I asked, rather foolishly indeed, of what possible use could they be to him, the answer was, he would like to die with his full meed of honours. Well, he got them at last; and after a few months his regret was that he had spent nine pounds on the rochet and mozetta."

" Do you think he would be satisfied to go back to the condition of a ' simplex sacerdos ' again, and to be called ' Father '? " said my curate.

" I do. He had received recognition and was satisfied," I replied.

" There must be something in it. I remember now

that bitter letter about Fame, which Tennyson wrote
when he had attained a world-wide reputation. He found
Fame to be hostility from his peers, indifference from his
superiors, worship from those he despised. He would
barter all his Fame for £5,000 a year; and was sorry he
ever wrote a line."

" What then is it all? Of what consequence was it to
Horace that a poor old priest, in the Ultima Thule of the
earth, should find a little pleasure in his lines, some eighteen hundred years after his death? " I said, half musingly.

" None whatever. But these passions are the minor
wheels of human action, and therefore of human progress,
when the great motor, religion, is set aside."

" And you think God permits them for that reason? "

" Possibly. By the way, Father Dan, allow me to
congratulate you on your excellent taste. Why, you have
made this little parlour a nest of luxury and refinement."

" Alas! yes. But all my comfort is gone. I blame
you for it all, you rascal. Why did you come introducing
your civilization here? We were happy enough without
it. And like Fame, luxury brings its trials. Hannah
wasn't easy until she rivalled your splendid establishment; and when taste came in, comfort went out by the
window. God bless me! All I have suffered for the
last fortnight! I must wipe my boots at the door, and
hang up my hat in the hall, and walk on tip-toe on these
waxed floors. I am afraid to sit down, lest I should break
these doll's chairs. I am afraid to get up lest I should
slip and break my old bones. I am afraid to eat lest I
should soil those new napkins. I am afraid to drink lest
I should break one of these new gilt cups. I have no
comfort but in bed. What in the world did I do that you
should have been sent here? "

" There's something in it," he said, laughing. " It
is the universal law of compensation. But, honestly, it
is all very tasteful and neat, and you'll get used to it.
You know it is one of the new and laughable arguments

against the eternity of punishment, that you can get used
to anything."

"I can't get that poor fellow, Lloyd, out of my head,"
I said, changing the subject. "That was a pitiful letter. And the pity is that a strictly private document,
such as that was, should see the light and be discussed
fifty years after it was written, by two priests on the west
coast of Ireland. To whom did he write it?"

"To Sir Robert Peel, then Prime Minister."

"There was a dear old friend of my youth," I said,
"who was fond of giving advice. I suppose I picked up
the evil habit from him. But his summary of all wisdom was this:—

"Never consult a doctor!

"Never go security!

"Never write a letter that may not be read in the
market square!"

"I hope you have followed this sapient, but rather
preternatural advice," said Father Letheby.

"No," I replied. "It would have been well for me
if I had done so."

We both lapsed into a brown study.

"It is not easy for us priests to take advice," he said
at last; "I suppose our functions are so magisterial that
we cannot understand even the suggestion of inferiority
in reproof. Was it not Dean Stanley who said that the
Anglican clergy are polished into natural perfection by
domestic interchanges of those silent corrections that are
so necessary, and that it is the absence of these cor-
rectives that accounts for the so many nodes and excre-
scences of our social characteristics?"

"True. But we won't take correction. Or rather,
no one dare give it. The Bishop can and will; but then
a word from a bishop smites like a Nasmyth hammer,
and he is necessarily slow of reproof. A Parish priest
nowadays dare not correct a curate—— "

"I beg pardon, sir," Father Letheby said; "I am

sure you'll do me an infinite favour if you kindly point
out my many imprudences and inconsistencies."

" And you'll take it well? "

" Well," he said dubiously, " I won't promise that I
shall not be nettled. But I'll take it respectfully."

" All right. We'll commence this moment. Give up
that coffee-drinking, and take an honest glass of punch."

He laughed in his own musical way. He knew the
anguish that coffee had cost Hannah. She had taken
to Father Letheby wonderfully. He had found for her a
new brand of snuff, and had praised her cooking. And
lo! a miracle. Hannah, the Parish priest's housekeeper,
had actually gone down and visited his servant. It was
a tremendous condescension, involving a great deal of
thought. But there was a new alliance—dual again; it
is almost like the kaleidoscopic changes of European poli-
ticians. Then for several days there were conferences
and colloguings, the result being that, as a reward of
humility, which indeed always brings its reward even in
this world, Hannah has her house furnished à la mode,
and has learned the science of coffee-making—a science
little known as yet in Ireland. Of course, there have
been crosses. It is not pleasant, when a brother priest
comes in, to see him stand in amazement and appear
quite distracted whilst his politeness will not allow him
to demand explanations. And when a more demonstrative character shouts Hallo! when he comes into your
parlour, and vents his surprise in a prolonged whistle, and
looks at you curiously when your attention is engaged,
it is slightly embarrassing. Then, again, I'm told that
the villagers are making sarcastic remarks about my little
ménage: " Begor, Hannah won't be left a pinny "; or,
" Begor, Kilronan is looking up "; or, " Begor, he'll be
expecting an incrase of the jues "; and one old woman,
who gets an occasional letter from America with an en-
closure, is quite sure I have embezzled her money, and
she comes to the door three times a week with—" that
little letther, your reverence? Sure, I don't begredge

it to you. You're welcome to it over and over again; but whin 'tis convanient, sure you won't see me wantin'? But sure, Mary will think it quare that I never wrote to thank her." I have given up protesting that I have received no letter lately from Mary; but the " purty boys " down at the forge have set the poor woman crazy. "Yerra, where 'ud he get de money for all them grand tings he has?" " Yerra, Kate, you'll never see dat post-office order." " Write to the Bishop, 'oman, and he'll see you rightified." And then, to crown all, comes the bill, just double what I expected. But it is wonderful how many extras there were, and how wages and the price of material went up. Alas! my little deposit of fifty pounds, which was to secure a few masses after my death, where is it? And poor old Hannah? Well, she'll have it all after my death, and that will make her doubly careful, and me—doubly miserable.

" Now," I said to Father Letheby, as he daintily balanced his spoon over his cup, and I leisurely stirred the sugar in—well, no matter, " I don't like that coffee. It is not sociable. It makes you too cautious, while we, under the potent and expanding influence of native manufacture, are inclined to develop. Now, if you want to succeed in life, give up that Turkish drug and do what all your predecessors did."

" I'm too Irish for that," he said, rather paradoxically, I thought. " I'm afraid I should be talking about my ancestors, and asking some one to be good enough to tread on the tail of my coat."

He knew well that I did not wish to interfere with his tastes.

" Well, however, think kindly of us who cling to old traditions. We too had our day."

I was silent, thinking of old times.

" You never slept in a lime-kiln, I presume," said I, starting from a long reverie.

" God forbid," he said with a start.

" Well, I did. It happened in this way. It was nearly

ten o'clock at night when I arrived at the door of the old
pastor, to whose care I was committed on my first mission. I knocked, and knocked, and knocked. No answer. 'Twas all the same. Father L—— had but one
room and the kitchen; and that room was parlour, library, drawing-room, bedroom, and all. I dismissed the
jarvey, left my portmanteau at the door, and wandered
out into the night. I dared not rouse up the farmers
around. It was the time of the Whiteboys, and I might
get a charge of shot or a thrust of a pike for my pains.
The night was cold and starry. And after wandering
about for some time I came to a kiln. The men—the
lime-burners—were not long gone, and the culm was still
burning. I went in. The warmth was most grateful.
I lay down quietly, took out my beads, and whilst saying
the Rosary I fell fast asleep. I awoke to hear: ' Come,
get out of this.' And, then, ' Good God! it is a priest.'
Ah! well, how times have changed! But think kindly of
us old men. We too have borne the burden and the
heat—the *pondus diei et œstus.*"

A deep silence fell upon us both, broken only by the
crackling of the turf and wood fire, I busy with the past,
and he sunk in his own reflections. At length I said:—

" Would I trouble you to hand me down that ' Pars
Verna ' with the morocco cover? Thanks! This little
time-stained book saw some curious scenes. It was my
companion in many a rough adventure. In these old
times it was quite a common experience for myself to
leave home at six o'clock in the morning so as to be at
the station-house by seven. By the way, you did murder
the names of the mountain town-lands when calling the
stations last Sunday. You must try and get the ' bloss '
of the Irish on your tongue. Well, we usually heard
confessions from seven to three o'clock in the afternoon,
with just an interval for breakfast—— "

" Pardon me, sir, but do you mean to say the people
remained fasting and received Holy Communion at three
o'clock? "

" Yes, my dear young man, that was an every-day experience. I remember a mission that was given in the
town of N——, where I was curate in '54, the year the
first great missions were given by Fathers Bernard and
Petcherine. One evening, dead tired after a continuous
day's work, I was crossing the church toward the sacristy,
when a huge shaggy countryman stopped me. It was just
half-past ten o'clock. ' I'm for Communion, your reverence,' said he. I was a little irritable and therefore a
little sarcastic at the time. ' It is usually the habit of
Catholics to receive Holy Communion fasting,' said I,
never dreaming but that the man was after his supper.
' For the matter of that, your reverence,' said he, ' I
could have received Communion any minit these last
three days; for God is my witness, neither bite nor sup
has crossed my lips, not even a spoonful of wather.' But
to come back. Dear me, how easy it is to get me off the
rail ! After three o'clock I used to start out for my sick-
calls; and, will you believe me, I was often out all night,
going from one cabin to another, sometimes six or seven
miles apart; and I often rode home in the morning when
the larks were singing above the sod and the sun was
high in the sky. Open that quarto.''
He did. The leaves were as black as the cover, and
clung together, tattered as they were.
" The rain and the wind of Ireland,'' I said. " It was
no easy job to read Matins, with one hand clutching the
reins and the pommel of the saddle, and the other holding that book in a mountain hurricane. But you are not
a Manichæan, are you? ''
He looked at me questioningly.
" I mean you don't see Mephistopheles rising in that
gentle cloud of steam from my glass? ''
" Oh, no,'' he said; " you have your tastes, and I
mine. Both are equally innocuous. But the fact is,''
he said, after a pause, " I cannot touch wine or spirits,
because I want to work at night, and I must have all my
faculties clear.''

" Then you are working hard. God bless you! I saw your notes the other day. But don't forget your Greek. French is the language of diplomacy, Italian the language of love, German the language of philosophy, English the language of commerce, Latin the language of the Church, Greek the language of the scholar, and Hebrew the language of God. But I remember it gave a new zest to my studies long ago, when I read somewhere that our Divine Lord spoke Greek, at least amongst the learned, for Greek in the East was what Latin has been in the West."

" Yes, but 'tis pitiful," he replied, with a blush; " I did get a gold medal from all Ireland in Greek; and yet, when I took up such an easy book as Homer the other day, why, 'twas all Greek to me."

Here Hannah broke in, opening the door.

" Won't you take another cup of coffee, sir? " Awaiting the reply, Hannah poked up the fire and sent the blazes dancing merrily up the chimney. Then she raised the flame of the lamp, and did a great many other unnecessary things; but the kitchen is lonesome.

" Well, Hannah," said Father Letheby enthusiastically, " I will. You have made me a confirmed teetotaler. I would not even think of punch when your fragrant coffee is before me."

" Wisha, then, sir, but there's more life in the little drop of sperrits. However, your reverence is welcome to whatever you like in this house."

This is not the first time Hannah has assumed a tone of proprietorship in my little establishment. Well, no matter. It is our Irish communism—very like that of the Apostles, too.

" You must not be disheartened about that," I said. " I read some time ago that no less a person than Lord Dufferin declared that, although he had taken a degree in Greek, he could not read a line of it in after years till he had learned it all over again, and in his own way."

" I am delighted to hear that," said Father Letheby.

D

" And when you do master your Greek," I said, " use your knowledge where it will profit you most."

He waited.

" On the Greek Fathers. Believe me, there is more poetry, science, philosophy, and theology there than in all modern literature, since Shakespeare. We don't know it. The Anglican divines do. I suspect that many a fairly sculptured sermon and learned treatise was cut from these quarries."

I suppose the poor fellow was weary from all the lecturing. Indeed, I think too his mind had rather a practical cast; for he began to ply me with questions about the parish that fairly astonished me.

" Did Pat Herlihy's big boy make his First Communion? What about establishing a First Confession class? He heard there was a night-dance at the cross-roads, half-ways to Moydore. Why don't the Moydore priests stop it? Did I know Winifred Lane, a semi-imbecile up in the mountains? He did not like one of the teachers. He thought him disrespectful. What was the cause of the coolness between the Learys and the Sheas? Was it the way that one of the Sheas, about sixty years ago, served on a jury, at which some disreputable Leary was convicted? What about a bridge over that mountain torrent at Slieveogue? He had written to the surveyor. Did I think the nuns in Galway would take a postulant? He heard that there was a sister home from New Zealand who was taking out young girls—— "

" My dear young friend," I said, when I had tried to answer imperfectly this catechism, " I know you are a saint, and therefore endowed with the privilege of bilocation; but I did not know that you could dictate to six amanuenses at the same time, like Cæsar or Suarez."

" Oh, by the way," he said, putting up his notebook, " I was near forgetting. With your permission, sir, I intend to put up a little crib at Christmas. Now, the roof is leaking badly over St. Joseph's Chapel. If you allow me, I shall put Jem Deady on the roof. He says you know him well, and can recommend him, and there are a few pounds in my hands from the Living Rosary."

It was true. I knew Jem Deady very well, as a confirmed dipsomaniac, who took the Total Abstinence Pledge for life regularly every three months. I also knew that that leak over St. Joseph's Chapel had been a steady source of income to Jem for the last ten years. Somehow it was an incurable malady, a kind of stone and mortar scrofula that was always breaking out, and ever resisting the science of this amiable physician. Sometimes it was "ground-damp," sometimes the "weeping wall"; and there were dread dissertations on barge courses and string courses, but there the evil was, ugly and ineradicable.

" I dare say, Jem told you that I had been putting cobblers from the village every winter for the last ten years on that roof and that he alone possesses the secret that will make that wall a ' thing of beauty and a joy for ever ' ? "

" Well, indeed, he said something of the kind. But I have taken a fancy to the fellow. He sings like an angel, and since the Concert he entertains me every night with a variety of melodies, amongst which I think ' Her Bright Smile Haunts Me Still ' is his masterpiece."

" He does not sing ' Two Lovely Black Eyes'? " I asked.

" No," said Father Letheby, seriously.

" I think his wife sings that," I said, as Father Letheby rose to go.

" By the way," I said, as I helped him on with his greatcoat in the hall, for he is one for whom I would make any sacrifice, " how have you acquired such a minute knowledge of my parishioners in such a short time ? "

" Well," said he, tying a silk handkerchief around his neck, " I was once at a military review in England, having been invited by some Catholic officers. I stood rather near the Duke of Cambridge. And this struck me. The

Duke called out, ' Who commands that company? ' ' I,
sir.' ' What is the name of the third man on the right?
Married or single? Term of service? Character? Trade? '
And I was utterly amazed at the accurate information of
the officers.   Now, I often thought, if our great Com-
mander-in-Chief questioned us in that manner, could we
reply with the same precision?   And I determined to
know, as soon as possible, the name, history, and position
of every man, woman, and child in this parish."

" And you have succeeded," I said admiringly. "You
know them better than I, who have spent thirty years
amongst them.   But "—I could not resist the temptation of a little lecture—" if you are asked, accept no
responsibility in money matters; and if two cocks are
fighting down the street, and consequently diplomatic
courtesies are suspended between the neighbours, I
would not, if I were you, trouble much to ascertain
which of the belligerents had ethical and moral right
on his side; and if Mrs. Gallagher, by pure accident,
should happen to be throwing out a pail of particularly
dirty water just at the psychological moment when Mrs.
Casey is passing her door; and if the tailormade gown
of the latter is thereby desecrated, and you see a sudden eclipse of the sun, and hear the rumble of distant
thunder, don't throw aside your Æschylus to see the
' Furies '; and if Mrs. Deady—— "

" Thank you! thank you, Father," he said, abruptly,
" never fear.   'Twill be all right! "

I closed the door on his fine, manly figure, and went
back to my arm-chair, murmuring:—

" *Pathemata—mathemata*.   So shall it be to the end,
O Father of history! "

CHAPTER XI

BESIDE THE SINGING RIVER

FATHER LETHEBY was coming home a few nights ago, a little after twelve o'clock, from a hurried sick-call, and he came down by the cliffs; for, as he said, he likes to see the waters when the Almighty flings his net over their depths, and then every sea-hillock is a star, and there is a moon in every hollow of the waves. As he skirted along the cliff that frowns down into the valleys of the sea on the one hand, and the valleys of the firs and poplars on the other, he thought he heard some voices deep down in the shadows, and he listened. Very soon the harsh rasp of a command came to his ears, and he heard: "'Shun! 'verse arms," etc. He listened very attentively, and the tramp of armed men echoed down the darkness; and he thought he saw the glint of steel here and there where the moonbeams struck the trees.

"It was a horrible revelation," he said, "that here in this quiet place we were nursing revolution, and had some secret society in full swing amongst us. But then, as the little bit of history brought up the past, I felt the tide of feeling sweeping through me, and all the dread enthusiasm of the race woke within me:—

> 'There beside the singing river
>   That dark mass of men are seen,
> Far above their shining weapons
>   Hung their own immortal green!'

But this is a bad business, sir, for soul and body. What's to be done?"

"A bad business, indeed," I echoed. "But worse for

soul than body. These poor fellows will amuse themselves playing at soldiers, and probably catching pneu-
monia; and there 'twill end. You didn't see any police-
men about?''

"No. They could be hiding unknown to me."

"Depend upon it, they were interested spectators of
the midnight evolutions. I know there are some fellows
in the village in receipt of secret service money, and all
these poor boys' names are in the Castle archives. But
what is worse, this means anti-clericalism, and consequently abstention from Sacraments, and a long train of
evils besides. It must be handled gently.''

"You don't mean to say, sir,'' he replied, "that that
Continental poison has eaten its way in Ireland?''

"Not to a large extent; but it is there. There is no
use in burying our heads in the sands and pretending not
to see. But we must act judiciously. A good surgeon
never acts hastily—never hurries over an operation.
Lente—lente.''

I saw a smile faintly rippling around the corners of his
mouth. But I was afraid he might rush matters here,
and it would be dangerous. But where's the use? He
understood but one way of acting—to grapple with an
abuse and strangle it. "You drop stones,'' he used to
say, " and they turn up armed men.''

How he learned their place of meeting I don't know.
But Sunday afternoon was a favourite time for the rebels;
and the coursing match on the black hills and the rabbit
hunt in the plantations were only preliminaries to more
important and secret work. Whether by accident or de-
sign, Father Letheby stumbled on such a meeting about
four o'clock one Sunday afternoon. A high ditch and a
strong palisade of fir trees hid him from sight, and he
was able to hear a good deal, and had no scruple in playing the listener. This is what he heard. The village
tailor, lame in one leg, and familiarly known as "Hop-
and-go-one,'' was the orator:—

"Fellow countrymen, de time for action has come.

From ind to ind of the land, the down-trodden serfs of
Ireland are rising in their millions. Too long have dey
been juped by false pretences; too long have the hire-
lings of England chated and decaved them. We know
now what a shimmera,[1] what a fraud, was Home Rule.
Our counthry has been dragged at the tail of English par-
ties, who were purshuing their own interests. But 'tis
all past. No more constitutional agitation, no more
paceful struggle. Lead will do what fine speeches didn't.
And if the black militia, wid dere ordhers from Rome,
attimpt this time to interfere, we know what answer to
give dem. De West's awake, and 'tisn't priests will
set us to sleep agin—— "

At this juncture the orator was caught by the nape of
the neck, and lifted bodily off the turf ditch, which was
his forum. When he looked around, and saw who was his
captor, he shrieked for mercy; and Father Letheby, drop-
ing him, as one would drop a rat, he scurried off as fast
as his lame leg would permit, whilst the priest, turning
round to the stupefied boys, warned them of their folly
and madness:—

" God knows, boys," he said, " I pity you. You are
bent on a desperate and foolish course, the end of which
no man can foresee. I know it is useless to reason with
you on the score of danger; but I warn you that you are
violating the laws of God and the Church, and that no
blessing comes from such action. And yet," he continued, placing his hand in the breast-pocket of his coat,
and drawing out a blue official paper, " this may convince you of your folly; at least, it may convince you of
the fact that there is a traitor and informer in your midst.
Who he is I leave yourselves to conjecture! "

He read out slowly the name of every young man that
had been sworn in that secret society in the parish. The
young men listened sullenly, and swore angrily between
their teeth. But they could not deny their betrayal.

[1] Chimera.

They were vexed, humbled, disgraced; but they had to
make some defence.

"The priests are always agin the people," said one
keen-looking fellow, who had been abroad.

"That's an utter falsehood," said Father Letheby,
"and you know it. You know that priests and people
for seven hundred years have fought side by side the
battle of Ireland's freedom from civil and religious dis-
abilities. I heard your own father say how well he remembered the time when the friar stole into the farmyard
at night, disguised as a pedlar, and he showed me the
cavern down there by the sea-shore where Mass was said,
and the fishermen heard it, as they pretended to haul
in their nets."

"Thrue enough for you, your reverence," said a few
others; " 'tis what our fathers, and our fathers' fathers,
have tould us."

"And now," continued Father Letheby, "look at
the consequences of your present folly. Possible im-
prisonment in the dungeons of Portland and Dartmoor;
exile to America, enforced by the threats of prosecution;
and the sense of hostility to the Church, for you know
you are breaking the laws. You dare not go to confession, for you cannot receive absolution; you are a constant terror to your mothers and sisters—and all at the
dictation of a few scoundrels, who are receiving secret
service money from the government, and a few newspapers that are run by Freemasons and Jews."

"Ah, now, your reverence," said one of the boys, a
littérateur, "you are drawing the long bow. How could
Irish newspapers be run by Freemasons and Jews?"

"Would you be surprised to hear," said Father Letheby, "that all the great Continental papers are the property of Freemasons and Jews; that all the rancour and
bitterness stirred up against the Church for the past fifty
years has been their work; that the anti-clerical feeling
in Germany and in France has been carefully originated
and fostered by them; that hatred of the Holy See is

their motto; and that they have got into Ireland. You can see the cloven foot in the virulent anti-religious and anti-clerical articles that you read by the light of the fire at the forge; and yet, the very prayer-books you used at Mass to-day, and the beads that rolled through your mothers' fingers, have been manufactured by them. But the Irish are always fools—never more so than now.''

It was a magnificent leap of imagination on Father Letheby's part—that which attributed to Jews and Free-masons the manufacture of beads and prayer-books on the one hand, and anti-clericalism on the other. Yet there was truth in what he had said. Indeed, there were many indications, as I could point out to him to his sur-prise, which proved that the anti-Catholic agencies here in Ireland were pursuing exactly the same tactics which had led to the extinguishing of the faith in parts of France and Italy—namely, the dissemination of pornographic literature. They know well that there is but one thing that can destroy Irish faith, and that is the dissemina-tion of ideas subversive of Catholic morality. Break down the earthworks that guard the purity of the nation, and the citadel of faith is taken. He was very silent all that evening, as I notice all Irish priests grow grave when this awful fact, which is under their very eyes, is made plain to them. It is so easy to look at things with-out seeing them. Then, as the full revelation of this new *diablerie* dawned upon him, he grew very angry. I think this is the most charming thing about my curate, that he is a thorough hater of everything cunning and concealed, and breaks out into noble philippics against whatever is foul and vicious. But I know he will be now on the alert; and God help any unfortunate that dares to peddle unwholesome wares under the necklaces and matches of his basket!

The tailor came duly to report Father Letheby for the drastic treatment he had received. He was rather too emphatic in demanding his immediate removal, and hinting at suspension. In lieu of that satisfaction, he

would immediately institute proceedings in the Court of
Queen's Bench for assault and battery, and place the
damages at several thousand pounds. I listened to him
patiently, then hinted that an illiterate fellow like him
should not be making treasonable speeches. He bridled
up at the word " illiterate," and repudiated the vile in-
sinuation. He could read and write as well as any priest
in Connaught.

" But you cannot read your own writing? " I said,
tentatively.

" Couldn't he? Try him! "

I thrust under his eyes his last letter to the sub-inspec-
tor of the district. I thought he would get a fit of
apoplexy.

" Now, you scoundrel," I said, folding the letter and
placing it beyond reach, " I forgive you all your deception and treason. What Father Letheby has got in store
for you I cannot say. But I'll never forgive you, you
most unscientific and unmathematical artist, for having
given me so many shocking misfits lately, until I have
looked like a scarecrow in a cornfield; even now you are
smelling like a distillery. And tell me, you ruffian, what
right had you to say at Mrs. Haley's public house that
I was ' thauto—thauto—gogical ' in my preaching? If
I, with all the privileges of senility, chose to repeat myself, to drive the truths of Christianity into the numskulls
of this pre-Adamite village, what is that to you—you
ninth part of a man? Was it not the immortal Homer
that declared that every tailor—— "

" For God's sake, spare me, your reverence, and I'll
never do it again."

" Do you promise to cut my garments mathematically
in the future? "

" I do, your reverence." He spoke as emphatically
as if he were renewing his baptismal vows at a great
mission.

" Do you promise to speak respectfully of me and my
sermons for the future? "

" I do, your reverence."

" Now, go. *Exi, erumpe, evade,* or I'll turn you into
a *Sartor Resartus.* I hand you over now, as the judge
hands the culprit, to Father Letheby. Don't be too much
surprised at eventualities. Do you know, did you ever
hear, what the women of Marblehead did to a certain
Floyd Ireson? Well, go ask Father Letheby. He'll tell
you. And I shall be much surprised if the women of
Kilronan are much behind their sisters of Marblehead in
dealing with such a scoundrel as you."

I proposed this conundrum to Father Letheby that
same evening: " Why is it considered a greater crime
to denounce and correct an evil than to commit it? " He
looked at me as if he doubted my sanity. I put it in a
more euphemistic form: " Why is success always the
test of merit? To come down from the abstract to the
concrete, Why is a gigantic swindler a great financier,
and a poor fellow that steals a loaf of bread a felon and a
thief? Why is a colossal liar a great diplomatist, and a
petty prevaricator a base and ignoble fraud? Why is
Napoleon a hero, and that wretched tramp an ever to be
dreaded murderer? Why is Bismarck called great,
though he crushed the French into a compost of blood
and rags, ground them by taxation into paupers, jested
at dying children, and lied most foully, and his minor
imitators are dubbed criminals and thieves? Look
here, now, young man! If you, by a quiet, firm, in-
domitable determination succeed in crushing out and
stamping out for ever this secret society here, it will re-
dound to your infinite credit in all men's eyes. But
mark, if with all your energy and zeal you fail, or if you
pass into a leaderette in some Freemason journal, and
your zeal is held up as fanaticism and your energy as
imprudence, the whole world will regard you as a hot-
headed young fool, and will ask with rage and white lips,
What is the Bishop doing in allowing these young men
to take the reins into their own hands and drive the
chariot of the sun? It is as great a crime to be a young

man to-day as it was in the days of Pitt. Nothing can
redeem the stigma and the shame but success. Of
course, all this sounds very pagan, and I am not identi-
fying myself with it. I believe with that dear bare-
footed philosopher, St. Francis, who is to me more than
fifty Aristotles, as à Kempis is more than fifty Platos,
that a man is just what he is in the eyes of God, and no
more. But I am only submitting to you this speculative difficulty to keep your mind from growing fallow
these winter evenings. And don't be in a hurry to answer
it. I'll give you six months; and then you'll say, like the
interlocutor in a Christy Minstrel entertainment: ' I
give it up.' "

CHAPTER XII

CHURCH IMPROVEMENTS

I AM afraid Father Letheby is getting irritable. Perhaps he is studying too hard, and I don't spare him there, for he has the makings of a bishop in him; or perhaps it is that wretched coffee—but he is losing that beautiful equanimity and enthusiasm which made him so attractive.

" I cannot understand these people," he said to me, soon after his adventure with the " boys." " Such a compound of devotion and irreverence, meanness and generosity, cunning and childlike openness, was never seen. When I give Holy Communion with you, sir, on Sunday morning, my heart melts at the seraphic tenderness with which they approach the altar. That striking of the breast, that eager look on their faces, and that ' Cead milé failté, O Thierna! '¹ make me bless God for such a people; but then they appear to be waiting for the last words of the *De Profundis*, to jump up and run from the church as if in a panic. I can understand now how *extemplo* came to mean *in a hurry*, for if the roof were falling they could not rush from the building more promptly. Then an old woman will haggle over sixpence in buying a pair of chickens, and then come to you the following day and offer you in a stocking all she had saved in this world. I give them up. They are unintelligible."

From which I perceive that our good schoolmaster, experience, is trying the rod on this most hopeful and promising pupil.

¹" A hundred thousand welcomes, Lord."

" I hope you did not perceive any such abrupt and sudden contrasts in your protégé, Jem Deady," I said. " He has realized your ideas of a nineteenth century *Goban Saor*."[1]

He laughed loudly.

" There's no use in talking," he said. I notice he is coming down gradually from his polished periods to our village colloquialisms.

" Thou shalt lower to their level." God forbid! 'Twas bad enough with myself; but with this bright, accomplished fellow, 'twould be too bad. He then told me with delight and chagrin, rage and laughter, his experiences with Jem.

It would appear that he made a solemn contract with his architect to stop the leak and restore the wall in St. Joseph's Chapel for twenty-five shillings. " 'Twas too little," said Jem, " but what can you do with a gintleman that doesn't know a trowel from a spade." All materials were to be found by the contractor.

On Monday afternoon there was a knock at Father Letheby's door, and Jem was announced.

" Well, Jem," said Father Letheby, cheerfully, " getting on with the job? "

" Yes, your reverence, getting on grand," said Jem. " But I come to you about the laddher."

" The-e ladder? " echoed Father Letheby.

" Yes, your reverence," echoed Jem confidentially, " the laddher to get up on the roof, you know."

" But I understood you to say that you were getting through with this little job."

" Oh, of course, your reverence, we're getting through the preliminaries; but I must get on the roof, you know."

" I presume so," said Father Letheby, a little nettled, " and why don't you go there? "

" Does you reverence take me for an aigle, and want me to fly? "

[1] A famous Irish architect.

"Well, not exactly," said Father Letheby, with a slight touch of flattery and sarcasm, " 1 am more disposed to take you for a nightingale! "

"Well, then, your reverence," said Jem, melting under the happy allusion, " a gintleman of your grate expayrince in building should know that, of all things else, a laddher is the wan thing necessary."

"Then you expect me to construct a ladder for your convenience? "

"Oh, not at all, your reverence; but if you gave me a little note up to the ' Great House,' I'd have it down while you'd be saying ' trapsticks.' "

There were some reasons why it was not at all desirable that he should ask favours from the "Great House"; but there was no help, and Jem got the letter.

"Now, this is all you require," said Father Letheby, with determination.

"That is all," said Jem. "Do you think I'd be throubling your reverence every minit. Long life to your reverence. May you be spared long in the parish."

About four o'clock that afternoon, Father Letheby was startled by a sudden commotion in the village. All the dogs were barking, and there are as many dogs in Kilronan as in Constantinople, and they are just as vicious; all the women were at the doors, rubbing their hands in their aprons; and the village loafers were all turned towards where a solemn procession was moving through the street. First came a gang of youngsters singing, " Sure, We're the Boys of Wexford," then a popular ditty; then came two labourers, dragging along a ladder with as much show of expended energy as if it were a piece of heavy ordnance; then the cart on which the ladder was placed; then two more labourers behind, making desperate efforts to second the arduous endeavours of their mates in front; then a squadron of bare-legged girls, trying to keep the hair out of their eyes; and finally, the captain of the expedition, Jem Deady, leisurely walking along, with his hands in his pockets, a wheaten straw in his mouth, whilst he looked from cabin to cabin to receive the admiration of the villagers. It was expressed in various ways:—

" Wisha, thin, Jem 'tis you're the divil painted."

" Where is he taking it? "

" To the chapel."

" Wisha, thin, I thought the priests had some sinse."

" Whist, 'uman, he's come around the new cojutor and got a job."

" Th' ould job? "

" Th' ould job! "

' Wisha, God help his poor wife now. 'Tis she'll suffer," etc.

The men made desperate efforts as they passed Father Letheby's windows. He looked on hopelessly, as you look at a charade of which you have not got the key.

At six o'clock there was a deputation at the door, consisting of four labourers and the owner of the cart.

" We come for our day's hire, your reverence," said the foreman, unabashed.

" Oh, indeed," said Father Letheby, " I am not aware that you are in my employment."

" We dhrew the laddher down from the Great House to the chapel; and I may tell you reverence 'twas a tough job. I wouldn't do it again for five shillings."

" Nor I, ayther."

" Nor I, ayther."

" Nor I, ayther, begor."

" Well, look here," said Father Letheby, " I'm not going to submit to this infamous extortion. I didn't employ you, and I acknowledge no responsibility whatsoever."

" That manes you won't pay us, your reverence? " said the foreman, in a free translation.

" Precisely," said Father Letheby, closing the door abruptly.

He heard them murmuring and threatening outside, but took no notice of them. Later in the evening he took his usual stroll. He found these fellows loafing around the public house. They had been denouncing him vigorously, and occasionally a Parthian shaft came after him:—

" Begor, 'tis quare, sure enough."

" Begor, we thought the priests couldn't do any wrong."

But when he turned the corner he met a good deal of sympathy:—

" Wisha, begor, 'tis your reverence was wanted to tache these blackguards a lesson."

" Wisha, 'twas God sent you," etc., etc.

Now, one shilling would have given these fellows lashings of porter, and secured their everlasting fealty and an unlimited amount of popularity. I told him so.

" Never," he said, drawing back his head, and with flashing eyes, " I shall never lend myself to so demoralizing a practice. We must get these people out of the mire."

The next day, he thought he was bound to see how Jem was progressing with his contract. He went down to the little church and passed into the sacristy, whence he had a clear view of the roof of St. Joseph's Chapel. Jem was there, leisurely doing nothing, and on the graveyard wall were eight men, young and old, surveying the work and offering sundry valuable suggestions. They took this shape:—

" Wisha, Jem, take the world aisy. You're killing yerself, man."

" What a pity he's lost his wice (voice); sure 'twas he was able to rise a song."

' Dey say," interjected a young ragamuffin, " dat Fader Letheby is going to take Simon Barry into his new choir. Simon is a tinner, and Jem is only a bannitone."

" Hould your tongue, you spalpeen," said a grown man, " Jem can sing as well as twinty Simons, dat is if he could only wet his whistle."

" Thry dat grand song, Jem, ' Tis Years Since Last
We Met.' "

" No, no," said the chorus, " give us ' Larry
McGee.' "

"Wisha, byes, wouldn't wan of ye run over to Mrs.
Haley's for a pint. 'Tis mighty dhry up here."

" Here ye are," said the chorus, chipping in and making up the requisite " tuppence." " Don't be long about
it, ye young ruffian."

" But what about the pledge, Jem? " asked a conscientious spectator. " Shure your time isn't up yet."

" 'Tis up long ago," cried another. " 'Twas three
months yesterday since he took the pledge."

" Byes," said Jem, who was troubled at the possible
scandal he was about to give, " I promised not to dhrink
in a public house; and shure this isn't a public house,
glory be to God! "

They took off their hats reverently; and then the pint
came, was taken up the ladder with great care and
solemnity, and a few minutes after, Father Letheby
heard : —

" What is it going to be, byes? I've left me music
on the pianney! "

" ' Larry McGee! ' ' Larry McGee! ' No. No. ' 'Tis
Yares Since Last——.' No. No. ' The Byes of Wexford.' "

" Byes, I think the majority is in favour of ' Larry
McGee.'—Here's to yer health! "

And then came floating from the roof in various
quavers and semiquavers and grace-notes, the following,
which is all Father Letheby can remember.

" I—in the town of Kilkinny lived Larry McGee,
　Oh—oh the divil's own boy at divarshion was he,
　He—he had a donkey, a pig, but he hadn't a wife,
　His cabin was dreary, and wretched his life."

Then the notes came wavering and fitful, as the wind
took them up, and carried them struggling over the moorland; and all that Father Letheby could hear was about

a certain Miss Brady, who was reared up a lady, and who was requested to accept the name of Mrs. McGee. This suit must have been successful, because, as the wind lulled down, the words came clearly:—

" Sure the chickens were roasted—the praties was biled,
    They were all in their jackets, for fear they'd be spiled;
    And the neighbours came flockin', for to fling up the stockin',
    And dance at the weddin' of Larry McGee."

It was interesting; but Father Letheby's temper was rising with the undulations of the song. He came out into the graveyard, and there was a stampede of specta- tors. Jem was lifting the porter to his lips, and looked down calmly and philosophically at the young priest.

" Mr. Deady," said the latter, putting on his strongest accent, " I do not think I engaged you to entertain the village with your vocal powers, much as I esteem them. I engaged you to work—to do honest work for honest wages."

" Begor," said the unabashed Jem, " if I was a Turk, or a Armaynian, I'd be allowed to ate my dinner."

" But this is not your dinner hour! "

" Twelve to wan is the dinner hour, except when I dines at the Grate House, whin, for my convaynience, they puts it off till aight."

It was a sly cut at Father Letheby, and he felt it.

" And your dinner, I presume, is the usual quantity of filthy porter, such as I see represented in your hand."

" It is, your reverence, excep' whin I dines with the Captain. Den we haves roast beef and champagne."

All this Father Letheby told me, with a look of puzzled anger, and with many exclamations.

" I never saw such a people; I'll never understand them," etc. His magnificent impetuosity again.

" Tell me," I said, for he had given me most cordially the privilege of speaking freely, " do you make your meditation regularly? "

" Well, I do," he replied, " in a kind of way."

" Because," I went on to say, " apart from the spiri- tual advantages it affords, that closing of our eyes daily

and looking steadily into ourselves is a wonderfully soothing process. It is solitude—and solitude is the mother
country of the strong. It is astonishing what an amount
of irritation is poured from external objects through the
windows of the soul—on the retina, where they appear
to be focussed, and then turned like a burning-glass on
the naked nerves of the soul. To shut one's eyes and
turn the thoughts inward is like sleep, and, like sleep,
gives strength and peace. Now, would you accept from
me a subject of meditation? "

" Willingly, sir," he said, like a child.

" All that you want to be perfect is to curb your impetuosity. I notice it everywhere. Probably it is natural; probably it is accentuated by your residence in
feverish cities. Now, I have a right to give an advice
on this matter, for I got it and took it myself. When I
was as young as you I said Mass in twenty minutes, and
said the Office in forty minutes. How? Because I slurred
over words, spoke to the Almighty as a ballad-singer,
and for a few years went through these awful and sacred
duties without ever resting or dwelling on their sublime
signification. One day a holy old priest said to me:—

" ' Father, would you kindly give me an easy translation of the first stanza of the hymn for Terce? '

" I was completely at sea. He saw it.

" ' Ah, never mind. But what means *factus sum,
sicut uter in pruina*? You say it every day nearly.'

" I couldn't tell him.

" ' *Herodii domus dux est eorum.*' What is that? "

" I made a feeble attempt here, and translated boldly,
' The house of Herod is their leader.'

" The venerable man looked smilingly at me; and
then asked me to look up my Bible. I did, and found
that I had been speaking an unknown language to Almighty God for years, and I called it prayer."

Father Letheby looked humbled. He said: " True,
Father, I fear; and if you had to say the entire Office,
commencing Matins at eleven o'clock at night; or if you

had to crush Vespers and Compline, under the light of a street lamp, into the ten minutes before twelve o'clock, you'd see the absurdity of the whole thing more clearly. A strictly conscientious confrère of mine in England used always commence Prime about ten o'clock at night; but then he always lighted a candle, for consistency, before he uttered *Jam lucis orto sidere*. It is a wonder we were never taught the very translation of the psalms in college."

" Well, we're wandering. But set apart, *hic et nunc*, a half-hour for Matins and Lauds; twenty minutes for the Small Hours; a quarter of an hour for Vespers and Compline; and take up no other duty until that time has expired. Then never say your Office from memory, even the parts you know best. Read every line from your Breviary. It is not my advice, but that of St. Charles Borromeo. Take half an hour for the celebration of Mass. It will be difficult at first, but it will come all right. Lastly, train yourself to walk slowly and speak slowly and deliberately—— "

" You are clipping my wings, Father," said he, " and putting soles of lead on my feet."

" Did you ever hear of Michael Montaigne? " I said.

" Yes. But that's all I know about him."

" Quite enough, indeed. He hardly improves on acquaintance. But his father trained himself to wear leaden shoes in order that he might leap the higher. That's what I want from you. But where's this we were? Oh, yes! You must take these poor people more easily. You cannot undo in a day the operations of three hundred years—— "

" Yes, but look how these people spring into the very van of civilization when they go to England or America. Why, they seem to assume at once all the graces of the higher life."

" Precisely—the eternal question of environment. But under our circumstances we must be infinitely patient."

" What vexes me most," said Father Letheby, " is

that we have here the material of saints; and yet—look now at that wretched Deady! I don't mind his insolence, but the shifty dishonesty of the fellow."

"Let him alone! By this time he is stung with remorse for what he said. Then he'll make a general confession to his wife. She'll flay him with her tongue for having dared to say a disrespectful word to God's minister. Then he'll go on a desperate spree for a week to stifle conscience, during which orgies he'll beat his wife black and blue; finally, he'll come to you, sick, humbled, and repentant, to apologize and take the pledge for life again. That's the programme."

"Tis pitiful," said the young priest.

But the following Sunday he recovered all his lost prestige and secured immortal fame at the football match between the "Holy Terrors" of Kilronan and the "Wolf Tones" of Moydore. For, being asked to "kick off" by these athletes, he sent the ball up in a straight line seventy or eighty feet, and it struck the ground just three feet away from where he stood. There was a shout of acclamation from the whole field, which became a roar of unbounded enthusiasm when he sent the ball flying in a parabola, not six feet from the ground, and right to the hurdles that marked the opposite goal. The Kilronan men were wild about their young curate, and under his eye they beat their opponents hollow; and one admirer, leaning heavily on his *caman*, was heard to say:—

"My God, if he'd only lade us!"

CHAPTER XIII

" ALL THINGS TO ALL MEN "

IN pursuing my course of lectures to my young curate—
lectures which he returned with compound interest by
his splendid example of zeal and energy—I put into his
hands the following lines, addressed by that gentle saint,
Francis de Sales, to some one in whom he had a similar
interest:—

> " Accustom yourself to speak softly and slowly, and to go—
> I mean walk—quite composedly; to do all that you do gently
> and quietly, and you will see that in three or four years you
> will have quite regulated this hasty impetuosity. But care-
> fully remember to act thus gently and speak softly on occa-
> sions when the impetuosity is not urging you, and when there
> is no appearance of danger of it, as, for example, when
> sitting down, rising up, eating, when you speak to N. N.,
> etc.; and in fact everywhere and in everything dispense not
> yourself from it. Now, I know that you will make a thou-
> sand slips a day over all this, and that your great natural
> activity will be always breaking out; but I do not trouble
> myself about this provided that it is not your will, your de-
> liberation; and that, when you perceive these movements,
> you always try to calm them. Equableness of mind and of
> outward demeanour is not a particular virtue, but the interior
> and exterior ornament of a friend of Jesus Christ. (Letter VII.)

Now, here's the difficulty. Undoubtedly he is impetuous, he rushes at conclusions too rapidly, he judges
hastily; and with an imperfect knowledge of human nature, which is a mass of irregularities, he worries himself because he cannot bring a whole parish up to his
level in a few weeks. That impetuosity shows itself
everywhere. He is an anachronism, a being from

111

another time and world, set down in sleepy Kilronan. For the first few weeks that he was there, whenever he slammed his hall door and strode down the village street with long, rapid, undulating steps, all the dogs came out and barked at him for disturbing their slumbers, and all the neighbours came to their doors and asked wildly, " Who's dead? What happened? Where's the fire? " etc., and the consequence was that the wildest rumours used to be circulated; and then, when a few days' experience disproved them, the cumulative wrath of the disappointed villagers fell on Father Lethbey's devoted head.

" Why the mischief doesn't he go aisy? Sure, you'd think he was walking for a wager. He'll kill himself in no time if he goes on that way."

He used to laugh airily at all this commotion. And now here was the puzzle. No doubt whatever he can do more work in one day than I or Father Tom Laverty could do in a month. And if I clip his wings, and put lead in his shoes, as he remarked, he may take to slippers and the gout, and all his glorious work be summarily spoiled. That would never do. I have no scruple about what I said regarding the Office and Mass; but if I shall see him creeping past my window in a solemn and dignified manner, I know I shall have qualms of conscience. And yet——

It was in the beginning of December, and one day I had occasion to go down through the village. It was not a day to attract any one out of doors; it was one of those dreadful days which leave an eternal landmark behind them in the trees that are bent inwards toward the mountains from the terrible stress of the southwest winds. Land and sea were wiped out in the cataracts of rain that poured their deluges on sea and moor and mountain; and the channels of the village ran fiercely with brown muddy water; and every living thing was housed, except the ducks, which contemptuously waded through the dirty ruts, and only quacked melodiously when the storm lifted their feathers and flung them from pool to pool of the deserted street. I called on Father Letheby.

" This is dismal weather," I said, " enough to give any one a fit of the blues in this awful place."

He looked at me, as if this were an attempt to draw him. There was a roar of wind that shook his window-sashes, as if it said, " We will get in and spoil your pleasure, whether you like it or not "; and there was a shower of bullets, as from a Maxim, that threatened to smash in and devastate all the cosy comforts.

" By Jove," said he, turning round, " I never felt happier in my life. And every roar and splash of the tempest makes me draw closer and closer to this little nest, which I can call my own home."

It was a cosy nest, indeed. The first burned merrily —a little coal, a good deal of bogwood and turf, which is the cleanest fire in the world; there was cleanliness, neatness, tidiness, taste everywhere; the etchings and engravings gave tone to the walls; the piano lay open, as if saying, " Come, touch me "; the books, shining in gold and red and blue and purple, winked in the fire-light; and, altogether, it was a picture of delight accentuated by the desolation outside.

' What do I want? " he continued. " Ease? here it is; comfort? here it is; health? thank God, perfect; so-ciety? here are the kings of men on my shelves. I have only to summon them—here Plato, Aristotle, Æschylus, Virgil, Dante, Shakespeare! come here, and they come; speak, and they open their dead lips; be silent, and back they go to their shelves. I have not got your Greek Fathers yet; but they'll come. You notice that my theological library is rather scant. But I can bor-row St. Thomas, Lugo, Suarez; I cannot borrow the others, for you are so jealous about your books."

" Rather clever economy! " I said. " But now tell me what you do without the morning paper? "

" Well, now, there you touched a sore point. At least it was; but it is healing. For the first few weeks

it was my daily penance. I used always breakfast in
England with the paper propped against the teapot.
They said it was bad for digestion, but it made me eat
slowly; and you may perhaps have perceived—indeed,
you have perceived—that I am rather quick in my
habits."

I nodded oracularly.

"Well, the first few weeks I was here that was my
only misery. Without the paper everything looked
lonely and miserable. I used to go to the door every
five minutes to see whether there was a newsboy on the
horizon; but you cannot understand the feeling."

"Can't I? I know it well. You remember what the
uprooted tree was to the blinded giant in Virgil:

> 'Ea sola voluptas,
> Solamenque mali.'

Well, that was the newspaper to me. But how do you
get on now?"

"I never care to see one. Nay, I should rather have
a feeling of contempt for any one whom I should see
wasting valuable time on them."

"But the news of the world, politics, wars, the amenities of Boards of Guardians, Town Commissioners, etc.;
the suicides, the divorces, stocks and shares, etc.;—don't
these things interest you?"

"No. My only regret is, when the boys ask me about
the war, I am afraid I appear awfully ignorant. And
they're so learned. Why, every fellow down at the forge
thinks himself a General or an Admiral. 'Ah, if I had
dem troops, wouldn't I settle so and so!' Or, 'Why
the d—— didn't Gineral S—— bring out his cavalry?
'Tis the cavalry does it. Bourbaki—he was the Gineral!'
'Yerra, what was he to Skobeloff?' And they look at
me rather mournfully."

Here an awful blast swept the house, as if to raze it
to its foundations,

" A pleasant day for a sick-call to Slieveogue! " I
said.

" I shouldn't mind one bit. 'Twould make the fire
the merrier when I returned. I enjoy nothing half so
much as walking in the teeth of wind and rain, along
the smooth turf on yonder cliffs, the cool air lapping you
all round, and the salt of the sea on your lips. Then,
when you return, a grand throw-off, and the little home
pleasanter by the contrast. By the way, I was out this
morning."

" Out this morning? Where? " I exclaimed.

" Up at Campion's."

" Nonsense! "

" Quite true. And would you guess for what, sir? "

" Go on. I am a poor hand at conundrums."

" You don't know Mrs. C——, a constable's widow
at Moydore? "

" I can't say I have that pleasure. Stop! Did she
come about a licence? "

" She did."

" And you helped her?—No! God forbid! That
would be too great a somersault! "

" I did."

" What? "

He looked embarrassed, and said, apologetically:
" Well, pardon me, sir, and I'll tell you all. She came
in here this morning, wet and bedraggled. Her poor
widow's weeds were dripping with the rain. She sat
there. You see where her boots have left their mark.
She said her husband had just died, and left her, of
course, penniless, with four young children. There was
nothing before her but the workhouse, unless I would
help her—and she heard that I was good to the poor;
sure every one was talking about me—you understand? "

I nodded.

" Well, there was but one possible way in which she
could be helped, and that was to get her a licence to

sell porter and spirits. I stopped her abruptly, and said:
' My dear woman, you might as well ask me to get you
appointed lady in waiting to the Queen. But in any case
I'd rather cut off my right hand than help any one to
get a licence. Nay, I am fully determined to cut down
every licence in this parish until but one is left.' She
looked at me in amazement. Then her Celtic temper
rose. ' Wisha, 'tis aisy for you to lecture poor people
who have not a bite or a sup, nor a roof over their heads,
wid your carpets, and your pictures, and your pianney,
and your brass fire-irons; but if you had four little *gar-
lachs* to feed, as I have, you'd have a different story.'
Here she arose to go; and, as a parting shot: ' God help
the poor, however; sure they have no one to go to when
their priests desart them.   ɪ don't know what it was,''
continued Father Letheby, '' but I softened a little here,
and said: ' Now, I have told you that I cannot do anything towards getting you a licence—it's against all my
principles; but I'll tell you what I'll do. I'll go up to
Captain Campion's with you, and introduce you on the
strength of these letters from your parish priest; but remember, not one word shall I say in favour of your demand. Do you understand? ' ' I do, your reverence,'
she said; ' may God bless you! ' The hot fires were
ashes again. We both went up in the awful rain. It
was rather early even for a morning call, and Captain
Campion was not yet downstairs. So I left the widow
in the hall, and went out to a sheltered spot, where I
could watch the action of the storm on the waves. In
half an hour I returned. There was no necessity for an
introduction. The good woman had introduced herself,
and secured Captain Campion's vote and influence for
the next licensing sessions. I was never so sorry—nor
so glad.''

'' 'Tis a bad business,'' I said mournfully. '' Imagine
eight public houses in this wretched village of three hundred souls! ''

'' 'Tis, sir! '' he said, as if his conscience stung him;

" but I did some good by my visit; I think I have
brought Captain Campion around."

" To what? " I exclaimed.

" To recognize his duty to the Church, and the people,
and God, by going to his duty."

" You don't say so? " I said, and I *was* surprised. I
could not help thinking of what a glorious triumph it
would be to that gentle saint, whose brow was never
troubled but with the thought of her father's perversity.
How often, how ardently, she had prayed for that day;
how many Masses, how many Communions, she had
offered to obtain that grace! Many a time I have seen
her, after Holy Communion, straining her eyes on the
Tabernacle, and I knew she was knocking vigorously at
the Heart of Christ; and many a time have I seen her,
a Lady of Sorrows, imploring the Queen of Sorrows to
take that one trouble from her life. Oh! if men could
only know what clouds of anguish and despair their indifference to the practices of their holy religion brings
down upon gentle hearts, that dare not speak their sorrow, the Church would not have to mourn so many and
such faithless and rebellious children.

I said to Father Letheby: " God bless you; but how
did you work the miracle? "

" Well." he said bashfully, " it was not the work of
one day or of one visit. I have been laying my train to
the citadel; to-day I fired it, and he capitulated. Tell
me, sir, did you ever hear of the *Halcyone*? "

Did I ever hear of the *Halcyone*? Who didn't? Was
there a man, woman, or child, from the Cliffs of Moher
to Achill Island, that did not know the dainty five-ton
yacht, which, as a contrast to his own turbulent spirit,
he had so named? Was it not everywhere said that Campion loved that yacht more than his child—that he spoke
to her and caressed her as a living thing—and how they
slept on the calm deep on summer nights, whilst phos-
phor-laden waves lapped around them, and only the dim
dawn, with her cold, red finger woke them to life? And

was it not told with pride and terror in every coracle
along the coast with what fierce exultation he took her
out on stormy days, and headed her straight against the
billows, that broke into curtsies on every side, and
how she leaped up the walls of water which lay down
meekly beneath her, and shook out her white sail to the
blast, until its curved face brushed the breakers, and her
leaden keel showed through the valleys of the sea? and
men leaned on their spades to see her engulfed in the
deep, and the coast-guards levelled their long glasses, and
cried: " There goes mad Campion and the witch again!"

" What do you know about the *Halcyone*? " said I.

" A good deal by hearsay; not a little by personal experience," he replied.

" Why, you don't mean to say that you have seen the
famous yacht? " I asked, in amazement.

" Seen her, steered her, laughed at her, feared her,
like Campion himself."

" Why, I thought Campion never allowed any one but
himself and his daughter to cross her gunwale? "

" Well, all that I tell you is, I have been out several
evenings with the Captain; and if you want to examine
me in jibs, and mainsails, and top-gallants, now is your
time."

Look here! This curate of mine is becoming quite
humorous, and picking up all our Celtic ways. I don't
at all like it, because I would much rather he would keep
up all his graceful dignity. But there again—the eternal
environments. How far will he go?

" Don't mind your lessons in navigation now," I said,
" but come to the point. How—did—you—catch—
Campion? "

" Well, 'tis a long story, but I shall try to abridge it.
I knew there was but one way to this man's heart, and I
was determined to try it. Has not some one said, ' All
things to all men '? Very well. Talk to a farmer about
his crops, to a huntsman about his horses, to a fisherman about his nets, you have him in the palm of your

hand. It is a kind of Christian diplomacy; but I would
much rather it were not necessary."

He was silent, leaning his head on his hands.

" Never mind," I said, " the question of honour. Human nature is a very crooked thing, and you can't run
a level road over a hill."

" I never like even the shadow of deception," he said;
" I hate concealment; and yet I should not like Campion to know that I practised even so innocent a strata-
gem."

" Oh, shade of Pascal! " I cried, " even you could
detect no casuistry here.   And have you no scruple,
young man, in keeping an old gentleman on the tenter-
hooks of expectation whilst you are splitting hairs? Go
on, like a good fellow, I was never so interested in my
life. The idea of landing Campion! "

" Well, 'twas this way. I knew a little about boats,
and made the Captain cognizant of the fact. I expected
an invitation. He did not rise to the bait. Then I tried
another plan. I asked him why he never entered the
Halcyone for the Galway regatta. He muttered something of contempt for all the coast boats. I said quietly
that I heard she tacked badly in a strong gale, and that
it was only in a light breeze she did well. He got furi-
ous, which was just what I wanted. We argued and
reasoned; and the debate ended in his asking me out the
first fresh day that came last September. I don't know
if you remember that equinoctial gale that blew about
the 18th or 19th. It was strong, much stronger than I
cared for; but I was pinned to my engagement. I met
him down at the creek. The wind blew off the land. It
was calm enough in the sheltered water; but when we
got out, by Jove, I wished a hundred times that I was
here. I lay down in the gangway of the yacht whilst
Campion steered. From time to time great waves broke
over the bow of the yacht, and in a little while I was
drenched to the skin. Campion had his yellow oil-skins,
and laughed at me. Occasionally he asked, " Does she

tack well? '' I answered coolly. I knew he was trying
my nerve, as we mounted breaker after breaker and
plunged down into awful valleys of the sea. Then, as
one great squall broke round and the yacht keeled over,
he turned the helm, until she lay flat on a high wave,
and her great sail swept the crest of its foam, and her
pennon dipped in the deep. I thought it was all over, as
I clutched the gunwale to prevent my falling into the sea.
He watched me narrowly, and in a moment righted the
yacht.

" ' We were near Davy Jones's locker there? ' he said
coolly.

" ' We wouldn't remain long together,' I replied.

" ' How? '

" ' Well, you know, you'd go a little deeper, and I
should hope I would get a little higher.'

" ' You mean I'd have gone to Hell? '

" ' Certainly,' I replied.

" ' I'm not a bad man,' he said, taken aback.

" ' You are,' I replied; ' you persecute the poor and
drag their faces through the dust. You're an irreligious
man, because you never kneel to God; you're a dishonest
man, because you profess to belong to a faith whose
doctrines you do not accept, and whose commands you
disobey.'

" ' Hallo, there! ' said he, ' I'm not used to this kind
of language.'

" ' Perhaps not,' I said; for with the thorough drench-
ing and the fright I was now thoroughly angry. ' But
you'll have to listen to it. You cannot put your fingers
in your ears and steer the *Halcyone*. It will take us an
hour to reach land, and you must hear what you never
heard before.'

" ' I've a strong inclination,' he said, ' to pitch you
overboard.'

" ' I'm quite sure you're perfectly capable of murder,'
I said. ' But again, you cannot let go the ropes in this
gale. Besides, there are two sides to that question.'

" Then and there I pitched into him, told him how he
was breaking his child's heart, how he was hated all along
the coast, etc., etc.; but I insisted especially on his
dishonesty in professing a creed which he denied in daily
practice. I was thoroughly angry, and gave my passion
full swing. He listened without a word as we went
shoreward. At last he said :

" ' By Jove! I never thought that a priest could speak
to a gentleman so boldly. Now, that damned old landlubber '—I beg your pardon, sir," broke in my curate,
" the words escaped me involuntarily."

" Never mind," I said, " go on."

" But it was very disrespectful—— "

" Now, I insist on hearing every word he said. Why,
that's the cream of the story."

" Well, he said : ' That damned old landlubber and
bookworm never addressed me in that manner '—but perhaps he meant some one else."

" Never fear! He meant his respected old pastor.
The ' landlubber ' might apply to other natives; but I
fear they could hardly be called ' bookworm ' with any
degree of consistency. But go on."

" Well, you know, he spoke rather jerkily, and as if
in soliloquy. ' Well, I never! ' ' Who'd have thought
it from this sleek fellow? ' ' Why, I thought butter
would not melt in his mouth! ' ' What will Bittra say
when I tell her? ' At last we pulled into the creek; I
jumped ashore from the dingey, as well as my dripping
clothes would let me, and lifting my hat, without a word,
I walked towards home. He called after me :—

" ' One word, Father Letheby! You must come up
to the house and dry yourself. You'll catch your death
of cold.'

" ' Oh! 'twill be nothing,' I said. He had come up
with me, and looked humbled and crestfallen.

" ' You must pardon all my rudeness,' he said, in a
shamefaced manner. ' But, to be very candid with you,
I was never met so boldly before, and I like it. We men

E

of the world hate nothing so much as a coward. If some
of your brethren had the courage of their convictions and
challenged us poor devils boldly, things might be different. We like men to show that they believe in Hell by
trying to keep us from it.' But now I am sounding my
own praises. It is enough. to say that he promised to
think the matter over; and I clinched the whole business
by getting his promise that he would be at the altar on
Christmas morning.''

I thought a good deal, and said : " It is a wholesome
lesson. We have no scruple in cuffing Jem Deady or Bill
Shanahan; but we don't like to tackle the big-wigs. And
they despise us for our cowardice. Isn't that it? Well,
my dear fellow, you are a *tetragonos aner*, as old Aristotle would say—an idea, by the way, stolen by Dante in
his ' sta come torre ferma.' In plainer language, you're
a *brick*! Poor little Bittra! how pleased she'll be! "

CHAPTER XIV

FIRST FRIDAYS

I NOTICE, as I proceed with these mnemonic scraps from my diary, and try to cast them into shape, a curious change come over me. I feel as one waking from a trance, and all the numbed faculties revive and assert their power; and all the thoughts and desires, yea, even the capabilities of thirty years ago, come back and seem to claim their rightful places, as a deposed king would like to sit on his throne, and hold his sceptre once more before he dies. And so all my ideas are awakening; and the cells of memory, as if at some magic *Sesame*, yield up their contents; and even the mechanical trick of writing, which they say is never fully lost, appears to creep back into my rheumatized fingers as the ink flows freely from my pen. I know, indeed, that some say I am passing into my second childhood. I do not resent it; nor would I murmur even at such a blessed dispensation. For I thank God I have kept through all the vicissitudes of life, and all the turbulence of thought, the heart of a child.

There is nothing human that does not interest me. All the waywardness of humanity provokes a smile; there is no wickedness so great that I cannot pity; no folly that I cannot condone; patient to wait for the unravelling of the skein of life till the great Creator willeth, meanwhile looking at all things *sub specie æternitatis*, and ever finding new food for humility in the barrenness of my own life. But it has been a singular intellectual revival for me to feel all my old principles and thoughts shadowing themselves clearer and clearer on the negatives of memory where the sunflames of youth imprinted them, and from which, perhaps, they will be transferred to the tablets that last for eternity. But here God has been very good unto me in sending me this young priest to revive the past. We like to keep our consciousness till we die. I am glad to have been aroused by so sympathetic a spirit from the coma of thirty years.

It is quite true, indeed, that he disturbs, now and again, the comforts of senile lethargy. And sometimes the old Adam will cry out, and sigh for the leaden ages, for he is pursuing with invincible determination his great work of revival in the parish. He has doubled, trebled, the confessions of the people on Saturday, and the subsequent Sunday Communions. He has seized the hearts of all the young men. He is forever preaching to them on the *manliness* of Christ—His truthfulness, His honour, His fearlessness, His tenderness. He insists that Christ had a particular affection for the young. Witness how He chose His Apostles, and how He attached them to His Sacred Person. And thus my curate's confessional is thronged every Saturday night by silent, humble, thoughtful young fellows, sitting there in the dark, for the two candles at the altar rails throw but a feeble light into the blackness; and Mrs. Darcy, under all improvements, has retained her sense of economy.

" Where's the use," she says, " of lighting more than wan candle, for wan candle is as good as fifty? "

She has compromised with Father Letheby for two, for his slightest wish is now a command.

And so the young girls and all the men go to Father Letheby's confessional. The old women and the little children come to me. They don't mind an occasional growl, which will escape me sometimes. Indeed, they say they'd rather hear one roar from the " ould man " than if Father Letheby, " wid his gran' accent," was preaching forever. But young men are sensitive; and I am not sorry.

Yet, if my Guardian Angel were to ask me, What in the world have you to grumble about? I couldn't tell him. For I never come away from that awful and sacred duty of the confessional without a sense of the deepest humiliation. I never sit in " the box," as the people call the confessional. A slight deafness in one ear, and the necessity of stretching occasionally a rheumatized foot, make it more convenient for me to sit over there, near and under the statue of our Blessed Mother. There in my arm-chair I sit, with the old cloak wrapped round me that sheltered me many a night on the mountains. And there the little children come, not a bit shy or afraid of old " Daddy Dan." They pick their way across the new carpet with a certain feeling of awkwardness, as if there were pins and needles hidden somewhere; but when they arrive at safe anchorage, they put their dirty clasped fingers on my old cassock, toss the hair from their eyes, and look me straight in the face, whilst they tell their little story to me and God. They are now well trained in the exact form of confession. Father Letheby has drilled them well. But dear me! what white souls they are! Poverty and purity have worked hand in hand to make them angelic, and their faces are transfigured by the light that shines within. And their attenuated bodies show clearly the burning lamp of holiness and faith, as a light shines soft and clear through the opal shades of porcelain or Sèvres. And the little maidens always say, " Tank you, Fader," when they receive their penance; and the boys say, " All right." I sometimes expect to hear " old fellow " added. Then the old women come; and, afraid to touch the grand carpet with their feet, they leave rather vivid impressions in brown mud on the waxed floor, which is the very thing that Miss Campion does not want; and they throw themselves backward whilst they recite in the soft, liquid Gaelic the *Confiteor;* and then raise themselves erect, pull up their black cloaks or brown shawls with the airs and dignity of a young barrister about to address the jury, arrange

the coif of shawl or hood of cloak around their heads, and
then tell you—nothing! God bless them, innocent souls!
No need for these elaborate preparations.   Yet what contrition, what sorrow, what love they pour forth over some
simple imperfections, where even a Jansenist cannot detect the shadow of a venial sin!   No wonder that my
curate declares that we have material in Ireland to make
it again a wonder to the world—an Island of Saints once
more! But something is wanting. He does not know
what, nor do I. But he says sometimes that he feels as
if he were working in the dark. He cannot get inside the
natures of the people. There is a puzzle, an enigma
somewhere. The people are but half revealed to us.
There is a world of thought and feeling hidden away
somewhere, and unrevealed. Who has the key? He is
seeking for it everywhere, and cannot find it. Now, you
know, he is a transcendentalist, so I don't mind these
vagaries; yet he is desperately in earnest.

But he is very kind and tender towards his old pastor.
When he " started " the devotion of the Nine Fridays in
honour of the Sacred Heart, of course he set them all
wild. Their eternal salvation depended on their performing
the Nine Fridays successively. And so one Thursday night,
when the wind was howling dismally, and the rain patter-
ing on the windows, and the fire in my little grate looking all the brighter from the contrast, a timid knock
came to my door. I put down the *Pensées* of Pascal—
a book for which I have a strange predilection, though I
do not like the man who wrote it.

" Some children want to see you, sir," said Hannah.
" I hope you're not going to leave the house in this
weather."

" Send them in and let us see," I replied.

They came to the door reluctantly enough, one pushing
the other before her, and there they stood bashfully, their
fingers in their mouths, staring at the lamp, and the
pictures, and the books, like Alice in Wonderland.

" Well, what's up, now? " I said, turning around.

" 'Tis the way we wants to go to confession, Fader."

" Hallo! are ye going to die to-night that ye are in such a mighty hurry? "

" No, Fader, but to-morrow is the fust Friday."

" Indeed! so it is. What has that to do with the matter? "

" But we are all making the Nine Fridays, Fader; and if we break wan, we must commence all over again."

" Well, run down to Father Letheby; he'll hear you."

" Father Letheby is in his box, Fader; and "—— here there was a little smile and a fingering of the pinafores—" we'd rader go to you, Fader."

I took the compliment for what it was worth. The Irish race appear to have kissed the Blarney stone *in globo*.

" And have you no pity on a poor old man, to take him out this dreadful night down to that cold church, and keep him there till ten or eleven o'clock to-night? "

" We won't keep you long, Fader. We were at our juty last month."

" All right, get away, and I'll follow you quickly. Mind your preparation."

" All right, Fader."

" 'Tisn't taking leave of your seven sinses you are, going down to that cowld chapel this awful night," said Hannah, when she had closed the door on the children. " Wisha, thin, if I knew what them whipsters wanted, 'tis long before they crossed the thrishol of the door. Nine Fridays, begor! As if the Brown Scaffler and the first Sunday of the month wasn't enough for them. And here I'll be now for the rest of the winter, cooking your coughs and cowlds. Sure, you're no more able to take care of yerself than an unwaned child."

She brought me my boots, and my old cloak, and my muffler, and my umbrella all the same; and as I passed into the darkness and the rain, I heard anathemas on " these new fandangos, as if there weren't as good priests in the parish as ever he was."

I slipped into the church, as I thought, unperceived; but I was hardly seated, when I heard the door of Father Letheby's confessional flung open; and with his quick, rapid stride, and his purple stole flying from his shoulder, he was immediately at my side, and remonstrating vigorously at my imprudence.

" This is sheer madness, sir, coming out of your warm room on this dreadful night. Surely, when I got your permission to establish this devotion, I never intended this."

" Never mind, now," I said, " I'm not going to allow you to make a somersault into heaven over my head. In any case, these little mites won't take long."

They looked alarmed enough at his angry face.

" Well, then, I shall ask you to allow me to discontinue this devotion after to-night."

" Go back to your confessional. Sufficient for the day is the evil thereof. There's plenty of time to consider the future."

He was much annoyed over my indiscretion; but he resumed his work. Mine was quickly gone through, and I passed up the dimly lighted aisle, wondering at myself. Just near the door, I could not forbear looking around the deep sepulchral gloom. It was lit by the one red lamp that shone like a star in the sanctuary, and by the two dim waxlights in tin sconces, that cast a pallid light on the painted pillars, and a brown shadow farther up, against which were silhouetted the figures of the men, who sat in even rows around Father Letheby's confessional. Now and again a solitary penitent darkened the light of the candles, as he moved up to the altar rails to read his penance or thanksgiving; or the quick figure of a child darted rapidly past me into the thicker darkness without. Hardly a sound broke the stillness, only now and then there was a moan of sorrow, or some expression of emphasis from the penitents; and the drawing of the slides from time to time made a soft sibilance, as of shuttles, beneath which were woven tapestries of human souls that were fit to hang in the halls of heaven. Silently the mighty work went forward; and I thought, as there and then the stupendous sacrifice of Calvary was brought down into our midst, and the hands of that young priest gathered up the Blood of Christ from grass, and stone, and wood—from reeking nails and soldier's lance, and the wet weeping hair of Magdalen, and poured it softly on the souls of these young villagers—I thought what madness possesses the world not to see that this sublime assumption of God's greatest privilege of mercy is in itself the highest dogmatic proof of the Divine origin of the Church; for no purely human institution could dare usurp such an exalted position, nor assume the possession of such tremendous power.

As I knelt down, and turned to leave the church, I felt my cloak gently pulled. I looked down and faintly discerned in the feeble light some one huddled at my feet. I thought at first it was one of the little children, for they used sometimes to wait for the coveted privilege of holding the hand of their old pastor, and conducting him homeward in the darkness. This was no child, however, but some one fully grown, as I conjectured, though I saw nothing but the outline of wet and draggled garments. I waited. Not a word came forth, but something like the echo of a sob. Then I said:—

" Whom have I here, and what do you want? "

" Father, Father, have pity ! "

" I do not know who you are," I replied, " and wherefore I should have pity. If you stand up and speak, I'll know what to say or do."

" You know me well," said the woman's voice, " too well. Am I to be cast out forever? "

Then I recognized Nance, who had followed and blessed Father Tom the evening he left us. She did not bless me nor address me. I had to speak publicly of poor Nance; perhaps, indeed, I spoke too sharply and strongly —it is so hard to draw the line between zeal and discretion, it is so easy to degenerate into weakness or into

excess. And Nance feared me. Probably she was the
only one of the villagers who never dared address me.

" What do you want here? " I gently said.

" What do I want here? 'Tis a quare question for a
priest to be afther asking. What did the poor crature
want when she wint to a bigger man dan you, and she
wasn't turned away aither? "

" Yes, Nance; but she repented and loved Christ, and
was prepared to die rather than sin again."

" And how do you know but I'm the same? Do you
know more than the God above you?—and He is my
witness here to-night before His Blessed and Holy Son
that all hell-fire won't make me fall again. Hell-fire,
did I say? " Her voice here sunk into a low whisper.
" It isn't hell-fire I dread, but His face and yours."

I stooped down and lifted her gently. The simple
kindness touched the broken vase of her heart, and she
burst into an agony of passionate tears.

" Oh, wirra! wirra! if you had only said that much to
me three months ago, what you'd have saved me. But
you'd the hard word, Father, and it drove me wild to
think that, as you said, I wasn't fit to come and mix with
the people at Mass. And many and many a night in the
cowld and hunger, I slept there at the door of the chapel;
and only woke up to bate the chapel door, and ask God
to let me in. But sure His hand was agin me, like yours,
and I daren't go in. And sometimes I looked through
the kayhole, to where His heart was burnin', and I
thought He would come out, when no one could see Him,
and spake to me; but no! no! Him and you were agin
me; and then the chapel woman 'ud come in the cowld
of the mornin', and I would shlink away to my hole
agin? "

" Speak low, Nance," I whispered, as her voice hissed
through the darkness. " The men will hear you! "

" They often heard worse from me than what I am
saying to-night, God help me! 'Tisn't the men I care
about, nor their doings. But whin the young girls would

crass the street, les' they should come near me, and the
dacent mothers 'ud throw their aprons over their childres'
heads, les' they should see me, ah! that was the bitter
pill.   And many and many a night, whin you wor in your
bed, I stood down on dem rocks below, with the say calling for me, and the hungry waves around me and there
was nothin' betune me and hell but that—— "

She fumbled in her bosom and drew out a ragged, well-
worn scapular with a tiny medal attached, and kissed it.

" And sure I know if I wint with 'em, I should have
to curse the face of the Blessed and Holy Mary forever,
and I said then, ' Never! Never! ' and I faced the hard
world agin."

I detected the faintest odour of spirits as she spoke.

" 'Tis hardly a good beginning, Nance, to come here
straight from the public house."

" 'Twas only a thimbleful Mrs. Haley gave me, to
give me courage to face you."

" And what is it to be now? Are you going to change
you life? "

" Yerra, what else would bring me here to-night? "

" And you are going to make up your mind to go to
confession as soon as you can? "

" As soon as I can? This very moment, wid God's
blessing."

" Well, then, I'll ask Father Letheby to step out
for a moment and hear you."

" If you do, then I'll lave the chapel on the spot, and
maybe you won't see me again."   She pulled up her
shawl, as if to depart.

" What harm has Father Letheby done you? Sure
every one likes him."

" Maybe! But he never gave me word or look that
wasn't pison since he came to the parish.   I'll go to
yourself."

" But," I said, fearing that she had still some dread
of me that might interfere with the integrity of her confession, " you know I have a bad tongue—— "

"Never mind," she said, "if you have. Sure they say your bark is worse than your bite."

And so, then and there, in the gloom of that winter's night, I heard her tale of anguish and sorrow; and whilst I thanked God for this His sheep that was lost, I went deeper down than ever into the valleys of humiliation and self-reproach: "Caritas erga homines, sicut caritas Dei erga nos."[1] Here was my favourite text, here my sum total of speculative philosophy. I often preached it to others, even to Father Letheby, when he came complaining of the waywardness of this imaginative and fickle people. "If God, from on high, tolerates the unspeakable wickedness of the world—if He calmly looks down upon the frightful holocaust of iniquity that steams up before His eyes from the cities and towns and hamlets of the world—if He tolerates the abomination of paganism, and the still worse, because conscious, wickedness of the Christian world, why should we be fretful and impatient? And if Christ was so gentle and so tender towards these foul, ill-smelling, leprous, and ungrateful Jews, why should we not be tolerant of the venial falls of the holy people—the kingly nation?" And I was obliged to confess that it was all pride—too much sensitiveness, not to God's dishonour, but to the stigma and reproach to our own ministrations, that made us forget our patience and our duty. And often, on Sunday mornings in winter, when the rain poured down in cataracts, and the village street ran in muddy torrents, and the eaves dripped in steady sheets of water, when I stood at my own chapel door and saw poor farmers and labourers, old women and young girls, drenched through and through, having walked six miles down from the farthest mountains; and when I saw, as I read the Acts and the Prayer before Mass, a thick fog of steam rising from their poor clothes and filling the entire church with a strange incense, I thought how easy it ought to be for us to condone the thoughtlessness or the inconsiderate weaknesses

[1] Charity towards men, as the charity of God towards us.

of such a people, and to bless God that our lot was cast amongst them. I heard, with deeper contrition than hers, the sins of that poor outcast; for every reproach she addressed to me I heard echoed from the recesses of that silent tabernacle. But all my trouble was increased when I insisted on her approaching the Holy Table in the morning. The thought of going to Holy Communion appalled her. " Perhaps in eight or twelve months she'd be fit; but to-morrow—— "

Her dread was something intense, almost frightful :—

" Sure He'll kill me, as He killed the man who towld the lie ! "

I tried to reassure her :—

" But they say he'll *bleed* if I touch Him."

I gently reasoned and argued with her. Then her objections took a more natural turn : —

" Sure the people will all rise up and lave the chapel."

Then it became a question of dress. And it was with the greatest difficulty, and only by appealing to her humility, and as a penance, that I at last induced her to consent to come up to the altar rails after all the people had received Holy Communion. There was a slight stir next morning when all the people had reverently retired from the Holy Table. I waited, holding the Sacred Host over the Ciborium. The people wondered. Then, from the farthest recess of the church, a draped figure stole slowly up the aisle. All knew it was Nance. So far from contempt, only pity, deep pity, filled the hearts of old and young; and one could hear clearly the *tchk* ! *tchk* ! that curious click of sympathy which I believe is peculiar to our people. The tears streamed down the face of the poor penitent as I placed the Sacred Host upon her tongue. Then she rose strengthened, and walked meekly, but firmly, back to her place. As she did, I noticed that she wore a thick black shawl. It was the quick eye of my curate that had seen all. It was his gentle, kind heart that forestalled me.

I got an awful scolding from Hannah when I came home that night in the rain.

"Never mind, Hannah," I said, when she had exhausted her diatribe, "I never did a better night's work in my life."

She looked at me keenly; but these poor women have some queer way of understanding things; and she said humbly:—

"Than' God!"

CHAPTER XV

HOLLY AND IVY

THE progress of my curate and myself in our study of the Greek authors is not so steady or so successful as we had anticipated. Somehow or other we drift away from the subject-matter of our evening lessons, and I am beginning to perceive that his tastes are more modern, or, to speak more correctly, they tend to less archaic and more interesting studies. Then again I have read somewhere that the Hebrew characters, with their minute vowel-points, have driven blind many an enthusiastic scholar, and I fear these black Greek letters are becoming too much for my old sight. There now, dear reader, don't rush to the conclusion that this is just what you anticipated; you knew, of course, how it would be. You never had much faith in these transcendental enterprises of reviving Greek at the age of seventy-five, and you shook your incredulous head at the thought of an Academia of two honorary members at Kilronan. Now we *have* done a little. If you could only see the " Dream of Atossa " done into English pentameters by my curate, and my own " Prometheus "—well, there, this won't do —*Vanity of vanities*, said the Preacher.

But this much I shall be pardoned. I cannot help feeling very solemn and almost sad at the approach of Christmas time. Whether it is the long, gloomy tunnel that runs through the year from November to April— these dark, sad days are ever weeping—or whether it is the tender associations that are linked with the hallowed time and the remembrance of the departed I know not; but some indescribable melancholy seems to hover around and hang down on my spirits at this holy season; and it is emphasized by a foreboding that somewhere in the future this great Christian festival will degenerate into a mere bank holiday, and lose its sacred and tender and thrice-sanctified associations. By the way, is it not curious that our governments are steadily increasing the number of secular holidays, whilst the hands of Pharisees are still uplifted in horror at the idleness and demoralization produced amongst Catholics by the eight or ten days that are given in the year to the honour of God's elect?

Well, we shall stand by the old traditions to the end. And one of my oldest habits has been to read up at Christmas time every scrap of literature that had any bearing whatever on the most touching and the most important event in all human history. And so, on the Sunday evening preceding the celebration of Father Letheby's first Christmas in Kilronan, I spoke to him at length on my ideas and principles in connection with this great day; and we went back, in that rambling, desultory way that conversation drifts into—back to ancient prophecies and forecastings, down to modern times—tales of travellers about Bethlehem, the sacrilegious possession of holy places by Moslems, etc., etc., until the eyes of my curate began to kindle, and I saw a possible Bernard or Peter in his fine, clear-cut face, and a " Deus vult " in the trembling of his lips. Ah me! what a glorious thing is this enthusiasm of the young—this noble idealism, that spurns the thought of consequences, only sees the finger of God beckoning and cares not whither!

" Hand me down that Virgil," I said, to avert an explosion, for when he does break out on modern degeneracy he is not pleasant to hear.

" Now spare my old eyes, and read for me, with deliberation, those lines of the Fourth Eclogue which forecast the coming of our Lord! "

He read in his fine sonorous voice, and he did full justice to the noble lines :—

> " Ultima Cumæi venit jam carminis ætas;
> Magnus ab integro sæclorum nascitur ordo.
> Jam redit et Virgo, redeunt Saturnia regna;
> Jam nova progenies cælo demittitur alto,"—

down to the two lines which I repeated as a prayer :—

> " O mihi tam longæ maneat pars ultima vitæ
> Spiritus et, quantum sat erit tua dicere facta."

" No wonder," he said, at length, " that the world of the Middle Ages, which, by the way, were *the* ages of enlightenment, should have regarded Virgil as a magician and even as a saint."

" But," he said, after a pause, " the ' Dream of the Dead Christ ' would be almost more appropriate nowadays. It is terrible to think how men are drifting away from Him. There's Ormsby now, a calm, professed infidel; and absolutely nothing in the way to prevent his marriage with Miss Campion but his faith, or want of faith."

" Ormsby! " I cried. " Infidel! Marriage with Miss Campion!—want of faith!!! What in the world is this sudden discharge of fireworks and Catherine-wheels upon your pastor? Or where has all this gunpowder been hitherto stored? "

" I thought I had told you, sir," he said, timidly, " but I have so many irons in the fire. You know that Ormsby's marriage is only a question of weeks but for one thing."

" And, if I am not trespassing too much on the secrecy of your confidential intercourse with these young people," I said (I suppose I was a little huffed), " may I ask how long is all this matrimonial enterprise in progress, and how does Campion regard it? "

" I am afraid you are offended, sir," he said, " and indeed quite naturally, because I have not spoken about this matter to you before; but really it appears so hopeless, and I hate speaking of things that are only conjectural. I suppose you had set your heart on Miss Campion's becoming a nun? "

" God forbid! " I said fervently. " We don't want to see all our best girls running into convents. I had set my heart on her being married to some good, excellent Catholic Irishman, like the Chief over at Kilkeel."

" Neil Cullen? Campion wouldn't listen to it. His name is a red rag to a bull. He never forgave Cullen for not firing on the people at that eviction over at Labbawally, some two or three years ago."

" And what does the person most interested think of the matter? " I asked.

" Well, I think she is quite in favour of it," he said. " Her father likes him, he will live in the old house, and she likes him—at least, she asked me to do all in my power to bring him into the Church."

" The little puss," I could not help saying. " Who would ever have thought it? And yet, would it not be best? I pity her living with that old sea-dog—that Viking in everything but his black mane of hair. But now, look here; this matter is important; let us talk it over quietly. Who or what is Ormsby? You have met him? "

" Several times. He is a young Trinity man, goodlooking, gentlemanly, correct, moral. He has a pension of two hundred a year, his salary as Inspector of Coast Guards, and great expectations. But he has no faith."

" And never had any, I suppose. That's the way with all these fellows—— "

" On the contrary, he was brought up a strict Evangelical, almost a Calvinist. Then he began to read, and like so many others he has drifted into unfaith."

" Well, lend him some books. He knows nothing, of course, about us. Let him see the faith, and he'll embrace it."

" Unfortunately, there's the rub. He has read everything. He has travelled the world; and reversing the

venerable maxim, *Cœlum, non animum mutant*, he has
taken his faith from his climate. He has been a Theoso-
phist in London, a ' New Light ' in 'Frisco, as he calls
it, a Moslem in Cairo (by the way, he thinks a lot of
these Mussulmans—fine, manly, dignified fellows, he
says, whose eloquence would bring a blush almost to the
cheek of a member of Parliament). Then he has been
hand in glove with Buddhist priests in the forests of
Ceylon, and has been awfully impressed with their secret
power, and still more with their calm philosophy. I
believe," said my curate, sinking his voice to a whisper
of awe and mystery, " *I believe—he has kissed—the—
tooth—of—Buddha!* "

" Indeed," I replied, " and what good did that operation do him? "

" Not much, I suppose, except to confirm him in that
gospel of the sceptic : ' There are more things in heaven
and earth, Horatio, than are dreamt of in your philosophy ! ' "

" Humph! Here, then, stands the case. Our most
interesting little parishioner has set her heart on this
globe-trotter. There is a big wall in the way, and it
won't do to repeat the tragedy of Pyramus and Thisbe.
Now, what is to be done to make the young fellow a
Catholic? Has he any prejudices against us? "

" Not one. On the contrary, he rather likes us. He
has received all kinds of hospitality from Catholic priests
the wide world over, and he thinks us a right honest,
jolly lot of fellows."

" H'm! I am not sure that that is exactly what St.
Liguori or Charles Borromeo would fancy. But never
mind! Now does he know what we hold and believe? "

" Accurately. He has read our best books."

" Has he had any intercourse with Catholics? "

" A good deal. They have not impressed him. Look
at Campion now. Would any man become a Catholic
with his example before him? "

" Hardly indeed, though we must speak kindly of him

now, since you converted him. Had you any chat with
him about his difficulties? "

" Yes, several. I walked home with him a few evenings from Campion's. You know that path over the
cliff and down to the coast-guard station? "

" Well. And what is his special trouble? Does he
think he has an immortal soul? "

" There you struck it. That's his trouble; and how
to convince him of that beats me. I asked him again
and again whether he was not self-conscious, that is,
perfectly cognizant of the fact that there was a something, an Ego, outside and beyond the brain and inferior
powers that commanded both? Was there not some intellectual entity that called up memory, and bade it un-
seal its tablets? And did he not feel and know that he
could command and control the action of his brain, and
even of every part of it? Now, I said, if the brain is
only dumb matter, which you admit, and cannot create
thought, where is this volition, or what is it? It is not
cerebral, for then matter would create thought; that is,
be the creator and the created at the same time."

" Well? "

" He listened attentively and then said quietly:
' Quite true. But if the Ego is different from the brain
and is self-conscious, where does the self-consciousness
go when the brain becomes anæmic and sleeps, or when
the faculties are chloroformed? ' ' Oh,' I said, ' the
organ is shut down, the stops are closed.' ' Yes,' he
said, ' but where goes the performer? ' By Jove, I was
stranded. I tell you what it is, Father Dan, though
you'll call it treason, I'll pitch Æschylus to the mischief,
and study what is of human and vital interest to us
priests."

" That little objection needn't alarm you," I said,
" you'll find the answer in every handbook of Catholic
philosophy."

" What manual of Catholic philosophy in English could
I get for Ormsby? " asked my curate.

" Alas! my dear young friend, I don't know. There is the great hiatus. You cannot put a folio calf-bound volume of Suarez in his hands—he may not understand Latin. I know absolutely no book that you can put into the hands of an educated non-Catholic except Balmez's ' Letters to a Sceptic.' "

" *He has read it*," said my curate.

We were both silent.

" Now, you know," he continued, after a long pause, " I don't attach the least importance to these objections and arguments. I lived long enough in England to know that faith is a pure, absolutely pure gift of the Almighty, not to be acquired by learning or study, but possibly by prayer. I see, therefore, only one hope, and that is, in our Lord and His Blessed Mother."

" A profound and true remark," I replied, as he rose up to depart. " Get these mites of children to pray, and to say the Rosary for that particular purpose. I can't understand how God can refuse them anything."

" By the way," he said, as he put on his greatcoat, " it is a curious fact that, with all his incredulity, he is exceedingly superstitious. You can hardly believe how troubled he is about some gibberish of that old hag that sets charms for lame horses, etc. I'm not at all sure but that she set charms in the other way for my little mare."

" Well, what has she told Ormsby? "

" Her language was slightly oracular. Out of a joke, he crossed her palm with a sixpence. She looked him all over, though she knew well what he had in his mind, examined the lines of his hand minutely, and then delivered three Sibylline sentences:—

' Set a stout heart to a steep brae.'

That did not disconcert him. Then she said:—

' He that tholes, overcomes.'

He quite agreed with her. It was a naval simile, and it pleased him.

'But a white cloth and a stain never agree.'

He was struck as if by a blow. ' Mind you,' he said, ' I am very candid. I have had my own faults and human weaknesses; but I never did anything immoral or dishonourable. What did she mean? ' ' She meant,' I said, to reassure him, ' that you have kept her carefully out of the coast-guard station; that you have not allowed her to interfere with the men, or their wives, or their servants; that therefore you have put many a sixpence out of her pocket; and that she must have her revenge. Dismiss her jargon from your mind as soon as you can.' ' More easily said than done, Father,' he replied, and he then began to mutter: ' A white cloth and a stain never agree.' What *does* she mean? "

" The old story of Voltaire," I said, when my curate had finished. " Don't forget the children's prayers."

On Christmas eve he called at noonday, just as we were going out to the midday confessional. He had nothing new to tell. He was rather gloomy.

" You'll meet Miss Campion in the church," he said; " she'll tell you all."

" I don't think," I said, to cheer him—for where is the use of fretting in this queer world?—" there was so much need for Ormsby to go as far as Ceylon to find Buddha and the Nirvana. Look there."

Leaning against the blank wall opposite my house were three silent figures. They were a little distance apart, and they leaned against their support with the composure of three cabinet ministers on their green benches on the night of a great debate. Their feet were slightly parted, and they gazed on the road with a solemn, placid expression, as of men to whom the Atlantean weight of this weary world was as the down on a feather. Calmly and judicially, as if seeing nothing, yet weighing all things, they looked on pebble and broken limestone, never raising their heads, never removing their hands from their pockets. They had been there since breakfast time that morning, and it was now past noon.

" My God," said Father Letheby, when I told him, " 'tis awful! "

" 'Tis the sublime," I said.

" And do you mean to tell me that they have never stirred from that posture for two long hours? "

" You have my word for it," I replied; " and you know the opinion entertained about my veracity—' he'd no more tell a lie than the parish priest.' "

" I notice it everywhere," he said, in his impetuous way. " If I drive along the roads, my mare's head is right over the car or butt, before the fellow wakes up to see me; and then the exasperating coolness and deliberation with which he draws the reins to pull aside. My boy, too, when waiting on the road for a few minutes whilst I am attending a patient, falls fast asleep, like the fat boy in Pickwick; down there, under the cliffs, the men sleep all day in, or under, their boats. Why does not Charcot send all his nervous patients to Ireland? The air is not only a sedative, but a soporific. 'Tis the calm of the eternal gods—the sleep of the immortals."

" 'Tis the sleep of Enceladus in Etna," I replied. " When they wake up and turn, 'tis hot lava and ashes."

" That's true, too," he said, musingly; " we are a strange people."

My own voice again echoing out of the dead past.

Miss Campion and " her friend from Dublin," Miss Leslie, were very busy about the Christmas decorations. Mrs. Darcy helped in her own way. I am afraid she did not approve of all that was being done. Miss Campion's and Mrs. Darcy's ideas of " the beautiful " were not exactly alike. Miss Campion's art is reticent and economical. Mrs. Darcy's is loud and pronounced. Miss

Campion affects mosaics and miniatures. Mrs. Darcy
wants a circus-poster, or the canvas of a diorama. Where
Mrs. Darcy, on former occasions, put huge limbs of holly
and a tangled wilderness of ivy, Miss Campion puts three
or four dainty glistening leaves with a heart of red coral
berries in the centre. Mrs. Darcy does not like it, and
she thinks it her duty to art and religion to remonstrate.

" Wisha, Miss, I wouldn't be sparin' the holly if I
was you. Sure 'tis chape."

" Ah, well, now, Mrs. Darcy, don't you think this looks
neat and pretty? "

" As nate and purty as yourself, Miss; but sure the
parish priest won't mind the expinse. 'Tis Christmas
times, and his heart is open."

This wasn't too kind of Mrs. Darcy; but it does not
matter. She looked ruefully at the fallen forest of green-
ery that strewed the chapel floor.

Miss Campion saw her distress, and said, kindly :—

" Now, Mrs. Darcy, is there any improvement you
would kindly suggest before we conclude? "

" Wisha, Miss, there isn't much, indeed. You have
made it lovely. But I'd like to see a little bit of holly
in the Blessed Virgin's crown, and just a weeshy little
bit in her Child's fingers. Sure, whatever is going these
Christmas times, them have the best right to it."

Miss Campion smiled, and yielded to the pious wishes
of the chapel woman, and then said :—

" Now, Mrs. Darcy, we'll put a few noble branches
around the front porch, and whatever is left you must
take it home, and let Jemmy decorate the dresser."

The first suggestion met Mrs. Darcy's tastes to perfection; the second went straight to her mother's heart.

" May God bless you, Miss; and may it be many a long
day till throuble or sorrow crass the thrishol' of your
dure."

The neighbours flocked in on Christmas eve to see Mrs.
Darcy's cabin. Jemmy had risen to the occasion. The
polished pewter vessels and the brass candlesticks shone

resplendent from the background of black holly and veined
ivy, and the red pearls of the berries. The comments,
like all human criticisms, varied according to the sub-
jectivity and prejudices of the visitors.

" Wisha, 'tis purty, indeed. God bless those that gave
it to the poor widow."

" Wisha, Jemmy, agra, there's no knowing what you'll
be when you grows up."

" Wisha, thin, Mrs. Darcy, you wor always the good
nabor. Would it be asking too much, ma'am, to give us
thim few kippeens on the floor? Sure Abby says she'd
like to have a little bit of holly to stick round the Infant
Jesus this holy and blessed night."

" 'Tis aisy for some people to be proud. Aisy got,
aisy gone. But 'tis quare to be taking what ought to go
to the house of God to make a babby-show for ourselves."

" Yerra, whisht, 'uman, we must hould our heads as
high as we can while we have it. It may go soon, and
Mary Darcy may wish to be no betther thin her nabors."

Ah me! Here is the great world in miniature.

" There is not a word of news going? " I said to Miss
Campion, as we walked up and down the moss-covered
walk that lay to the south side of the little church.

" Nothing, Father," she said, " except, indeed, that
father makes his Christmas Communion in the morning;
and oh! I am so thankful to God and to Father Letheby."

" It is really good news, Beata," I replied. I sometimes called her Beata, for Bittra sounds horrid. I intend to compromise on her wedding morn by calling her
Beatrix. " Really good news. It will add considerably
to the happiness of one, whose only object in life appears
to be to make every one around her happy. But there
is no other news that may be supposed to interest in a
far-off way the old pastor, who gave Beata her First
Communion, and——? "

She blushed crimson, and held down her head.

" Now," I said, " give your old parish priest your
arm, for I am getting more and more feeble every day,

and tell him all.   Perhaps he could help you too."

" Oh, father, if you could; but it is almost too much to expect from God.   Perhaps I'd forget Him."

" Not much fear of that," I exclaimed fervently; "but now let us calculate the chances."

" But oh, Father, if you only knew Rex—he is so good, so gentle, he takes so kindly to the poor (" the clever rascal," I ejaculated under my breath), and he likes us so much, I'm sure it needs but little to make him an excellent Catholic."

Well, now, what is a poor old man to do?   Here am I, prepared to calculate and balance chances of this young man's conversion—the *pros* and *cons* of a serious matter; and here this young lady branches off into a magnificent apotheosis of her young demigod!   What has the cold yellow candle light of reason to do in the *camera obscura* of the human heart?   Let us fling open the shutters, and let in the golden sunshine.

" So I've heard," I said.   " And I also know this, Beata, that is, I've read something like it in good books, written by holy and thoughtful men, that the gift of faith is given freely by the Holy Spirit to those who, like your *fiancé*, have led pure and unsullied lives."

She started at the word *fiancé*, and the smile on her face was a study.   Poor old Dante! no wonder you walked on air, and lightly spurned the stars, when your lady beckoned.

" Beatrice in suso, ed io in lei guardava."

So shall it be to the end.

Well, we talked the whole thing over; debated all possibilities, laughed at difficulties, cut through obstacles, leaped over obstructions, and, at last, saw in imagination, written on the cold, frosty air of December, the mystic legend, I WILL, surrounded by a gorgeous corona of orange blossoms.

Then, of course, the superb unreason of women. Beata began to cry as I handed her over to Miss Leslie, who looked daggers at me, and I am quite sure called me, in her own mind, " A horrid old thing! "

Father Letheby, after his unusually heavy confessional, was jubilant. Nothing exhilarates him like work. Given a scanty confessional, and he is as gloomy as Sisyphus; given a hard, laborious day, and he is as bright as Ariel. He was in uncommonly good spirits to-day.

" By Jove, Father Dan," he said, as we walked home together to our little bit of fish, " I have it. I'll try him with the *Kampaner Thal!* "

" The very thing," I replied.

" Don't you think it would do? You know he regards all our arguments as so much special pleading, and he discounts them accordingly."

" Of course," I said. " Wonder you never thought of it before! "

" That is curious now. But you always find things in unexpected quarters. But you're sure 'twill do? "

" Quite sure. By the way, what *is* the *Kampaner Thal?* "

He looked squarely at me.

" 'Pon my word, Father Dan, I confess I sometimes think you are rather fond of a joke."

" Come along, never mind," I replied. " After air and water, the power of a pleasant and kind word is the best and cheapest thing God gives us, His children."

CHAPTER XVI

VIOLENT CONTRASTS

CHRISTMAS DAY was a day of undiluted triumph for Father Letheby. There were great surprises in store for me. That is one of my curate's few faults—is it a fault?—that he is inclined to be dramatic. As he says, he hates to speak of a thing until it is beyond the reach of failure. Of all criticisms, the one he most dreads is, "I told you so." And so, on this Christmas morning, I had a series of mild, pleasant shocks, that made the bright, crisp, frosty, sunny morning all the more pleasant. It was a slight, because expected, surprise to see Captain Campion at the altar rails. He appeared at eight o'clock Mass. Thanks be to God! I manage still to use the sublime privilege given by the Church that morning, of being allowed to celebrate three times. I have not omitted it for fifty years. When I shall fail to say my three Christmas Masses, then you may take up your *Exequiæ*, and practise the *Requiem æternam* for poor Daddy Dan.

Well, I had said the first two Masses, commencing at seven o'clock. It is a curious experience, that of seven o'clock Mass on Christmas morning. The groping through the dark, with just the faintest aurora on the horizon, the smell of the frost in the air, the crunching of icicles under one's feet, the shadowy figures, making their way with some difficulty to the church, the salutations of the people: "Is that you, Mick?" "'Tis, Mrs. Grady; a happy Christmas to you, ma'am." "The same to you, Mick, and manny of them." "Good morning, Mrs. Mulcahy; 'tis a fine Christmas morning, glory be to God."

" 'Tis indeed, ma'am, glory be to His Holy Name."
" Hurry up, Bess, you'll never catch the priest at the
altar." " Yerra, sure, haven't we three Masses to-day."
The more polite people said: " The compliments of the
saison to you, ma'am." " The same to you, sir; may we
be all alive and happy this time twelvemonth."

Well, just as I commenced the hymn of the angels at
my first Mass, there was a crash of music and singing
from the gallery over the door, that made my old heart
leap with joy and pride. I never expected it; and the
soft tones of the harmonium, and the blending of the
children's voices, floating out there in the dark of the
little chapel, made tears of delight stream down the
wrinkles of my cheeks. And what was the *Gloria*, do
you think? From Mozart's " Twelfth Mass," if you
please. Nothing else would do. The pride of Kilronan
is gone so high since that famous concert, that I am
almost sure they would challenge the seraphim to a fair
contest, that is, if the latter would put aside their golden
viols and sambucæ, and compete only with their voices
against the " new choir of Kilronan." I violated egregi-
ously one strict rubric at the *Dominus vobiscum*. I raised
my eyes and took a good long look at choir and people.
I couldn't help it. If Martinucci and Baruffaldi, Gavan-
tus and Merati, Gardellini and Bauldry, and the whole
Congregation of Sacred Rites were there in the front
bench, I couldn't help myself. I kept my hands open
for at least a quarter of a minute, whilst I surveyed my
little congregation. It was a pathetic sight. The lights
from the altar shone on the faces of Captain Campion
and Bittra, and one or two of the better-class parishioners
on the front bench; but all behind were buried in a deep
well of darkness. I could barely distinguish the pale
faces of the confused mass that stretched in the deep
gloom towards the door; but overhead, about a dozen
dark figures were outlined against the light of the two
wax candles on the harmonium, over which, on this eventful morning, Father Letheby presided. And this was the

object of the concert at last. I should have known that
there was some supernatural object behind it.   This
young man does not care much to develop or elicit the
dormant energies of the people, unless he can turn therewith the mills of God. But what trouble it must have
given him! How many a cold night did he leave his
room, and there, on that gallery, contend with the rough
and irregular voices, until he brought them into that
stream of perfect unison. I can imagine what patience
he exercised, what subtle flatteries he administered, what
gentle sarcasm he applied, before he succeeded in modu-
lating the hoarse thunders of Dave Olden's voice, that
rose like a fog-horn over the winds and waves whenever
he ventured upon the high seas; and how he cut off re-
morselessly the grace-notes of Abby Lyden, who has begun to think herself an Albani; and how he overcame
the shyness of the fisher lads, and brought clear to the
front the sweet tenors of the school boys, on whom, he
said, all his hopes depended. And how his own rich bari-
tone ascended strongly and softly over all, blending into
perfect harmony all discordance, and gently smothering
the vagrant and rebellious tones that would sometimes
break ambitiously through discipline, and try to assert
their own individuality. He sang an Offertory solo, accompanying himself on the harmonium. Who will say
it was not sweet? Who will say it was not appropriate?

" O Vergine bella!
Del ciel Regina,
A cui s'inchina
La terra ed el mar.

" O Tu che sei stella
Del mare si bella,
Ci guido nal porta
Col tuo splendor."

And then when Bethlehem was repeated, with all its

lowliness and humility, there in that humble chapel; and
the Divine Babe lay white and spotless on the corporal,
the glorious *Adeste* broke forth. Ah me! what a new experience for myself and people. Ah me! what a sting of
compunction in all the honeyed delights of that glorious
morning, to think that for all these years I had been
pastor there. Well, never mind; *meâ maximâ culpâ!
Ignosce, Domine!*

I placed the Sacred Host on Captain Campion's tongue,
and most heartily forgave him his unflattering epithets.
Tears of joy streamed down Bittra's face as she knelt beside him at the altar rails. I was wearied and tired from
the large number of Communions I administered that
morning. The last communicant was poor Nance. She
was hidden away in the deep gloom; but I am not at all
sure that the Child Jesus did not nestle as comfortably
in the arms of the poor penitent as in those of His virgins
and spotless ones. And there were many such, thank
Gód, amongst my Christmas congregation that morning.

But the great surprise of all was in store. For, after
Mass was over, there was a great rush to St. Joseph's
Chapel; and I am afraid I cut my own thanksgiving short,
to move with silent dignity in the same direction. I
heard gasps of surprise and delight, exclamations of wonder, suppressed hallelujahs of joy; I saw adoration and
tenderness, awe and love on the dimly lighted faces of
the people. No wonder! For there, under a rough,
rustic roof of pines and shingles, was the Bethlehem of
our imaginations in miniature. Rough rocks lined the
interior, wet green mosses and lichens covering them
here and there; in front of the cave a light hoar-frost lay
on the ground, and straw and stubble littered the palace
floor of Him who walks on the jasper and chalcedony par-
quetting of the floors of heaven. And there was the
gentle Joseph, with a reverent, wondering look on his
worn features; and there the conscious, self-possessed,
but adoring expression on the sweet face of the Child·

Mother; and there the helpless form and pleading hands of Him whose omnipotence stretches through infinity, and in whose fingers colossal suns and their systems are but the playthings of this moment in His eternal existence, which we call Time.   Three shepherds stood around, dazed at some sudden light that shone from the face of the Infant; one, a boy, leaned forward as if to raise in his arms that sweet, helpless Babe; his hands were stretched towards the manger, and a string held the broad hat that fell between his shoulders.   And aloft an angel held in his hand a starry scroll, on which was inscribed *Gloria in excelsis Deo*.   I stood amongst my awe-struck congregation for a few minutes. Some were kneeling, and uttering half-frantic ejaculations of adoration, pity, and love; some leaned against a pillar, silent, but with tearful eyes; little children pointed out to each other the different features of this new wonder-world; but all around, the fervid Celtic imagination translated these terra-cotta figures into living and breathing personalities. It was as if God had carried them back over the gulf of nineteen centuries, and brought them to the stable door of Bethlehem that ever memorable night.   I think it is this realization of the Incarnation that constitutes the distinguishing feature of Catholicity.   It is the Sacred Humanity of our Lord that brings Him so nigh to us, and makes us so familiar with Him; that makes the Blessed Eucharist a necessity, and makes the hierarchy of Bethlehem, Jerusalem, and Calvary so beloved—beloved above all by the poor, and the humble, and the lowly.   Listen to this!

" Oh, dear, dear, and to think of our Lord with the straw under Him, and His feet covered with the frost of that cowld night—— "

" And the poor child!   Look at her; why, she's only a little girl, like Norah; and not a woman near to help her in her throuble."

" Look at His little hands stretched out, like any

ordinary child. Glory be to His Holy Name. Sure, only for Him where 'ud we be? ''

'' And poor St. Joseph! No wondher he's fretting. To think of thim two cratures in his hands, and he not having house or home to shelter thim! ''

'' Wisha, Mary, 'twas a pity we worn't there that blessed night. Sure, 'tis we'd give 'em the best we had in the world, an' our hearts' blood.''

I shared to the full this feeling about St. Joseph. And when, after Father Letheby's Mass, I came down, and brought over my old arm-chair, and placed it in front of the crib, and put down my snuff-box, and my breviary, and my spectacles, and gave myself up to the contemplation of that wonderful and pathetic drama, St. Joseph would insist on claiming the largest share of my pity and sympathy. Somehow I felt that mother and child understood each other perfectly—that she saw everything through the eyes of God, and that therefore there was not much room for wonderment; but that to St. Joseph the whole thing was an unspeakable mystery of humiliation and love, infinite abasement and infinite dignity; and I thought I saw him looking from the child-face of his spouse to the child-face of the Infant, and somehow asking himself, '' What is it all? '' even though he explicitly understood the meaning and magnitude of the mighty mystery.

Father Letheby has a new series of pictures of the Life of our Lord, painted by a French artist, whose name I can never recall except when I sneeze—Tissot. I do not like them at all. They are too realistic—and, after all, the ideal is the real. I have a special, undiluted dislike of one picture—the *Magnificat*. I'd have torn it up, and put the fragments in the fire, but that it was not mine. But how in the world any Catholic could paint my beautiful child-prophetess of Hebron as Tissot has done baffles comprehension. But he has one lovely picture, '' Because there was no Room.'' The narrow lane of the Jewish city—the steep stairs to the rooms—the blank

walls perforated by a solitary, narrow window—the rough
stones, and the gentle animal that bore Mary, treading
carefully over them—the Jewish women, regretfully refusing admission—the sweet, gentle face of the maiden
mother—and the pathetic, anxious, despairing look on
the features of St. Joseph—make this a touching and
beautiful picture. Poor St. Joseph! " Come, take the
reins of the patient animal, and lead him and his sacred
burden out into the night! There is no room in the City
of David for the children of David. Out under the stars,
shining brilliantly through the frosty atmosphere, over
the white, rugged road, into an unknown country, and
' Whither, O my God? ' on thy lips, as the child at thy
side shuddered, and no finger from heaven nor voice from
earth directed thee; unless, indeed, that faint flashes of
light athwart the net of stars told thee that the angels
were cutting their way down through the darkness, and
into the spheres of men, and that all heaven was in a
tumult of expectation, whilst in yonder city men slept, as
they always sleep unconscious when God is near. And
then, when the feeble plaint broke from Mary's lips, " I
cannot go further," and the gentle beast turned aside into
the rocks and whins, and called to his companions of the
stable, and the meek-eyed ox looked calmly at the in-
truders, and there—there—dear God! to think of it all—
In mundo erat, et mundus eum non cognovit."

I sat quietly there until Benediction at three o'clock,
and then I remained rolling my beads through my fingers, and singing in my heart the grand majestic O's of
the preceding day's offices, at the end of every decade,
until five o'clock struck. From time to time my little
children would come, and leaning on my knee, would
gaze with wonder and affection at the Child of Bethlehem; and then, looking up into my face, put wonderful
questions about deep mysteries to their old Father. For
all day long, a stream of visitors passed before the crib;
and the next day, and the next, crowds trooped over from
Moydore and the neighbouring parishes, for the fame of

it had gone abroad over the land; and men and women came, jealous of their own pastors, and wondering at the sudden uprise of Kilronan. Then the climax was reached on the twelfth day, when the Kings appeared, and the group in the stable was complete. The " black man " from Nubia came in for more than his share of honours; and it was admitted all round that Kilronan was immortalized and the other parishes were forever in the background.

" May God bless the man that gave us such a sight," said an old woman fervently, as I left the wondering crowd and went home to dinner.

" May God bless all our priests," said another, fearing that I might be offended.

" Wisha, thin, Father Dan," said a third, " what a wondher you never tould us what you had in store for us. Wisha, thin, it wasn't worth while keeping it such a grate sacret."

There is no end to the ingenious charity of these people. On my plate at the dinner table, amidst a pile of Christmas cards, was a dainty little duodecimo. I took it up. It was from Father Letheby. And what was it? The *Imitation* in Greek, by a certain George Mayr, S.J. Wasn't this nice? My pet book done into my favourite language! It was the happiest Christmas I ever spent. *Quam bonus Israel Deus!* So too said Father Letheby. But I had some dim presentiment that all his well-merited pleasure would not be quite unalloyed—that some secret hand, perhaps a merciful one, would pluck a laurel leaf or two from his crown. We had a pleasant academic discussion after dinner about the honourable retention of ancient Irish customs—he quite enthusiastic about them, I rather disposed to think that the abuses which invariably accompanied them made their final extinction altogether advisable. We put our respective theories in practice next morning with the most pe·fect

consistency; for Hannah drove indignantly from the door
the wren-boys, just as they were commencing:

> "A thrate, a thrate, if of the best,
> We hope in heaven your sowl will rest;
> But if you give it of the small
> It won't agree with our boys at all."

And, on his part, Father Letheby listened with intense
delight to this dithyrambic, which ushers in St. Stephen's
day all over Ireland; and he dispensed sundry sixpences
to the boys with the injunction to be always good Irishmen and to buy sweets.

That night, just as I was thinking of retiring, for I
am an early riser, I heard a gentle tap at the hall door,
then a hurried colloguing in the hall; and Hannah put in
her head and whispered:—

"Lizzie is afraid, sir, that the priest is sick. Would
you mind coming down to see him?"

"God bless me! no," I said, quite alarmed. I followed the servant rapidly and was ushered into Father
Letheby's parlour, unexpected and almost unannounced.

"What's the matter, sir?" he cried; "what's the
matter?"

"Nothing particular," I replied. "'Tis a rather fine
night, is it not?"

"Lizzie must have sent for you?" he answered.

"Yes," I said, "she did. She thought you were unwell. Are you?"

He looked ill enough, poor fellow, and at these words
he sank wearily into a chair.

"I am afraid you're unwell," I repeated.

"I'm not unwell," he said, blubbering like a child,
"but—but—my heart is broken."

"Oh," I cried, "if that's all, it's easily mended.
Come now, let's hear all, and see if we can't put the
pieces together."

"I wouldn't mind," he cried, standing up and strid-
ing along the little room, his hands tightly clasped behind

his back, " but the poor little altar boys—the poor little beggars—they looked so nice yesterday, and oh to think of it! Good God! "

" Very dramatic, very dramatic," I said, " but not the quiet narrative and consecutive style that I affect. Now, supposing you told me the story. There's balm in Gilead yet."

And this was the story, told with much impressiveness, a fair amount of gesticulation, and one or two little profane expressions, which made the Recording Angel cough and look away to see how was the weather.

It appears that about seven o'clock Father Letheby had a sick-call outside the village. There are generally a fair share of sick-calls on the day succeeding the great festivity, for obvious reasons. He was returning home through the village, when the sound of singing arrested his steps just outside Mrs. Haley's public house. His heart gave a bound of delight as he heard the familiar lines and notes of the *Adeste*. " Thank God! " he said, " at last, the people are beginning to bring our Catholic hymns into their own homes." As he listened intently there was a slight reaction as he recognized the sweet liquid notes, with all the curls and quavers that are the copyright and strictly legal and exclusive possession of Jem Deady.

" Good heavens! " said the young priest, in a frenzy of indignation, " has that ruffian dared to introduce into the taproom our Christmas melodies, and to degrade them into a public-house chorus? "

He stepped into the shop. There was no one there. He turned softly the handle of the door, and was in the taproom for several minutes before he was recognized. What he witnessed was this. Leaning in a tipsy, maudlin way against the wall were the holly bushes, which, decorated with pink ribbons, and supposed to conceal in their dim recesses the " wren, the wren, the king of all birds," had been the great attraction of the morning.

Leaning on the deal table, with glasses and pints of
porter before them, as they sat and lounged or fell in
various stages of intoxication, were the wren-boys; and
near the fire, with his back turned to the door, and his
fingers beating time to the music in pools of dirty porter,
was Jem Deady. As Father Letheby entered he was
singing:—

> " Deum de Deo, Lumen de Lumine,
>   Gestant puellæ viscera—— "

the most awful and tender lines of the glorious hymn.

He was unconscious of the priest's presence, and quite
unconscious of his horrible sacrilege. Father Letheby
continued gazing on the sad scene for a few minutes,
with mingled feelings of anger, horror, and disgust. Then,
closing the door softly after him, he strode through the
street, and knocking peremptorily at all the doors, he
soon had a procession of the fathers and mothers of the
children following him to the public house. What occurred then has passed into the historical annals of Kilronan. It is enough to say here that its good people
heard that night certain things which made their ears
tingle for many a day. Mrs. Haley came up to my house
the following morning to give up her license; and there
was a general feeling abroad that every man, woman, and
child in Kilronan should become total abstainers for life.

" But that's all," said Father Letheby; " and now I
am really sick of the entire business; and to-morrow I
shall write to the Bishop for my *exeat*, and return to England or go to Australia, where I have been promised a
mission."

It was rather late, and I should have been long ago in
my comfortable bed; but the text was too good to miss.

" My dear Father Letheby," I said, " it is clear to me
that you are working not for God's honour, but for your
own *kudos*."

He started at these strong words, and stared at me.

" Because," I continued calmly, "if it was the honour

of God you had at heart, this calamity, the intensity of
which I have no idea of minimizing, would have stimu-
lated you to fresh efforts instead of plunging you into
despair. But your pride is touched and your honour is
tarnished, and you dread the criticism of men. Tell me
honestly, are you grieved because God has been offended,
or because all your fine plans have *ganged aglee*? There!
Dear St. Bonaventure, what a burden you laid on the
shoulders of poor humanity when you said, *Ama nesciri,
et pro nihilo reputari*. You did not know, in the depths
of your humility, that each of us has a pretty little gilded
idol which is labelled *Self*! And that each of us is a
fanatic in seeking to make conversions to our own little
god. And I am not at all sure but that education only
helps us to put on a little more gilding and a little more
tawdry finery on our hidden deity; and that even when
we sit in judgment upon him, as we do when preparing
for Confession, it is often as a gentle and doting mother,
not as an inflexible and impartial judge. Here are you
now (turning to Father Letheby), a good, estimable, zeal-
ous, and successful priest; and because you have been
touched in a sore point, lo! the voice from the inner
shrine demanding compensation and future immunity.
Everything has prospered with you. Religion has pro-
gressed, with leaps and bounds, since you came to the
parish; the people adore you, and you have the satisfaction of knowing that you are that most difficult of heroic
successes, a conqueror because a reformer; and because
you have met one reverse, you are going to turn your
back on your work, and seek the curse of those who put
pillows under their armpits and garlands of roses in their
hair. Did you imagine that Satan, a living, personal, and
highly intelligent force, was going to allow you to have
everything your own way here—to fold his arms while
you were driving back his forces in utter rout and confusion? If you did, you were greatly mistaken. You have
met a slight reverse, and it has become a panic. *Sauve
qui peut*! And the commander—the successful general—

is the first to turn his back, throw down his sword, and flee."

" Say no more, Father Dan, for God's sake. I am heartily ashamed of myself."

A good scolding is almost equal to a cold bath as a tonic for disordered nerves.

I went home with a satisfied conscience, murmuring, *Per la impacciata via, retro al suo duce.* I think I know whither he is tending.

A demoralized, woe-begone, wilted, helpless figure was before me in the hall. If he had been under Niagara for the last few hours he could not be more hopelessly washed out. It was Jem Deady in the custody of his wife, who was now in the ascendant.

" Here he is, your reverence—a misfortunate anga-shore! For the love of God make him now a patthern to the parish! Cling him to the ground, or turn him into somethin'; make him an example forever, for my heart is broke with him."

Whilst I was turning over in my mind into which of the lower animals it would be advisable to cause the immortal soul of Jem to transmigrate and take up a temporary residence, I thought I saw a glance upwards from his eye, visibly pleading for mercy.

" It is quite clear, Jem," I said, " that your Christmas dinner disagreed with you."

" Begor, thin, your reverence," broke in Mrs. Deady, setting herself in a rather defiant attitude, " he had as good a dinner as any poor man in your parish. He had a roast goose, stuffed by thim two hands with praties and inguns, until the tears ran down my face; and he had a pig's cheek, and lashins of cabbage."

" And why don't you tell his reverence about the rice puddin'? " said Jem, in a tone of honest indignation. " 'Tis a shame for you, Bess! She made a rice puddin', your reverence, that was fit for the Grate House; and begor, your reverence might sit down to worse yourself. Sich raisons and currans! "

" Begor, I'm thinking you're thrying to put the comedher on me, you blagard, with your blarney," said Mrs. Deady with angry suspicion, drawing back and scrutinizing his face.

" Thrying to put the comedher on *you*, Bess? Begor, I'd like to see the man that could do it. But I'll say this, in the presence of his reverence, and wid yerself to the fore, that there isn't in this parish, nor in the nex', nor in the nex' again, nor widin the four walls of Ireland, a betther wife nor a betther housekeeper den you, Bess Clancy." And to emphasize this panegyric, Jem threw his battered hat on the floor and brushed away a tear.

It was a pity not to come to the aid of such a superb diplomatist. No wonder the British diplomatic service is manned by Irishmen from Singapore to Halifax. What would Melikoff, and Von Schaffterhausen, and De Laborie be in the hands of Jem Deady? He'd twist them around his little finger. I saw the angry wrinkles smoothing themselves on the brow of Mrs. Deady, as she melted under the gentle rain of flattery.

" I'd forgive you a good deal, Deady," I said; "your repeated violations of solemn pledges, your sacrilege in bringing down to a public house the most sacred melodies of the Church—— "

" They were *at* me," said Jem. " They said as how I couldn't get my tongue around the Latin, and that Father Letheby—— "

" I understand," I interrupted; " but even that I'd forgive. But to take the innocent lambs of my flock, my choir boys and altar boys, the children of sober and religious parents, whose hearts are broken by your misconduct—— "

" Childre' of sober and religious parents—whose hearts are broken," chimed in Mrs. Deady. " Wisha, thin, without manin' any disrespect to your riverence, would you be plazed to mintion these dacent people? An' if these religious parents wor mindin' their childre', insted of colloguing and placin' their nabors, their religious childre' wouldn't be lying drunk in Mrs. Haley's public house. But of coorse 'tis Jim Deady here and Jim Deady there; and if the truth wos towld, he's as good as any of 'em, though I shouldn't say it to his face. Come along, you poor fool."

" I must do what I came for," said Jem, solemnly.

Then, with an air of awful determination, as if he were binding iron bars and padlocks on his thirsty lips, Jem took the pledge. Mrs. Deady, in high dudgeon, had gone down the street. Jem and I were alone.

" Tell me, yer reverence," he whispered, " did that mane scut of a tailor insult ye the other night? "

" Oh, not at all, Jem," I cried, fearing the consequences to the tailor.

" I have an eye on him this long time," said Jem, " and faith, he'll come to grief soon."

" Now, Jem," I warned emphatically, " no violence, mind. The unfortunate fellow is sorry."

" All right, your reverence; we are not going to waste violence on the likes of him. But—— "

Here Jem fell into a profound reverie.

" Begor, your reverence, ye did that little job nately," he cried, waking up. " That woman's tongue didn't lave me worth tuppence. God bless yer reverence, and spare ye long to us."

He took my hand, and kissed it till it was blistered by the sharp bristles of his unshaven lips. Poor fellows! how they warm to us! and how, with all their faults, we fling around them something more than maternal love!

CHAPTER XVII

A CLERICAL SYMPOSIUM

THERE is no law, supernatural or natural, forbidding us
(who, if we have not many of the crosses, neither have we
many of the pleasures of this life) from meeting sometimes, and carrying out St. Paul's prescriptions in the
matter of hospitality. I believe, indeed, his words—and
he was a wise, kind saint—apply principally to bishops;
but why should not we imitate our superiors afar off,
and practise the kindly virtue? It is good to meet sometimes and exchange opinions; it softens the asperities of
daily life, makes the young think reverently of the old,
and the old charitably of the young. At least, these are
my views, and acting upon them there is always an open
door and a *Cead Milé Failté* for a brother; and a few times
in the year I try to gather around me my dear friends,
and thus to cement those bonds of friendship that make
life a little more pleasant, and, perhaps, may keep our
memories green. Sometimes, indeed, my dear old
friends object to face a drive of eight or ten miles on a
cold night in winter; but the young fellows always come.
Nothing but extreme urgency would keep them away
from an evening with Daddy Dan. Now, we have no
nonsense—no soups, nor entrées, which some of my more
fashionable confrères are at present affecting, if you
please; but a plain turkey and ham, and a roast leg of
mutton, and a few little trimmings to fill up vacant
spaces. There is an old tradition, too, in Ireland, which
I keep to pretty closely—never to invite more than the
Muses, nor less than the Graces; but on this occasion—
it was during the Octave of the Epiphany—I departed

from the custom, and, owing to a few disappointments, the ominous number of thirteen sat down to dinner. I must say, however, it had not a paralyzing effect on the appetites of my guests, nor did they appear to have any apprehensions of a sudden call to the places where turkeys and good mutton are not appreciated. There were a few jokes about the intolerable longevity of certain parish priests; and when my curate, who occupied the vice-chair with infinite grace and dignity, remarked in his own grand style that " really Da Vinci's ' Last Supper ' was responsible for that unhallowed superstition, and there really was nothing in it," some few wags professed themselves greatly relieved, and showed it by newborn zeal in the avocations of the evening. My duties as host engrossed all my attention, until the table was cleared for action; and the call for coffee from eight out of thirteen guests recalled me to my favourite meditation on the mighty yet silent revolution that is progressing in the Irish Church.

I have been now in touch with three generations of Irish priests, each as distinct from the other, and marked by as distinctive characteristics, as those which differentiate an Anglican parson from a mediæval monk. My early education was coloured by contact with the polished, studious, timid priests, who, educated in Continental seminaries, introduced into Ireland all the grace and dignity and holiness, and all the dread of secular authority with the slight tendency to compromise, that seemed to have marked the French clergy, at least in the years immediately succeeding the revolutions and the Napoleonic wars. These were the good men who fraternized with landlords, and lent their congregations to a neighbouring parson on the occasion of some governmental visitation; who were slightly tinged with Gallican ideas, and hated progress and the troubles that always accompany it. They were holy, good, kindly men, but they could hardly be called officers of the Church Militant. Then came Maynooth, which, founded on governmental sub-

sidies, poured from its gates the strongest, fiercest, most
fearless army of priests that ever fought for the spiritual
and temporal interests of the people—men of large
physique and iron constitutions, who spent ten hours a
day on horseback, despised French claret, loved their
people and chastised them like fathers, but were prepared
to defend them with their lives and the outpouring of
their blood against their hereditary enemies. Intense in
their faith, of stainless lives and spotless reputations,
their words cut like razors, and their hands smote like
lightning; but they had the hearts of mothers for the
little ones of their flocks. They had the classics at their
fingers' ends, could roll out lines from Virgil or Horace
at an after-dinner speech, and had a profound contempt
for English literature. In theology they were rigorists,
too much disposed to defer absolution and to give long
penances. They had a cordial dislike for new devotions,
believing that Christmas and Easter Communion was
quite enough for ordinary sanctity. Later on they became more generous, but they clung with tenacity to the
Brown Scapular and the First Sunday of the month. I
am quite sure they have turned somersaults in their
graves since the introduction of the myriad devotions that
are now distracting and edifying the faithful. But they
could make, and, alas! too often perhaps for Christian
modesty, they did make, the proud boast that they kept
alive the people's faith, imbued them with a sense of the
loftiest morality, and instilled a sense of intense horror
for such violations of Church precepts as a *communicatio
cum hereticis in divinis*, or the touching of flesh meat on
a day of abstinence. I believe I belong to that school,
though my sympathies are wide enough for all. And as
in theology, I am quite prepared to embrace Thomists,
and Scotists, and Molinists, Nominalists and Realists in
fraternal charity, so, too, am I prepared to recognize and
appreciate the traits and characteristics of the different
generations of clerics in the Irish Church. Sometimes,
perhaps, through the vanity that clings to us all to the

end, I play the part of " laudator temporis acti," and
then the young fellows shout :—

" Ah, but Father Dan, they were giants in those days."

And the tags and shreds of poor human nature wave in
the wind of flattery ; and I feel grateful for the modest
appreciation of a generation that has no sympathy with
our own.

Then, down there, below the water-line of gray heads
is the coming generation of Irish priests, who, like the
lampadephoroi of old in the Athenian games, will take
the torch of faith from our hands and carry it to the
Acropolis of Heaven—clean-cut, small of stature, keen-
faced, bicycle-riding, coffee-drinking, encyclopædic young
fellows, who will give a good account of themselves, I
think, in the battles of the near future. It is highly
amusing to a disinterested spectator, like myself, to
watch the tolerant contempt with which the older generation regards the younger. They have as much contempt for coffee as for ceremonies, and I think their mistakes in the latter would form a handsome volume of
errata, or add another appendix to our valuable compen-
diums. To ask one of these old men to pass a cup of
coffee is equivalent to asking a Hebrew of the strict ob-
servance to carve a ham, or a Hindoo to eat from the
same dish with a Christian. And many other objects
that the passing generation held in high esteem are "gods
of the Gentiles" to the younger. They laugh profanely
at that aureole of distinction that used hang around the
heads of successful students, declaring that a man's education only commences when he leaves college, and that
his academical training was but the sword exercise of the
gymnasium ; and they speak dreadful things about evolution and modern interpretation, and the new methods of
hermeneutics, and polychrome Bibles ; and they laugh
at the idea of the world's creation in six days ; and altogether, they disturb and disquiet the dreams of the staid
and stately veterans of the Famine years, and make
them forecast a dismal future for Ireland when German

metaphysics and coffee will first impair, and then destroy, the sacred traditions of Irish faith. And yet, these young priests inherit the best elements of the grand inheritance that has come down to them. Their passionate devotion to their faith is only rivalled by their passionate devotion to the Motherland. Every one of them belongs to that great world-wide organization of Priests Adorers, which, cradled in the dying years of our century, will grow to a gigantic stature in the next; for at last it has dawned upon the world that around this sacred doctrine and devotion, as around an oriflamme, the great battles of the twentieth century will rage. And they have as tender and passionate a love for the solitary isle in the wintry western seas as ever brought a film to the eyes of exile, or lighted the battle fires in the hearts of her heroes and kings. And with all my ancient prejudices in favour of my own caste, I see clearly that the equipments of the new generation are best suited to modern needs. The bugle-call of the future will sound the retreat for the ancient cavalry and the Old Guard, and sing out, Forward the Light Brigade!

This evening, as usual, the conversation was discursive. It ranged over the whole area of human knowledge and experience, from the price of a horse to Lehmkuhl's Latinity, and from the last political speech to the everlasting question, ever discussed and never decided, What is meant by the month's residence as a condition for the acquisition of a domicile? That horrible drug was irritating the nerves of the younger men, until I heard, as in a dream, a Babel of voices:—" The two Ballerini "— " They'll never arrest him "—" He'll certainly fire on the people "—"Daniel never wrote that book, I tell you" —" 'Tis only a ringbone "—" Fifty times worse than a sprain "—" He got it in the Gregorian University "— " Paddy Murray, George Crolly "—" I admire Balfour for his profound knowledge of metaphysics "—" Did you see the article in the *Record* about the Spanish dispensation? "—" He's got a first-class mission in Ballarat "—

" No, the lessons were from the Scripture occurring "—
" I don't think we're bound to these Masses "—" 'Twas
a fine sermon, but too flowery for my tastes "—" Yes, we
expect a good Shrove this year "—" His *Data of Ethics*
won't stand examination "—" Our fellows will lick yours
well next time "—" Picking the grapes and lemons at
Tivoli"—"Poor old Kirby, what an age he is"—" ' 'Twilight and evening bell, and after that the dark, And may
there be no sadness of farewell, when I embark,' that's
the way it runs "—" He cut in his physic year, and is
running a paper in Boston "—" It is up now to thirty-
five shillings a ton, and will go higher," etc., etc. The
older men, under the more kindly influence, were calm
as sophomores.   Amidst the whirlpool of words, they
clung to two sheet-anchors—O'Connell in politics, and St.
Alphonsus in theology.

At last, the conversation simmered down into an academic debate, whether the centripetal system, which con-
centrates all Irish students in Maynooth, or the centri-
fugal, which sends them scampering over the Continent
to the ancient universities, was the better. This was a
calm, judicious tournament, except now and again, when
I had to touch the gong, and say :—

" Gentlemen, only three at a time, if you please."

It was a curious thing to notice that those who had
studied in Maynooth were very much in favour of a Continental education; and those who had been in foreign
universities were rather inclined to give the verdict for
Maynooth.

" You see," said one, " it is an education in itself to
go abroad. It means expansion, and expansion is education. Then you have the immense advantage of being
able to learn and master the foreign languages and literature, and nowadays a man that can't speak French at
least is a very helpless creature."

" You take it for granted," replied another, " that residence abroad insures a knowledge of French. I spent
six years in the seminary at N——, and except *cela va*

sans dire, tant pis, and a few other colloquialisms, which you will find on the last page of an English dictionary, I might as well have been in Timbuctoo."

" Well," said my curate—and though he is not very popular, somehow or other his words appear to carry great weight—" I must confess that the regret of my life is that I had not an opportunity of studying in Rome, just as the hope of my life is that I shall see Rome before I die. I consider that the greatest Irish college in the world, in numbers and in the influence that arises from intellectual superiority, should be somewhere within the shadows of the Seven Hills."

" Why not transfer the Dunboyne, with all its endowments and emoluments, to Rome? " asked a young, eager fellow, who says he can read the Office, going ten miles an hour on the bicycle.

" 'Twouldn't ever do," said a Roman student; " you must be brought up in Rome to understand its spirit. Transplanted shoots never thrive there."

" Psha! " said an old Maynooth man, who had been listening impatiently to these suggestions; " we forgot more theology in Maynooth than you ever learned."

" I don't want to disparage your knowledge of theology, Father," said my curate, sweetly, " but you know there are other elements in priestly education besides the mere propositions, and the *solvuntur objecta* of theology. And it is in Rome these subtle and almost intangible accomplishments are acquired."

Now, this was getting a little warm; so I winked at a young fellow down along the table, and he took the hint promptly, and cried out: " Look here, Father Dan, this is tiresome. Tell us how you managed the Irish Brigade in France in the fifties. Weren't they going to throw Marseilles into the sea? "

" Now, now," said I, " that won't do. I'm not going to be trotting out that old chestnut at every dinner party. Let us have a song! "

And we had, and a good many of them—dear old Irish

melodies that would melt an icicle and put blood into a
marble statue. No nonsense at my table, I assure you.
No operatic rubbish, but genuine Irish music, with the
right lilt and the right sentiment. I did let a young fellow once sing, "I Dreamt that I Dwelt in Marble Halls";
but I told him never to repeat it. But it was worth while
going miles to hear my curate singing, in his own fine
voice, that superb ballad of that true and gentle patriot,
Thomas Davis, " The mess-tent is full, and the glasses
are set."

Dear me! what a mercurial race we are; and how the
mercury runs up and down in the barometer of our human
hearts! I could see the young priests' faces whitening
at the words:

> " God prosper old Ireland! You'd think them afraid,
>   So pale grew the chiefs of the Irish Brigade! "

and softening out in lines of tenderness when the end
came:

> " For, on far foreign fields, from Dunkirk to Belgrade,
>   Lie the soldiers and chiefs of the Irish Brigade."

Then we had " The West's Awake," and " Dear Land,"
and then we all arose and sang together, " God bless
the Pope, the great, the good." I was going to say " sang
in unison," but I am afraid I should be trespassing on
the sacred precincts of truth; yet if that grand old man
in Rome, that electric spark in the vase of alabaster,
sitting in that lonely chamber, behind the long, empty,
gas-lit state apartments, could hear those voices there
above the western seas, he would surely realize more
keenly what he understands already, that he can always
call upon his Irish reserves to ring, as with a fence of
steel, the chair and the prerogatives of Peter.

Then came the " Good-nights." I pulled aside an old
friend, a great theologian, who has all kinds of musty,
dusty, leather-bound, water-stained volumes on his
shelves.

"Did you ever hear," I whispered, "of a mysterious thing, called the *Kampaner Thal?*"

"Never," he said, emphatically.

"You couldn't conjecture what it is?"

"No," he said, with deliberation; "but I can aver it is neither Greek, Latin, nor Irish."

"Would you mind looking up your cyclopædias," I pleaded, "and letting me know immediately that you find it?"

"Of course," he replied. Then, jerking his thumb over his shoulder: "I suppose it is this chap?"

"It is," I said. "He reads a good deal——"

"Look here, Father Dan, I don't know what we're coming to. Did you ever see such a sight as that table to-night?"

"Never," I replied, resignedly.

"Would any one believe, when we came on the mission, that we'd live to see such things? Why, these fellows talk up to us as if we were their equals. Don't you remember when a curate daren't open his mouth at table?"

"Of course," I replied, demurely.

"And it is only now I am beginning to discover the vagaries of this chap of mine. Do you know what he wants? A shrine, if you please—some kind of picture, with candles lighting before it all day. 'Can't you say your Rosary,' I said, 'like your betters?' No, he should have the shrine. And now he wants to force on Benediction every Sunday—not every first Sunday of the month, but every Sunday, if you please. And he has a big red lamp, burning in what he calls his oratory. You can see it miles away. I say to the boys, 'Don't be afraid to put to sea at night now, boys. Begor, ye've got a lighthouse at last.' Well, good-bye! What's this thing you want?"

And he jotted down the name, I presume phonetically, in his note-book. Now, mind, that man has not had a scandal in his parish for fourteen years; and he is up to his neck in securities for half the farmers of the district.

All this time, shrinking into an obscure corner of the hall, was my Curé d'Ars, as I call him. He now came forward to say good night, his thin face wreathed in smiles, and his two hands stretched out in thankfulness.

" Good night, Father Dan, and a thousand thanks. I never spent a pleasanter evening. What fine young fellows! So clever, so jolly, and so edifying! Won't it be a satisfaction for us when we are going to leave behind us such splendid safeguards of the faith? "

His curate was waiting respectfully. He now got the little man into his great-coat, and buttoned it from collar to boot: the latter murmuring his thanks all the time :—

" Dear me! dear me! what a trouble I am! Many thanks! Many thanks! There, now I am all right! "

Then his muffler was wrapped carefully around his neck by this big grenadier, and his gloves were drawn over his hands.

" Dear me! dear me! how good! how kind! I'm a regular mummy! a real Egyptian mummy, Father Dan! Good night! good night! Dear me, what a pleasant gathering! "

And the stalwart curate lifted him on his car, as if he were an infant.

A few days later we had a long chat over many things, I and my curate.

When he was going he said :—

" That was a real jolly evening. Father Dan! I never enjoyed anything so much! "

" Yes," I said, " and you had a splendid audience for that noble song! "

" Yes, indeed; they were very kind."

" Oh, I don't mean *in foro interno*," I said, " but *in foro externo*. There was a crowd outside the window! "

" My God! " he cried, quite shocked. " What a scandal! "

" Not a bit of it," I said; " you've gone up a hundred

per cent. in the estimation of the villagers. There was a real fight for the window-sill. But your friend, Jem Deady, captured it."

He looked dreadfully annoyed.

" Jem says that he kept awake all night trying to remember the notes; and if you'd give him the words of the song and whistle it—— "

" What! " said Father Letheby, like a pistol-shot.

" And if you'd give him two or three audiences—I suppose he means rehearsals on the piano—he is quite sure—— "

!   !!   !!!

Dear me; how some people despise popularity !

CHAPTER XVIII

THE KAMPANER THAL

EVENTS are thickening around me these winter days; and much oftener than in past years am I compelled to lay aside my pet authors, when my lamp is lighted, and my fire is sparkling merrily, whilst the earth is waking up from its winter's sleep, and stretching out its hands in the feeble lengthening of the evenings towards the approaching spring. This evening I had an unexpected visitor—no less a person than Reginald Ormsby, the betrothed of Bittra. He came in modestly and apologetically, with all that gentlemanly deference that is so characteristic of the British officer. He made a nice little speech, explaining his reasons for visiting me so late, and mildly deprecating the anger of such a potentate as the parish priest of Kilronan. I had pulled the bell in the mean time, and Hannah had brought in the "materials"; and in reply to his pretty eloquence, I merely pushed the decanter towards him, and said:—

" Go ahead! "

He filled his wine-glass with a firm hand, until the blessed liquor made an arc of a circle on the summit; then tilted it over into the tumbler, without spilling a drop, then filled the tumbler to the top with hot water, and I said in my own mind, " He'll do."

" Of course," I said, after this little ceremony had been proceeded with, " you smoke? "

" I shouldn't venture to think of smoking in your pretty parlour, sir," said he. " You know cigar smoke hangs around the curtains for days, and—— "

" Never mind the curtains," I replied. " I don't keep
Havanas here, though I suppose we must soon, as that
appears to be a constituent in the new education to which
we old fossils are being subjected. But if you have a
cigar-case about you, light up, like a good fellow. You
have to say something of importance, I think, and they
say a cigar promotes easy and consecutive thought."
" Very many thanks, sir," he said. " Then, with
your permission, I will."
He smoked quietly for a few seconds, and it was a
good cigar, I can tell you. The fragrance filled the
whole house. Then I broke the ice:—
" Now, my curate has had several conferences with
you about religion, and he told me he was going to try the
Kampaner Thal."
" Oh, yes! so he did, indeed. He has been very kind."
I should say here that my theological friend and neigh-
bor had written me: " I have hunted up all my cyclopædias, and can find, no trace whatever of that thing
about which you were inquiring. From the word *Kampaner*, I suspect it has something to do with bells. Perhaps your curate wants a chime for your cathedral at
Kilronan. When you get them, select C sharp, or B
flat, and put it around his neck, that we may know
where to find him. Yours truly——"
" Now," I said to Mr. Ormsby, " I do not know
whether that *Kampaner Thal* is bird, beast, fish, or in-
sect; whether it is a powerful drug or a new system of
hypnotism."
" Oh, 'tis none of these dreadful things," he said,
laughing; " 'tis only a little book. Here it is! I always
carry it about with me. It is really very beautiful."
I handled the little duodecimo with suspicion; then
gave it back.
" It has done you a lot of good, I suppose?" I said, I
am afraid, with a certain amount of contempt.
" I can't say it has," he replied sadly; then lapsed
into moody reflection.

Now, gloom is the one thing I cannot tolerate; so to rouse him from his reverie, and possibly from a slight, venial prompting of curiosity, I asked him to read some passages for me.

" My old sight cannot bear much of a strain," I said, " and the print is mighty small. Now, like a good fellow, pick cut some good things, and read them slowly, for perhaps I may require to punctuate them."

So he read in a calm even monotone, without inflection, but with many pauses, whilst I watched every syllable and measured it.

" I have a strong objection to a *voyage pittoresque* through the planets; we bear in our own breasts a heaven full of constellations. There is in our hearts an inward, spiritual world, that breaks like a sun upon the clouds of the outward world. I mean that inward universe of goodness, beauty, and truth— three worlds that are neither part, nor shoot, nor copy of the outward. We are less astonished at the incomprehensible existence of these transcendental heavens because they are always there, and we foolishly imagine that we create, when we merely perceive them. After *what model*, with what *plastic power*, and *from what*, could we create these same spiritual worlds? The atheist should ask himself how he received the giant idea of God, that he has neither opposed nor embodied. An idea that has not grown up by comparing different degrees of greatness, as it is the opposite of every measure and degree. In fact, the atheist speaks as others of *prototype* and *original*."

" Stop there," I cried; " why that is the ontological argument of St. Anselm, adopted afterwards by a soldier philosopher like yourself, called Descartes. There's nothing new under the sun. It is wonderful how modern artists can refurbish our old Masters and make wonderful pictures from them! "

" Quite so," he replied, " in lieu of yourselves. There, now, I am always too precipitate; pardon me, sir, if I am too bold; but you Catholics have a wonderful talent for burying your treasures in napkins. Have you any treatise on the immortality of the soul in English, and in such a style as this? "

" I am afraid," I replied, as I looked askance at the volume, " that just now I cannot mention one. But go

on, if it does not tire you. Time is the cheapest thing we
have in Ireland."

He continued :—

" ' The inward world, that is indeed more splendid and admirable than the outward, needs another heaven than the
one above us, and a higher world than that the sun warms;
therefore, we say justly, not a second *earth*, or globe, but a
second world beyond this universe.'

" Gione interrupted me : ' And every virtuous and wise man
is a proof of another world.'

" ' And,' continued Nadine quickly, ' every one who unde-
servedly suffers.'

" ' Yes,' I answered; ' that is what draws our thread of
life through a long eternity. The threefold echo of virtue,
truth, and beauty, created by the music of the spheres, calls
us from this hollow earth to the neighbourhood of the music.
Why and wherefore were these desires given us? Merely
that, like a swallowed diamond, they should slowly cut through
our earthly covering. Wherefore were we placed upon this
ball of earth, creatures with light wings, if instead of soaring
with our wings of ether, we are to fall back into the earth-
clods of our birth? . . . . Is an angel to be imprisoned in the
body to be its dumb servant, its stove-warmer and butler, its
cuisinier and porter at the door of the stomach? Shall the
ethereal flame merely serve to fill the circular stove with life's
warmth, obediently burn and warm, then become cold and
extinguished? "

" Very good, indeed," I interrupted. " He knows
how to put things in a virile way."

" ' The discrepancy between our wishes and our relations,
between the *soul* and the *earth*, remains a *riddle* if we continue; and if we cease to live, a *blasphemy*. Strangers, born
upon mountains, we consume in lowly places, with unhealthy
heimweh (home-sickness). We belong to higher regions, and
an eternal longing grows in our hearts at music, which is the
Kuhreigen of our native Alps. . . . '

" ' From hence what follows? ' asked the chaplain (a Kan-
tian).

" ' Not that we are unhappy, but that we are immortal;
and this world *within* us demands and manifests a *second* without us. . . . I cannot tell how painful, how monstrous and
horrible the thought of an annihilating death, of an eternal
grave, now appeared to me. Men often bear their errors, as

their truths, about in words, and not in feeling; but let the
believer in annihilation place before him, instead of a life of
sixty years, one of sixty minutes; then let him look on the
face of a beloved being, or upon a noble or wise man, as upon
an aimless hour-long appearance; as a thin shadow that melts
into light and leaves no trace; can he bear the thought? No!
the supposition of imperishableness is always with him; else
there would hang always before his soul, as before Mahomet's
in the fairest sky, a dark cloud; and, as Cain upon the earth,
an eternal fear would pursue him. Yes, if all the woods upon
this earth were groves of pleasure; if all the valleys were
Kampaner valleys; if all the islands were blessed, and all the
fields Elysian; if all eyes were cheerful and all the hearts joy-
ful—yes, then—no! even then, had God, through this very
blessedness, made to our spirits the *promise*, the *oath* of eternal duration! But, now, O God! when so many houses are
houses of mourning, so many fields battlefields, so many cheeks
pale, when we pass before so many eyes red with weeping or
closed in death: Oh! can the grave, that haven of salvation,
be the last swallowing, unyielding whirlpool? No, the trampled
worm dares raise itself towards its Creator, and say, " Thou
durst not create me only to suffer! " ' "

I was listening with closed eyes to the reading, the
quiet rhythm of the sentences, and the calm, deep music
of his voice, sounding ineffably soothing, when a quaver,
then a break in his voice, just as he repeated the last
words, made me look toward him. The calm, strong
man was weeping silently; and just then he broke into a
paroxysm of sobs that shook his strong frame as by a
palsy. Dear Lord! what hidden grief there is in the
world! Who would ever dream that the calm exterior of
this reasoning, cultivated atheist concealed such hidden
fires? It was no time to talk; I let the poor fellow alone.
After a few moments he dried his eyes, and said:—

" I am quite ashamed of this snivelling, Father. I
shouldn't have attempted to read this. It always upsets
me."

" Never mind, my poor boy," I said. " It is good for
men sometimes to weep." I thought in my own mind,
My little child will be in safe hands.

" Now, put it aside," I said gently, " and let us talk."

" One sentence more, Father, just to get over this
weakness,"

" ' Ah, Carlson (Carlson stands for myself), upon what a beautiful world do you throw your immeasurable gravestone, that no time can lift. Your difficulties, which are founded on the *necessary* uncertainties of men, if solved, would only have the effect to destroy our *faith;* which is the solution of a thousand other difficulties ; without which our existence is without aim, our pains without solution, and the Godlike Trinity within our breasts three avenging angels. From the formless earthworm up to the beaming human countenance ; from the chaos of the first day up to the present age of the world ; from the first faint motion of the heart to its full, bold throbbing in the breast of manhood, the invisible hand of God leads, protects, and nourishes the inward being ; the *nursling of the outward* educates and polishes and makes it beautiful—and wherefore? That when it stands as a demgiod in the midst of the ruins of the temple of the body, the blow of death may prostrate it forever, that nothing shall remain from the corpse-veiled, the mourning and mantled immeasurable universe, but the eternally sowing, never harvesting, solitary spirit of the world! One eternity looking despairingly at the other ; and in the whole spiritual universe no end, no aim! And all these contradictions and riddles, whereby not merely the harmony, but the very *strings* of creation are tangled, must we take, merely on account of the difficulties, that, indeed, our annihilation cannot solve? Beloved Carlson! into this harmony of the spheres, that is not *over,* but ever *around* us, will you bring your shrieking discord? See how gently and touchingly the day departs, and how holily the night comes! Oh, can you not believe that even thus our spirits shall arise from the dust, as you once saw the full moon arise over the crater of Vesuvius? '

" Gione took his hand and said :—

" ' Amongst us all, will you alone be tormented with this despairing faith? '

" Two hot drops fell from his blinded eyes ; he looked at the mountains, and said :—

" ' I can bear no annihilation but my own. My *heart* is of your opinion ; my *head* will slowly follow.' "

" And that, sir," said Ormsby, closing the book and putting it into his side pocket, " is just where I am. My heart is with you ; if only my head would follow. Put Bittra for Gione, and you will understand my emotion."

" Even that won't do," I said ; " the head might follow, and you might be as far from us as ever."

" I don't understand," he said in a bewildered way. " Surely all that's wanting now is a conviction of the truth of your teaching? "

" There's your grave mistake," I replied; " conviction is not faith. There are thousands of your countrymen filled with conviction of the truths of Catholicity; but they are as far outside the Church as a Confucian or a Buddhist. Faith is not a matter to be acquired by reading or knowledge. It is a gift, like the natural talent of a great painter or musician—a sixth sense, and the pure gratuity of the All-Wise and the All-Good."

This appeared to him to be a revelation which he could not comprehend; it seemed to be such an inevitable logical sequence—conviction and profession.

" I am attracted by everything," he said, " in your Church. The whole thing appears to be such a well-connected scheme, so unlike the religion in which I was born and educated, where you had to be for ever searching after a missing link. And then your Church seems to be founded on love—love of a supernal kind, of course, and almost un'ntelligible; but it is the golden chain in the string of pearls. You will have noticed how rapidly sometimes the mind makes comparisons. Well, often, at our station over there, I have thought, as I searched the sea, that we Protestants look at God through the large end of a telescope and throw Him afar off, and make Him very small and insignificant; whilst you look at Him through the narrower end, and magnify Him and bring Him near. Our God—that is, the God in whom I was taught to believe—is the God of Sinai, and our Christ is the historic Christ; but that won't do for a humanity that is ever querulous for God, and you have found the secret."

I was quite astonished at the solemn, thoughtful manner in which this young fellow spoke, and his words were so full of feeling and self-sympathy for his great privation. He was silent for a long time, smoking freely, whilst I was pondering many things, mostly in humility for our slow appreciation of the great gift of divine faith. At last, he said:—

" I do not quite follow you, sir, in your remark about

a sixth sense; for this is not a question of sense, but of the soul."

We were now getting into deep water, and when an old gentleman hasn't opened a book of philosophy for nearly thirty years, he may be well excused for a certain timidity in approaching these deep questions. But, "keep to the metaphorical" has always been a great rule of mine, which never failed me.

"Let me explain," I said. "Have you ever been to an ophthalmic hospital or a blind asylum?"

"Yes," he replied, "principally abroad."

"Well," I continued, "you might have noticed various forms of the dread disease of blindness. Some are cases of cataract; in some the entire ball is removed; some have partial sight behind the ugly film. But the most pathetic case to my mind is that of the young boy or girl who comes toward you, looking steadily at you with large, luminous eyes, the iris perfectly clear, the pupil normally distended, and even the white of the eye tinged with that delicate blue that denotes perfect health in the organ; but in one moment the truth flashes upon you—that poor patient is stone-blind. Now, where's the disease?"

"The optic nerve is destroyed," he answered promptly.

"Precisely. And now, if you were to pour in through the dark canal of the pupil the strongest sunlight, or even the flash of your electric searchlight, would it make any difference, do you think?"

"None," he said, "so far as sight was concerned; but it might possibly paralyze the brain."

"Precisely. And if you, my dear young friend, were pouring, till the crack of doom, every kind of human light —philosophical, dogmatic, controversial—upon the retina of the soul without the optic nerve of faith, you will be blind, and go blind to your grave."

Somehow this appeared to be a relief, though it looked like discouragement.

" It is something to know," he said, " that the fault
is not altogether my own. But," after a pause, " this
demands a miracle."

" Quite so. A pure light from God. And that is the
reason that my excellent curate is storming the citadels
of heaven for you by that terrible artillery—the prayers
of little children. And if you want to capture this grace
of God by one tremendous *coup*, search out the most
stricken and afflicted of my flock (Bittra has a pretty
good catalogue of them), and get him or her to pray for
you, and very soon the sense of faith will awaken within
you, and you will wonder that you were ever blind."

" Ten thousand thanks," he said, rising; " I had no
anticipations of so pleasant and instructive an evening."

" You were told to expect to meet a funny old fellow,"
I said, " with as many quips, and cranks, and jests, as
old Jack Falstaff? "

" Well," he said, pulling his moustache nervously, " I
should not like to put it so brusquely."

" Of course not. But there lies a big mistake, my dear
boy. Democritus was as much a philosopher as Hera-
clitus, and he lived fifty years longer. There is a good
deal of philosophy behind a laugh, and we put our gargoyles on the outside of our churches."

" Indeed, I must say, from a long experience," he replied, " and a grateful experience, that your men are the
most cheerful class I have met—if I except our own
sailors—although the comparison sounds grotesque. And,"
he said hesitatingly, " that just reminds me; if I may
take the freedom of showing my gratitude in a small
way, permit me to say to you as pastor, what I have
already hinted to himself, that your most excellent curate
will involve himself in a great deal of trouble and possible
expense if he perseveres in that matter of the fishing-
boat. Indeed, I have been working the matter for him,
because his heart is set on it; but I have misgivings. I'm
not sure that I am quite right in mentioning the matter

to you, sir; but I am really anxious, and I speak from long experience."

He lighted another cigar at the door, and I returned to think somewhat anxiously whether I had done credit to Catholic philosophy. But my thoughts would revert to these last words of Ormsby's. What if Father Letheby should get into a bad mess, and everything so promising? How little these young men reflect what a trouble they are to their old pastors!

CHAPTER XIX

LITERARY ATTEMPTS

I BROKE Captain Ormsby's advice to Father Letheby as gently as I could; and I flatter myself I have the talent of putting things in as roundabout a way as any professional diplomat. He took it badly. He is clearly overworking himself, for he now becomes irritable on the slightest provocation.

"Blocked everywhere!" he said, walking up and down his little room. "Father Dan, you are right; and I am a fool. There is no use attempting to do any good in Ireland."

"Now, this was not exactly the conclusion I wanted him to come to; but we have a national failing of generalizing from rather minute particulars.

"I'm not so sure of that," I said. "I think you have a fair share of work to do here, and that you have done it and are doing it remarkably well."

Absurd! There was not half enough to do to satisfy his Napoleonic ambition. Nothing but the Vicariate of the whole of the Dark Continent for this young man.

"Look here, Father Dan. My parochial work is over every day at four o'clock; and you have taught me to finish the Office, even by anticipation, before dinner. Now what on earth is a young fellow to do between four o'clock of a winter's evening and ten o'clock, when he retires? Once in a month I dine at Campion's; but the rest of the time, except when I run up to you——"

"And you don't come half enough, you, sir," I said.

" I never saw anything like the—pride of young fellows nowadays."

" That's all right, Father Dan," he replied, somewhat more calmly; " but even with all your kindness, what in the world am I to do with my leisure time? "

" Read, and read, and read," I said. " Have you not the whole ocean of human knowledge to dip into? "

" Ah! *cui bono?* " he replied.

" *Cui bono?* from you! I never thought I'd hear that fatal word again. *Cui bono?* from you! *Cui bono?* from you! "

I was never so startled in my life. It was a dread revelation of dissatisfaction and ennui, that might lead no one knew whither.

" *Cui bono?* " I said. " Is there any pleasure on this earth comparable to the pleasure of acquiring knowledge? Is there any satisfaction equal to the continuous pursuit of ideas—always coming up to them, and passing them in the insatiable thirst and pursuit? Now, I see clearly that my tastes are not your tastes, and I was wrong in forcing the studies of the classics upon you. But take up philosophy, arrange a *horarium* for the evenings—so much time for reading, so much for thinking, so much for writing—— "

" Ah! there you've struck it," he broke in.   " If I could only write, I should always have an incentive, and a strong incentive for reading and studying what I read."

" And why don't you write? " I repeated. " Paper is cheap; pens and ink don't cost much—— "

" Write for what, and for whom? " he cried.

" Write for the magazines," I said. " Write brisk, crisp, lively articles for our reviews and periodicals; get paid for them; and then the ineffable pleasure of seeing your own work in print! "

" And what if they were rejected contumeliously? "

" Impossible," I replied; " there is room and to spare for good writers. Why, we are always crying out about the barrenness of our literature! "

G

He had gone over to a portfolio, and had taken out a few rolls of manuscript, to each of which a letter was tagged. He handed them to me without a word. It needed only a glance to see that if the editors had used up all the polite words of the language, nevertheless, " Rejected! " was written in capital letters on every page. I knew well what it meant to a proud, sensitive spirit; and although it was only the usual probation for literary novices, it might have a different effect from successful training in the case of a thoughtful if irritable mind. I pretended to read carefully the two essays, the three short stories, and the half-dozen poems that had come back to the author's hands without proofs, whilst I was rapidly turning over in my mind what I should say or do; for the recollection of my own experience at his age led me to believe that this was a critical moment for him. Happy the stupid souls that can gaze, without the constant fretting of thought, into the fire for hours together! Happy we, who, going down the decline of life, have the brake put on by a merciful Providence, and the wheels move slowly, and day blends with night, and night dawns to day, almost imperceptibly! But thrice unhappy they in whose souls the mills of thought whirl round and round without ceasing the wheelstones that grind together, if the grist is not between! How often to dreaming poet and idealist has the eternal fretting of the wheels become intolerable, and then——

" I shouldn't mind," he interjected on my reverie, " but these papers issue such lamentable stuff! Such vapid essays, such aimless stories, such bread-and-butter school-girl poetry—' sing ' and ' spring,' ' bird ' and ' heard '—not an elevating idea or thought through the whole thing from beginning to end; and then look at these: ' We consider your story too long;' ' We regret that the style of your article is unsuited to our pages; ' ' We see some promise in your poem, but it is not quite up to the level of our requirements; ' ' Try blank verse. . . . . We shall be glad to hear from you again.' Did you ever hear such mockery, and these very men printing such intolerable rubbish! "

Of course, he never thought of the poor editor, leaning over his chair in a brown study, biting the pen-handle, and wondering how he can please " A Constant Subscriber," who objects to the rather light nature of the articles he is now giving to the public; or, " Sacerdos," who does not like poetry; or, " Senex," who asks sarcastically: Is he putting himself in rivalry with the " Edinburgh " or " Quarterly," or who the mischief cares one brass pin about " Aristotle's Constitution of Athens; " and wouldn't he give them something light and agreeable to help to digest their dinners? Oh no! he only thought then and there that there should be an *auto da fe*—a summary crematory process of all the editors under the sun.

" Look here, young man," said I, at last, " there is only one thing for you to do. You must write a book."

" Look here, Father Dan," said he, " I'm not in much humour for joking. Any priest that would attempt to write a book nowadays should have the spirit of the martyrs, who stepped on to the sands in the Coliseum and saw the brutal Romans in the *auditorium* and wild beasts in the cages beneath! "

" Well, my dear boy," I replied, " you *will* write the book; but for goodness sake write it in your present humour, before the fires die down."
He laughed.

" Write a book? What in the world should I write about? The world is deluged and drowned by books. And if I wrote it, who could or would publish it? Imagine me hawking around a wretched manuscript from publisher to publisher, until it was tattered, yellow, and undecipherable. Why, the big London fellows accept only ten MSS. out of five hundred on the average, and you know I cannot publish at my own risk."

" Who the mischief spoke about publishing? " I replied, trying to keep up the flame; " I only asked you
to write. Write, write, write, and leave the publishing
to God."

" And what am I to write about? Every subject
under the sun is threshed out and threadbare, from the
origin of ideas down to the microbe of typhoid fever.
Not at all; the world is grown too wise for books; we must
devise something else."

" It is not many days ago," I replied, " since I heard
you lament the awful and culpable defects in our popular
Catholic literature. Hadn't you to fall back upon that
barbarous book to enlighten Ormsby on the existence of
his immortal soul? "

" Barbarous? I wish to heaven that I could write
anything half as good. But, as you see, there are whole
fields of literature yet untrodden by us, but where heretics and others are reaping rich harvests. Yet, who
would dare make the attempt? Don't you know that
the ablest professors in your own time in Maynooth never
ventured into print? They dreaded the chance shots
from behind the hedge from the barrels of those masked
banditti, called ' critics.' "

" Dear me, how you do run on! One would think you
had the MS. cut and dry in your pocket, you talk so
glibly about publishers and critics. Can't you write the
book first and then take circumstances as they occur? "

" Well, go on, suggest a subject, sir."

" Now, this is rather sudden, young man. Give me
one day, and I'll give you a list of subjects that would
bewilder you! Only promise me you'll take one up."

" All right! " said he; " I promise. Hallo! where are
you taking those papers? "

" I'm taking them home for the present. They are
confiscated to the Crown."

He looked at them wistfully, as if they were going to
the holocaust, as we might imagine the great mother of

the Maccabees watched half with pain, half with pride, wholly with resignation, her sons mount the funeral pyre.

" Never fear," I replied, " they won't go up the chimney. At least, I'll answer for the prose. I'm not so sure about the poetry. Now, good day! I'll keep you to your promise."

And I did, but with what cost to myself. I had to search in the cemeteries of the past for the skeletons of designs, once gladly adopted, then as gladly laid to rest. At last, I found, hidden away amongst episcopal documents, dispensations, etc., a yellow, frayed paper, tied up in string that once was red, but now was white and fragile. It broke in my fingers and revealed the little dreams and ambitions of nearly forty years ago. Need I say they never ripened, or came within even measurable distance of perfection. They were three large quarto sheets, and they were darkened thus:—

A. M. D. G.

Subjects for Articles and Papers to be written, wholly or partially, during the Coming Years.

I. MENTAL PHILOSOPHY.

I. The Influence of Plato on the Early Christian Church.

II. The Influence of Aristotle on the Mediæval Church.

III. The Neo-Platonists.

IV. The Argument in St. Augustine on the Immortality of the Soul. (Is it Tenable?)

V. The Atomic Theory of Democritus, and the Modern Discoveries in Astronomy.

VI. The Influence of the Inductive Philosophy on Modern Disbelief.

VII. Was Spinoza an Atheist?

VIII. Is Descartes the Father of Modern Rationalism?

IX. St. Anselm's Proof of the Existence of God.

Rather a large order, I thought, as I looked with pitying eyes on the far vision of a curly-headed young priest
of forty years ago, and thought of the day-dreams of
youth; and what a very slender precipitate of work fell
from the vast effervescence of the idealism of inexperi-
ence. There remained another page of projected inspiration on the scope and meaning of Holy Scripture; but
this I put aside. I found my knowledge, little as it was,
was derived from such obsolete and antique commentators as à Lapide, Maldonatus, Estius, and the *Triplex;*
and I was ashamed to produce such fossilized literature to the advanced thinkers of the present day. I did
not like to face this ordeal : —

" Then you haven't heard of the new schools of interpretation? You know that the great thinkers of Germany, Bahrdt, and Semler, and Eichhorn, have upset
all our preconceived ideas about the Bible. The Wolfian
ideas have been expanded and developed; and advanced
Catholic apologists have set themselves to the task of
reconciling our ancient traditions with the discoveries of
modern science. The tremendous advances made by
philological scientists and experts during these last years
—— "

I don't say, indeed, that my curate would indulge in
this affectation, for he is rather disposed to take the old,
unlearned modes of saving souls and going with them to
Heaven, than the new, brilliant mimetism of a world that
knows not God. But still I know he would think it waste
of time to pursue such studies, until the modern *Luci-
feri* tell us exactly what they have placed beyond the
borderland of conjecture, and into the certain and un-

shaken fields of mathematical demonstration. So I left
my Scriptural syllabus at home.

He looked slightly appalled at the large schedule of
science I showed him. I reassured him by telling him
I insisted positively on his taking only one subject in
each department.

" The grand mistake," I declared, " made by us,
Catholics, is in taking too wide, too bird's-eye a view of
human history and philosophy, instead of mapping them
into sections, as the astronomical photographers are mapping the skies from the Papal Observatory in Rome to
the Lick Observatory in California. What we want most
is sectional treatises on single subjects. Now, what you
are to give us is not a vast diorama from Thales to Ros-
mini, and from the persecutions of Julian to the *Kultur-
kampf* of Bismarck, but a neat etching of some particular persons and events, and a clear photograph of some
practical point of Catholic philosophy. If you throw in
a few side-lights from the errors of non-Catholic thinkers, so much the better. Now, look it over carefully ; as
the strolling player declares—' You pays your money,
and you takes your choice.' "

He thought that question of inductive philosophy very
nice. He had read something about it in Macaulay.
He liked that Platonic question very much. It bordered
upon poetry and mysticism. Then St. Augustine! That
would be charming. He had always such a love for St.
Augustine! But Fénelon? The " dove of Cambrai "
versus the " eagle of Meaux! " What a delightful idea!
No good housekeeper, at a cheap sale, was ever so
puzzled. Finally, we decided that, in philosophy, he was
to take up the question of " Modern Aspects of Pantheism ; " and in Ecclesiastical History he selected " The
Cappadocians."

" But what about books? " he asked in dismay. " I
haven't a single book on these blessed subjects."

" Buy them," I said. " Every good workman buys
his tools and materials."

" I have a strong suspicion, Father Dan," he said, " that this is all a practical joke. Why, that means a whole library. And if I had money, which I have not, I do not know the name of a single blessed Catholic author on these subjects."

" Why, my dear fellow, there are hundreds. Let me see! On the Fathers, Basil, and the two Gregories. Let me see! Haven't you—my memory is failing—haven't you Cardinal Newman's essays on these Fathers? "

" Well? You don't want me to give a verbatim version of Cardinal Newman, surely, do you? "

" Let me see! Why, we have hundreds of English Catholic writers on these subjects. What in the world is becoming of my memory? Why, we have whole libraries in the English language on these subjects! Isn't there Alzog and—and—Darras?—— "

" I have Darras," he cried triumphantly.

" Well, look it up, and see all you can get about St. Basil."

" But their writings! Wouldn't it be nice to give Greek extracts from their sermons and homilies? "

" 'Twould indeed. Well, I'll look up all the old catalogues I have kept, and let you know about books of reference. Meanwhile, commence somewhere by way of preface. Now, what are you going to do about that fishing-boat? Ormsby says it is certainly a troublesome and may be a perilous enterprise! "

" It's gone too far now to draw back," said Father Letheby. " The Board has yielded at last, thanks to Ormsby himself."

" They'll advance all the money? "

" No; two thirds; four hundred pounds."

" That's very kind of them; and no interest, no security. I did not think Boards could be so generous."

" No, indeed. They have full security to be paid back, principal and five per cent. interest, in less than five years."

" By Jove! You are a clever fellow. And where have you got all this Midas wealth? "

He asked me to be good enough to move with him to the window. True enough, even under the cold light, the broad sea stretched sparkling before us, with all its magic and glamour, but unruffled and unploughed by even one Nautilus-sail of busy man.

" There," he cried, " there lie the gold mines of Ireland, unworked and neglected. In these depths is wealth enough to make Kilronan a busy emporium of merchandise for half the world! "

" I see. And the other two hundred? Where do they come from? "

" Subscribed by twenty merchants, who have taken shares in the boat."

" And you never asked your old pastor to invest in this patriotic bank. Shame! Shame! And I wanted a little return as well as the rest of the world."

He laughed.

" The mackerel fishery alone," he continued, in a calculating way, " is worth a hundred pounds each for each boat in the Manx and French fishing-fleets that anchor off our shores every year, and take our wealth back to their thriving villages. I calculate another cool hundred on cod, hake, etc. I think we shall pay back the Board's loan in three years, besides paying handsome dividends to our shareholders. The boat is in the hands of a Belfast firm. She will be ready by the first of May. On that day she will be christened the ' Star of the Sea,' and will make her first run to the fishing-fleet."

" And what about the shirt-factory? "

" That's all right, too," he said, though his face grew a little clouded. " I shall have twenty sewing-machines in full swing by the middle of April. The manager was here and dined with me last Thursday; he's a fine fellow. He assures me that, after the initial expenses are over, the girls can earn from eight to ten shillings a week easily."

" By Jove! That's good. That will be a great help
to the poor people."

" Yes; he sends the shirts here, ready and cut for sewing, by the new system of scientific shirt-making. Then
all they have to do is to tack them together with the
machines."

" God bless you! " I said fervently. " You're a wonderful fellow."

I was sorry that I gave him Ormsby's message of
warning.

CHAPTER XX

MADONNA MIA

THE winter had nearly rolled by, and the sky was opening out its eyelids wider and wider, and letting in light to
man and all his wondrous train of servitors. It was a
cold, steely light indeed, particularly on those March
evenings; and the sunsetting was a dreary, lonesome
thing, as the copper-coloured rays rested on hamlet or
mountain or tinged the cold face of the sea. But it was
light, and light is something man craves for, be it never
so pale. Will not one of heaven's delights be to see the
" inaccessible light " in which God—our God—is
shrouded, and to behold one another's faces in the light
that streams from the Lamb? And so, very tempting as
my fire is—and I am as much a fire-worshipper as an
Irish Druid or a Peruvian Inca—I always like to go out
as the days are lengthening and the sun is stretching out
his compasses to measure in wider arcs the sky.

This evening, too, I had a little business with Father
Letheby. As I entered his parlour, I carried a tiny slip
of printed paper in my hand.

" You'd hardly guess what it is? " I said, holding it
from the light.

" A check for a hundred pounds, or my removal! " he
exclaimed.

" Neither. Read it! "

I am quite sure it was infinitely more gratifying than
the check, to say nothing of the removal; and I am quite
sure the kindly editor, who had sent me that proof of

Father Letheby's first poem, would have been amply repaid for his charity if he had seen the shades and flushes of delight and half-alarm that swept like clouds across the face of the young priest. And it was not all charity, either. The good editor spoke truly when he declared that the poem was quite original and out of the beaten track, and would probably attract some attention. I think, next to the day of his ordination, this was the supreme day in Father Letheby's life hitherto.

" It was very kind," he said, " very kind indeed. And how am I to thank you, Father Dan? "

" By keeping steadily at the work I pointed out for you," I replied. " Now, let me see what you have done."

" Do you mean about the books? " he asked.

" Yes," I said determinedly, " and about the *horarium* I marked out and arranged for you. Have you conscientiously studied during the two hours each evening, and written from 11 A.M. to noon every day, as I appointed?"

" To be candid," he said at once, " I have not. First came the lack of books. Except Butler's ' Lives of the Saints,' I cannot come across a single indication of what Basil and the Gregories did or wrote; and my edition of Butler is expurgated of all the valuable literary notes which, I understand, were in the first editions. Then the moment I take the pen into my hand, in comes Mrs. Luby to know wouldn't I write to the colonel of the Connaught Rangers to get her little boy discharged and sent home. He enlisted in a fit of drink. Then comes Mrs. Moriarty with the modest request to write to the pastor of Santa Barbara about her little girl who emigrated to America sixteen years ago. Then comes—— "

" Never mind," I said, " I have been there. But I won't accept these excuses at all. You *must* work, whether you like or no. Now, I am going to take away all excuses. I have been searching a lot of old catalogues, and I have discovered that these are the books

for you. On the subject of ' Modern Pantheism ' we will
get :—

" (1) Lewes' ' History of Philosophy,' 4 vols.

" (2) Brucker's ' Historia Critica Philosophiæ,' 6 vols.

" (3) Tenneman's ' History of Philosophy ' (Cousin).

" (4) Émile Saisset's ' Modern Pantheism,' 2 vols.

" (5) ' History of Pantheism ' (Plumtre).

" (6) ' An Essay on Pantheism,' by J. Hunt, D.D.

" (7) ' Spinoza,' by Principal Caird, LL.D.

" (8) ' Spinoza,' by D. J. Martineau.

" (9) ' Spinoza, his Ethics and Correspondence,' by R.
Willis, M.D.

" (10) ' Spinoza,' by Nourrisson.

" Now, on the subject of Ecclesiastical History we will
get, read, and consult :—

" (1) ' Historia Literaria Ecclesiæ,' by Cave.

" (2) Farrar's ' Lives of the Fathers,' 2 vols.

" (3) Cave's ' Lives of the Fathers,' 3 vols.

" (4) ' Lives of the Fathers,' by the S. P. C. K.

" (5) The Bishop of Lincoln (Kaye) on ' The Fathers
and Early Councils.'

" (6) ' Lives of the Fathers,' by the author of ' A Dominican Artist,' 3 vols.

" (7) Neander's ' Church History,' 8 vols.

" (8) Neale's ' Oriental Church.' "

Here Father Letheby stopped me, as he broke from a
suppressed chuckle into uncontrollable laughter.

" Why, Father Dan, what in the world are you reading?
Don't you know that you are calling out a list of the
most rampant heretics and disbelievers, every one of
whom is probably on the Index? Is it possible that you
cannot discover any English Catholic authorities on these
subjects? "

" I have not seen them," I said mournfully. " And
do you mean to say that all these Protestants, and many
of them, you say, infidels, have not been interested in
these subjects? "

" Well, I presume they would not have gone to the

vast trouble of accumulating material, and writing 'ponderous volumes otherwise.''

" And what are we doing? And if ever these grave
subjects become of importance or interest to our youth,
say in the higher systems of education, what books can
we put into their hands? ''

We were both in a brown study. These things make
men thoughtful. At last Father Letheby said :—

" How do they manage in the German and French
universities, I wonder? ''

" Depend upon it," I replied, " there is no lack of
Catholic authors on every subject there. And I'm told
the Italian priests take an extraordinary interest in these
higher studies. And in France every French priest
thinks he is bound to write at least one book.''

" I never understood the importance of this matter till
I met Ormsby," said Father Letheby. " He opened my
eyes. By the way, Father Dan, I must congratulate
you on the impression you have made there. Some
things you said have made a vivid impression on him.
He keeps on saying: ' A sixth sense! A sixth sense.
Perhaps he is right, after all.' And the dependence on
the prayers of little children and the afflicted touched
him deeply. Do you know, I think he'll come round.''

" God grant it," I said, rising. " But I suppose this
little project of ours is knocked on the head.''

" You mean the books? ''

" Yes.''

" I fear so. The fact is, Father Dan, I find I have no
time. Between my two hours with the choir on Tues-
days and Fridays, the Saturday and Sunday evenings in
the church, the occasional evening out, and my correspondence, I don't know where to get time to fit in everything. And now that you have been so good as to
secure the sympathy of the editor of the —— for me, I
think I may do something for him at intervals.''

" I have regretted a few things during my life, young
man," I said; " but I never regretted anything so much

as to have sent on that poem of yours instead of sending it up the chimney."

" My dear Father Dan," said he, " what are you saying? Don't you know that the Pope himself writes poetry, and writes it well? "

" May God forgive him! " I said fervently. Then I got sorry, as this was not reverent, and a bright thought struck me.

" What kind of poetry does His Holiness write? "

" Why, the most beautiful Latin elegiacs and hexameters."

" I thought so," I said triumphantly. " I knew that the Holy Father would write nothing but in the style of the divine Mantuan. If you do anything that way, my boy, I'll forgive you. Keep to your classics, keep to your classics, and you're all right."

It was delightful to find us, the last remnant of the great generation of the classical priests of Ireland, backed up by the first authority in the world.

It was twilight when I left, and I made my usual detour around our hamlet. Outside the village and just beyond the school-house, in a little cottage whose diamond windows are almost hidden under green creepers, lived Alice Moylan, the head monitress in our little school. I rather liked Alice, for when she was a little child of seven years, she gave me an idea of something for which I had been long seeking. It was a few years back, when I had not laid up my pen finally, but still retained the belief, with a certain author, that " there is no greater mental excitement, and scarcely a sweeter one, than when a young man strides up and down his room, and boldly resolves to take a quire of writing paper and turn it into a manuscript." And in these latter days of life I still sought for a vision of our Lady, which I could keep before my imagination when writing certain things in her honour. Now (perhaps I have already said it), I had a peculiar devotion to the Child-Virgin of the Temple and

of the House of Nazareth, where in the noontide the
Archangel entered and spoke his solemn words. And I
never said the *Magnificat* but on my knees and with a
full heart, as I thought on the Child-Prophetess of
Hebron and the wondering aged saints. But I sought
her face everywhere in vain—in pictures, in the faces of
my little children; but not one came up to my ideal of
what the little maiden of the Temple and Nazareth was
like. At last, one day, little Alice came, and in her
sweet oval face, and calm, entreating eyes and raven
hair, subdued beneath such a dainty frilled head-dress, I
saw our Blessed Lady and wondered and was glad. And
in those days of her simple childhood, before the awful
dawn of self-consciousness, I used dream and dream, and
put into form my dreams; and the face that haunted all
my sacred and poetic conceptions of our dear Queen was
the face of little Alice. But the child grew, and waxed
in strength, but waned in beauty—at least the beauty I
regarded when the white soul looked out of the beautiful
childish face. But Alice grew to be the village beauty,
and she knew it. Every one told her of it; but her chief
admirer was the little milliner, who lived down near the
post-office, and whose simple life was a mixture of very
plain, prosaic poverty, and very high and lofty romance.
From this Miss Levis, who was a confirmed novel-reader,
Alice learned that " she had the face and form of an
angel "; that " her eyes had a velvety softness that drew
you like an enchanted lake "; that these same eyes were
" starry in their lustrous beauty "; that she had " the
complexion of a creole, or rather the healthy pallor of
the high-born aristocracy of England "; that " her figure
was willowy and swayed like a reed in the wind "; and
all the other curious jargon of the novelette—the deadly
enemy of simplicity and innocence. Then Alice grew
proud and vain, and her vanity culminated on the night
of our concert in November, when she drew up for the
first time her luxuriant black hair and tied it in a knot
and bound it in a fillet, which was said to be the *mode à*

la Grecque.   But she was a very pure, innocent girl withal, and exceedingly clever in her work at school.

I had missed her recently, but had been occupied with other thoughts until the time came for the quarterly salaries of the teachers; and I noticed in the returns from the principal teacher that Alice had been absent the greater part of the time.   This evening, after leaving Father Letheby, I determined to call, unprepared to witness the little tragedy that was before me—one of those little side-scenes in the great drama of existence, which God turns suddenly to the front lest we should ever mistake the fact that our little world is a stage, and that we have all the denizens of the veiled eternities for our audience.   Mrs. Moylan was one of those beautiful Irish mothers, who, having passed through the stress and storm of life, was moving calmly into the great sea of Death and Eternity.   She had one of those Irish faces that were so typical of our race some years ago, and the intense resignation and patience of which rivalled the sweet innocence of our little Irish children for the admiration of such a keen and sympathetic observer as Dr. Newman.   There were a few wrinkles in the pallid cheeks, and one or two lines across the white forehead, crowned with the clean white cap which our Irish mothers wear. She looked, I thought, a little reproachfully at me as I entered, but only welcomed me with that courteous reverence which makes us priests so often humbled and ashamed.   After a few words I inquired for Alice.

" My poor child hasn't been well, your reverence. We were jealous that you never asked for her."

I protested my utter ignorance of her illness, and inquired what was the ailment.

" You can see yourself, your reverence," the poor mother said, silently wiping away a tear.   " But," she whispered, " don't pretend to see anything. She feels it very much."

I passed into the little chamber and was making my

apologies to the poor child, when, in spite of her mother's warning, I started back, shocked and horror-stricken.

" Good God," I could not help crying out, " what has happened to you, my poor child? "

She smiled faintly, and then a tear rolled down the leprous cheek. Ay! indeed! my poor little Madonna, my little child, whose beauty was such a dream of Paradise, was changed. The large, lustrous eyes were untouched; but the fair cheek was one hideous, leprous sore. The black, glossy hair was now a few dirty wisps. The child, whose face and figure everyone turned around to look at a second time, was now a revolting mummy, seamed and scarred by some terrible disease. I had presence of mind enough to take up the thin, white hand; she picked the coverlet and said nothing. Her heart was too full of her misery to utter a word. I could only say :—

" My poor child! my poor child! "

I turned to the mother.

" This is too dreadful! What has happened? "

" Dreadful enough, your reverence," she cried; " but welcome be the will of God! "

" But what has happened? " I cried.

Then I thought it would be a relief to the poor child's feelings to tell me her own sad tale, so I said :—

" Never mind! Alice will tell me all herself. Now, my child, tell me all."

She did, with all the humility and such gentle submission to God's decree that I wept freely. It would appear that on the afternoon of that November concert, Alice, like so many other girls, was very much engrossed in her preparations for the evening. She had studied the " Young Lady's Journal " and several other works of interest and usefulness, and all day long was highly excited over her appearance. Once, when she was particularly engaged at the looking-glass, she heard someone fumbling at the half-door, as if anxious to come into the kitchen. Angry at being disturbed, she burst from her room, and saw in the framework of the door an awful sight. It was a poor woman, whose face was completely eaten away by a dread disease called nasal polypus. The nose was completely gone and the upper lip. The eyes stared out as if from a death's-head. The poor creature begged for alms; but Alice, flushed at the thought of her own beauty, and in a rage from being called away from her glass, clapped her hands and shouted:—

" Well, you *are* a beauty."

" Not so handsome as you, alanna," said the afflicted one. " There was wance when, perhaps, I was. But your time may come. Mockin' is catchin'. Mockin' is catchin.' "

And with these words the woman strode away.

" I could not get the thought of my sin out of my head all that day," continued Alice; " her face was always coming before me, until at last I gave up looking at the glass. But when the night came and we were all in the concert-room, my vanity came back again, for I heard people whisper as I was passing, and my foolish head was turned. Then, when it was all over, and the girls broke into groups, and the people were all around, I tried to attract more attention. And I had been reading of a trick in the novels for making one's self more interesting by standing on tiptoe and opening the eyes widely; and, God help me! I was practising this foolishness, thinking that some of the young men were admiring me for it, when suddenly Father Letheby saw me, and he gave me a look that struck me like a flash of lightning. I felt dazed and blinded, and asked one of the girls to take me from the room and lead me home. But all that night I never slept, the woman's face and the awful look that Father Letheby gave me were staring at me out of the curtains and out of the dark, until late in the morning I fell into a sleep, only to dream the same dreadful things."

Here the poor girl broke down and sobbed in an agony of remorse.

" Well, then, Father, I got up sick and sorrowful, and before my breakfast I went over there to the Blessed Virgin's altar and said a Rosary, and begged and prayed her not to punish me for what I had done. Sure, I said, 'twas only a girl's foolishness and I was young; and I promised then and there to give up novel-reading and to be good, and to let my hair fall down, and to drop all my foolish notions; but 'twas no use. I saw something in the face of the Blessed Virgin that frightened me, and I knew I was in for something. I didn't think my punishment would be so dreadful."

Here the poor child sobbed again, and picked the coverlet mournfully as she tried to choke down her emotion. I looked over at that statue of the Blessed Virgin and shook my head reproachfully.

" Oh! Father, why does God punish us so terribly for such small sins? " the poor girl went on. " And what must purgatory be, and what must hell be when He punishes us so dreadfully here! I thought 'twas all over and my fear was vanishing, when one Sunday morning, dressing for Mass, I noticed a tiny pimple here on my cheek. It wasn't as big as the head of a pin; but it gave me great trouble. Not that I suspected anything; but when our poor heads are turned with vanity, you don't know, Father, what a worry these little blemishes are. I just touched it with my finger and it bled. That night 'twas an angry spot. I used everything I could think of —lard, and butter, and ointment. No use. Every day it grew and grew and grew into an ugly sore. Then I wrote, as Miss Levis advised me, to a London doctor, recommended in the journals; he sent me a prescription—— "

" For nothing? " I interjected.

" No, indeed, Father. Before I was done with him it cost me a pound. But I applied his cosmetics and became daily worse. Then my mother spoke of making

rounds. But I wouldn't leave her. I went to the school
every day, but I saw the girls watching me. I heard
them whisper to each other, and sometimes I caught
their words. They weren't kind. Then I stopped away.
One day, while I was sitting at the door knitting, suddenly the sun was darkened, and there was the dreadful
face of that woman over me.

"'I'm asking charity for God's sake,' she said.

"I got up humbly and gave her bread and two-pence.
She looked at me keenly and said: 'God save you, alanna,
and purtect you from misfortune. Sure, 'twas only a
hasty word you said. God save you and purtect you,
alanna!'

"Then the frightful anger of God coming down upon
me suddenly flashed upon me, and I flung aside my
knitting and rushed into this room, and cried and
screamed, and bit the counterpane until I tore it in
threads, and shrieked:—

"'Don't! don't, O Lord; Oh, don't! don't!'

"And then I turned to the Blessed Virgin and said
the little prayer 'Remember;' and then I said:—

"'You won't let Him, Mother! you won't let Him!
Didn't you say you wouldn't let Him?'

"But the face stared down at me pitilessly, pitilessly.
There was no hope."

The poor child stopped again, and to relieve her from
the pain of memory I said:—

"But wasn't the doctor called in all this time? The
doctor is very clever, you know."

"Oh, he was, Father! And he was very kind. But
he was very angry; and I think, Father, he cursed when
I told him about these London cosmetics. And one day
he asked mother a lot of queer questions about father
and grandfather; and then he said something about 'stru-
mous' and 'hereditary;' and he has done me no good."

"Did Father Letheby call?" I asked.

"Oh, dear, yes, that was my only consolation. He
calls twice a week, sometimes three times; and he

brought Miss Campion, and she comes every day and
reads for hours with me; and look at those violets and
lilies of the valley—'twas she brought them; and sometimes a strange gentleman comes with her, and he sits
down and talks and puts queer questions to me—all about
God, and what I do be doing, and what I do be thinking.
But since Father Letheby told me that there is something behind it all that I don't understand, and that
some day I will understand it, and see it is all God's love
and not His anger, I am quite resigned, Father, and I do
be saying all day: ' Thy Will be done! Thy Will be
done.' But I break down when I think of all I've gone
through."

" Let me see," I said, as a light began to dawn upon
me; " you are now perfectly resigned, my poor child,
are you not? "

" Oh! yes, Father; and really happy. Only for mother, who frets about me so much, I wouldn't care to be
well again. Sure, as Father Letheby says, I don't know
but that something dreadful was in store for me; and
that God, in His mercy, has just saved me."

" Quite right! quite right! my child. And tell me
now—this strange gentleman—has he ever asked you to
pray for him? "

" He did, Father. And I didn't like it at first; but
Father Letheby said I should. And I have been saying
a Rosary for him every day since. And the last day he
was here he asked me: ' Now, Alice, tell me the plain
truth. Are you glad this has happened you?.' I hesitated for a moment, then I looked at the Wounds of our
Lord, and I said firmly: ' I am.' And he said: ' Do
you believe God will give you back your beauty, and
make it a hundred times greater in heaven for all you
have suffered here? ' And I said confidently: ' I do.'
' Alice, my child, will you pray and pray strongly for
me? ' I said: ' I will, sir.' And he went away looking
happy. But, you know, Father, these are my good
times, when I feel resigned and think God is using me

for His own wise purposes; welcome be His Holy Will!
But I am sometimes bad, and I get unhappy and miserable, and I ask myself: ' Why did God do it? Why did
God do it? ' And once I said to our Blessed Lady, when
she looked so cold and stern—I said—— "

" What did you say, dear? "

" I said: ' If Daddy Dan was here, he wouldn't let
you do it.' "

And the poor child smiled at her own childishness and
simplicity.

" But that's not all, Father. I have told no one but
mother and you; but I'm all one running sore down to
my feet, and the doctor said something about an operation the other day. Sure, you won't allow that, Daddy
Dan, will you? "

She was rolling one of the buttons in my sleeve round
and round in her thin fingers, and looking wistfully at me.

" No, my child, no operation! You have gone through
too much for that. But now cheer up, Alice, it will all
come right. Some of these days you will see how our
dear Lord and His Holy Mother love you. Why, don't
you know, you little goose, that these are signs of your
predestination? Don't you remember all that you have
learned about the saints, and how they prayed to be
afflicted? "

" I do, Daddy Dan."

" And don't you remember all about those holy women
that were marked with the wounds of our Divine Lord?"

" I do, Daddy Dan."

" Very well! Now you're one of them. The Lord
has made you His own. Now, good-bye. I'll come to
see you every day in future. But pray! pray! pray!
won't you? "

" I will, Daddy Dan! Will you come to-morrow? "

This was all very well; but I was as cross as a bear
with a sore head, notwithstanding.

" Wisha, then, Mrs. Moylan," I said, as I was leaving the house, " aren't you the mighty proud woman entirely, never to call in your parish priest, nor send him word about your poor child! What are we coming to, I wonder, when poor people are getting so much above themselves? "

" Well, then, I didn't like to be troubling your reverence. And sure, I thought you knew all about it, and that Father Letheby told you."

" He didn't, then. You and he have kept it a great secret—a great secret entirely. Never mind. But tell me, is the poor child really resigned? "

" Well, indeed she is, your reverence, excep' now and then, when the whole thing comes back to her. In fact, she's less trouble than when she was well. Then nothing could please her. She was always grumblin' about her clothes, an' her food; and she was short and peevish. Now she is pleased with everythin'. 'Tis ' whatever you like, mother; ' or ' 'tis too good for me, mother; ' or ' thank you kindly, mother,' until sometimes I do be wishing that she had some of the old sperrit, and take me short in her answers. But, sure, 'tis all God's Blessed and Holy Will. Glory be to His Holy Name! "

I went back through the village again and called upon Father Letheby. He was just sitting down to dinner.

" I don't want to take away your appetite," I said, refusing the chair which he proffered; " but I am for the first time genuinely angry with you. I suppose you had your reasons for it; but you ought to know that a parish priest has, by every law, natural and canonical, the right to know about his sick or distressed poor people, and that a curate has no right to be keeping these things a secret from him. Reticence and secretiveness are excellent things in their way; but this too may be overdone. I have just been down to Mrs. Moylan's to learn for the first time that her child has been sick for nearly two months. You knew it and you never told me. Now, I'll insist for the future that a sick-call book shall be

kept in the sacristy, and that the name of every patient
in the parish shall be entered there. Good evening."

He flushed up, but said nothing.

I passed the chapel door and went in straight up to the
altar of the Blessed Virgin.

" Now," I said, " you've carried this entirely too far.
Is this the return I've got for all I've done for you for
the past fifty years? Think of all the Rosaries I said for
you, all the Masses I offered for you, all the May devotions I established for you, all the Brown Scapulars I
gave for you—all—all—and this is your return; and she
your own child, that I thought was so like you. 'Pon
my word, I think I'll blow out that lamp and never light
it again."

The mild, brown eyes looked down on me calmly, and
then that queer thing called Conscience, that jumps up
like a jack-in-the-box when you least expect it, started
at me and began :—

" What folly is this, Father Dan? Do you think you
know more than God and His Blessed Mother? Do
you? Your head is so turned with heathen vanity that
you think you ought to get the reins of the universe into
your hands. Here's your classics, and your Spinoza,
and your Cappadocians, and your book-writing, and all
your castles in the air, and your little children lying on
their sick-beds and you knowing nothing about it. Look
sharp, old man, your time is at hand, and think what the
Judge may do with you when His hand presses so tightly
on His little children."

I sat down to my dinner, but couldn't touch a bit. It
was a nice little dinner, too—a little roast chicken and a
scrap of bacon and some nice floury potatoes. No use.
The thought of that child would come before me, and her
piteous cry : "Oh, don't, dear Lord, don't!" and, "Sure
you won't let Him, Mother; you said you wouldn't;"
and with a great big lump in my throat I pushed aside
the plate and went over to the darkening window.

After a time Hannah came in, looked at the dishes, and looked at me.

" Was there anything wrong with the chicken? " she said, thinking I was reflecting on her cookery.

" No, Hannah, 'twas all right; but I'm not in a humour for eating."

She was surprised. So was I. It was the first time for many years that I bolted. Thank God, a good appetite and His Divine Grace have never deserted me.

" I'm thinkin' you're in for somethin'," she said. " And no wondher! I niver knew a man to timpt Providence like you. Will you have the hot wather, as you ate nothin'? "

" Don't mind, Hannah. I'll have a cup of tea by and by."

I sat down to the fire, looking into all its glowing crevices and crannies, thinking, thinking of many things. By and by, in came Father Letheby. He was subdued and deferential, but evidently very much hurt at my unaccustomed rudeness. He stood with his back to the fire, looking down on me, and he said, in his best Sunday accent, smoothed and ironed :—

" I confess, sir, I am still quite at a loss to understand your rather—well—forcible remarks this evening. I can see, certainly, a great deal of reason in your irritation; and I am not at all disposed to contravene the principle that you have an indefeasible right to be acquainted with the sorrows and trials of your parishioners; but pardon me for saying it, I was only carrying out, perhaps too logically, your own reiterated teaching."

" Look here," said I, " have you had your dinner? "

" Yes, sir," said he.

" Well, then, sit down, and have your coffee here. Touch that bell."

He sat down, and somehow this took a lot of the starch out of him.

" You were saying something," said I, " about my teaching. When did I ever teach you to keep the most vital interests of these poor people a secret from me? "

" Well," said he, balancing the sugar in his spoon over the cup, " if there was one lesson more than another that was continually dinned into my ears, it was: ' When a young man comes into a strange parish, he must be all eyes and ears, but no tongue,' and I think you quoted some grave authorities for that aphorism."

" Quite so," I replied. " I think it is a most wholesome advice. For there never yet was a young man that was not disposed to think that he could run a parish better than all the pastors that lived for generations there. But did you understand me to say that we were never to talk over and discuss parochial affairs? "

" Well, I confess," said he, " I did not. But you see, sir, your thoughts were running in quite another channel. You were interested in the classics and in literary matters."

" My conscience, my dear boy, has already made me aware of that, and in somewhat more forcible and less polite language than you have used. Now, I admit that I have been a surly old curmudgeon this afternoon, and I am sorry for it; but hereafter, don't leave me in the dark any longer about my parishioners. It seems to me that, if we dropped our occasional uncharitableness about each other and our more occasional criticisms on our superiors, and addressed ourselves to the work God gives us to do in that limited circle He has drawn about us, it would be all the better."

" Well, sir, I quite agree with you. But I must say that for the few months I have been here, I do not remember to have heard much uncharitableness about our brethren from you."

There now! How can you be angry with a fellow like that? The black cloud turned softly into gray, and the gray turned slowly round, and showed only the silver lining.

CHAPTER XXI

THE FACTORY

NOTWITHSTANDING my gloomy forebodings, I find that Father Letheby has eagerly grasped the idea of writing on the historical and philosophical subjects I had suggested. Where he got books of reference I know not, nor can I conjecture; but he has a silent way of accomplishing things that would seem to a slow-moving mind like my own little short of a miracle. When, therefore, one fine day in April I strolled in to see him (for that little tiff about the sick child has only cemented our friendship), I gasped to see a huge pile of quarto manuscript paper in a fair way to be soon well blackened, and by the side of his writing-table several heavy, leather-lined folios, which a certain visitor described as " just the kind of book you would take with you for a stroll by the seashore, or your annual holiday at Lisdoonvarna."

" Hallo! " I cried; " so you're at it. I thought you had given it up."

" I'm in for it," he replied modestly, " for good or ill. You see, I recognized some truth in what you said, and I determined to do a little to take away our reproach."

." I must say you are a singularly acute and deep thinker to recognize my far-seeing, almost Promethean wisdom; but to tell you the truth, I haven't the faintest idea of what I said to you, except to recommend you to do something for the spread of Catholic literature."

" Never mind, Father Dan," he replied, " the seed is sown; the die is cast. I intend to scribble away now and to submit my manuscript to the editor of some ecclesiastical journal. If he accepts it, well and good; if he doesn't, no harm done. By the way, you must help me, by looking over this translation of the funeral oration of St. Gregory Nazianzen on St. Basil. I depend on your knowledge of Greek a great deal more than on these garbled versions of Scotch or Oxford translators."

Isn't that a nice young man? What could I do but go over, then and there, that famous panegyric, that has made the author as great as his subject. At the end of his papers on the "Three Cappadocians," Father Lethe-by intends to give in Greek, with English translation, passages from their sermons and poems. A happy idea!

"Now, so far so good!" said Father Letheby, after this little conference. "The metaphysical subject is more difficult to tackle—a fellow can be tripped up so easily; but we'll postpone that for the present. Now here are three matters that concern us. I think Ormsby is on the point of coming over. The prayers of the little children and of that poor Dolores, Alice, have nearly pushed open the gates of the Kingdom. At least, they're creaking on their hinges. Secondly, I'm beginning to get afraid of that young girl. Under her awful cross she's developing such sanctity as makes me nervous about guiding her any longer. She is going up the eternal hills, and my spiritual sight cannot follow. Thirdly, we open the shirt-factory on the 20th. I give you timely warning, Father Dan, for you are to be chairman, and your speech is to be the event of the occasion."

"Quite an anti-climax from the eternal hills," I said, noticing his tendency to practical issues rather than to supernatural evolutions; "but now, let us see. Are you sure of Ormsby?"

"Nearly so. I have left him severely alone—told him the matter concerned himself altogether. He has given up reading and argumentation of every kind. He says the *Veni Creator* every day. But I think, under Heaven, it is the patience and divine serenity of this poor child that affect him most deeply."

" Then he isn't shocked at her appearance? "

" Oh, dear, yes! He cannot bear to look at her. He
says it is more like Oriental leprosy than anything he
has seen in these countries. But her gentleness and
patience and her realization of the unseen startle him— "

" It has startled me more than once," I replied.

" And me. I begin to feel almost nervous about
directing so high a soul. I am glad you have noticed it,
because you can give me lights."

" H'm. You are becoming sarcastic, young man. But
I feel we are treading on holy ground. Let us look to
ourselves. How often do you give the child Holy Communion? "

" Every Sunday and holiday."

" Has she asked for more frequent Communion? "

" Yes, indeed; but I hesitated."

" Hesitate no longer. *Digitus Dei est hic.*"

Of course, I had seen all this myself; for in a quiet,
unconscious way this poor child had manifested even to
my purblind eyes the dealings of God's munificence with
her. By degrees all the old vain regrets after her beauty
had yielded to perfect resignation; and resignation had
grown into peace, and peace had been transformed into
rapture.

" I used be thinking, Daddy Dan, a good deal of what
you said to me—how these poor bodies of ours were but a
little lime, and phosphorus, and water; and that we must
all go through the terrible changes of death; and what you
told me of that great saint in Spain and the dead queen;
but it was only when Father Letheby read to me about
our Lord, ' a worm and no man,' ' a leper and accursed
by God and afflicted '; ' and one huge sore from the
crown of his head to the sole of his feet '—that I began
to think He had made me like Himself, welcome be His
Will, and Holy be His Name! "

Then I got her a fine big brass Crucifix from the Pas-
sionist Fathers at Mount Argus, and left her to her
wonder-working and merciful Master. But she has im-

pressed Ormsby profoundly. " The weak things of the
world hast Thou chosen to confound the strong." " Thy
ways are upon the sea, and Thy pathway on the mighty
waters, and Thy footsteps are unknown."

" Well, now," I said to Father Letheby, getting out
of my reverie, " to come down from the Holy Mountain,
what's this you are saying about the shirt-factory? You
don't mean to aver it is a *fait accompli*? "

" Certainly," he replied, " everything is arranged; and
on the 20th a dozen sewing-machines will be clicking
merrily in the old mill."

" You have the lamp of Aladdin," I said admiringly.
" Now, who's to be there? "

" All the gentry and the *élite* of the neighbourhood,"
he said.

" Rather a limited audience for a great occasion," I
couldn't help saying.

" No matter," he cried, rising up; " it is a good work,
however. But you'll take the chair, Father Dan, won't
you? "

" All right," I replied, but with a little misgiving, for
no one knows what necromancy this fellow is capable of,
and I had already conjured up visions of the Lord Lieutenant and the Dowager This and the Countess That—
" but mind you, my speech is to come in at the end;
and I promise you they won't have to look long at their
watches."

" Very good, sir," he replied, " all is now arranged."

I went down to see my little martyr, for she is pleased
to say that I do her good by my visits. There she lay
meekly, the big crucifix in her hands, and her lips always
moving in silent prayer. The children often come in to
see her, she told me, and read by her bedside; for now
there is no jealousy, nor triumph, but all have begun to
think that there is a saint in the parish. The little milliner used come at the beginning, and bring her little
novelettes and journals, and talk about the fashions,
which only made the sufferer unhappy. All that is now

stopped; and the " Clock of the Passion " and the " Visions of Catherine Emmerich " are now her only reading.

" Mr. Ormsby was here again to-day," she said.

" Indeed. And was he as inquisitive as usual? "

" Nearly," she said, with a smile. " But do you know, Daddy Dan, I think he'll become a Catholic. Isn't it an awful thing not to be a Catholic, Daddy Dan? "

" 'Tis, my child. It's worse than being born blind."

" Now, what would I do if I had not our dear Lord "— kissing the crucifix—" and His holy Mother? I'd rather a thousand times be as I am than Queen of England."

" Of course. Who brought these flowers? "

" Miss Campion. She calls them lilies of the valley. Is it a sin to smell them, Daddy Dan? "

" No, child, it is no sin. Nay, 'tis a prayer if you glorify God for the wonders He has wrought in these tiny leaves."

" But they'll fade away and die in a day or two, Daddy Dan! "

" So shall all beautiful things, my child, only to be transplanted where there is no rust or fading."

" Thank you, Daddy Dan. That's just what I said to Mr. Ormsby. ' Do you really believe,' he said, ' that it is the love of God that has smitten you? ' ' Yes,' I said firmly. ' Do you believe that you are all the dearer to Him for that He has smitten you? ' ' Yes,' I said, ' I'm sure of it.' ' And do you believe that God will take you out of the grave and build you up far fairer than you have been? ' ' I believe it most certainly,' I re- plied. ' It's the sublime and the impossible,' he cried. And then he said—but I shouldn't repeat this, Daddy Dan—' Mind, little one, if I become a Catholic, it's you have made me one.' But it would be so nice, if only to repay Miss Campion for all her goodness."

Then I began to think of some holy man that said : There should be an invalid and an incurable one in every

H

religious community, if only to bring God nearer to them in His great love.

As I was leaving, Mrs. Moylan pulled me aside.

" Is there any chance at all, your reverence, of her recovery? "

She looked with a mother's wistfulness at me.

" For I do be praying to the Lord morning, noon, and night, that if it be His Blessed and Holy Will, He would take her out of suffering, or restore her to me."

I made no answer.

" You could do it, your reverence, if you liked. Sure, I don't want you to do any harm to yourself, God forbid; but you could cure her and restore her to me, if you plazed."

" I couldn't, Mrs. Moylan," I replied; " and what is more, I wouldn't now take her away from God if I could. I was as bitter as you about it; but now I see that God has His own designs upon your child, and who am I that I should thwart Him? "

" Perhaps your reverence is right," she replied; " but the mother's heart will spake up sometimes whin it ought to be silent."

I passed by my little chapel as I went home, and knelt down for a prayer. I thought the Blessed Virgin looked queer at me, as if to say :—

" Well, are you satisfied now? Who was right—you or my Son? " And I went home very humbled.

The great day at last arrived. And if I was surprised the evening of the concert at the transformation effected in the old mill, I was still more surprised when, entering its precincts on the opening day of the Kilronan Shirt-Factory, I came face to face with quite a distinguished gathering. There were carriages drawn up at the door, the liveried coachmen hardly able to hold the prancing horses' heads; and the owners were in the great room upstairs, chatting in groups or examining the machines, that, clean and bright and polished, only awaited the soft touch of human fingers to work wonders. And there, on the large table filling up the whole centre of the room, was displayed an assortment of linen and flannels cut up into as many sections as you could take out of all the diagrams of Euclid. And there, of course, was the stage, undisturbed since the evening of the concert; and there were the same flowers and palms, and the same little girls dressed in satin, and the same piano, and Miss Campion, only waiting the signal to commence.

I moved up through the long hall, making my bows to right and left. Father Letheby was chatting gaily with some very grand people, and pointing out his little improvements here and there. He was in his best optimistic humour, and was quite at his ease in the groups that surrounded him. It is curious how we differ. I did not feel at all comfortable, for I'd rather be talking over the cross-door to any old woman about her chickens, or settling the price of a bonham, or lecturing about the measles and the croup, than conversing with the grandest people of the land. But every one to his tastes; and sure, I ought to be proud that my good curate——

" I move that the parish priest take the chair."

" I beg to second the proposal," said a dapper young fellow, who looked as if he had stepped out of a band-box. And before I knew where I was, I was on the stage ensconced in a comfortable chair; and then there was a burst of music around me, which gave me leisure to look about and take stock. It was all very nice. There was a great group of fine ladies in front, and they were all staring at me as if I were a dime-museum prodigy. I was " Gorgonized from head to foot with a stony, British stare "; a cool, unblushing, calculating stare, that made me feel as if I were turning into stone. I did not know what to do. I tried to cross my legs coolly, but the armchair was too low, and I fell back in a most undignified manner. Then I placed my hands on my knees, thinking that this was the correct thing; but it struck me immediately that this was the attitude at High Mass,

and I gave it up as out of place. Then I assumed an air
of frigid composure, and toyed with my watch-chain. But
a little girl screwed her eyes into me, and said, evidently,
in her mind: " That old gentleman is a fidget." Then I
leaned back gracefully, but something whispered:
" That's all right at home, Father Dan, but please remember that the convenances of society require a different posture;" and I sat bolt upright in a moment. My
eye caught in a blissful moment my new handsome umbrella that lay against my chair. I took it up and leaned
with dignity upon it; but the aforesaid little girl looked
at me, and looked at her mamma, and said—I know she
said in her own mind—" That old gentleman thinks it is
going to rain, and he wants to open his umbrella. Mamma, tell him that there is no danger of rain here." I
put down my umbrella. Then Miss Campion—God bless
her! she always comes to my relief—tore her little fingers along the keys in a grand finale, and then tripped
over to her old pastor, and said gaily:—

" Hurrah! Now, Father Dan, for the grand speech.
Won't you astonish these heretics? "

I believe I did astonish them. For, after a few preliminaries, I settled down coolly into a quiet, deliberate
talk; and I saw by degrees the stony stare melt away
into sunny smiles, and the sunny smiles broadened into
genteel laughter, and there was great clapping of hands,
and suppressed cheers, and altogether I felt that I held
them all in the palms of my hands. But that wicked
little girl in the front seats held out a long time. She
did not know whether to laugh or to cry. She blinked
her eyes at me, as if to be sure it was not a spectral
vision; then looked dreadfully alarmed; then consulted
her mother's face, now wreathed in smiles; and then,
when her brother was falling off the seat laughing, and
poking her with his stick, she condescended to relax her
awful stare, to smile, to look surprised at herself for
smiling—at last, to laugh. I knew then I had the victory, and I sang, *Io Triumphe!* in my own mind.

It is curious and interesting to notice how thoroughly these Protestant folk warm to a priest the moment they discover he is not quite an ogre. All these great people gathered round me; they were so delighted, etc.

" What's your name, my dear? " I said to the wicked little girl.

" Nonna! " she replied.

" By Jove! " I exclaimed, " St. Gregory's mother! "

" Naw," she said, " it's grandmaw's name."

" It's a pretty name all the same," I replied; " may you wear it as long as grandma."

The girls were all sitting at the machines waiting. Down near the end of the hall were two individuals in close conversation. They looked prosaic and dull amid all the excitement. When I got near them I saw the man, who was looking at me steadily, with one eye closed, whilst I was speaking. He was an infidel, a Giaour, an incredulous, questioning, calculating unbeliever in all my rosy forecastings. He was the manager over from Loughboro'. The lady was manageress, and had come over to superintend the initial proceedings at Kilronan. Somehow I didn't like them. They chilled the atmosphere. There was that cool, business-like air about them, that L. S. D. expression that shears off the rays of imagination, and measures and weighs everything by the same low standard. I saw Father Letheby buoyant, enthusiastic, not merely hopeful, but certain of the success of his enterprise. I saw those two business people chatting and consulting together, and I knew by their looks that they were not quite so sanguine. It was " the little rift within the lute."

As I went home, pondering and thinking—for I didn't wait for the tea and cake that are supposed to be essential to all these gatherings—I heard the patter of a light foot behind me, and in a minute Bittra was by my side.

" Dear me! " she panted, " you are so young and active, Father Dan, it is hard to keep up with you."

By which kind sarcasm I knew that Bittra had something good to tell me.

" Shall I call you Bittra or Beata? " I replied, looking down at her flushed face.

" Beata! Beata! Beatissima! " she said, in a kind of ecstasy; " it is all right; and God is *so* good! "

" I always object to the fireworks style of elocution on the part of my curate," I said, " and if you could shed a calm, lambent light on this ecstatic episode, it would suit my slow intellect."

" Slow," she said, stopping—" do you know, Father Dan, that is, you *do* know, that you have just made one of the nimblest, wittiest, drollest, most eloquent speeches that ever was made. I heard Mrs. S—— say that she never could have believed—— "

" Beata," I interrupted seriously, " my purgatory will be long enough, I believe. Indeed, if I get out in the general exodus on the Day of Judgment I shall consider myself happy. Where's the use in your adding to it, and making an old vain man so much vainer? Tell me about what is nearest to your heart to-day."

Thus soberized, she gave me a fairly consecutive account of what had happened. I say " fairly," because, of course, there were many exclamations, and notes of interrogation, and " asides," which I let pass without comment.

Ormsby had paid the suffering child a visit that morning, and had put his final theses and difficulties before her. Disbeliever in miracles, he was face to face with a miracle. That such an awful affliction as befell Alice should be accepted, not only with resignation, but with joy; that she would consider it a positive misfortune to be restored to her old beauty, and that she was for ever thanking God that He had elected her to suffering, was either of two things—insanity or inspiration. And her faith in the supernatural—her intense realization of the existence and the daily, hourly influence of our Lord and His Blessed Mother, and her profound conviction that

one day her physical shame and torment would intensify
her glory in Heaven—all this struck him as a revelation, before which the antics of spiritualists, and the fore-
knowledge of Brahmins, and the blank agnosticism of
science paled into contemptible insignificance.

Bittra, as usual, had been speaking to Mrs. Moylan
in the kitchen. Sitting on the straw chair, she spoke for
the hundredth time her words of consolation to the poor
mother. The murmur of voices came clear, but indi
stinct, from the little chamber of the sick girl. Then,
after a long conference, Ormsby came out, grave and collected as usual, and Bittra having said good-bye to the
mother, and kissed the leprous face of the sick girl, they
both walked on in silence, until they came to the bridge
that spanned the fiord near the " great house." Ormsby
leaned on the parapet of the bridge looking out over the
tumbling waters for a long time. Then, turning, he
said : —

" Bittra, I *must* become a Catholic."

Then Bittra put her hand in his gloved palm, and that
was all.

" And was that all? " I exclaimed incredulously.

" That's all," said Bittra, " and wasn't it enough? "

" That's not the way a novelist would wind up such a
delightful romance," I said. " There would have been
at least twenty or thirty pages of lurid description."

" Ah! but this is not a romance," said Bittra; " this
is stern reality."

And she tried ineffectually to frown.

" It only remains now," she continued, " that Rex
shall be instructed, and that won't take long; and then
received, and make his First Communion, and that won't
take long; and then—and then—— "

She paused. I was studying attentively a seagull that
was poised motionless over the heaving waters.

" Father Dan, you're becoming very unkind."

" Indeed? I was only waiting for the date and circumstances of the ' then.' "

" Well, you see, it can't be May; because the people have a foolish superstition about May; though I should *so* like to be—to be—married under our Lady's auspices. But the first day in June. Won't that be delightful? And it must be right under the statue of the Sacred Heart; and I shall put there such a mass of roses that day; and we shall both go to Holy Communion, and you'll say the nuptial Mass, Father Dan—— "

" I? "

" Yes, of course. Who else, I should like to know? "

" I thought you would be bringing down an Archbishop or even a Cardinal—— "

" Now, you're jesting as usual. I'll have no one but you—you—you—to marry me; and perhaps, if I were not asking too much, the choir might sing—— "

" Certainly! They *must*. But I won't promise you that wedding-march by that German fellow—— "

" Mendelssohn? "

" Yes. That's his name, I believe. Nor that other march of that other fellow, whom we see on the papers."

" I know. You mean the grand march in ' Lohengrin.' Why, Father Dan, what a musician you are! Who would ever think it? "

" Ah, my dear, I'm not understood at all. But I'll promise you one thing, my little child, such an ovation from the poor of Kilronan as will make the angels cry with envy."

Here Bittra was silent.

" One word more, Father Dan," she said, wiping away a happy tear, " I must be running back. Rex is waiting. But he doesn't speak enthusiastically about this sewing business. You know he has great experience of the world—— "

I nodded " Of course."

" And he has seen all kinds of things, and he is awfully shrewd and clever, and he knows people so well, and he understands business matters so thoroughly—— "

" Go on," I said, admiringly.

" Well," she continued, with a laugh, " he does not like this affair at all, nor the boat business at all. He's afraid that Father Letheby, for whom he has the greatest admiration, will become embarrassed in money matters, and that there will be trouble—— "

" Don't let this imaginary shadow darken your sunshine, Bittra. It will be all right. Trust Father Letheby. He is very far-seeing."

" Well, good-bye, Father Dan. Pray for me. And won't you go see our little saint, and tell her? I have no time to-day."

" Good-bye, and God bless you! " I said fervently.

It is these white souls that brighten the gray landscapes of life, and make death desirable; for shall we not meet their sisters and compeers in Heaven?

CHAPTER XXII

THE MAY CONFERENCE

My mail is not generally a heavy one, thank God! and when I do see a sheaf of letters on my table, I feel pretty certain that there is something unpleasant amongst them. I make it a rule, therefore, never to read a letter until breakfast is over; for I think we ought to take our food, as the Lord intended, with a calm mind. And I am not one of those ascetics whom every mouthful they swallow seems to choke. I take what God sends with a thankful heart, and bless Him for it. And sure it was well I followed this wholesome practice the following morning; for I do not think I ever lost my equanimity so thoroughly as when, on opening a circular, I saw a formal and extended and appalling syllabus of our Conferences for that year. Up to this, our Conferences had been conferences —informal conventions, where we met, talked over our little troubles, discussed a rubrical or theological question in an academic fashion, and listened with patience and edification to some young man, who nervously read for an hour or so some carefully prepared paper on a given subject. Then, if the Master of Conferences wanted to show how well read he was, he put a few questions here and there around the table. But if he was very persistent, and the chase became too hot, it was easy to draw a red herring across the track, the aforesaid red herring generally taking the shape of one of those venerable questions, which, like the trisection of an angle, or the quadrature of a circle, or the secret of perpetual motion, shall never be finally solved. The red herring that did us most service, and was now, after the lapse of forty years' discussion, a battered skeleton, was "whether invincible ignorance on the part of the penitent as to the reservation of a particular sin excused from the reservation, or whether faculties in every case were withdrawn from the confessor." I believe the question has been warmly debated in the schools; but there it remains, suspended, like the Prophet's coffin (I am afraid my metaphors are getting mixed), between heaven and earth.

But altogether these conferences were nice, pleasant occasions for meeting the brethren and exchanging ideas. What was my consternation this morning to read a series of new rules, as dogmatic as an Act of Parliament, which put an end for ever to the old order of things, and reduced our delightful meetings to a number of monthly examinations on Rubrics, Sacred Hermeneutics, Theology, and Ecclesiastical History. Our names were all to go into a hat, and the unfortunate prizeman was to be heckled and cross-examined by the chairman for ten minutes, like any ordinary Maynooth student at the Christmas and Easter examinations. Then came *the* Conference, after three or four poor fellows had been turned inside out. This was a paper to be read for three-quarters of an hour. Then came another cross-examination of that unhappy man; then a series of cross-questions, after we had all gone into the hat again. "And then," I said to myself with chagrin and disgust, "they will gather up all that remains of us from the floor and send us home for decent interment." Here is one little trifle, that would easily fill up a half-year's study in a theological seminary :—

PRO MENSE AUGUSTO.
(*Die I^{ma} Mensis.*)
1. Excerpta ex Statutis Dioecesanis et Nationalibus.
2. De Inspiratione Canonicorum Librorum.
3. Tractatus de Contractibus (Crolly).

"Good heavens," I exclaimed, as Father Letheby came in and read down the awful list in the second copy which I handed him, " imagine that! What in the world do bishops think? It is easy for them to be twirling their rings around their little fingers and studying the stones in their mitres. They have nothing else to do, as we all know, except the occasional day's amusement of knocking curates around, as you would pot balls on a billiard-table. But what consideration have they for us, poor hard-working missionary priests? What do they know about our heavy confessionals, our sick-calls, our catechising in the schools, our preparing for our sermons, our correspondence for our people, with Europe, Asia, Africa, America, and Oceanica, our—our—our—look at this! ' Excerpta ex Statutis ! ' That means reading over every blessed diocesan and national statute, that is, two ponderous volumes. Again, ' De Inspiratione '— the whole question of the Higher Criticism, volume after volume, Bull after Bull, articles in all the magazines, and the whole course of German exegetics. That's not enough! But here, as dessert, after junks of Rubrics, and indigestible slabs of controverted hermeneutics, come the light truffles and *pâté de foie gras* of Crolly's ' Contracts.' Begor, the next thing will be they'll want us to preach our sermons before them; and then this Master of Conferences—he's a good fellow and an old classmate of my own; but of course he must exhibit his learning, and bring in all his Christy minstrel conundrums, as if any fool couldn't ask questions that twenty wise men couldn't answer—and then he'll cock his head, like a duck under a shower, and look out of the window, and leave me stuck dead—— "

There was a quiet smile around Father Letheby's mouth during this philippic. Then he said, smoothing out the paper:—

" There is a little clause here at the end, which I think, Father Dan, just affects you."

" Affects me? If there is, it didn't catch my eye, Show it to me."

I took the paper, and there, sure enough, was a little paragraph:—

"6° The privilege, in virtue of which parish priests of a certain standing on the mission are exempted from the obligations of the Conference, will be continued."

I read that over three times to make quite sure of it, my curate looking down smilingly at me.

"If *you* are not of a certain standing, Father Dan, I'd like to know who is."

"True for you," I replied musingly. "I believe I am called the Patriarch of the Conference."

Visions of an old man, leaning back in his chair, whilst he was proof-protected against theological bullets, swam before me; and I began to feel like a man on a safe eminence, overlooking the battlefield, or a Spanish lady at a bull-fight.

"'Pon my word," I said, at length, "I'm beginning to think there is something in it, after all. The Holy Ghost has something to say to our good and holy prelates. There is no doubt there was a great waste of time at these Conferences, and young men got into idle habits and neglected their theology; and, you know, that's a serious matter. In fact, it reaches sometimes to a mortal sin. We must *all* study now. And you see how practical the bishop is. There's Rubrics. Now, there's no doubt at all that a good many of us don't respect the ceremonies of the Mass. Go to Lisdoonvarna, and every fellow appears to have his own idea of—"

"Pardon me, sir," said Father Letheby, "I cannot quite follow you there. I must say I never saw the Rubrics half so well carried out in England as here at home. In fact, this complaint appears to be one of these satires on racial characteristics that are only half true, and take all their force from traditional misrepresentations."

Isn't that fine language? You see, he's taking a leaf or two out of my book.

"Well, but you can't deny that this question of Scriptural exegesis is one of these dominant questions that must arrest the attention of all who are interested in ecclesiastical or hieratical studies," said I, trying to keep pace with him.

" Quite true," he said; " and yet I should like to see these new-fangled theories about Scriptural inspiration, plenary or otherwise, lifted from the shaking quagmires of conjecture on to the solid ground of demonstration."

" You cannot deny whatever," I replied, just before giving in, " that Crolly's ' Contracts ' is solid and well-reasoned and coherent argument; and look at its vast importance.   It touches every question of social and civil life—— "

" It is an excellent heliograph in sunny weather," he said; " but what about a muggy and misty day? "

" Well, God bless the bishop, whatever," I replied, throwing up the sponge; " if we haven't the ablest theologians, the smartest Master of Ceremonies, and the best Orientalists in Ireland, it won't be his fault.   Dear me, how far-seeing and practical he is! "

" But about his ring and his mitre, sir? " said my curate.   " You were pleased to make some observations a few minutes ago—— "

" That'll do now," I replied.   " My mare will be ready the morning of the Conference.   You'll drive, and we must be in time."

That was a pleasant drive.   May in Ireland!   What does it mean?   It means coming out of a dark tunnel into blinding sunshine; it means casting off the slough of winter, and gliding with crest erect and fresh habiliments under leafy trees and by the borders of shining seas, the crab-apple blossoms, pink and white, scenting the air over your head, and primroses and violets dappling the turf beneath your feet; it means lambs frisking around their tranquil mothers in the meadows, and children returning at evening with hands and pinafores full of the scented cowslip and the voluptuous woodbine; it means the pouring of wine-blood into empty veins, and the awakening of torpid faculties, and the deeper, stronger pulsations of the heart, and the fresh buoyancy of drooping and submerged spirits, and white clouds full of bird-music, as the larks call to their young and shake out the raptures of their full hearts, and the cheery salutations of the ploughmen, as the coulter turns over the rich, brown soil, and the rooks follow each furrow for food.

" A grand day, Mick! "

" Grand, your reverence, glory be to God! "

" Good weather for the spring work."

" Couldn't be better, your reverence."

We're out of hearing in a flash, for the little mare feels the springtime in her veins, and she covers the road at a spanking pace.

" You've thrown off twenty years of age, to-day, Father Dan," said Father Letheby, as he looked admiringly at his old pastor, then turned swiftly to his duty, and shook out the ribbons, and then drew them together firmly, and the little animal knew that a firm hand held her, and there was no fear.

" No wonder, my boy," I cried; " look at that! " And I pointed to the *anerithmon gelasma* of old Æschylus; but what was his Ægean or even his Mare Magnum to the free and unfettered Atlantic? Oh! it was grand, grand! What do I care about your Riviera, and your feeble, languid Mediterranean? Give me our lofty cliffs, sun-scorched, storm-beaten, scarred and seamed by a thousand years of gloom and battle; and at their feet, firm-planted, the boundless infinity of the Atlantic!

We were in time, and I was snugly ensconced in my old corner up near the bishop's chair before the priests began to throng in. Now, I'd like to know this. If an old gentleman, not hitherto very remarkable for dandyism, chooses to brush his white, silvered hair over his coat-collar, and has put on a spotless suit of black cloth, and sports his gold chain and seals conspicuously, and wears his spectacles easily, and drops them in a genteel manner on the silk ribbon that is suspended around his neck; and if he is altogether neat and spruce, as becomes

an ecclesiastic of some standing in his diocese, is that a
reason why he should be stared at, and why men should
put their hands in their pockets and whistle, and why
rather perky young fellows should cry " Hallo! " and
whisper, " Who's the stranger? " And even why the
bishop, when he came in, and we all stood up, should
smile with a lot of meaning when I kissed his sapphire
ring and told him how well he looked?

" And I can reciprocate the compliment, Father Dan,"
his Lordship said; " I never saw you look better. All
these vast changes and improvements that you are making at Kilronan seem to have quite rejuvenated you."

Father Letheby, at the end of the table, looked as
demure as a nun.

" I must congratulate your Lordship also," I said, "on
these radical changes your Lordship has made in the constitution of our Conference. It is quite clear that your
Lordship means to give full scope to the budding talent
of the diocese."

A groan of dissent ran round the table.

" I'm afraid you must give up your Greek studies,
Father Dan," said the bishop; " you'll have barely time
now to master the subject-matter of the Conference."

" That's true, my Lord, indeed," I replied, " it would
take twenty hours out of the twenty-four, and seven days
out of every week to meet all these demands, at least for
a valetudinarian (' Oh! Oh! ' from the table). But your
Lordship, with your usual consideration, has taken into
account the nimble intellects of these clever young
men, and exempted the slow-moving, incomprehensive
minds of poor old parish priests like myself." (" No!
No!! No!!! " from the table).

" Now, now," said the Master of Conferences, a thin,
tall, high cheek-boned, deep-browed, eagle-eyed priest,
whom I have already introduced as " a great theologian,"
" this won't do at all. We're drifting into the old ways
again. I mustn't have any desultory conversation, but

proceed at once to business. Now, my Lord, would you
kindly draw a name? ''

"Put in Father Dan! Put in Father Dan!" came
from the table.

The bishop smilingly drew up number four; and the
chairman called upon Father Michael Delany.

Father Michael squirmed and twisted in his seat. He
was a very holy man, but a little peppery.

"Now, Father Michael," said the chairman blandly,
"we'll take the Rubrics first. Let me see. Well, what
do you do with your hands during the celebration of the
Holy Sacrifice? ''

"What do I do with my hands? " said Father Michael
sullenly.

"Yes; what do you do—do—with your hands? ''

"That's a queer question," said Father Michael. "I
suppose I keep them on me."

"Of course. But I mean what motions—or shall we
call them gestures?—do you use? ''

"What motions? ''

"Yes. Well, I'll put it this way. There's an admirable book by an American priest, Father Wapelhorst, on
the Ceremonies. Now, he wisely tells us in the end of
the book what things to avoid. Could you tell me what
to avoid—what *not* to do in this matter? ''

"Don't you know, Father Michael? " said a sympathetic friend; " go on. *Elevans et extendens——* ''

"Young man," said Father Michael, " thank you for
your information, but I can manage my own business.
What's this you were saying? " he cried, turning to the
Master of Conferences.

"What mistakes might a priest make with his hands
during celebration? ''

"What mistakes? Well, he might put them in his
pocket or behind his back, or—— ''

"Never mind, never mind. One question more. If
you wore a pileolus, zucchetto, you know, at what part
of the Mass would you remove it? ''

" I wouldn't wear anything of the kind,". said Father Michael; " the five vestments are enough for me, without any new-fangled things from Valladolid or Salamanca."

The chairman had graduated at Salamanca.

" My Lord," I interposed charitably, " I don't want to interfere with this interesting examination, but my sense of classical perfection and propriety is offended by this word in the syllabus of to-day's Conference. There is no such word in the Latin language as ' Primigeniis '— ' De Primigeniis textibus Sacræ Scripturæ——' "

" Now, Father Dan, this won't do," shouted the chairman. " I see what you're up to. There must be no interruptions here. Very good, Father Michael, very good indeed ! Now, we'll take another. Father Dan, if you interrupt again, I'll put you into the hat. Well, number eighteen ! Let me see. Ah, yes. Father Irwin ! "

Poor Father Michael looked unhappy and discomfited. It is a funny paradox that that good and holy priest, who, his parishioners declared, " said Mass like an angel," so that not one of his congregation could read a line of their prayer-books, so absorbed were they in watching him, couldn't explain *in totidem verbis* the Rubrics he was daily and accurately practising.

Which, perhaps, exemplifies a maxim of the Chinese philosopher :—

" One who talks does not know.
One who knows does not talk.
Therefore the sage keeps his mouth shut,
And his sense-gates closed."

Before Father Irwin was questioned, however, there was a delightful interlude.

Someone asked whether it was lawful for anyone, not a bishop, to wear a zucchetto during the celebration of Mass. As usual, there was a pleasant diversity of opinion, some contending that the privilege was reserved to the episcopate, inasmuch as the great rubricists only contemplated bishops in laying down the rules for the removal and assumption of the zucchetto; others again maintained that any priest might wear one; and others limited the honour to regulars, who habitually wore the tonsure. The chairman, however, stopped the discussion peremptorily, and again asked (this time a very aged priest) the question he had put to Father Delany. The old man answered promptly:—

" The zucchetto, or pileolus, is removed at the end of the last secret prayer, and resumed after the ablutions."

" Quite right," said the chairman.

" By the way," said the old man, " you pronounce that word pileōlus. The word is pileŏlus."

" The word is pileōlus," said the chairman, whose throne wasn't exactly lined with velvet this day.

" Pardon me. The word is pileŏlus. You find it as such in the scansions of Horace."

" This is your province, Father Dan," said the bishop. " There's no one in the diocese so well qualified to adjudicate here—— "

" ' Vixere fortes ante Agamemnona
Multi— '

my Lord! " said I. I was drawing the bishop out. " There were ironical cheers at ' Agamemnona.' "

" ' Mutato nomine, de te
Fabula narratur,' "

said the bishop, smiling. " Of course, we have many a rich depository of classical lore here,

' At suave est ex magno tollere acervo.' "

" My Lord," said I, pointing around the table,

" ' Omnes hi metuunt versus, odere poetas,' "—

(" Oh! Oh! Oh! " from the Conference.)

" ' Nec recito cuiquam nisi amicis, idque coactus
Non ubivis coramve quibuslibet.' "

Here the Master of Conference, seeing that the bishop
was getting the worst of it, though his Lordship is a profound scholar, broke in :—

" ' Ohe!
Jam satis est! Dum æs exigitur, dum mula ligatur,
Tota abit hora.' "

He looked at me significantly when he said, " dum
mula ligatur," but I had the victory, and I didn't mind.

" Now, look here, Father Dan, you're simply intolerable. The Conference can't get along so long as you are
here. You are for ever intruding your classics when we
want theology."

" I call his Lordship and the Conference to witness,"
I said, " that I did not originate this discussion.   In
fact, I passed over in charitable silence the chairman's
gross mispronunciation of an ordinary classical word,
although I suffered the tortures of Nessus by my for-
bearance—— "

" There will be no end to this, my Lord," said the
chairman.   " That'll do, Father Dan.   Now, Father
Irwin."

I was silent, but I winked softly at myself.

CHAPTER XXIII

A BATTLE OF GIANTS

" Now, Father Irwin," said the chairman, addressing a smart, keen-looking young priest who sat at the end of the table, " you have just come back to us from Australia; of course, everything is perfect there. What do you think—are the particles in a ciborium, left by inadvertence, outside the corporal during consecration consecrated? Now, just reflect for a moment, for it is an important matter."

" Unquestionably they are," said the young priest confidently.

" They are *not*," replied the chairman. " The whole consensus of theologians is against you."

" For example? " said Father Irwin coolly.

" Wha-at? " said the chairman, taken quite aback.

" I doubt if all theologians are on your side," said Father Irwin. " Would you be pleased to name a few?"

" Certainly," said the chairman, with a pitying smile at this young man's presumption. " What do you think of Benedict XIV., Suarez, and St. Alphonsus? "

The young man didn't seem to be much crushed under the avalanche.

" They held that there should be reconsecration? "

" Certainly."

" Let me see. Do I understand you aright? The celebrant intends from the beginning to consecrate those particles? "

" Yes."

" The intention perseveres to the moment of consecration? "

" Yes! "

" And, the *materia* being quite right, he intends to consecrate that objective, that just lies inadvertently outside the corporal? "

" Quite so."

" And you say that Benedict XIV., Suarez, and St. Alphonsus maintain the necessity of reconsecration? "

" Yes."

" Then I pity Benedict XIV., Suarez, and St. Alphonsus."

There was consternation. The bishop looked grave. The old men gaped in surprise and horror. The young men held down their heads and smiled.

" I consider that a highly improper remark, as applied to the very leading lights of theological science," said the chairman, with a frown. And when the chairman frowned it was not pleasant. The bishop's face, too, was growing tight and stern.

" Perhaps I should modify it," said the young priest airily. " Perhaps I should have rather said that modern theologians and right reason are dead against such an opinion."

" Quote one modern theologian that is opposed to the common and universal teaching of theologians on the matter! "

" Well, Ballerini, for example, and the Salmanticenses—— "

" Psha! Ballerini. Ballerini is to upset everything, I suppose? "

" Ballerini has the Missal and common sense on his side."

" The Missal? "

" Yes. Read this—or shall I read it?

" ' Quidquid horum deficit, scilicet materia debita, forma cum intentione, et ordo sacerdotalis, non conficitur Sacramentum; et his existentibus, quibuscunque aliis deficientibus, veritas adest Sacramenti.' "

" Quite so. The whole point turns on the words *cum intentione.* The Church forbids, under pain of mortal sin, to consecrate outside the corporal; consequently, the priest cannot be presumed to have the intention of committing a *grave* just at the moment of consecration; and, therefore, he cannot be supposed to have the intention of consecrating."

" Pardon me, if I say, sir," replied the young priest, " that that is the weakest and most fallacious argument I ever heard advanced. That reasoning supposes the totally inadmissible principle that there never is a valid consecration when, inadvertently, the priest forgets some Rubric that is binding under pain of mortal sin. If, for example, the priest used fermented bread, if the corporal weren't blessed, in which case the chalice and paten would be outside the corporal, as well as the ciborium; if the chalice itself weren't consecrated, there would be no sacrifice and no consecration. Besides, if you once commence interpreting intention in this manner, you should hold that if the ciborium were covered on the corporal, there would be no consecration—— "

" That's only a venial sin," said the chairman.

" A priest, when celebrating," said Father Irwin sweetly, " is no more supposed to commit a venial than a mortal sin. Besides—— "

" I'm afraid our time is running short," said the bishop; " I'll remember your arguments, which are very ingenious, Father Irwin. But, as the chairman says, the *consensus* is against you. Now, for the main Conference, *de textibus Sacræ Scripturæ.*"

" Father Duff will read his paper, my Lord, and then we'll discuss it."

" Very good. Now, Father Duff! "

Father Duff was another representation of the new dis-

pensation, with a clear-cut, smooth-shaven face, large
blue-black eyes, which, however, were not able to fulfil
their duties, for, as he took out a large roll of manuscript
from his pocket, he placed a gold-rimmed *pince-nez* to
his eyes, and looking calmly around, he began to read in
a slow, rhythmic voice. It was a wonderful voice, too,
for its soft, purring, murmurous intonation began to have
a curious effect on the brethren. One by one they began
to be seized by its hypnotic influence, and to yield to its
soft, soporific magic, until, to my horror and disgust, they
bowed their heads on their breasts, and calmly slept.
Even the Master of Conference, and the bishop himself,
gently yielded, after a severe struggle. " I shall have it
all to myself," I said, " and if I don't profit much by its
historical aspects, I shall at least get a few big rocks of
words, unusual or obsolete, to fling at my curate." And
so I did. Codex Alexandrinus, and Codex Sinaiticus,
and Codex Bezæ, and Codex Vaticanus rang through my
bewildered brain. Then I have a vague recollection that
he actually laughed at the idea of six literal days of creation, which made an old priest, out of his dreams, turn
over to me and whisper : " He's an infidel "; then, again,
he ridiculed the idea of the recognized authorship of the
Pentateuch ; spoke of Chaldean and Babylonian interpolations ; knocked on the head the Davidical origin of the
Psalms ; made the Book of Daniel half-apocryphal ; introduced the Book of Job, as a piece of Arabian poetry, like
the songs of some man called Hafiz ; talked about Johan-
nine Gospels and Pauline Epistles ; and, altogether, left
us to think that, by something called Ritschlian inter-
pretations, the whole Bible was knocked into a cocked
hat. Then he began to build up what he had thrown
down ; and on he went, in his rhythmical, musical way,
when just as he declared that " the basal document on
which everything is founded is the ur-evangelium, which
is the underlying cryptic element of the Synoptic Gospels "—just as he reached that point, and was going on
about Tatian's " Diatessaron," a deep stertorous sound,

like the trumpeting of an elephant, reverberated through
the conference room. They all woke up, smiling at me,
and as they did not seem inclined to apologize to Father
Duff for their misbehaviour, I said gravely and most
angrily : —

" My Lord, I think the Conference should be a little
less unconscious of the grave discourtesy done to one of
the most able and erudite papers that I have ever heard
here—— "

There was a shout of irreverent laughter, in which,
I am sorry to say, the bishop joined. At least, I saw his
Lordship taking out a silk handkerchief and wiping his
eyes.

" I propose now, my Lord, as an *amende* to the most
cultured and distinguished young priest, that that valuable paper be sent, with your Lordship's approbation, to
some ecclesiastical journal in Ireland or America. Its
appearance in permanent print may give these young
men some idea of the contents of the document, the
main features of which they have lost by yielding, I
think too easily, to the seductions of ill-timed sleep—— "

Here there was another yell of laughter, that sounded
to my ears ill-placed and discourteous; but the chairman
again interposed : —

" Now, Father Duff, if you are not too highly flattered
by the encomiums of Father Dan, who was your most
attentive and admiring listener, I should like to ask you
a few questions on the subject-matter of your paper."

" Surely," I declared, " you are not going to attack
such a stronghold? Besides, the time is up."

" There is a full hour yet, Father Dan," said the
bishop, consulting his watch; " but you won't mind it,
you are able to pass your time so agreeably."

I did not grasp his Lordship's meaning; but I never do
try to penetrate into mysteries. What's that the Scripture says? " The searcher after majesty will be over-
whelmed with glory."

But the little skirmishes that had taken place before

the paper was read were nothing to the artillery-duel that was now in progress.

" With regard to the Septuagint," said the chairman, " I think you made a statement about the history of its compilation that will hardly bear a test. You are aware, of course, that Justin, Martyr and Apologist, declares that he saw, with his own eyes, the cells where the Seventy were interned by order, or at the request, of Ptolemy Philadelphus. How, then, can the letter of Aristeas be regarded as apocryphal? "

" Well, it does not follow that the whole letter is authentic merely because a clause is verified. Secondly, that statement imputed to Justin may be also apocryphal."

" Do you consider the names of the seventy-two elders also unauthentic? "

" Quite so.."

" And altogether you would regard the Septuagint as a rather doubtful version of the Ancient Law? "

" I'd only accept it so far as it agrees with the Vulgate and Codices."

" But you're aware it was in common use amongst cultivated Jews years before the coming of our Lord; in fact, it may be regarded as a providential means of preparing the way of the Lord for the Jews of Greece and Alexandria."

" That proves nothing."

" It proves this. It is well known that the Hebrews were scrupulously exact about every title and letter, and even vowel-point—— "

" I beg your pardon, sir; the Hebrews before Christ didn't use vowel-points."

" That's a strong assertion," said the chairman, reddening.

" It is true. I appeal to his Lordship," said Father Duff.

" Well," said the bishop diplomatically, " that appears

to be the received opinion; but the whole thing is wrapped up in the mists and the twilight of history."

I thought that admirable.

" To pass away from that subject," said the chairman, now somewhat nervous and alarmed, " I think you made statements, or rather laid down a principle, that Catholics can hardly accept."

Father Duff waited.

" It was to the effect that in studying the history of the Bible, as well as in interpreting its meaning, we must take into account the discoveries and the deductions of modern science."

" Quite so."

" In other words, we are to adopt the conclusions of German rationalistic schools, and set aside completely the supernatural elements in the Bible."

" Pardon me; I hardly think that deduction quite legitimate. There are two schools of thought in the Church on this question: the one maintains with Dr. Kaulen, of Bonn, that the conclusions of modern criticism are so certainly erroneous that young students should not notice them at all. The other holds that we must read our Bibles by the light of modern interpretation. The official Encyclical of the present Pope Leo XIII. (' Providentissimus Deus ') should have closed the controversy; but men are tenacious of their opinions, and both schools in Germany utilize the Encyclical for their own ends. Professor Aurelian Schöpfer, of the Brixen, at once published his book (' Bible and Science '), in which he maintained that the teaching of the natural sciences may be used by Catholics not only to confirm Biblical statements, but to interpret them. As I have said, he was opposed by Kaulen, of Bonn. There was a second duel between Schantz of Tübingen, and Scholz of Würzburg. The former insisted that no new principle of Biblical interpretation has been introduced by the Encyclical; the latter that the principle of scientific investigation was recognized, and was to be applied. Now, a Protestant, König of Rostock, was interested in this Catholic controversy, and collected seventy reviews of Schöpfer's work by leading scholars in Germany, Austria, France, Ireland, America; and he found that five-sixths endorse the position of the author—— ''

'' You might add, Father Duff,'' said my curate, who was an interested listener to the whole argument, and who had been hitherto silent, '' that these reviewers found fault with Schöpfer for ignoring the *consensus patrum*, and for decidedly naturalistic tendencies.''

The whole Conference woke up at this new interlude. The chairman looked grateful; the bishop leaned forward.

'' But the ' Civiltà Cattolica,' '' said Father Duff, '' which we may regard as official, says, in its review of the same book: ' Biblical history cannot be any longer stated except in agreement with the true and correct teaching of the Bible and the reasonable conclusions of the natural sciences.' ''

'' Quite so,'' said Father Letheby, '' that applies to the certain discoveries of geology and astronomy. But surely you don't maintain that philology, which only affects us just now, is an exact science.''

'' Just as exact as the other sciences you have mentioned.''

'' That is, as exact as a mathematical demonstration?''

'' Quite so.''

'' Come now,'' said my curate, like a fellow that was sure of himself, '' that's going too far.''

'' Not at all,'' said Father Duff; '' I maintain that the evidence of history on the one hand, and the external evidence of monuments on the other, combined with the internal evidence of Scriptural idiomatisms of time and place, are equivalent to a mathematical demonstration.''

'' You'll admit, I suppose,'' said Father Letheby, ''that languages change their structures and meanings very often? ''

'' Certainly.''

" The English of Shakespeare is not ours."

" Quite so."

" Even words have come to have exactly antithetical meanings, even in a lapse of three hundred years."

" Very good."

" And it is said that, owing to accretions, the language we speak will be unintelligible in a hundred years' time."

" Possibly."

" Now, would you not say that a contemporary of Shakespeare's would be a better judge of his poetry and its allusive and natural meaning than ever so learned a linguist, after an interval of change? "

" Well, I should say so. I don't know where you are drifting."

" What is the reason that we never heard of these ' internal evidences,' these ' historical coincidences,' these ' exclusive idioms,' from Origen or Dionysius, or from Jerome or Augustine, from any one of the Fathers, who held what we hold, and what the Church has always taught, about the authorship of the Sacred Books, and to whom Hebrew and Greek were vernacular? "

" But, my dear sir, there are evident interpolations even in the Gospels. Do you really mean to tell me that that canticle of the *Magnificat* was uttered by a young Hebrew girl on Hebron, and was not rather the deliberate poetical conception of the author of St. Luke's Gospel?"

I jumped from my seat; but I needn't have done so. I saw by the whitening under my curate's eyes, and the impression of his lips, and his eyes glowing like coal, that our dear little Queen's honour was safe in his hands. Father Duff couldn't have stumbled on a more unhappy example for himself. Father Letheby placed his elbows on the table and, leaning forward, he said in a low, tremulous voice:

" You may be very learned, Father, and I believe you are; but for all the learning stored up in those German universities, which you so much admire, I would not

think as you appear to think on this sacred subject. If
anything could show the tendency of modern interpreta-
tions of the Holy Scriptures, it would be the painful and
almost blasphemous opinion to which you have just given
expression. It is the complete elimination of the supernatural, the absolute denial of Inspiration. If the *Magnificat* is not an inspired utterance, I should like to know
what is."

There was a painful silence for a few seconds, during
which I could hear the ticking of my watch. Then the
Master of Conference arose, and, kneeling, said 'the
Actiones nostras. We were all gathering up our books
and papers to disperse, when the Bishop said:—

" Gentlemen, the annual procession in honour of our
Blessed Lady will be held in the Cathedral and College
grounds on the evening of May the 31st. I shall be glad
to see there as many of you as can attend. Dinner at
four; rosary and sermon at seven o'clock. Father Letheby, would you do me the favour of preaching for us on
that occasion? "

Father Letheby blushed an affirmative; and then the
bishop, with delightful tact, turned to the humbled and
almost effaced Father Duff, and said:—

" Father Duff, leave me that paper; I think I'll adopt
the admirable suggestion of our friend, Father Dan."

Some of the young fellows, wits and wags as they
were, circulated through the diocese the report that I
tried to kiss the bishop. Now, there is not a word of
truth in that—and for excellent reasons. First, because
like Zacchæus, I am short of stature; and the bishop—
God bless him!—is a fine, portly man. Secondly, because I have an innate and congenital dread of that little
square of purple under his Lordship's chin. I'm sure
I don't know why, but it always gives me the shivers.
I'm told that they are allowing some new class of people
called " Monsignori," and even some little canons, to
assume the distinctive colour of the episcopate. 'Tis a
great mistake. Our Fathers in God should have their

own peculiar colours, as they have their own peculiar and tremendous responsibilities. But I'll tell you what I did. I kissed the bishop's ring, and I think I left a deep indentation on his Lordship's little finger.

The Master of Conference detained me.

" I'm beginning to like that young fellow of yours," he said. " He appears to have more piety than learning."

" He has both," I replied.

" So he has, so he has, indeed. What are we coming to? What are we coming to, at all? "

" Then I suppose," I said, " I needn't mind that bell? "

" What bell? "

" The bell that I was to tie around his neck."

" Father Dan, you have too long a memory; good-bye! I'm glad you've not that infidel, Duff, as curate."

We went home at a rapid pace, my curate and I, both too filled with thought to speak much. At last, I said, shaking up :—

" I'm beginning to think that I, too, took forty winks during the reading of that paper."

" I think about forty minutes of winks, Father Dan," he replied. " You slept steadily for forty minutes out of the forty-five."

" That's a calumnious exaggeration," I said; " don't I remember all about Job, and Daniel, and the synoptic Gospels."

" These were a few preliminaries," replied my curate.

" But who was that undignified and ungentlemanly fellow that woke us all with such a snore? I suppose it was Delaney? "

" No; it was not Delaney. He was too agitated after his rencontre with the chairman to fall asleep."

" Indeed? Perhaps it would be as well for me not to pursue the subject further. This will be a great sermon of yours."

" I'm very nervous about it," he said, shaking the reins. " It is not the sermon I mind, but all the dislike and jealousy and rancour it will cause."

" You can avoid all that," I replied.

" How? "

" Break down hopelessly and they'll all love you. That is the only road to popularity—to make a fool of yourself."

" I did that to-day," he said. " I made a most determined cast-iron resolution not to open my lips unless I was interrogated, but I could not stand that perkiness and self-sufficiency of Duff, especially when it developed into irreverence."

" If you had not spoken I should have challenged him; and I am not sure I would have been so polite as you were. The thing was unpardonable."

We dined at Father Letheby's. Just after dinner there was a timid knock at the door. He went out, and returned in a few minutes looking despondent and angry. I had heard the words from the hall:—

" She must give it up, your reverence. Her little chest is all falling in, and she's as white as a corpse."

" One of the girls giving up work at the machines," he replied. " She's suffering from chest trouble, it appears, from bending over this work."

" Who is she? " I queried.

" Minnie Carmody—that tall girl who sat near the door."

" H'm," I said. " I think it would be nearer the truth to say that Minnie Carmody's delicacy comes from the vinegar bottle and white paper. She was ashamed of her red face, and this is the latest recommendation of the novelette to banish roses, and leave the lilies of anæmia and consumption."

" It augurs badly, however," he replied. " The factory is not open quite a month yet."

CHAPTER XXIV

THE SERMON

I AM quite sure that sermon cost me more anxiety and
trouble than Father Letheby suffered. I was deeply interested in its success, of course. But that was not the
point. I am probably the feeblest and worst preacher in
my diocese. This gives me the indefeasible right to dog-
matize about preaching. Just as failures in literary attempts are the credentials of a great critic, so writers on
sermons can claim the high authority and ambassador-
ship to dictate to the world, on the grounds that they are
incapable of producing even a catechetical discourse. But
they fall back upon that universal and indisputable privilege of our race—the belief in their own infallibility. It
often surprised me that the definition of Papal Infallibility, which concentrated in the Vicegerent of the Most
High the reputed privilege of our race, did not create a
greater outcry. It was the final onslaught of the Holy
Spirit on the unspeakable vanity of the race. It was the
death-blow to private judgment. At least, it ought to
have been. But, alas! human vanity and presumption
are eternal and indestructible. From the corner-boy here
at my window, who asks indignantly, " Why the deuce
did not Gladstone push his Bill through the House of
Lords, and then force the Commons to accept it? " to the
flushed statesman, whose dream is Imperialism; from the
little manikin critic, who swells out his chest, and demands summary vengeance on that idiot of an author
who has had the daring presumption to write a book on
the Greek accent, or binary stars, up to the *Jupiter*

I

Tonans of the world-wide circulating journal, which dictates to the universe, it is all the same. Each from his own little pedestal—it may be the shuffling stilts of three feet high, or it may be the lofty security of the Vendôme column—shrieks out his little opinion, and demands the silence or assent of the universe. Would that our modern Stylites, like to those of old, might, from their eminences, preach their own nothingness! Would that, like the Muezzins of Islam, they might climb the minarets of publicity and fame, only to call the world to praise and prayer!

But I, sharing the weaknesses, and, therefore, the privileges of a common humanity, claim the right to the luxury of preaching, which comes nearest to that of criticising, and is only in the third degree of inferiority from that supreme pleasure that is involved in *I told you so*.

And so, here by the western seas, where the homeless Atlantic finds a home, do I, a simple, rural priest, venture to homilize and philosophize on that great human gift of talk. Imagine me, then, on one of those soft May evenings, after our devotions in my little chapel, and with the children's hymns ringing in my ears, and having taken one pinch of snuff, and with another poised in my fingers, philosophizing thus:—

" I think—that is, I am sure—that the worst advices I ever heard given in my life were these:—

" ON PREACHING.—Try to be simple; and never aim at eloquence.

" ON MEDITATION.—Keep your fingers in your Breviary, and think over the lessons of the Second Nocturn.

" And they are evil counsels, not *per se*, but *per accidens;* and for precisely similar reasons. They took no account of the tendency of human nature to relax and seek its ease. When the gray-haired counsellor said, ' Be simple,' he said, ' Be bald and vulgar.' For the young men who listened aimed at simplicity, and therefore naturally argued, the simpler the better; in fact, the

conversational style is best of all. Where, then, the need
for elaborate preparation? We shall only vex and con-
fuse the people, consequently preparation is superfluous.
We know the results. ' A few words ' on the schools;
an *obiter dictum* on the stations; a good, energetic, Demo-
sthenic philippic against some scandal. But instruction
—oh, no! edification—oh, no! That means preparation;
and if we prepare, we talk over the people's heads, and
we are ' sounding brasses and tinkling cymbals.' "

" But surely, sir, you wouldn't advise young men to
study the eloquence of Massillon, or Bourdaloue, or Lacordaire? That would be talking over their heads with
a vengeance."

" Do you think so? " I said. " Now, listen, young
man. Which is, you or I, the elder? I am. All right.
Now, my experience is that it is not the language, however eloquent, the people fail to follow, but the ideas, and
they fail to follow the ideas because they are ill-instructed
in their religion. Of course, I'm involved in the censure
myself as well as others. But I proved this satisfactorily
to myself long ago. We were in the habit of ' reading a
book ' at the Lenten exercises in the last town wherein
I officiated as curate. Now, the people hate that above
all things else. They'd rather hear one word from a
stuttering idiot than the highest ascetical teaching out
of a book. Nevertheless, we tried it; and we tried the
simplest and easiest books we could find. No use. They
couldn't follow one paragraph with intelligence. One
evening I read for them—it was in Passion week—the last
discourse of our Lord to His disciples—words that I
could never read without breaking down. I assure you,
they failed to grasp the meaning, not to speak of the
pathos and divine beauty, of those awful words. They
told me so."

" Do you mean then to conclude that we, young
priests, should go in for high, flowery diction, long
phrases, etc.? I could hardly imagine any man, least of
all you, sir, holding such a theory! "

" You're running away with the question, my boy. The eloquence that I recommend is the eloquence of fine taste, which positively excludes all the ornaments which you speak of."

" By Jove, we don't know where to turn," said my curate. " I never ventured, during my late English experience of seven years, to stand in the pulpit and address the congregation, without writing every word and committing it to memory. I daren't do otherwise; for if I made a mistake, fifty chances to one, some Methodist or Socinian would call at the presbytery next morning and challenge me to deadly combat."

" And why should you give up that excellent habit here," I said, " and go on the *dabitur vobis*? "

" Because you may conjecture easily that I shall be talking over their heads."

" Better talk over their heads, young man, than under their feet. And under their feet, believe me, metaphorically, they trample the priest who does not uphold the dignity of his sacred office of preacher. ' Come down to the level of the people! ' May God forgive the fools who utter this banality! Instead of saying to the people : ' Come up to the level of your priests, and be educated and refined,' they say : ' Go down to the people's level.' As if any priest ever went down in language or habit to the people's level who didn't go considerably below it."

" 'Pon my word, Father Dan," said Father Letheby, " if I did not know you so well, I would think you were talking nonsense."

" Hear a little more nonsense! " I said. " I say now that our people like fine, sonorous language from the altar; and they comprehend it! Try them next Sunday with a passage from Lacordaire, and you'll see what I mean. Try that noble passage, ' Il y a un homme, dont l'amour garde la tombe '—' There is a man whose tomb is guarded by love —and see if they'll understand you. Why, my dear fellow, fifty years ago, when the people were a classical people, taught only their Homers and Virgils by the side of the ditch, they could roll out passage after passage from their favourite preachers, and enjoy them and appreciate them. It was only a few days since, I was speaking on the subject to a dear old friend, who, after the lapse of fifty years, quoted a passage on Hell that he had heard almost as a child: ' If we allowed our imagination, my dear brethren, to dwell persistently on this terrific truth, Reason itself would totter on its throne.' But the people of to-day cannot quote, because they cannot get the opportunity. The race of preachers is dead.''

I shut him up, and gave myself time to breathe.

'' Would you say then, sir,'' he said meekly, '' that I should continue my habit of writing out verbatim my sermons, and then commit them to memory? ''

'' Certainly not,'' I replied, '' unless you find it necessary to maintain the high level on which all our utterances should be placed. And if now, after the practice of seven years, you cannot command your language, you never will. But here is my advice to you, and, as you are a friend, I shall charge nothing for it, but I make it copyright throughout the universe:—

    I. STUDY.

    II. PREACH NOT YOURSELF, BUT GOD.

    III. LIVE UP TO YOUR PREACHING.

That's all.''

He appeared thoughtful and dissatisfied. I had to explain.

'' A well-filled mind never wants words. Read, and read, and read; but read, above all, the Holy Scriptures. Never put down your Breviary, but to take up your Bible. Saturate yourself with its words and its spirit. All the best things that are to be found in modern literature are simple paraphrases of Holy Writ. And interweave all your sentences with the Sacred Text. All the temporal prosperity of England comes from the use of the Bible, all its spiritual raggedness and nakedness from its misuse. They made it a fetish. And their commentators are proving, or rather trying to prove, that it is only a little wax and pasteboard—only the literature of an obscure and subjugated race. But, even as literature, it has had a tremendous influence in forming the masculinity of the British character. They are now giving up the Bible and the Sabbath. And the *débâcle* is at hand. But I often thought we would have a more robust piety, a tenderer devotion, a deeper reverence, if we used the Sacred Scriptures more freely. And our people love the Sacred Writing. A text will hang around them, like a perfume, when all the rest of our preaching is forgotten. Why, look at myself. Forty years ago I attended a certain Retreat. I forget the very name of the Jesuit who conducted it; but I remember his texts, and they were well chosen:—

' I have seen a terrible thing upon the earth: a slave upon horseback, and kings walking in the mire.'
' You have taken my gold and silver, and made idols unto yourselves.'
' If I am a father, where is my honour? '
' If I am a master, where is my fear? '

I have made hundreds of meditations on these words, and preached them many a time. Then, again, our people are naturally poetic; the poetry has been crushed out of their natures by modern education. Yet they relish a fine line or expression. And again, their own language is full of aphorisms, bitter and stinging enough, we know, but sometimes exquisite as befits a nation whose forefathers lived in tents of skins. Now give them a few of the thousand proverbs of Solomon, and they will chew them as a cow chews the cud. But I should go on with this subject for ever."

" But what about the use of sarcasm, sir? Your allusions to the Gaelic sarcasms reminded me of it. I often heard people say that our congregations dread nothing so much as sarcasm."

" I'm glad you reminded me of it. I can speak on the matter like a professor, for I was past-master in the

science. I had a bitter tongue. How deeply I regret it,
God only knows. I have often made an awful fool of
myself at conferences, at public meetings, etc.; I have
often done silly and puerile things, what the French call
bêtises; I think of them without shame. But the sharp,
acrid things I have said, and the few harsh things I have
done, fill me with confusion. There's the benefit of a
diary. It is an examination of conscience. I remember
once at a station, a rather mean fellow flung a florin on
a heap of silver before me. He should have paid a half-
crown. I called his attention to it. He denied it. It
was the second or third time he had tried that little
game. I thought the time had come for a gentle remon-
strance. I said nothing till the people were about to
disperse. Then I said I had a story to tell them. It was
about three mean men. One was an employer of labour
in America, who was so hard on his men that when his
factory blew up he docked them, or rather their widows,
of the time they spent foolishly up in the sky. There
was a titter. The second was a fellow here at home, who
stole the pennies out of the eyes of a corpse. There was
a roar. ' The third, the meanest of the three, I leave
yourselves to discover. He isn't far away.' The bolt
went home, and he and his family suffered. He never
went to a fair or market that it was not thrown in his
face; and even his little children in the schools had to
bear his shame. I never think of it without a blush.
Who wrote these lines?—

> ' He who only rules by terror
> Doeth grievous wrong;
> Deep as Hell I count his error,
> Listen to my song.' "

" I'm not sure," said Father Letheby. " I think it
was Tennyson."

" Thank God, the people love us. But for that, I
should despair of our Irish faith in the near future."

" You said, ' Preach not yourself, but God '? "

" Aren't you tired? "

" No ! " he said ; " I think you are speaking wisely."
Which was a direct implication that this was not in my
usual style. But never mind!

" Let me carry out my own suggestion," I said.
" Take down that Bible. Now, turn to the prophecy of
Ezekiel—that lurid, thunder-and-lightning, seismic, mag-
netic sermon. Now find the thirty-third chapter. Now
find the thirtieth verse and read."

He read :—

" And thou, son of man : the children of thy people, that
talk of thee by the walls and in the doors of the houses, and
speak, one to another, each man to his neighbour, saying:
Come and let us hear what is the word that cometh forth from
the Lord. And they come to thee, as if a people were coming
in, and my people sit before thee; and hear thy words, and
do them not; for they turn them into a song of their mouth,
and their heart goeth after their covetousness. And thou
art to them as a musical song that is sung with a sweet and
agreeable voice; and they hear thy words and do them not."

" Very good. Now, there is the highest ambition of
many a preacher : ' to be spoken of by the walls, and in
the doors of the houses.' And, when judgment came,
the people did not know there was a prophet amongst
them."

" It isn't easy to get rid of ourselves in the pulpit,"
said Father Letheby.

" No, my dear boy, it is not. Nowhere does the *ego*
cling more closely to us. We are never so sensitive as
when we are on ceremonies, never so vain as in the pulpit. Hence the barrenness of our ministry. The mighty
waters are poured upon the land, to wither, not to fer-
tilize."

" You said, thirdly, ' Live up to your preaching.'
That's not easy, either."

" No; the most difficult of the three. Yet here, too,
your words are barren, if they come not supported by the
example of your life. A simple homily from a holy man,
even though it were halting lame, and ungrammatical,

will carry more weight than the most learned and eloquent discourse preached by a worldly priest. I know nothing more significant in all human history than what is recorded in the Life of Père Lacordaire. In the very zenith of his fame, his pulpit in Toulouse was deserted, whilst the white trains of France were bringing tens of thousands of professional men, barristers, statesmen, officers, professors, to a wretched village church only a few miles away. What was the loadstone? A poor country parish priest, uninformed, illiterate, uncouth—but a saint. And I know nothing more beautiful or touching in all human history than the spectacle of the great and inspired Dominican, coming to that village chapel, and kneeling for the blessing of M.. Vianney, and listening, like a child, to the evening catechetical lecture, delivered in a weak voice, and probably with many a halt for a word, by the saint of Ars."

Here I could proceed no further. These episodes in the lives of our holy ones fill me up to the throat, for my heart swells for their beauty. And I am a soft old fool. I can never read that office of St. Agatha or St. Agnes without blubbering; and St. Perpetua, with her little babe, kills me outright.

We had a great debate, however, the following evening about the subject-matter of the sermon. He wanted to preach on the *Magnificat*. I put down my foot there, and said, No!

" That poor Duff will be there; and you'll be like the victor rooster crowing over a fallen antagonist."

" But Duff and I are the best friends in the world."

" No matter. I suppose he has nerves and blood, like the rest of us. Try something else! "

" Well, what about the *Ave Maria*, or *Tu gloria Jerusalem, tu lætitia Israel*, etc.? "

" The very thing."

" Or, the place of the Blessed Virgin in Scripture? "

" You've hit the nail on the head. That's it! "

" Well, now," said he, taking out a note-book, " how long shall it be? "

" Exactly forty-five minutes."

" And I must write every word? "

" Every word ! "

" How many pages will that make? "

" Twenty pages—ordinary copy-book. The first fifteen will be expository; the last five will be the peroration, into which you must throw all the pathos, love, fire, and enthusiasm of which you are capable."

" All right. Many thanks, Father Dan. But I shall be very nervous."

" Never mind. That will wear off."

I said to myself, you have heavier troubles in store; but why should I anticipate? The worst troubles are those that never arise. And where's the use of preaching to a man with the toothache about the perils of typhoid fever?

I went down to see my little saint.

She was " happy, happy, oh ! so happy ! But, Daddy Dan, I fear 't won't last long ! "

" You are not going to heaven so soon, and leaving us all desolate, are you? "

" No, Daddy Dan. But Mr. Ormsby, who thinks that I have made him a Catholic, says he will bring down a great, great doctor from Dublin to cure me. And I don't want to be cured at all."

" If it were God's Holy Will, dear, we should be all glad. But I fear that God alone can cure the hurt He has made."

" Oh, thank you ! thank you ! Daddy Dan. You have always the kind word. And sure you know more than all the doctors. And sure, if God wished me to be cured, you'd have done it long ago."

" I'm not so sure of that, my child," I said; " but who is the great doctor? "

" He's a doctor that was in the navy—like my poor father—and he has seen a lot of queer diseases in India, and got a lot of cures."

" Well, we're bound to try every natural specific, my child. But if all fails, we must leave you in the hands of the great Physician."

" That's what I should like best, Daddy Dan! "

" You must pray now for Father Letheby. He is going to preach a great sermon."

" On what? "

" On our Blessed Lady."

" I should like to be there. The children tell me he preaches lovely. They think he sees the Blessed Virgin when he is talking of her. I shouldn't be surprised."

" I think he'll have crosses, too, like you, my dear. No, no, I don't mean illness; but crosses of his own."

" I should be sorry," she said, her eyes filling with tears.

" Of course, you want heaven all to yourself. Aren't you a selfish saint? "

" I'm not a saint at all, Daddy Dan; but Father Letheby is, and why should he be punished? "

" Why, indeed? Except to verify that line of Dante's of the soul in Paradise:

" ' E dal martirio venni a questa pace.' "

CHAPTER XXV

MAY DEVOTIONS

I OFTEN wonder if the May devotions in other countries are as sweet and memory-haunting and redolent of peace as here in holy Ireland. Indeed, I suppose they are; for there are good, holy Catholics everywhere. But somehow the fragrance and beauty of these May evenings hang around us in Ireland as incense hangs around a dimly lighted church, and often cling around a soul where faith and holiness have been banished. I cannot boast too much of the picturesqueness and harmony of our evening prayers at Kilronan, at least until Father Letheby came. We had, indeed, the Rosary and a little weak homily. Nevertheless, the people loved to come and gather around the beautiful statue of our Mother. But when Father Letheby came, he threw music and sunshine around everything; but I believe he exhausted all his art in making the May devotions attractive and edifying. He said, indeed, that they were imperfect, and would always remain imperfect, until we could close them with Benediction of the Most Blessed Sacrament; and he urged me again and again to apply for permission, but, to tell the truth, I was afraid. And my dear old maxim, which had done me good service during life —my little pill of all philosophy—*lente! lente!* came again to my aid. But I'll tell you what we had. The Lady altar had all its pretentious ugliness hid under a mass of flowers—great flaunting peonies burning in the background, beautiful white Nile lilies in the front, bunches of yellow primroses between the candles, great tulips stained in flame colours, like the fires of Purgatory around the holy souls in our hamlet pictures. And hidden here and there, symbolical of the Lily of Israel, and filling the whole church with their delicate perfumes, were nestled lilies of the valley, sweetest and humblest of all those "most beautiful things that God has made and forgot to put a soul in." Then such hymns and litanies! I do not know, I am sure, what people feel in grand city churches, when the organ stops are loosed and the tide of music wells forth, and great voices are lifted up; but I think, if the Lord would allow me, I would be satisfied to have my heaven one long May devotion, with the children singing around me and the incense of flowers in the air, and our dear Mother looking down on us; only I should like that there were life in those wondrous eyes of Mother and Child, and I should like that Divine Child, who holds us all in the palms of His little hands, would get a little tired sometimes of contemplating His Mother's beauty and turn in pity towards us.

Our order of service was: Rosary, Hymn, Lecture. Hymn, Litany of Loretto. Did you ever hear:

> "Oh, my Mother, still remember
> What the sainted Bernard hath said—
> None hath ever, ever found thee wanting
> Who hath called upon thine aid."

or:

> "Rose of the Cross! thou mystic flower!"

or Father Faber's splendid hymn:

> "Hark, hark, O my soul! angelic songs are swelling."

Well, if you didn't, God help you!

I used to read a book sometimes—sometimes Father Gratry's "Month of May," sometimes that good little book by the Abbé Berlioux. But when the people began to yawn I flung the book aside, and said a few simple words to the congregation. And I spoke out of a full

heart, a very full heart, and the waters flowed over, and
flooded all the valleys.

The 31st of May fell on Sunday; and it was on this
Sunday evening Father Letheby was to preach in the
cathedral. I told the people all about it; and we offered
the evening devotions for his success. Somehow I
thought there was a note of emphasis in the " Holy
Marys " that evening; and a little additional pathos in
the children's voices. Miss Campion presided at the harmonium that evening in place of Father Letheby. I
think, indeed, that the people considered that prayers for
their young curate were a little superfluous; because, as
we came out I was able to hear a few comments and
predictions : —

" Faith, you may make your mind aisy about him.
They never heard anything like it before, I promise you."

" I heard they used to say over there in England that
Father Burke himself couldn't hould a candle to him."

" If he'd spake a little aisier," said a village critic,
who had a great opinion of himself, since he was called
upon to propose a resolution at a Land-League meeting,
" and rise his wice, he'd bate thim all."

" Did you ever hear Father Mac? " said an old
labourer, dressed in the ancient Irish fashion, but old
Father Time had been snipping at his garments as he
couldn't touch himself. " That was the pracher! He
hadn't his aiqual in Ireland. I rimimber wance a Good
Friday sermon he prached in Loughboro'. Begor, you
couldn't stick a pin between the people, they were so
packed together. He kem out on the althar, and you
could hear a pin dhrop. He had a crucifix in his hand,
and he looked sorrowful like. ' In the Name av the
Father,' sez he; thin he shtopped and looked round; ' and
av the Holy Ghost,' sez he, and he shtopped ag'in; ' but
where's the Son? ' sez he, rising his wice; and begor,
'twas like the day of gineral jedgment. Thin he tore off
a black veil that was on the crucifix, and he threw it on
the althar, and he held up the crucifix in the air, and he

let a screech out of him that you could hear at Moydore; and—— "

" Was that all the sarmon? " said a woman who was an interested listener.

" Was that all? " cried the narrator indignantly. " It wasn't all. He prached that night two mortial hours, and "—he looked around to command attention and admiration—" *he never tetched a sup of wather the whole time, though it was under his hands.*"

" Glory be to God," said the listeners; " sure 'twas wandherful. And is he dead, Jer? "

" Dead? " cried Jer, rather contemptuously, for he was on the lofty heights of success; " did ye never hear it? "

" Wisha, how could we, and 'tis so far back? "

" Some other time," said Jer, with a little pitying contempt.

" Ye may as well tell it now," said an old woman; " I hard the people shpake av him along ago; but sure we forget everything, even God sometimes."

" Well," said Jer, sitting on a long, level tombstone, " maybe ye don't know how the divil watches priests when they are on a sick-call. He does, thin. Fram the time they laves the house till they returns he is on their thrack, thrying to circumwent them, ontil he gets the poor sowl into his own dirty claws. Sometimes he makes the mare stumble and fall; sometimes he pulls down a big branch of a three, and hits the priest across the face; sometimes he hangs out a lanthern to lade him into a bog. All he wants is to keep him away, and WHAT he has wid him, and thin he gobbles up that poor sowl, as a fox would sling a chicken over his shoulder, and takes him off to his din. Well, this night Father Mac was called out late. It was as dark as the caves down there by the say av a winter's night. As he wint along the road, he began praying softly to himself, for he knew the divil was watching him. All of a suddint he was taken out av his saddle and pitched head foremost in a brake of

briars. When he recovered himself he looked around
him and saw at a distance—— "

" I thought it was dark, Jer," said a young mason,
who knew that Jer was drawing the long bow.

" Av coorse it was, but couldn't ye see a light shining even on a dark night, my fine young man? " said Jer,
in a temper.

" Oh, was it a light? " said the mason.

" Ye ought to think twice before intherrupting yer
elders," said Jer. " Well, as I was saying, when he
come to himself, he looked around, and he asked, in a
loud wice, ' Is there anny wan there who could sarve
Mass for a priest? ' There was no answer. Thin he said
a second time, ' For the love av God, is there anny wan
there who could sarve Mass for a priest? "

" Begor, I always thought that was the shtory about
the priest that forgot to say the Masses for the dead,
and kem out av of his grave on Christmas night," said
an old woman.

" Thrue for ye, so it is," said another. " Many and
many's the time we heard it."

" Begor, Jer," said a young man, " ye're getting
mixed."

" There's a hole in the ballad and the song fell out,'
said another.

" Jer could tell that story betther, if he had a couple
of glasses in, I'm thinking," said the young mason, as
they strolled away and left Jer sitting on the monu-
ment.

" Yes; or if he had the clay in his mouth, and the
pint on the dresser," said his companion.

So was this great actor hissed off the stage. It was a
bad breakdown, and there was no mercy. It turned the
women's conversation back to their curate.

" May the Lord stringthen and help him in his endeavour, our darlin' man," said one.

" Amin, thin, and may the Blessed Vargin put the
words into his mouth that he has to shpake," cried an-

other. The children listened gravely. All that they could conjecture was that Father Letheby was engaged on a great and dangerous enterprise.

I never had a moment's doubt but that their prayers were heard and their predictions verified, although when Father Letheby called the next day he looked depressed and gloomy enough.

" Well," I said, " a great success, of course? "

" I'm afraid not," he said moodily.

" You broke down badly just in the middle? "

" Well, no, indeed; there was certainly no breakdown, but the whole thing was evidently a failure."

" Let me see," I cried. " There are certain infallible indications of the success or failure of a sermon. Were there any priests present? "

" About twenty, I think," he replied. " That was the worst of it. You don't mind the people at all."

" And weren't they very enthusiastic," I asked, " when you returned to the sacristy? "

" No, indeed. Rather the contrary, which makes me think that I said something either perilous or ill-advised."

" Humph! Didn't any fellow come up to you and knock the breath out of your body by slapping you on the back? "

" No! " he replied sadly.

" Didn't any fellow say: *Prospere procede, et regna?*"

" No! " he said. " It was just the other way."

" Didn't any fellow shake you by the hand even, and say: *Prosit! prosit!! prosit!!!* "

" I'm afraid not," he said gloomily.

" That's bad. Nor even, *macte virtute esto, Titus Manlius?* "

" No," he said. " There was no indication of sympathy whatsoever."

" Didn't any fellow drop into the vernacular, and say: ' Put the hand there. Sure I never doubted you,' and wring your hand as if he wanted to dislocate it? "

" No, no, no! There was simply dead silence."

" And perhaps they looked at you over their shoulders, and whispered together, as they put their surplices into their bags, and stared at you as if you were a sea-monster? "

" Something that way, indeed," said my poor curate.

" Did the bishop make any remark? "

" Yes. The bishop came over and said he was very grateful, indeed, for that beautiful sermon. But that, of course, was purely conventional."

" And the people? How did they take it? "

" They were very quiet and attentive, indeed : apparently an intelligent congregation."

" You don't think you were talking over their heads? "

" No, indeed. Even the poor women who were gathered under the pulpit stared at me unmercifully; and I think a few persons in front were much affected."

I waited for a few minutes to draw my deductions. But they were logical enough.

" My dear boy," I said at length, " from a long and profound experience of that wilful thing called human nature, allow me to tell you that every indication you have mentioned points to the fact that you have preached not only an edifying and useful, but a remarkable sermon —— "

" Oh, that's only your usual goodness, Father Dan," he broke in. " I'm quite certain it was a failure. Look at the attitude of the priests! "

" That is just my strongest foundation," I replied. " If their enthusiasm had taken the other shapes I suggested, I should have despaired."

" Well, 'tis over, for better, for worse," said he; " I did my best for our Lady, and she won't blame me if I failed."

" That is sound Christian philosophy," I replied; " leave it there. But don't be too flushed if my predictions come true."

" I suppose we may have a procession of the children on Corpus Christi? " he said abruptly.

" Hallo! another innovation! Where are you going
to stop, I wonder? "

" Why not have it? " he said. " It will be a sermon
to the people! "

" Around the church, you mean," I conjectured, " and
back again to the High Altar? "

" No! but through the village, and out there along
the path that cuts the turf over the cliffs, and then back
to the mill, where we can have Benediction (I'll extem-
porize an altar), and down the main road, and to the
church."

" Go on! go on! " I said in a resigned manner; " perhaps you'll invite our pious friend, Campion, down to
Benediction—— "

" He'll be carrying the canopy."

I looked at this young prestidigitateur in a bewildered
manner. He was not noticing me.

" You know," he said, " I'll put Campion and Ormsby
and the doctor, and the old Tertiary, Clohessy, under the
canopy. It's time that these men should be made to understand that they are Catholics in reality as well as in
name."

I was dumbfounded at his audacity.

" I have got faculties from the bishop," he continued,
" to receive Ormsby, and to use the short form. He'll
be a noble Catholic. He is intelligent, and deeply in
earnest."

" And who is this great man he is bringing from
Dublin? " I asked.

" Oh! the doctor? An old chum. They have seen
some rough and smooth weather together. This fellow
is gone mad about his profession, and he studies eighteen hours out of the twenty-four—— "

" He ought to be a Master of Conference," I interrupted. " But won't our own man be jealous? "

" Not at all. He says he has done his best for Alice;
and if anyone else can help her on, he'll be delighted.
But he is not sanguine, nor am I."

" Nor I. It appears a deep-rooted affair. But what a visitation—God's angel, cloaked from head to foot in blackness, and with a flaming sword."

We were both silent, thinking of many things.

" Then the procession will be all right, sir? " he said at last, waking up.

" I hope so," I said resignedly. " Everything else that you have touched you have adorned. This will follow suit."

" Thank you, sir," he said. " It will be a glorious day for the children."

" By the way," I said, as he was going, " was Duff at the sermon? "

" He was, poor fellow; and I am afraid he got a wigging from the bishop. At least they were walking up and down there near the sacristy for at least half an hour before dinner. You know Duff is an awfully clever fellow. He has written some articles in the leading English magazines, in which, curiously enough, he quite agrees with Professor Sayce, the eminent Assyriologist, who has tried to disprove the theories about the Pentateuch originated by Graf and Wellhausen—— "

" My dear fellow, this is not a conference. Spare my old nerves all that nonsense. The Bible is God's own Word—that is enough for me. But what about Duff? "

" Well, at table, the bishop was specially and expressly kind to him, and drew him out about all these matters, and made him shine; and you know how well Duff can talk—— "

" I wouldn't doubt the bishop," I said; " he always does the kind and the right thing."

" By the way, I forgot a moment ago to say that Duff met me this morning at the station, and said, I am sure with perfect sincerity: ' Letheby, I must congratulate you. You taught me a sharp lesson the other day; you taught me a gentler lesson last evening. Pray for me that I may keep farther away from human will-o'-the-wisps, and nearer the Eternal Light than I have been.'

1 shook his hand warmly. *Sedes sapientiæ, ora pro nobis.*"

" Amen! " I said humbly.

" I've asked him over to dine on the day our fishing-boat will be launched," said Father Letheby, after a pause. " Some of the brethren are coming; and you'll come, sir? Duff is very anxious to meet you."

" Of course," I replied. " I never refuse so delightful an invitation. But why should Duff be anxious to meet me? "

" I really don't know, except that you are, as you know yourself, sir, a celebrity. He thinks a great deal of you."

" Probably a great deal more than I am disposed to think of myself. Did he say so? "

" Oh, dear, yes! He said: ' I must make the acquaintance of that pastor of yours, Letheby, he's an *immortal genius*!' "

" An immortal genius! Well, you must know, my innocent young man, that that expression is susceptible of a double interpretation—it may mean an immortal fame like William Shakespeare's, or an immortal fame like Jack Falstaff's; it may mean a Cervantes, or a Don Quixote, a foole who has eclipsed the name of his creator. But, as I am charitably inclined, I shall give your learned friend the benefit of the doubt, and meet him as one of my many admirers, rather than as one of my few critics. Perhaps he may change his opinion of me, for better, for worse, on a closer acquaintance."

" I'm quite sure, sir, that there will be a mutual appreciation. That's arranged, then—the procession on Corpus Christi, and dinner the day of our launch."

CHAPTER XXVI

AT THE ZENITH

FOR one reason or another, the great events to which our little history is tending were deferred again and again, until at last the Monday within the Octave of Corpus Christi was chosen for the marriage of Bittra Campion and the launch of the great fishing-boat, that was to bring untold wealth to Kilronan. Meanwhile our faculties were not permitted to rust, for we had a glorious procession on the great *Fête-Dieu*, organized, of course, and carried on to complete success by the zeal and inventive piety of my young curate. My own timidity, and dread of offending Protestant susceptibilities— a timidity, I suppose, inherited from the penal days— would have limited that procession to the narrow confines of the chapel yard; but the larger and more trusting faith of Father Letheby leaped over such restrictions, and the procession wound through the little village, down to the sheer cliffs that overhang the sea, along the narrow footpath that cuts the turf on the summit of the rocks, around the old mill, now the new factory, and back by the main road skirting the bog and meadowland, to the village church again. It would be quite useless to inquire how or where Father Letheby managed to get those silken banners, and that glittering processional cross, or the gorgeous canopy. I, who share with the majority of my countrymen the national contempt for minutiæ and mere details, would have at once dogmatically declared the impossibiilty of securing such beautiful things in such a pre-Adamite, out-of-the-way village as Kilronan. But Father Letheby, who knows no such word as impossibility, in some quiet way—the legerdemain of a strong character—contrives to bring these unimaginable things out of the region of conjecture into the realms of fact; and I can only stare and wonder. But the whole thing was a great and unexampled success; and, whilst my own heart was swelling under the influence of the sweet hymns of the children, and the golden radiance of June sunlight, and the sparkling of the sea, and the thought that I held the Lord and Master of all between my hands, my fancy would go back to that wondrous lake on whose waters the Lord did walk, and from whose shores He selected the future teachers of the world. The lake calm in the sunlight, the fish gleaming in the nets, the half-naked Apostles bending over the gunwales of their boats to drag in the nets, the stately, grave figure of our Lord, the wondering women who gazed on Him afar off with fear and love—all came up before my fancy, that only came back to reality when I touched the shoulders of Reginald Ormsby and the doctor, who, with two rough fishermen, belonging to the Third Order of St. Francis, held the gilded poles of the canopy. They manifested great piety and love and reverence all the way. Ormsby had brought over all his coast-guards except the two that were on duty at the station, and they formed a noble guard of honour around the canopy; and it was difficult to say which was the more beautiful and picturesque—the demonstrative love of the peasant women, who flung up their hands in a paroxysm of devotion, whilst they murmured in the soft Gaelic: " Ten thousand, thousand thanks to you, *O white and ruddy Saviour!* " or the calm, deep, silent tenderness of these rough men, whose faces were red and tanned and bronzed from the action of sun and sea. And the little children, who were not in the procession, peeped out shyly from beneath their mothers' cloaks, and their round, wondering eyes rested on the white Host, who in His undying words had once

said: " Suffer little children to come unto me! " Let
no one say that our poor Irish do not grasp the meaning
of this central mystery of our faith! It is true that their
senses are touched by more visible things; but whoever
understands our people will agree with me that no great
theologian in his study, no philosopher in his rostrum, no
sacred nun in her choir, realizes more distinctly the awful
meaning of that continued miracle of love and mercy
that is enshrined on our altars, and named *Emmanuel*.

But all things come around, sooner or later, in their
destined courses, and Monday dawned, fair and sunny
and beautiful, as befitted the events that were to take
place. There was a light summer haze on sea and land;
and just a ripple of a breeze blown down as a message
from the inhospitable hills. Father Letheby said early
Mass at eight o'clock; and at half-past nine, the hour for
the nuptial Mass, there was no standing or sitting-room
in the little chapel. Of course, the front seats were reserved for the gentry, who, in spite of an academical dislike to Ormsby's conversion, gathered to witness this
Catholic marriage, as a rare thing in Ireland, at least
amongst their own class. But behind them, and I
should say in unpleasant proximity (for the peasantry do
not carry handkerchiefs scented with White Rose or
Jockey Club—only the odour of the peat and the bogwood), surged a vast crowd of men and women, on whose
lips and in whose hearts was a prayer for her who was
entering on the momentous change in her sweet and tranquil life. And young Patsies and Willies and Jameses
were locked by their legs around their brothers' necks,
and trying to keep down and economize for further use
that Irish cheer or yell, that from Dargai to Mandalay is
well known as the war-whoop of the race invincible. I
presume that I was an object of curiosity myself, as I
awaited in alb and stole the coming of the bridal party.
Then the curiosity passed on to Ormsby, who, accompanied by Dr. Armstrong, stood erect and stately before
the altar-rails; then, of course, to the bride, who, accom-

panied by her father, and followed by a bevy of fair children, drew down a rose-shower of benedictions from the enthusiastic congregation. Did it rest there? Alas, no! Bridegroom and bride, parish priest and curate, were blotted out of the interested vision of the spectators; and, concentrated with absorbing fascination, the hundreds of eyes rested on the snowy cap and the spotless streamers of Mrs. Darcy. It was the great event of the day—the culmination of civilization in Kilronan! Wagers had been won and lost over it; one or two pitched battles had been fought with pewter weapons at Mrs. Haley's; ballads had been written on it in the style, but not quite in the polished lines, of "Henry of Navarre"; and now, there it was, the "white plume" of victory, the cynosure of hundreds of wondering eyes. I daresay the "upper ten" did not mind it; they were used to such things; but everything else paled into insignificance to the critical and censorious audience behind them.

"Didn't I tell you she'd do it?"

"Begor, you did. I suppose I must stand the thrate."

"Father Letheby cud do anything whin he cud do that."

"Begor, I suppose she'll be thinkin' of marryin' herself now, and Jem hardly cowld in the clay."

"Yerra, look at her! She thinks she's wan of the gintry. Oh my! she's blushin'. 'Twasn't so long ago that you could sow praties in her face."

"I suppose thim cost a lot of money. But, shure, it was the priests give 'em to her."

"Wisha, thin, there's many a poor creature that would want the money more."

Now, all this was not only sarcastic, but calumnious. The cap and streamers were Mrs. Darcy's own, bought out of her hard earnings, and donned to-day to honour the nuptials of her idol and benefactress. She knew the mighty ordeal that was in store for her; but she faced it, and thanked God she was "not behoulden to wan of thim for what she put into her mout and upon her back."

And she stood there at the altar-rails, erect and defiant, and there was not a tremor in the hand that held the holy-water vase, nor in the hand that held the aspergill.

But it was very embarrassing to myself. I am not disposed to be nervous, for I have always conscientiously avoided tea and too much study, and I have lived in the open air, and always managed to secure eight hours of dreamless, honest sleep; but I was "discomposed," as someone charitably explained it that morning; and Mrs. Darcy's cap was the cause. I couldn't take my eyes away from it. There it was, dancing like a will-o'-the-wisp before my dazzled vision. I turned my back deliberately upon it, and lo! there it was in miniature in the convex arc of my spectacles; and if I looked up, there was my grinning congregation, and their half-audible remarks upon this dread and unwonted apparition. At last I commenced:

"Reginald Darcy, wilt thou take Bittra Ormsby here present——"

A forcible reminder from Father Letheby brought me to my senses; but away they scattered again, as I heard Campion muttering something uncomplimentary under his black moustache.

"Ahem!—Reginald Ormsby, wilt thou take Mrs. Darcy——"

Here Father Letheby nudged me again, and looked at me suspiciously. I got a sudden and violent paroxysm of coughing, a remnant of an old bronchial attack to which I am very subject. But I managed to say:—

"For the love of God, send that woman into the sacristy."

She covered her retreat nobly, made a courtesy to the priests, genuflected calmly, laid down the aspergill, and, under pretence of having been sent for something which these careless priests had forgotten, retired with honours; and then I suppose had a good long cry. But poor Bittra was blushing furiously; Ormsby was calm as on the quarter-deck; but Dr. Armstrong was pulling at his moustache, as if determined to show the world that there was no use any more for razors or depilatories; and Miss Leslie had bitten right through her under lip, and was threatened with apoplexy. We got through the rest of the ceremony with flying colours: and the moment I said, *In nomine Patris, et Filii, et Spiritus Sancti*, the hush of death fell on the congregation. Then the nuptial blessing was given, the choir threw all their vocal strength into the grand *finale;* the registers were signed; Campion kissed his beloved child, and shook hands with Ormsby; and then commenced the triumphal march. I forgot to say that for the glorious procession on the Thursday before the village was *en fête.* Great arcades of laurel were stretched from chimney to chimney, because there were no upper rooms in the cabins; the posts and lintels of the humble doors were covered with foliage and flowers; and the windows were decorated with all the pious images that had been accumulating in the cabins for generations. Little *eikons* of the Sacred Heart, gorgeous statues of our Lady of Lourdes, coloured prints of Leo XIII., and crucifixes without number dappled the dark background of the windows—and all the splendour was allowed to remain untouched during the octave. And glad they were, poor people, to show their love for their young idol and mistress, even with the decorations of their Lord and King. But what a shout tore open the heavens as Bittra appeared, leaning on her husband's arm; and what prayers echoed round and round them, as Ormsby handed Bittra into the victoria that was waiting! No genteel showers of rice, no casting of slippers nor waving of jealous handkerchiefs here, but——

" Come down out o' dat, you grinning monkey," and the gorgeous coachman was hauled down ignominiously, and a score of strong arms replaced the panting horses under the bridal carriage. And so it moved on, this bridal procession, amidst a strange *epithalamium* of cheering and blessings, whilst rough hands from time to time grasped the strong fingers of the smiling bridegroom or the tiny gloved hand of the bride. Ay, move down the valley of life together, you two, linked hand-in-hand, having said your farewells to the world, for you are entering on a new and altogether consecrated life. No wonder that the Church insists on the sacramental nature of this stupendous compact between two human souls; no wonder that the world, anxious to break its indissolubility, denies its awful sacredness; no wonder that the Catholic girl enters beneath the archway of the priest's stole[1] with the fear of great joy, and that the Catholic bridegroom is unnerved with dread at undertaking the responsibilities of a little universe.

We had a little chat over this matter, my curate and I, the evening before Bittra's marriage. It came around quite naturally, for we had been debating all kinds of possibilities as to the future; and he had been inveighing, in his own tumultuous manner, against the new and sacrilegious ideas that are just now being preached by the modern apostles of free thought in novel and journal. We agreed in thinking that the Christian ideal of marriage was nowhere so happily realized as in Ireland, where, at least up to recent times, there was no lurid and volcanic company-keeping before marriage, and no bitter ashes of disappointment after; but the good mother quietly said to her child: " Mary, go to confession tomorrow, and get out your Sunday dress. You are to be married on Thursday evening." And Mary said: "Very well, mother," not even asserting a faintest right to know the name of her future spouse. But, then, by virtue of the great sacramental union, she stepped from the position of a child and a dependent into the regal position of queen and mistress on her own hearth. The entire authority of the household passed thereby into her hands, as she slung the keys at her girdle; she became bursar and *économe* of the establishment; and in on instance

---

[1]In many places in Ireland the priest places the broad ends of the stole on the heads of the newly married couple.

was her right to rule supreme ever questioned by husband or child, unless drink came in to destroy this paradise, as the serpent fouled with his slime the flowers of the garden of Eden. Married life in Ireland has been, up to now, the most splendid refutation of all that the world and its gospel, the novel, preach about marriage, and the most splendid and complete justification of the supernaturalism of the Church's dogmas and practices. But, reverting to the new phases in the ever-shifting emotionalism of a godless world, with which marriage has become a question of barter—a mere lot-drawing of lambs for the shambles—he compared the happy queenly life of our Irish mother with that of the victim of fashion, or that of uncatholic lands, where a poor girl passes from one state of slavery to another.

" I hope," he said, " that we never shall be able to compare Bittra, like so many other brides, to the sleeping child that Carafola has painted, with an angel holding over it a crown of thorns, and whom marriage, like the angel, would awake by pressing the thorns on her brow."

" God forbid! " I said fervently. How little I dreamed of the troubles that were looming up out of the immediate future to shroud her marriage sunshine in awful gloom!

As the marriage procession passed the door where Alice lived, Bittra gave a little timid, imperious command to her admirers to stop. She and Ormsby alighted and passed into the cottage. The orange blossoms touched the crown of thorns on the head of the sick girl; but, somehow, both felt that there was need of a sisterhood of suffering on the one part to knit their souls together. Ormsby remained in the kitchen, talking to Mrs. Moylan; and from that day forward she was secured, at least, from all dread of dependence or poverty for ever more.

At the breakfast table it was, of course, my privilege to propose the health of the bride and bridegroom, which

I most gladly did; and, let me say, so successfully as to
bring back unwonted smiles to Campion's face, who now
freely forgave me for the *gaucheries* at the marriage service.   Then the guests strolled around, looking at the
marriage presents—the usual filigree and useless things
that are flung at the poor bride.   Bittra took me into a
little boudoir of her own to show me her *real* presents.

" Father," she said, " who is a great artist, wanted
me to give back all this rubbish, as he calls it; but I
would much rather sacrifice all that *bijouterie* outside."
And she exhibited with glistening eyes the bridal offer-
ings of the poor fisherwomen and country folk of Kilronan.   They were fearfully and wonderfully made.
Here was a magnificent three-decker battleship, complete from pennant to bowsprit, every rope in its place,
and the brass muzzles of its guns protruded for action.
Here was a pretty portrait of Bittra herself, painted by a
Japanese artist from a photograph, surreptitiously ob-
tained, and which had been sent 15,000 miles across the
ocean for an enlarged replica.   Here were shells of all
sizes and fantastic forms, gathered during generations,
from the vast museums of the deep.   Here was a massive gold ring, with a superb ruby, picked up, the Lord
knows how, by a young sailor in the East Indian Islands.
Here, screaming like a fury, was a paroquet, gorgeous as
a rainbow, but ill-conducted as a monkey; and here was
a gauze shawl, so fine that Bittra hid it in her little palm,
and whispered that it was of untold price.

" But, of course, I cannot keep all these treasures,"
she said; " I shall hold them as a loan for a while; and
then, under one pretext or another, return them.   It is
what they indicate that I value."

" And I think, my little child," I said, " that if you
had them reduplicated until they would fill one wing of
the British Museum, they would hardly be an exponent
of all that these poor people think and feel."

" It should make me very happy," said Bittra.

And then we passed into the yard and dairies, where

the same benevolent worship had congregated fowl of strange and unheard-of breeds; and there was a little bonham; and above all, staring around, wonder-stricken and frightened, and with a gorgeous blue ribbon about her neck, was the prettiest little fawn in the world, its soft brown fur lifted by the warm wind and its eyes opened up in fear and wonder at its surroundings. Bittra patted its head, and the pretty animal laid its wet muzzle in her open hand. Then she felt a little shiver, and I said:—

"That bridal dress is too light. Go in and change." But she said, looking up at me wistfully:—

"It is not the chill of cold, but of dread, that is haunting me all the morning. I feel as if some one were walking over my grave, as the people say."

"Nonsense!" I cried. "You are unnerved, child; the events of the morning have been too much for you."

Here we heard her father's voice, shouting: "Bittra! Bittra! where are you?"

"Here, father," she said, as Ormsby came into the yard with Campion, "showing all my treasures to Father Dan."

She linked her arm in her husband's, and Campion looked from one to the other admiringly. And no wonder. They were a noble, handsome pair, as they stood there, and the June sunlight streamed and swam around them.

"Go in," he said at last. "The guests expect you."

He and I walked around the farmyard, noting, observing, admiring. He called my attention to this animal and to that, marked out all his projected improvements, and what he would do to make this a model country residence for his child; but I could see that he had something else to say. At last he turned to me, and there was a soft haze in his gleaming black eyes as he tried to steady his voice:—

"I have been a hard man," he said, "but the events of this morning have quite upset me. I didn't know that my child was so worshipped by the people, and it has

touched me deeply. You know, brought up in the school
where I graduated, I have never been able to shake off a
feeling of contempt for these poor, uneducated serfs; and
their little cunning ways and want of manliness have
always disgusted me. I am beginning to see that I have
been wrong. And then I have been a bad Catholic.
Ormsby, lately an unbeliever, has shown me this, not by
his words, for he is a thorough gentleman, but by his
quiet example. You know I did not care one brass pin
whether he was Turk, Jew, or atheist, so long as he married Bittra. Now I see that the Church is right, and
that her espousal would have been incomplete if she had
not married a Catholic, and a true one. All this has disturbed me, and I intend to turn over a new leaf. I am
running into years; and although I have, probably, thirty
years of life before me, I must brush up as if the end
were near. I am awfully sorry I was not at the rails
with Bittra and Ormsby this morning; but we shall all
be together at Holy Communion the Sunday after they
return from the Continent. By Jove! there goes the
Angelus; and twelve is the hour to start the boat!''

He took off his hat, and we said the *Angelus* in silence
together. I noticed the silver gathering over his ears,
and the black hair was visibly thinning on the top. I
watched him keenly for those few seconds. I did not
know that those musical strains of the mid-day Angelus
were his death-knell—the ringing up of the great stage-
manager, Death, for his *volté subito*—his leap through
the ring to eternity.

CHAPTER XXVII

THE "STAR OF THE SEA"

THERE was a vast crowd assembled down where the extemporized pier jutted into the creek, and where the new fishing-boat, perfect in all her equipments, lolled and rolled on the heaving of the tide. Her high mast made an arc of a circle in the warm June air, as the soft, round wavelets lifted her; and many was the comment made on her by those whose eyes had never rested but on the tarred canvas of the coracle.

"She has a list to port!" said an old mariner, critically.

"Where's yer eyes, Jur?" cried another. "Don't ye see she lanes to stabbord?"

"I'll bet dhrinks all round she's level as the althar," said a third.

"'Twill take six min to navigate her," cried an old salt, who had been around the world.

"'Tis aisy to get 'em for the big wages the priest is offering."

"How much?" cried a mariner from Moydore.

"Fifteen shillings a week, an' a share in the profits."

"Here's the capt'n and the priests. Now, boys, for a cheer."

And there was a cheer that made the ocean shiver, and fluttered the flags over the tents, and made even the trick-o'-the-loop men pause in their honest avocation, and the orange-sellers hold their wares suspended in mid-air.

"Is that him?" was the cry, as Father Letheby, his face aglow with excitement and pride, came down the by-path to the pier.

K

" That's him, God bless him! " said the Kilronan men. " 'Twas a lucky day brought him among us. What are yere priests doing? "

" Divil a bit! " said the strangers, who felt themselves humiliated.

There was a ring of merchants around Father Letheby, the shopkeepers over from Kilkeel and Loughboro' who had subscribed to the balance of local aid required by the Board of Works. They scanned the boat critically, and shuffled, in imagination, the boundless profits that were to accrue.

A light breeze blew off the land, which was another favourable omen; and it was reported that the coast-guards had seen that morning the Manx fishing-fleet about twelve miles to the south'ard.

There had been a slight dispute between Father Letheby and Campion about the naming of the craft, the latter demanding that she should be called the " Bittra Campion of Kilronan," and Father Letheby being equally determined that she should be called the " Star of the Sea." Bittra herself settled the dispute, as, standing in the prow of the boat, she flung a bottle of champagne on the deck, and said tremulously : " I name her the ' Star of the Sea.' "

But she grew pale, and almost fainted, as the heavy bottle, without a break, pirouetted down between the sails and cordage, and seeking an opening in the gunwale of the boat flopped into six fathoms of sea-water.

It was a dread omen, and all felt it. Nothing could have been more inauspicious or unlucky. But the Celtic wit and kindness came to her aid.

" Never mind, Miss; 'tisn't you, but the d——d old hulk that's unlucky."

" Thim bottles are made of sheet-iron; they're so tick they don't hould a glassful."

" One big cheer, byes, for the ' Star of the Say.' "

It was a big cheer; but somehow there was a faltering note somewhere; and when Father Letheby handed Bittra ashore and the decks were cleared, and the crew summoned to make her ready to clear off, the men held back, cowed and afraid.

" You miserable cowards," said Father Letheby; " afraid of every little accident! I'll not let one of you now aboard; I'll get a crew of men from Moydore! "

This stung them to the quick; and when a few Moydore boys stood forward and volunteered, they were rudely flung aside by the four stalwart fishermen, and we went near having a good free fight to crown the morning's proceedings. Yet it was easy to see that their hearts were heavy with superstition and fear; and it was just at this crisis that Campion stepped forward and offered himself as captain and helmsman. There was a genuine ringing cheer when he walked down her deck; for every one knew what a splendid seaman he was, and it is exhilarating to see a strong man, self-reliant and confident, assume an authority and premiership by natural right, where weaklings are timid and irresolute. The clouds moved off from Father Letheby's face only to gather more deeply upon poor Bittra's. Campion saw it and came over to where she stood, leaning on Ormsby's arm.

" I would be miserable up at that old castle, mignonne," he said fondly, " when you and Ormsby depart. It is only a few hours at sea, and it will give nerve to these poor fellows."

" Father! father! " was all that she could say through her tears. What dreadful forebodings filled that gentle heart!

" Tell her it's all right, Ormsby! " Campion said, turning away from the tearful face. " You know all about the sea, and that there's no danger. What a noble craft she is! Good-bye, little woman! You have no time to lose if you want to catch the mail. Good-bye, Ormsby! Take care of her! "

He choked down his emotion as he kissed his child, and then sprang on deck.

" All right, lads!   Ease off her head first!   There,
cast away aft! "

And the pretty craft was caught up by the flowing
tide; and with the strong hand at the helm, floated calmly
down the deep creek until she reached a wider space,
where the wind could catch her.   Then they raised a
white sail, half-mast high, and she leaned over to the
pressure until she shot out amongst the breakers, and
her mainsail and topsail shook out to the breeze, and she
cut the calm sea like a plough in the furrow, and the
waters curled and whitened and closed in her wake.
Then, at a signal, her pennant was hauled to the mast-
head; and every eye could read in blue letters on a white
ground " Star of the Sea."   There was a tremendous
cheer, and the fishing-boat went forward to her fate.

Long after the crowd had dispersed, two figures leaned
on the battlements of the bridge that spanned the fiord
higher up near the great house.   Bittra fluttered her
little handkerchief as long as the dark speck at the helm
could be discerned.   Then the boat, now but a tiny white
feather in the distance, was lost in the haze; and Bittra
and her husband set out on their wedding journey.

As he went home, Father Letheby showed me a letter
received that morning from the manager of the great firm
at Loughboro', complaining that the work lately sent
from the Kilronan factory was very imperfect, and, indeed, unsaleable, and calling for the first instalment payable on the machines.

" I called the girls' attention to this," he said, " some
weeks ago, when the first complaints were made; and
some pouted, and some said they were doing too much
for the wages I gave them, although, to encourage them,
I gave them nearly double what I had stipulated for,
and have left myself without a penny to meet this first
instalment."

" Come," I said, " this won't do. Let us go in and see all about this! "

We went upstairs to the great room, to find it empty of workers. The girl who was placed in the position of superintendent was knitting in a corner, and rose as we entered.

" Where are the girls, Kate? " he said, not unkindly.

" I don't know, your reverence. They were saying yesterday that this should be a holiday."

" They knew all this work was waiting, and that the manager was complaining."

" They did, indeed, your reverence. I told them so, and one said: ' Let them wait.' They're grumbling about the wages, though they were never better off in their lives before."

" Are they all of the same mind in that matter? "

" Oh, no, your reverence. Nine of the girls are anxious, and are really grateful for the work; but there are three doxies, who have bachelors, if you please, and they think themselves quite above the work."

" I see. I think I know them. They won't come here again. Can you supply their places? "

" Easy enough, your reverence, but—— "

" Never mind. I'll do that myself."

He did. He dismissed the recalcitrants promptly; but when it became a question of obtaining substitutes, it was not so easy.

The rest of the girls went to work the following day; but as they passed through the village in the evening on the way home, they were hooted unmercifully, called " staggeens," " thraitors," " informers," and, as a result, remained at home, and sent in their resignation to Father Letheby. Not that the entire body of villagers sympathized with this disgraceful conduct; but the powers of evil are more aggressive than the agents of goodness; and the children of darkness are wiser in their generation than the children of light. I suppose it is the same the wide world over; but, of a surety, in Ire-

land one rebel makes a thousand. No one thinks himself called upon to be a martyr or witness to the right.
Of course, Father Letheby had sympathizers; but they
limited their sympathy to kindly criticism:—

" He was well in his way, making ladies of thim that
ought to be diggin' praties in the fields."

" He's young, Maurya; when he gets oulder, he'll
know betther."

" Shure, they were bad enough to say he was puttin'
the money in his own pocket, and dem goin' to their juty
every month."

" I hard my lady with the fringes and the curls and
the cuffs say that the poor priest was turning a good
pinny by it; and that he larned the thrade from his
father."

" The dirty whipster; an' I saw the chops and the
steaks goin' in her door, where a fryin'-pan was never
known to sing before."

" An' her kid gloves an' her bonnet on Sunday. Begor,
the Lady G—— is nothin' to her."

" Well, the poor priest is well rid av thim, however.
I suppose 'twill be shut up now."

Nevertheless, the girls never came back. The terror
of some nameless, undefined apprehension hung over
them.

But I am anticipating. We dined with Father Letheby the evening of this eventful day. We had a pretty
large party of priests; for a good many had come over to
witness the launch of the fishing-boat. And, Father
Letheby's star being in the ascendant, he had a few wor-
shippers, unenvious, except with the noble emulation of
imitating him. This is the rarest, but most glorious success that life holds forth to the young and the brave.
Fame is but a breath; Honour but the paint and tinsel
of the stage; Wealth an intolerable burden; but the fire
of noble rivalry struck from the souls of the young in the
glow of enthusiasm—here is the only guerdon that the

world can give to noble endeavour, and the kingly promises of success. And my brave curate, notwithstanding the reverses of the morning, rose to the occasion,
kindled by the sincere applause that rang around him for
noble efforts that had passed into completeness and frui-
tion; and I, an old man, just about to make my bow and
exit, felt almost young again, as the contagion of youth
touched me, and I saw their eyes straining afar after
the magnificent possibilities of the future. God bless
them! for they need every square inch of energy and enthusiasm to meet the disappointments and defeats, the
lack of sympathy and appreciation, and the superabun-
dance of criticism that await them. Dear me! if only
the young had fair play and the tonic of a kindly word—
but no, kind words appear to be weighed out like gold;
and then comes deadly depression and heart-searching
and all brave courage is extinguished, and all noble aspi-
rations checked, until in middle age we find only the
dried-up, cauterized, wizened soul, taught by dread experience to be reticent and cautious, and to allow splendid opportunities to pass unutilized rather than risk the
chances of one defeat. And the epitaph on these dead
souls is: *Foris pugnæ, intus timores.*

This evening we let ourselves out bravely. It was a great
occasion; we were all proud of the success of my brave
young confrère; and when Father Duff rose to propose his
health, the table rang and rocked with our applause.
The westering sun threw a soft glory over the beautiful
flowers and plants that decorated the table, and lingered
long in the ruby flames of the glasses; the room was
filled with a hundred odours from plant and shrub, and
the blood of grapes that were crushed in the wine-presses
of Languedoc and Dauphiny; and from afar through the
open window came the scented June air and the murmurs of the ever restless sea. Father Duff spoke well,
and feelingly, and generously, and wound up a fine, eloquent speech with the words: —

" And whilst we heartily wish him many years of increased utility in wider and loftier spheres of action, and,
with successful work, the laurels and the prizes that
should follow it, may we be tempted to follow his noble
initiative, and to learn that the very war against difficulties, and their conquest, is one of the richest prizes of
labour and effort, and that toil and battle, even of themselves, have the faculty of ennobling and refining."

Then we all stood up, with our glasses poised, and
sang: " For he's a right good fellow." There were
greetings of " Ad multos annos," etc.; and just then
there came across the fields from the direction of the pier
a low, wailing sound, so thin and faint that we almost
doubted the testimony of our ears. Presently it was renewed, in increased volume, then died away again as the
land breeze caught it and carried it out to sea. We looked
at one another in surprise, and Father Letheby, somewhat disturbed, said:—

" I did not know that any of our people was dead."

" You expected no funeral this evening? "

" No! I got no intimation that anyone was to be
buried."

Then he rose to respond to the toast of his health. He
spoke well, and with a good deal of grateful feeling; and
he seemed to appreciate mostly the generous congratulations of the younger clergy, whom he had gathered
around him. But ever and anon, that wail for the dead
broke over the moorland, and interrupted his glowing
periods, until it came quite close to the village, and appeared to be circling round the house in dismal, funereal
tones of agony and distress.

" I must bring my remarks to an abrupt conclusion,
gentlemen," he said anxiously; " something is seriously
wrong in the village, and I must go and see."

He had not far to go. For now a tumultuous throng
had burst into the village, as we could feel by the hurried tramp of feet, and the sound of many voices, and
the awful accents of hysterical women raising that chant

for the dead that is so well known in Ireland. The crowd
gathered in thick masses around the door, and we went
out.

" She's gone, your reverence, and they are all
drowned."

" Sunk by a steamer—— "

" Struck her foreships—— "

" No! abaft—— "

" The captain's drowned—— "

" Can't you let the min spake for theirselves? " said
Jem Deady, who assumed at once the office of Master of
Ceremonies. " Bring these fellows for'ard, and let them
tell the priest."

They were brought forward, the four fishermen, but
were not too well able to sustain conversation, much less
to detail a thrilling narrative of events; for the poor fellows had been filled up to the epiglottis with whiskey,
and were in momentary peril of asphyxia. By piecing
and patching their ejaculations together, however, it was
ascertained that the " Star of the Sea " had a glorious
run to the fishing-fleet, was welcomed cheerily by the
Manx boats, and even more enthusiastically by the Cher-
bourg fleet; had made all arrangements for the sale of
her fish; and then, with renewed vigour, was making for
home. The haze that had hung over the sea all the morning had deepened, however, into a thick fog; and one
wary old fisherman had ventured to warn Campion that
he had too much way on, and to keep a good look-out.
He laughed at the notion of their meeting any vessel in
those desolate waters, and had freed the helm for a moment whilst he lit a cigar, when just then there was a
shout, and a large steamer loomed out of the fog, running at right angles with the fishing-craft. Screams of
warning came from the steamer, her fog-whistle was
sounded, but Campion took it coolly.

" He thought it was the wather-witch, the 'Halcyonia,'
he had, your reverence, and she swung to the touch of a
baby's finger."

But the heavy craft was not so obedient, and Campion's attempt to show his seamanship was disastrous. He ran right under the steamer's nose, and had just almost cleared her when her prow struck the boat, six or eight feet from the stern, sheared off her helm and steering apparatus as if cut with a knife, and struck Campion as he fell. Then in a moment the boat filled and careened over, throwing her crew into the sea. The four fishermen were saved, two by clinging to the suspended anchors of the steamer, two by ropes flung from the deck. Campion went down.

" The last we saw of him was his black head bobbing in the wather; and, faith, it wasn't his prayers he was sayin'."

Here, indeed, was the dread descent of the sword on Damocles. And all looked to Father Letheby to know what he would say. He received the dread intelligence, which foreboded ruin to himself and others, like a man, and merely turned to the expectant crowd and said :—

" Get these poor fellows home as soon as possible. Their clothes are dripping wet, and they'll catch their death of cold."

True, indeed, there were little pools of water in the hall where the shipwrecked fishermen were standing.

As we turned to go in, whilst the crowd dispersed, Jem Deady took occasion to whisper :—

" Look here, your reverence, 'twas all dhrink."

Jem had kept his pledge for six weeks, and by virtue thereof assumed all the privileges of a reformer.

It was a dread ending of the day's business, and it came with crushing effect on the soul of Father Letheby. They were bad omens—the revolt at the factory and the destruction of the boat. We remained for hours talking the thing over, whilst my thoughts ran away to the happy girl who was just then speeding from Kingstown on her bridal tour. I followed her in imagination through smoky England to sunny France. I saw her, leaning on her husband, as he led her from church to

church, from gallery to gallery, in the mediæval cities of
the Continent; I saw her cross from the Riviera into
Italy, and I realized her enthusiasm as she passed, mute
and wonder-stricken, from miracle to miracle of art and
faith, in that happy home of Catholicism. I could think
of her even kneeling at the feet of the Supreme Pontiff
whilst she begged a special blessing on her father. and he,
rolling with the tide, a dead mass in ooze and slime, and
uncouth monsters swimming around him in curiosity and
fear, and his hands clutching the green and purple *algæ*
of the deep.

" Someone asked : —

" Was the boat insured? "

" No," said Father Letheby. " We were but waiting the result of her trial trip to make that all right."

" Then the committee are responsible for the whole
thing? "

" I suppose so," said Father Letheby, gloomily.

" I should rather think not," said Father Duff, who
was quietly turning over the leaves of an album. " Depend upon it, the Board of Works never allowed her to
leave her wharf without having her fully insured, at least
for the amount payable by the Board! "

" Do you think so? " said Father Letheby, as the
cloud lifted a little at these words.

" I know it," said Father Duff, emphatically.

After a little time, and ever so many expressions of
sympathy, the guests departed and left us alone. In a
few minutes a knock came to the door, and Lizzie summoned Father Letheby.

" You're wanting just for a minute, sir."

He went out, leaving the door ajar. I heard Father
Duff saying with emphasis : —

" I am deputed to tell you, Letheby, that we are all
determined to stand by you in this affair, no matter
what it costs. As for myself, I want to assure you that
if you are good enough to trust me, I can see my way
to tide you over the crisis."

"Ten thousand thanks, Duff," Father Letheby replied. "I shall show you my friendship for you by
demanding your assistance should I need it."

He came in to tell me.

"Never mind," I said; "I heard it all, God bless
them!"

I then regretted, for the first time in my life, that I
had not loved money; I would have given a good deal for
the luxury of drawing a big check with these brave young
fellows.

I remained till twelve o'clock, debating all possibilities, forecasting, projecting all manner of plans. Now
and then a stifled wail came up from the village. We
agreed that Bittra should be allowed to proceed on her
wedding trip, and that when she returned we would
break the dreadful news as gently as possible.

"No chance of seeing the dread accident in the London papers?"

"None! It cannot reach London before to-morrow
night. They will then be in Paris."

CHAPTER XXVIII

SUB NUBE

GLORIOUS summer weather, gold on sea and land, but gloom of death and dole on our hearts, and dark forebodings of what the future has in store. I could hardly believe it possible that one night's agony could work such a change in the appearance; but when, next morning, I saw the face of Father Letheby, white and drawn, as if Sorrow had dragged his rack over it, and the dark circles under his eyes, and the mute despair of his mouth, I remembered all that I had ever read of the blanching of hair in one night, and the dread metamorphoses that follow in the furrows where Anguish has driven his plough. It appeared, then, that between the buoyancy of the day's success, and the society of friends, and the little excitements of the evening, he had not realized the extent of his losses and responsibilities. But in the loneliness of midnight it all came back; and he read, in flaming letters on the dark background of his future, the one word: *Ruin!* And it was not the financial and monetary bankruptcy that he dreaded, but the shame that follows defeat, and the secret exultation that many would feel at the toppling over of such airy castles and the destruction of such ambitious hopes. He was young, and life had looked fair before him, holding out all kinds of roseate promises; and now, at one blow, the whole is shattered, and shame and disgrace, indelible as the biting of a burning acid, was his for all the long years of life. It was no use to argue: " You have done nothing wrong or dishonourable "; here was defeat and financial ruin, and no amount of whitewashing by reason or argument could cover the dread consequences.

" Come out," I cried, after we had talked and reasoned to no purpose; " sufficient for the day is the evil thereof. Let us have a walk; and the sea air will clear the cobwebs off our brains."

We strolled down by the sea, which to-day looked so calm and beautiful, its surface fluted with grooves where the sunlight reposed, and the coloured plaits of the waves weaving themselves lazily until they broke into the white lace-work of sandy shoals. Nothing was there to show the pitiless capacity or the deep revenge it takes from time to time on its helpless conquerors. As we passed down by the creek, the " Great House " came into sight, all its blinds drawn and the white windows staring blankly at the sea.

" This poor child has a heavier cross before her than you," I said.

" Yes, but hers shall be healed in time. But who will wipe out dishonour? "

" I cannot see where the dishonour comes in," I replied. " You have neither robbed nor embezzled."

" I am a hopeless insolvent," he said. " I am security, sole security, for those men over at Kilkeel, whom I promised and guaranteed to safeguard. That I am bound to do on every principle of honour."

" Well, looking at it in its worst aspect," I replied, " insolvency is not dishonourable—— "

" It is the very acme of dishonour in a priest," he said. Then I saw the inutility of reason in such a case.

We dined together that evening; and just as the Angelus bell rang, we heard the hootings and derisive shouts of the villagers after the new hands that had been taken on at the factory. In a few minutes these poor girls came to the door to explain that they could not return to work. It was the last straw. For a moment his anger flamed up in a torrent of rage against these miscreants whom

he had saved from poverty. Then it died down in meek
submission to what he considered the higher decree.

" Never mind, girls," he said; " tell Kate Ginivan to
close the room and bring me the key."

That was all, except that a certain listener treasured
up all this ingratitude in his heart; and the following Sunday at both Masses, the walls of Kilronan chapel echoed
to a torrent of vituperation, an avalanche of anger, sarcasm, and reproach, that made the faces of the congregation redden with shame and whiten with fear, and
made the ladies of the fringes and the cuffs wish to call
unto the hills to cover them and the mountains to hide
them.

Nothing on earth can convince the villagers that the
shipwreck was an accident and not premeditated.

" They saw us coming, and made for us. Sure we
had a right to expect it. They wanted to make us drunk
at the fishing-fleet; but the cap'n wouldn't lave 'em."

" You don't mean to say they dreaded your poor
boat? "

" Dreaded? They don't want Irishmen anywhere.
Sure, 'twas only last year, whin they wanted to start a
steamer between Galway and Newfoundland—the short-
est run to America—the captain was bribed on his first
trip, and tho' there isn't nothing but ninety fathoms of
blue say-wather betune Arran and Salthill, he wint out
of his way to find a rock, three miles out av his coorse,
and—he found it. The Liverpool min settled Galway."

" And didn't the cap'n cry: ' Port! d—n you, port! '
and they turned her nose right on us."

" But they were kind when they picked you up? "

" So far as talking gibberish and pouring whiskey into
us, they were; but whin they landed us, one dirty frog-
eater sang out:—

" It's addiyou, not O revwar! "

Just a week after these events, that is, the Wednes-
day after my great sermon, which is now a respectable

landmark, or datemark, at Kilronan, I got the first letter from Bittra.   Here it is, brief and pitiful:—

HOTEL BRISTOL, Paris, Sunday.

REV. DEAR FATHER DAN :—Here we are in the world's capital.
The air is so light that you should sift the heavy atmosphere
of Kilronan a hundred times to make it as soft and exhilarating.   We ran through London, seeing enough to make one
wish to escape it; and we are boulevarding, opera-seeing,
picture-gallery-visiting, church-going since.   The churches are
superb; but—the people! Fancy only two men at Mass at
Ste. Clotilde's, and these two leaned against a pillar the
whole time, even during the Elevation.   I had a terrible distraction; I couldn't help saying all the time: " If Father Dan
was here, he'd soon make ye kneel down "; and I fancied you
standing before them, and making them kneel down by one
look.   But the women are pious.   It's all beautiful; but I
wish I were home again! Rex is all kindness; but he's a
little shocked at our French customs.   "Are these Catholics?"
he says, and then is silent.   How is dear father?   I fear he'll
be lonesome without his *petite mignonne.*   Mind, you are
hereby invited and commanded to dine every evening with
papa, and also Father Letheby.   Love to St. Dolores! Tell
Mrs. Darcy I inquired for her.   What havoc she would make
of the cobwebs here!
Dear Father Dan,
                Always your affectionate child,
                                        BITTRA ORMSBY.
P.S.—Remember you dine with papa every day. No ceremony. He likes to be treated *en bon camarade!* Isn't that
good French?

" You never know what a pitiful thing human wisdom
is," said Father Letheby, one of these dismal days of
suspense, " until you come to test it in sorrow.   Now,
here's a writer that gives me most intense pleasure when
I have been happy; and I say to every sentence he writes:
' How true! How beautiful! What superb analysis of
human emotion and feeling! '   But now, it's all words,
words, words, and the oil of gladness is dried up from
their bare and barren rhetoric.   Listen to this:—

" ' A time will come, must come, when we shall be commanded by mortality not only to cease tormenting others, but
also ourselves. A time must come, when man, even on earth,
shall wipe away most of his tears, were it only from pride.
Nature, indeed, draws tears out of the eyes, and sighs out of

the breath so quickly, that the wise man can never wholly lay
aside the garb of mourning from his body; but let his soul
wear none. For if it is ever a merit to bear a small suffering
with cheerfulness, so must the calm and patient endurance of
the worst be a merit, and will only differ in being a greater
one, as the same reason, which is valid for the forgiveness of
small injuries, is equally valid for the forgiveness of the
greatest. . . . Then let thy spirit be lifted up in pride, and
let it contemn the tear, and that for which it falls, saying:
"Thou art much too insignificant, thou every-day life, for
the inconsolableness of an immortal—thou tattered, misshapen,
wholesale existence!" Upon this sphere, which is rounded
with the ashes of thousands of years, amid the storms of
earth, made up of vapours, in this lamentation of a dream, it
is a disgrace that the sigh should only be dissipated together
with the bosom that gives it birth, and that the tear should
not perish except with the eye from which it flows.' "

"It sounds sweetly and rhythmically," I replied,
"but it rests on human pride, which is a poor, sandy
foundation. I would rather one verse of the ' Imitation.'
But he seems to be a good man and an eloquent one."

"He apologizes for the defects of philosophy," said
Father Letheby. "He says:—

"' We must not exact of philosophy that, with one stroke
of the pen, it shall reverse the transformation of Rubens, who,
with one stroke of his brush, changed a laughing child into a
weeping one. It is enough if it change the full mourning of
the soul into half-mourning; it is enough if I can say to myself, "I will be content to endure the sorrow that philosophy
has left me; without it, it would be greater, and the gnat's
bite would be the wasp's sting.' "

"Now this is a tremendous admission from a philosopher in love with his science. It shows that he cares
for truth more than for mere wisdom—— "

"Look here, young man, something has brightened
you up; this is the first day for the fortnight that you
have condescended to turn your thoughts away from the
luxury of fretting."

"Ay, indeed," he said, and there was a faint halo
around his face. "Three things—work, Dolores, and my
weekly hour. I have trampled all my bitterness under
the hoofs of hard work. I have my first chapter of ' The

Cappadocians ' ready for the printer. I tell you work is a noble tonic. It was the best thing Carlyle wrote— that essay on Work. Then this afflicted child shames me. She takes her crucifixion so gloriously. And last, but not least, when I pass my hour before the Blessed Sacrament—an hour is a long time, Father Dan, and you think of a lot of things—and when all the Christian philosophy about shame, and defeat, and suffering, and ignominy comes back to me, I assure you I have been angry with myself, and almost loathe myself for being such a coward as to whimper under such a little trial."

" Very good! Now, that's common sense. Have you heard from the Board? "

" Yes; that's all right. They are going to hold an investigation to try and make that French steamer re sponsible, as I believe she is, for two reasons: she was going full speed in the fog; and she should have observed the rule of the road, or of the sea that a steamer is always bound to give way to a sailing vessel. And I am becoming thoroughly convinced now, from all that I can hear, that it was no accident. I should like to know what took that steamer away from the fleet, and five miles out of her ordinary course. I'm sure the Board will mulct her heavily."

" But has the Board jurisdiction over foreign vessels ten or twelve miles from shore? "

" That I don't know. I wish Ormsby were home."

" So do I, except for the tragedy we'll have to witness with that poor child."

" Have you heard lately? "

" Not since she wrote from Paris."

" Alice had a letter from Florence yesterday. Such a pitiful letter, all about her father. There was a good deal that Alice did not understand—about Dante, and Savonarola, and the Certosa—but she said I'd explain it. Clearly she knows nothing as yet."

But the revelation was not long delayed, and it came about in this wise. I had a letter—a long letter—from

Bittra from Rome, in which she wrote enthusiastically about everything, for she had seen all the sacred places and objects that make Rome so revered that even Protestants call it home and feel lonely when leaving it. And she had seen the Holy Father, and got blessings for us all—for her own father, for Daddy Dan, for Dolores, for Father Letheby. " And," she wrote, " I cannot tell you what I felt when I put on the black dress and mantelletta and veil, which are *de rigueur* when a lady is granted an audience with the Pope. I felt that this should be my costume, not my travelling bridal dress; and I would have continued to wear it but that Rex preferred to see me dressed otherwise. But it is all delightful. The dear old ruins, the awful Coliseum, where Felicitas and Perpetua suffered, as you often told us; and here Pancratius was choked by the leopard; and there were those dreadful emperors and prætors, and even Roman women, looking down at the whole horrible tragedy. I almost heard the howl of the wild beasts, and saw them spring forward, and then crouch and creep onwards towards the martyrs. Some day, Rex says, we'll all come here together again—you, and papa, and Father Letheby—and we'll have a real long holiday, and Rex will be our guide, for he knows everything, and *he'll charge nothing*." Alas! her presentiment about the mourning dress was not far from verification. They travelled home rapidly, up through Lombardy, merely glancing at Turin and Milan and the Lakes. At Milan they caught the Swiss mail, and passed up and through the mountains, emerging from the St. Gothard tunnel just as a trainful of passengers burst from the refreshment rooms at Goschenen and thronged the mail to Brindisi. Here they rested; and here Bittra, anxious to hear English or Irish news, took up eagerly the " Times " of a month past, that lay on a side table, and, after a few rapid glances, read:—

" A sad accident occurred off the Galway coast, on Monday, June——. The ' Star of the Sea,' a new fishing-smack, espe-

cially built for the deep-sea fisheries, was struck on her trial
trip by a French steamer and instantly submerged.　Her
crew were saved, except Captain Campion, the well-known
yachtsman, who had taken charge of the boat for the occasion.　He must have been struck insensible by the prow of the
steamer, for he made no effort to save himself, but sank instantly.　As the disaster occurred ten miles from land, there
is no hope that his body will be recovered."

How she took the intelligence, her blank stare of horror, when Ormsby entered the dining-room, whilst she
could only point in mute despair to the paper; how, the
first shock over, she fell back upon the sublime teach-
ings of religion for consolation; and how the one thing
that concerned her most deeply manifested itself in her
repeated exclamations of prayer and despair: " His
soul! his soul! poor papa! "—all this Ormsby told us
afterwards in detail.　They hurried through Lucerne to
Geneva, from Geneva to Paris, from Paris home, travelling night and day, his strong arm supporting her bravely,
and he, in turn, strengthened in his new-born faith by
the tenderness of her affection and the sublimity of her
faith.

Of course, we knew nothing of all this whilst the days,
the long days, of July drew drearily along with cloudless
skies, but, oh! such clouded hearts!　Suspense and un-
certainty weighed heavily on us all.　We did not know
what to-morrow might bring.　Occasionally a visitor
came over through curiosity to see the theatre of the accident, shrug his shoulders, wonder at the folly of young
men, and depart with an air of smug self-satisfaction.
There were a few letters from the factory at Loughboro',
complaining and then threatening, and at last came a
bill for £96 0s. 0d., due on the twelve machines, and an
additional bill for £30 0s. 0d., due on material.　Then
I wrote, asking the proprietor to take back machines and
material, and make due allowance for both.　I received
a courteous reply to the effect that this was contrary to
all business habits and customs.　There the matter
rested, except that one last letter came, after a certain

interval, peremptorily demanding payment and threatening law proceedings.

One shamefaced, dreary deputation came to me from the young girls who had been employed in the factory. They expressed all kinds of regrets for what they had done, promised amendment, guaranteed steady work for the future, would only ask half pay, would work for some weeks for nothing even until the debts were paid off. I referred them briefly to Father Letheby.

" They couldn't face him. If he was mad with them and scolded them, they could bear it and be glad of it; but they couldn't bear to see his white face and his eyes. Would I go and see him for them, and bring back the key to Kate Ginivan? "

I did, and came back with a laconic *No!* Then for the first time they understood that they had knocked their foolish heads against adamant.

" There's nothing for us, then, but America, your reverence," they said.

" It would be a good thing for the country if some of you went, whatever," I said.

The following Sunday a deputation appeared in the village—the good merchants from Kilkeel, who had subscribed the balance of two hundred pounds for the boat. They called just as Father Letheby was at breakfast, immediately after his last Mass. He received them courteously, but waited for what they had to say.

" That was an unfortunate thing about the boat, your reverence," said the spokesman.

" Very much so, indeed," said Father Letheby.

" A great misfortune, entirely," said another, looking steadily at the floor.

" We come to know, your reverence, what's going to be done," said the foreman.

" Well, the matter lies thus, gentlemen," said Father Letheby. " The Board of Trade is making careful investigations with a view to legal proceedings; and, I un-

derstand, are sanguine of success. They hope to make
that steamer responsible for the entire amount."

" The law is slow and uncertain," said the foreman.

" And we understand that the crew do not even know
the name of the steamer that ran them down," said
another.

" You may be sure, gentlemen," said Father Letheby, " that the Board will leave nothing undone to secure
their own rights and those of the proprietors. They have
already intimated to me that I shall be called upon to
prosecute in case the Inspector of the Board of Trade
finds that there was malice prepense or culpable negli-
gence on the part of the master of the steamer, and I am
fully prepared to meet their wishes. This means a prosecution, out of which, I am sanguine, we shall emerge
victorious; and then there will be no delay in discharg-
ing our obligations to you individually."

" Live horse, and you'll get grass," said one of the
deputation insolently, presuming on the quiet tone Father
Letheby had assumed.

" 'Tis hunting for a needle in a bundle of straw," said
another.

Father Letheby flushed up, but said nothing. The
foreman assumed a calm, magisterial air.

" You will remember, Reverend sir," he said, " that
this subscription to what some considered a Uropean[1]
idea was not, I may say, advanced on our part. It was
only at your repeated solicitations, Reverend sir, that we
consented to advance this sum out of our hard earnings
——— "

" Hard enough, begor," said a member; " 'tisn't by
booklarnin', but by honest labour, we got it."

" If you would kindly allow me, Mr. ———," said the
foreman, in a commiserating tone, " perhaps I could explain to the Reverend gentleman our views in a more—
in a more—in a more—satisfactory manner."

[1] " Utopian," I suppose, the poor man meant.

" There's simply nothing to be explained," said Father Letheby. " The boat is at the bottom of the sea; I am responsible to you for two hundred pounds. That's all."

" Pardon me, sir," said the eloquent foreman, who was nettled at the idea that his oratory was not acceptable—and he had once proposed a Member for Parliament—" pardon me, that is not all. We—a—are accustomed to repose in our clergymen the highest, and indeed, I may add, the deepest confidence. When that good lady—I quite forget her name, it is so long since I read my classics—perhaps, sir, you could help me—ahem! "

" I am quite at a loss to know to what excellent lady you refer," said Father Letheby.

" I'm very sorry to hear such a statement from the lips of a clergyman," said the foreman, with much severity; " for the lady to whom I refer is the representative, and, indeed, the personification of Justice—— "

" Oh, you mean ' Astræa,' " said Father Letheby.

" Quite so, sir," said the merchant, pompously. " When Astery left the earth she took refuge in the Church."

" Indeed! " said Father Letheby, " I was not aware of that interesting fact."

" Well, sir," said the merchant, nettled at this sarcastic coolness, " at least we, laymen, are accustomed to think so. We have been taught to repose unbounded confidence in our clergy—— "

" And how have I forfeited that confidence? " said Father Letheby, who began to see a certain deliberate insult under all this silliness.

" Well, you see, sir," he continued, " we relied on your word of honour, and did not demand the usual securities for the advance of our money. And now we find ourselves in a curious predicament—our money gone, and no redress."

" You doubt my word of honour now? " said Father
Letheby, who, to his own seeming, had been a miracle
of patience.

" We have been deceived, sir," said the merchant,
grandly.

" Pray, how? " said Father Letheby. " You may not
be aware of the meaning of your language, nor of the
usual amenities of civilized society, but you should at
least know that your language approaches very closely
to insult."

" We have been deceived, sir," said the other,
severely.

" Might I repeat my question, and ask you how? "
said Father Letheby.

" We got the most repeated assurance, sir," said the
merchant, " that this boat would be a mine of wealth.
Instead of that, it is, if I may so speak, a tornado of ruin
and misfortune. It lies, if I may use the expression, at
the bottom of the briny sea."

" To cut a long story short," said another of the deputation, " that boat was a swindle from beginning to
end, and I know it—— "

" Pardon me, gentlemen," said Father Letheby, rising, " but I must now cut short the interview, and ask
you to retire—— "

" Ask us to retire with our money in your pocket! "

" Turn us out, and we—— "

" Now, gentlemen, there is no use in prolonging this
unpleasantness. Be good enough to leave my house.
Lizzie, show these gentlemen the door." He had touched
the bell.

" We retire, sir, but we shall come again. We retreat, but we return. Like Marius "—the foreman was
now in the street, and there was a pretty fair crowd
around the door—" like Marius, like Marius—— "

" Who the d—l would marry the likes of you, you
miserable omadhaun," said Jem Deady, who knew by
instinct that this was a hostile expedition. " Give us

de word, your reverence, and we'll chuck the whole
bloomin' lot into the say.   It was many a long day since
they had a bat', if we're to judge by dere dirty mugs."
This was the signal for a fierce demonstration.   In a
moment the village was in arms, men rushed for stones,
women, hastily leaving the dinner-tables, gathered up
every kind of village refuse; and amidst the din of exe-
cration and abuse the shopkeepers of Kilkeel climbed on
their cars and fled; not, however, without taking with
them specimens, more or less decayed, of the *fauna* and
flora of Kilronan, in the shape of eggs redolent of sulphur-
etted hydrogen, a few dead cats, and such potatoes and
other vegetables as could be spared from the Sunday
dinner.   The people of Kilronan had, of course, a perfect right to annoy and worry their own priests, especially in the cause of Trades-Unionism; but the idea of a
lot of well-dressed malcontents coming over from Kilkeel
to insult their beloved curate was simply intolerable.

Nevertheless, that lonely walk by the sea-cliffs that
Sunday afternoon was about the most miserable experience in Father Letheby's life.   He did not know whither
to turn.   Every taunt and insult of these ignorant men
came back to sting him.   What would it be if the whole
thing came to publicity in the courts, and he was made
the butt of unjust insinuations by some unscrupulous
barrister, or the object of the lofty, moral indignation of
the bench!   Yet he felt bound, by every law of honour,
to pay these men two hundred pounds.   He might as
well be asked to clear off the national debt.   Now and
again he paused in his walk, and, leaning on his umbrella, scrutinized the ground in anxious reverie; then
he lifted up his eyes to the far horizon, beneath whose
thin and misty line boat and captain were sleeping. Then
he went on, trying in vain to choke down his emotion.
"Star of the Sea! Star of the Sea!" he muttered. Then,
half unconsciously: " Stella maris! Stella maris!! Porta
manes, et stella maris, succurre cadenti surgere qui curat
populo! "

CHAPTER XXIX

STIGMATA ?

I DO not think it was personal humiliation, or the sense of personal shame, or dread of further exposure, that really agitated Father Letheby during these dreary days, so much as the ever-recurring thought that his own ignominy would reflect discredit on the great body to which he belonged. He knew how rampant and how unscrupulous was the spirit of criticism in our days and with what fatal facility the weaknesses and misfortunes of one priest would be supposed, in the distorted mirrors of popular beliefs, to be reflected upon and besmirch the entire sacred profession. And it was an intolerable thought that, perhaps in far distant years, his example would be quoted as evidence of folly or something worse on the part of the Irish priesthood. " When Letheby wasted hundreds of pounds belonging to the shopkeepers of Kilkeel," or " Don't you remember Letheby of Galway, and the boat that was sunk? " " What was his bishop doing? " " Oh, he compelled him to leave the diocese!" These were the phrases, coined from the brazen future, that were flung by a too fervid or too anxious imagination at his devoted head; and if the consolations of religion healed the wounds rapidly, there were ugly cicatrices left behind, which showed themselves in little patches of silver here and there in his hair, and the tiny fretwork of wrinkles in his forehead and around his mouth. Then, whilst speaking, he grew frequently abstracted and would start and murmur: " I beg pardon! I didn't quite catch what you were saying." Then I understood

that he had sleepless nights as well as troublous days;
and all the time I was powerless to help him, though I
yearned to be able to do so. What was most aggravating
was the complete silence of Father Duff and his contem-
poraries during these days of trial, and the contemptuous
and uncharitable criticisms that reached me, but did not
reach Father Letheby, from quondam admirers and
friends.

" Sure, we knew well how it would all turn out! These
Utopian schemes generally do end in failure."

" If he had only followed the beaten track, there was
every prospect of success before him; for, mind you, he
had a fair share of ability."

" I wonder what will the bishop do? "

" I dare say he'll withdraw faculties and ask him to
seek a mission abroad."

" Well, it is a warning to the other young fellows, who
were tempted to follow him."

I was hoping that the return of Bittra and Ormsby
would wean him away from his anxiety. But this, too,
was pitiful and sad beyond words. I ventured to go see
her the morning after their arrival. Ormsby came into
the drawing-room first, and told me all particulars of
their journey, and prepared me to see a great change in
his young wife. Nevertheless, I was startled to see what
a transformation a few days' agony had caused. Bittra
had a curious habit of holding her face upwards, like a
child, when she spoke; and this innocent, ingenuous
habit, so typical of her candour and opennness of mind,
was now accentuated by the look of blank and utter despair that had crept over her. If she had wept freely, or
been hysterical, it would have been a relief; but no! she
appeared dazed, and as if stricken into stone by the magnitude of her sorrow; and all the little accidents of home
life—the furniture, the gardens, her father's room and
his wardrobe, his few books, his fishing-rods and fowling-
pieces—all were souvenirs of one whose place could not
be filled in her soul, and whose tragic end, unsupported

by the ministrations of religion, made the tender and reverent spirit of his child think of possibilities which no
one can contemplate without a shudder. How different
the Catholic from the non-Catholic soul! What an intense realization of eternity and the future of its immortal spirits in the one! How utterly callous and indifferent
to that immortality is the other! What an awful idea
of God's justice in the one. What cool contempt for
God's dispensations in the other! And how the one realizes the bursting of bonds and the setting free of the immortal spirit unto the vast environments and accidents
of life, whilst the other sees but dead clay with some dim
ideas of a shadowy and problematical eternity! "His
soul! his soul!" Here was the burden of Bittra's grief.
Ormsby could not understand it; he was frightened and
bewildered. I tried every word of solace, every principle of hope, that are our inheritance, only to realize
that—

> "Not all the preaching since Adam
> Can make Death other than Death!"

Then I took her out into the yard, and placed her where
her father had stood on the morning of her marriage, and
where he heard "the Mass of his sad life ringing coldly to
its end." I repeated every word he said—his remorse,
his faith, his determination for the future, his regret that
he was not with her on the morning of her nuptial Communion, his promise to be at Communion the Sunday
after they returned from the Continent. "And here,"
I said, "he stood when the Angelus rang, and, taking
off his hat, reverentially said it; and I counted the silver
in his hair. And do you think, you little infidel, that our
great Father has not numbered the hairs of his head also
—ay, and the deep yearnings of his heart?"
She looked relieved.
"Come now," I said, "put on your hat and let us see
Dolores. She knows eternity better than you or I."

" May I ask Rex to come with us? "

" Certainly," as I thought what a merciful dispensation it was that a new love had been implanted where an old love was rudely snatched away.

" And Dr. Armstrong? He journeyed down from Dublin with us."

" Of course. He intends, I believe, to see Alice professionally."

" Yes. He is to arrange for a consultation with our doctor."

" Very good. We shall all go together."

So we did. And I had the supreme consolation to see these two afflicted ones mingling their tears in the chalice that was held to them to drink.

" One little word, Father Dan," said Alice, as I departed. " I don't mind Mrs. Ormsby. There is to be no operation, you promised me."

" No my dear child, don't think of that. You will be treated with the greatest delicacy and tenderness."

The result of the investigation made next day was a curious one. It was quite true that her poor body was one huge sore; even the palms of her hands and the soles of her feet were not exempt. But Dr. Armstrong made light of this.

" I cannot promise to make her as handsome as I am told she was," he said; " but I can restore her health by powerful tonics and good food. That's no trouble. I've seen worse cases at least partially cured. But the poor girl is paralyzed from the hips down, and that is beyond human skill."

Here was a revelation. I told Alice about it after the doctors had left. She only said " Thank God! " But Dr. Armstrong's predictions were verified. Slowly, very slowly, in a few weeks, the external symptoms of the dread disease disappeared, until the face and forehead became thoroughly healed, and only a red mark, which time would wear off, remained. And her general strength came back, day by day, as fresh blood drove out all that was tainted and unwholesome, and even her hair began to grow, first in fluffy wisps, then in strong, glossy curls, whilst a curious, spiritual beauty seemed to animate her features, until she looked, to my eyes, like the little Alice I had worshipped as a child. In a mysterious way, also, Alice and Bittra seemed to pass into each other's souls; and as the thorns withered and fell away from each young brow and heart, little roses of Divine love, reflected in human sympathy and fellowship, seemed to sprout, and throw out their tender leaves, until the Rose of Love took the place of the red Roses of Pain; and Time, the Healer, threw farther back, day by day, the memories of trials surmounted, and anguish subdued in its bitterness to the sweetness of resignation. And when, one day in the late autumn, when all the leaves were reddening beneath the frosts of night and the hushed, hidden grays of sombre days, Alice was rolled to the door of her cottage, and saw the old, familiar objects again; and the children clustered around her bath-chair with all kinds of presents of lovely flowers and purple and golden fruits; and as the poor, pale invalid stretched out her thin hands to the sky, and drew in long draughts of pure, sweet air, she trembled under the joy of her resurrection, and seemed to doubt whether, after all, her close little room, and the weary bed, and her own dread cross, and her crucifix, were not better. But now she understood that this recovery of hers was also God's holy will, and she bowed her head in thankfulness and wept tears of joy.

And so the cross was lifted from the shoulders of two of my children, only to press more heavily on the third. As the dreary days went by, and no relief came to Father Letheby, his suspense and agitation increased. It was a matter of intense surprise that our good friends from Kilkeel seemed to have forgotten their grievance; and a still greater surprise that their foreman and self-constituted protagonist could deprive himself of the intense pleasure of writing eloquent objurgations to the priest.

But not one word was heard from them; and when, in
the commencement of the autumn, Father Letheby received a letter from the Board of Works, stating that the
Inspector of the Board of Trade despaired of making the
owners of the steamer amenable, and stated, moreover,
that they might be able to indemnify eventually the local
subscribers out of the receipts accruing from the insurance on the boat, no reply came to this communication
which he had immediately forwarded to Kilkeel.   He
had one other letter from the solicitor of the Loughboro'
Factory Company, stating that law proceedings were
about being instituted in Dublin, at the Superior Courts.
He could only reply by regretting his inability to meet
the demand, and offering, as an instalment, to auction
all his furniture and books, and forward the proceeds.
And so things went on, despair deepening into despair,
until one morning he came to me, his face white as a
sheet, and held out to me, with tremulous hands, a tiny
sheet, pointing with his finger to one particular notice.
It was not much, apparently, but it was the verdict, final
and irrevocable, of insolvency and bankruptcy. It was a
list of judgments, marked in the Superior Courts, against
those who are unable to meet their demands; and this
particular item ran thus:—

County.	Defendants.	Plaintiff.	Court.	Date of Judgment.	Amount.	Costs.
Galway.	Letheby, Rev. Edward, R.C. Clergyman.	Loughboro' Factory Co., L't'd.	Q. B.	Oct. 12, 187-	£126 0 0	£8 12 6

" This is the end," said he, mournfully.   " I have
written the bishop, demanding my *exeat*."

" It is bad, very bad," I replied.

" I suppose the Kilkeel gentlemen will come next,"
he said. " and then the bailiffs."

" The whole thing is melancholy," I replied; " it is

one of those cases which a man requires all his fortitude
and grace to meet."

" Well, I made a complete sacrifice of myself this
morning at Mass," he said, gulping down his emotion;
" but I didn't anticipate this blow from on high. Nevertheless, I don't for a moment regret or withdraw. What
is that you quote about suffering :—

> ' . . . aspera, sed nutrix hominum bona ' ?

I'll make arrangements now to sell off everything, and
then for

> ' Larger constellations burning, mellow moons, and happy
> skies,
> Breadths of tropic shade, and palms in cluster, knots of
> Paradise.'

But the name I leave behind me—Letheby!—Letheby!
It will go down from generation to generation—a word of
warning against shame and defeat. Dear me! how different the world looked twelve months ago! Who would
have foreseen this? And I was growing so fond of my
work, and my little home, and my books, and my choir,
and—and—the children! "

" Alice and Bittra have been pulled out of the fire un-
scathed," I said feebly. " Why may not you? "

" Ay, but they had physical and domestic troubles,"
he said; " but how can you get over disgrace? "

" That, too, may be overcome," I replied. " Is there
not something about ' opprobrium hominum et abjectio
plebis,' in Scripture? "

" True," he said, " there it is. I am for ever grasping
at two remedies, or rather support—work, work, work,
and the Example you have quoted; and sometimes they
swing me up over the precipices and then let me down
into the abysses. It is a regular see-saw of exultation
and despair! "

" Let me know, when you have heard from the
bishop," I said; " somehow I believe that all will come
right yet."

" No, no, Father Dan," he said, " it is only your good
nature which you mistake for a happy presentiment. Look
out for a new curate."

The events of the afternoon, indeed, did not promise
favourably for my forecast. About three o'clock, whilst
Father Letheby was absent, a side-car drove into the
village, from which two men alighted; and having made
inquiries, proceeded to Father Letheby's house, and told
the bewildered and frightened Lizzie that they had come
to take possession. Lizzie, like a good Irish girl, stormed
and raged, and went for the police, and threatened the
vengeance of the Superior Courts, at which they laughed
and proceeded to settle themselves comfortably in the
kitchen. Great fear fell, then, upon the village, and
great wrath smouldered in many breasts; and, as surely
as if they had lighted beacon-fires, or sent mounted
couriers far and wide, the evil news was flashed into the
remotest mountain nooks and down to the hermitages of
the fishermen. And there was wrath, feeble and impotent, for here was the law, and behind the law was the
omnipotence of England.

What Father Letheby endured that evening can only
be conjectured; but I sent word to Lizzie that he was to
come up to my house absolutely and remain there until
the hateful visitors had departed. This was sooner than
we anticipated. Meanwhile, a few rather touching and
characteristic scenes occurred. When the exact nature
of Father Letheby's trouble became known, the popular
indignation against the rebellious factory girls became so
accentuated that they had to fly from the parish, and
they finally made their way, as they had promised, to
America. Their chief opponents now were the very persons that had hooted their substitutes through the village, and helped to close the factory finally. And two
days after the bailiffs had appeared, an old woman, who
had been bed-ridden for years with rheumatism, managed to come down into the village, having got a " lift "
from a neighbour, and she crept from the cart to my

L

door. Father Letheby was absent; he hid himself in the
mountains or in the sea-caves these dread days, never
appearing in the village but to celebrate his morning
Mass, snatch a hasty breakfast, and return late at night,
when the shadows had fallen. Well, Ellen Cassidy made
her way with some difficulty into my little parlour, where,
after I had recovered from my fright at the apparition,
I ventured to address her:—

" Why, Nell, you don't mean to say that this is yourself? "

" Faith it is, your reverence, my own poor ould bones.
I just kem down from my cabin at Maelrone."

" Well, Nell, wonders will never cease. I thought
you would never leave that cabin until you left it feet
foremost."

" Wisha, thin, your reverence, naither did I; but God
give me the strinth to come down on this sorrowful
journey."

" And what is it all about Nell? Sure, you ought to
be glad that the Lord gave you the use of your limbs
again."

" Wisha, thin, your reverence, sure, 'tis I'm wishing
that I was in my sroud[1] in the cowld clay, before I saw
this sorrowful day. Me poor gintleman! me poor gintleman! To think of all his throuble, and no wan to help
him! "

" You mean Father Letheby's trouble, Nell? "

" Indeed, 'n' I do—what else? Oh! wirra, wirra! to
hear that me poor gintleman was gone to the cowld gaol,
where he is lying on the stone flure, and nothing but the
black bread and the sour wather."

Whilst Nell was uttering this lonely threnody, she was
dragging out of the recesses of her bosom what appeared
to be a red rag. This she placed on the table, whilst I
watched her with interest. She then commenced to un-
roll this mummy, taking off layer after layer of rags,

[1]Shroud.

until she came to a crumpled piece of brown paper, all the time muttering her Jeremiad over her poor priest. Well, all things come to an end; and so did the evolutions of that singular purse. This last wrapper was unfolded, and there lay before me a pile of crumpled banknotes, a pile of sovereigns, and a handful of silver.

" 'Tisn't much, your reverence, but it is all I have. Take it and give it to the good gintleman, or thim who are houlding him, and sind him back to us agin."

" 'Tis a big sum of money, Nell, which a poor woman like you could hardly afford to give—— "

" If it were tin millions times as much, your reverence, I'd give it to him, my darlin' gintleman. Sure, an' 'twas he came to me up on that lonesome hill in all the rain and cowld of last winter; and 'twas he said to me, ' Me poor woman, how do you live at all! And where's the kittle? ' sez he; but sure, I had no kittle; but he took up a black burnt tin, and filled it with wather, and put the grain of tay in it, and brought it over to me; and thin he put his strong arm under my pillow, and lifted me up, and ' Come, me poor woman,' sez he, ' you must be wake from fastin'; take this '; and thin he wint around like a 'uman and set things to rights; and I watchin' him and blessin' him all the time in *my* heart of hearts; and now to think of him without bite or sup—wisha, tell me, your reverence," she said, abruptly changing her subject, " how much was it? Sure, I thought there was always a dacent living for our priests at Kilronan. But the times are bad, and the people are quare."

It needed all my eloquence and repeated asseverations to persuade her that Father Letheby was not gone to gaol as yet, and most probably would not go. And it was not disappointment, but a sense of personal injury and insult, that overshadowed her fine old face as I gathered up her money and returned it to her. She went back to her lonely cabin in misery.

When Father Letheby came in and sat down to a late dinner, I told him all. He was deeply affected.

"There is some tremendous mine of the gold of human excellence in these good people," he said; "but the avenues to it are so tortuous and difficult, it seems hardly worth while seeking for. They are capable of the most stupendous sacrifices provided they are out of the common; but it is the regular system and uniformity of the natural and human law that they despise. But have you any letter for me?"

"None. But here is a tremendous indictment against myself from Duff."

"No letter from the bishop?" he said despondently, as he opened and read the letter, which ran thus:—

ATHELOY, 13/10/7—.

REV. DEAR FATHER DAN:—How has all this miserable business occurred? Well, to our minds, you alone are culpable and responsible. We must seem to Letheby to be utter caitiffs and cowards, to allow matters to come to such a horrible crisis, especially in the case of a sensitive fellow like him. But up to the date of that horrible exposure in Stubbs', we had no idea there were complications with those factory people—nothing, in fact, beyond the responsibilities of that unhappy boat. Now, why didn't you let us know? You may not be aware that the evening of the disaster I made a solemn engagement to stand by him to the end; and now all this must seem the merest braggadocio. And yet, the thing was a trifle. Would you tell Letheby now, that it will be all right in a few days, and to cheer up; no harm done, beyond a temporary humiliation! But we'll never dine with you again, and we shall, one and all, brave the Episcopal anger by refusing to be your curates when Letheby is promoted.

Yours, etc.,
CHARLES L. DUFF, C.C.

"He's very kind, very kind, indeed," said Father Letheby, meditatively; "but I cannot see how he is going to make it all right in a few days."

"It wouldn't surprise me much," I replied, "if that good young fellow had already put a sop in those calves' mouths over there at Kilkeel."

"Impossible!" he cried.

"Well, time will tell."

I called down to see Alice and talk over things. It
is wonderful what a *clairvoyante* she has become. She
sees everything as in a magic mirror.

"I think the Holy Souls will come to his relief," she
said, in a cool, calm way. "He has, I think, a great
devotion to the Holy Souls. He told me once, when we
were talking about holy things, that he makes a *memento* in every Mass for the most neglected and aban-
doned priest in purgatory; but, sure, priests don't go to
purgatory, Father Dan, do they?"

"Well, my dear, I cannot answer you in general terms;
but there's one that will be certainly there before many
years; and unless you and Father Letheby and Bittra
pull him out by your prayers, I'm afraid——. But continue what you were saying."

"He makes a *memento*, he said, for the most aban-
doned priest, and for the soul that is next to be released.
And whenever he has not a special intention, he always
gives his Mass to our Blessed Lady for that soul. Now,
I think, that's very nice. Just imagine that poor soul
waiting inside the big barred gates, and the angel, probably her warder for many years, outside. They don't
exchange a word. They are only waiting, waiting. Far
within are the myriads of Holy Souls, praying, suffering,
loving, hoping. There is a noise as of a million birds,
fluttering their wings above the sea. But here at the
gate is silence, silence. She dares not ask: When?—because the angel does not know. Now and again he looks
at her and smiles, and she is praying softly to herself.
Suddenly there is a great light in the darkness overhead,
and then there is a dawn on the night of purgatory; for
a great spirit is coming down swiftly, swiftly, on wings of
light, until he reaches the prison-house. Then he hands
the warder-angel a letter from the Queen of Heaven; and
in a moment, back swing the gates, and in plunges the
guardian angel, and wraps up that expectant soul in his
strong wings, and up, up, up, through starry night and
sunny day they go, until they come into the singing

heavens; and up along the great avenues of smiling angels, until at last the angel lays down that soul gently at the feet of Mary. And all this was done by a quiet priest in a remote, whitewashed chapel, here by the Atlantic, and there was no one with him but the little boy who rang the bell."

I had been listening to this rhapsody with the greatest admiration, when just then Bittra came in. She has got over the most acute period of her grief, " except when," she says, " she looks at the sea and thinks of what is there."

" Alice is prophesying," I said; " she is going to take Father Letheby out of his purgatory on Monday."

" Ah, no, Daddy Dan, that's not fair. But I think he will be relieved from his cross."

" And what about your own troubles, Alice? " said Bittra. " Is the healing process going on? "

" Yes, indeed, thank God," she replied, " except here and there."

Bittra was watching me curiously. Now it is quite a certain fact, but I never dreamed of attaching any importance to it, that this child had recovered her perfect health, so far as that dreadful scrofulous affection extended, except in the palms of her hands and the soles of her feet, where there remained, to the doctor's intense disappointment, round, angry sores, about the size of a half-crown, and each surrounded with a nimbus of raw, red flesh, which bled periodically.

" And here, also," she said innocently this evening, " here on my side is a raw sore which sometimes is very painful and bleeds copiously. I have not shown the doctor that; but he gets quite cross about my hands and feet."

" It is very curious," I said, in my own purblind fashion, " but I suppose the extremities heal last."

" I shall walk home with you, Father Dan, if you have no objection," said Bittra.

"Come along, child," I replied. "Now, Alice, we shall be watching Monday, All Souls' Day."

"Very well, Daddy Dan," she said, smiling. "Everything will come right, as we shall see."

As we walked through the village, Bittra said to me wonderingly:—

"Isn't it curious about those sores, Father? They won't heal."

"It is," I said musingly.

"I have been thinking a lot about it," she said.

"And the result of your most wise meditations?"

"You'll laugh at me."

"Never. I never laugh. I never allow myself to pass beyond the genteel limits of a smile."

"Then I think—but—— "

"Say it out, child. What are you thinking of?"

"I think it is the *stigmata*," she said, blushing furiously.

I was struck silent. It was too grand. Could it be? Had we a real, positive saint amongst us?

"What do you think, Father Dan? Are you angry?"

"God forbid, child. But tell me, have you spoken to Alice on the matter?"

"Oh, dear no! I wouldn't dream of such a thing. It would give her an awful shock."

"Well, we'll keep it a profound secret, and await further revelations. 'Abscondisti hæc a prudentibus, et revelasti ea parvulis.'"

But next evening, I think I threw additional fervour into the *Laudate's* and *Benedicite's* at Lauds.

But as I looked at Father Letheby across the table in the lamplight, and saw his drawn, sallow cheeks and sunken eyes, and the white patch of hair over his ears, I could not help saying to myself: "You, too, have got your *stigmata*, my poor fellow!"

CHAPTER XXX

ALL'S WELL

THE soul of Jem Deady was grievously perturbed. That calm and placid philosopher had lost his equanimity. It showed itself in many ways—in violent abstraction at meal-times, and the ghoulish way in which he swallowed cups of tea, and bolted potatoes wholesale; in strange muttered soliloquies in which he called himself violent and opprobrious names; in sacrilegious gestures towards Father Letheby's house. And once, when Bess, alarmed about his sanity, and hearing dreadful sounds of conflict from his bedroom, and such expressions as these: " How do you like that? " " Come on, you ruffian! " " You'll want a beefsteak for your eye and not for your stomach, you glutton! " when Bess, in fear and trembling, entered the bedroom, she found her amiable spouse belabouring an innocent bolster which, propped against the wall, did service vicariously for some imaginary monster of flesh and blood. To all Bess's anxious inquiries there was but one answer: " Let me alone, 'uman; I'm half out o' my mind! " There should be a climax, of course, to all this, and it came. It was not the odour of the steaks and onions that, wafted across intervening gardens from Father Letheby's kitchen, precipitated the crisis; nor the tears of Lizzie, who appeared from time to time, a weeping Niobe, and whose distress would have touched the heart of a less susceptible Irishman than Jem Deady; nor yet the taunts of the women of the village, who stung him with such sarcasms as these: " Yes; Faynians begor, with their drilling, an' their antics, an' their corporals, an' their sergeants—they couldn't hunt a flock of geese.

Dere goes de captain!—look at him an' his airs; and thim
Dublin jackeens above in the priest's house, atin' him
out o' house and home, and not a man in Kilronan able
to lay a wet finger on 'em." But, as in all great crises,
it is the simple thing that proves the last straw, so in
this. What steaks and onions, tears and taunts, could
not do, was done by an innocent Havana, whose odours,
sprung from a dainty weed, held between the lips of one
of these great representatives of Her Majesty's law, and
wafted to the senses of Jem Deady, as he bent over his
cabbages in his little garden, made him throw down his
spade with something that seemed like, and most unlike,
a prayer, and rush into the house and shout: " Tare an'
houns! Flesh and blood can't stand this! Don't shpake
a word, 'uman! Don't shpake a word! but get me soap,
and hot wather, and a towel, while you'd be saying thrap-
sticks! "

Bess did as she was directed; and then paused anxiously in the kitchen to conjecture what new form her
husband's insanity was taking. Occasionally a muttered growl came from the recesses of the bedroom; and
in about a quarter of an hour out came Jem, so transformed that Bess began to doubt her own sanity, and
could only say, through her tears:—

" For the love of God, Jem, is't yourself or your
ghost? "

It certainly was not a ghost, but a fine, handsome man,
over six feet high, his hair curled, and his whiskers shining with Trotter Oil, and his long pilot coat with the
velvet collar, which he had got from Father Laverty, and
on which the merciful night, now falling, concealed the
abrasions of time. Bess looked at him with all a wife's
admiration; and then, half crying, half laughing, said:—

" And what new divilmint are ye up to now? "

Jem answered not a word. He was on the war-path.
He only said sarcastically:—

" Ye needn't expect me home to tay, Mrs. Deady.
I'm taking tay with shupparior company to-night." ·

An hour later there were three gentlemen in Father
Letheby's parlour, who appeared to have known each
other in antenatal times, so affectionate and confidential
were they. The gentleman in the middle was sympa-
thizing with his brethren in the legal profession—for he
had introduced himself as the local bailiff—on their being
sent down from the metropolis and its gaieties, from
their wives and children, into this remote and forsaken
village called Kilronan.

" It ain't too bad," said one, with a strong Northern
accent. " A' have bun in wuss diggins thon thus! "

Then the conversation drifted to possible dangers. And
it appeared there was not, in Her Majesty's dominions,
a more lawless and fiendish set of ruffians than those who
lurked in Kilronan. Why, what did they do in the days
of the Lague? Didn't they take his predecessor, as
honest a man as ever lived, and strip him, and nail him
by the ears to his door, where his neighbours found him
in the morning? But " the poluss? the poluss? " " Oh!
they're always looking the other way. But let us get
the taste of these murderin' ruffians out o' our mout'!
Come down to Mrs. Haley's. There isn't a better dhrop
betune this and Dublin."

" But the proputty? the proputty? " said the bailiffs,
looking around anxiously.

" As safe as if ye had it in yere waistcoat pockets,"
they were assured.

The three well-dressed gentlemen moved with easy dignity down the one dark street of the village, piloted carefully by the central figure, who linked his arms affectionately in his comrades', and smoked his weed with as
much dignity as if he had been born in Cuba.

" Powerful dark hole! " said one; " one mut git a blow
o' a stun and nuvver be the wiser."

" Or the prod of a pike," suggested the middle gentleman.

" Huv tha' no gaws here? " cried his neighbour.

" No. But we're thinkin' of getting up the electric

light; at laste the parish priest do be talkin' about it, and sure that's the same as havin' it. But here we are. Now, one word. There's one ruffian here whose name mustn't pass yere mout', or we don't know the conse-kinces. He's a most consaited and outrageous ruffian, doesn't care for law or judge, or priest or pope; he's the only one ye have to be afeard of. Listen, that ye may remimber. His name is Jem Deady. Keep yere mouths locked on that while ye're here."

It was a pleasant little party in Mrs. Haley's " cosy " or " snuggery." There was warmth, and light, and music, and the odour of rum-punch and lemon, and the pungency of cigars, and the pleasant stimulus of agree-able conversation. Occasionally one of the " byes " looked in, but was promptly relegated to the taproom, at a civil distance from the " gintlemin." By and by, however, as more charity and less exclusiveness prevailed under the generous influences of good liquor, the " gintle-min " requested to be allowed to show the light of their glowing faces in the plebeian taproom; and the denizens of the latter, prompt at recognizing this infinite con-descension, cheered the gentlemen to the echo.

" 'Tis the likes of ye we wants down here," they cried; " not a set of naygurs who can't buy their tay without credit."

But the local bailiff didn't seem to like it, and kept aloof from the dissipation. Also, he drank only " limin-ade." It was admitted in after years that this was the greatest act of self-denial that was recorded in history. His comrades chaffed him unmercifully.

' Come, mon, and git out o' the blues. Whoy, these are the jolliest fullows we uver mot."

" And there isn't better liquor in the Cawstle cellars. Here's to yer health, missus."

So the night wore on.

But two poor women had an anxious time. These were Lizzie, who, in some mysterious manner, persuaded herself that she was responsible for the custody and safe

keeping of the bailiffs in the eyes of the law; and if anything happened to them she might be summoned up to
Dublin, and put on her trial on the capital charge. The
other was Mrs. Deady. When eleven o'clock struck,
she expected to hear every moment the well-known footsteps of her spouse; but no! Half-past eleven—twelve
struck—and Jem had not returned. At half-past twelve
there was a peculiar scratching sound at the back-door,
and Bess opened it and dragged Jem into her arms, whilst
she poured into his face a fire of cross-questions.

"Ax me no questions an' I'll tell ye no lies," said
Jem. "Have ye anythin' to ate?"

Bess had, in the shape of cold fat bacon. Jem set to
hungrily.

"Would ye mind covering up the light in the front
windy, Bess?" said Jem.

Bess did so promptly, all the while looking at her
spouse in a distressed and puzzled manner.

"Jem," said she at length, "may the Lord forgive
me if I'm wrong, but I think ye're quite sober."

Jem nodded. A knock came to the door. It was
Lizzie.

"Have ye no news of the bailiffs, Jem?"

"I have, acushla. I left them at your dure half an
hour ago, and they're now fast asleep in their warm and
comfortable beds."

"They're not in our house," said Lizzie, alarmed.
"Oh, Jem, Jem, what have ye done, at all, at all?"

"I'll tell ye, girl," said Jem, emphatically. "I left
the gintlemin at your dure, shook hands wid them, bid
them good-night, and came down here. Is that thrue,
Bess?"

"Every word of it," said Bess.

"Go back to your bed, alanna," said Jem, "and have
pleasant dhreams of your future. Thim gintlemin can
mind theirselves."

"'Tis thrue, Lizzie," said Bess. "Go home, like a
good girl, and make your mind aisy."

Lizzie departed, crying softly to herself.

" What mischief have ye done, Jem? " said Bess, when she had carefully locked and bolted the door. " Some day ye'll be dancin' upon nothin', I'm thinkin'."

" Nabocklish! " said Jem, as he knelt down and piously said his prayers for the night.

The following day was Sunday and All Saints' Day besides; and Jem, being a conscientious man, heard an early Mass; and being a constitutional man, he strolled down to take the fresh air—down the grassy slopes that lead to the sea. Jem was smoking placidly and at peace with himself and the world. One trifle troubled him. It was a burn on the lip, where the candle had caught him the night before at Mrs. Haley's, when he was induced to relax a little, and with his hands tied behind his back, grabbed at a rosy apple, and caught the lighted candle in his mouth. But that was a trifle. As Jem calmly strolled along, he became suddenly aware of a marine phenomenon; and Jem, as a profound student of natural history, was so interested in the phenomenon that he actually took the pipe from his mouth and studied the marvel long and carefully. About twenty yards from where he was standing, a huge pile of rock started suddenly from the deep—a square, embattled mass, covered by the short, springy turf that alone can resist the action of the sea. Beside it, a tall needle of rock, serrated and sharp, shot up. These two solitary islands, the abode of goats and gulls, were known in local geography as the Cow and Calf. Now the Cow and Calf were familiar to Jem Deady from his childhood. So were the deep, hollow caves beneath. So was the angry swirl of the tide that, parted outside the rocks, swept around in fierce torrents, and met with a shock of strength and a sweat of foam at the angle near the cliffs. Therefore, these things did not surprise the calm, equable mind of Jem. But perched on the sward on the top were two strange beings, the like of whom Jem had never seen before, and whom his fancy now at once recognized as the mermen

of fable and romance. Their faces were dark as that of
his sable majesty; their hair was tossed wildly. But
they looked the picture of despair, whereas mermen were
generally reputed to be jolly. It might be no harm to
accost them, and Jem was not shy about strangers.

"Hallo, there!" he cried across the chasm; "who
the —— are ye? Did ye shwim across from ole Vir-
ginny, or did ye escape from a throupe of Christy Min-
strels?"

"You, fellow," said a mournful voice, "go at once for
the poluss."

"Aisier said than done," said Jem. "What am I to
say suppose the gintlemin are not out of their warm
beds?"

"Tell them that two of Her gracious Majesty's servants are here—brought here by the worst set of ruffians
that are not yet hanged in Ireland."

"And what do ye expect the police to do?" said Jem,
calmly.

"To do? Why, to get a boat and tuk us out o' thus,
I suppose!"

"Look at yere feet," said Jem, "and tell me what
kind of a boat would live there?"

True enough. The angry waters were hissing, and
embracing, and swirling back, and trying to leap the
cliffs, and feeling with all their awful strength and agility
for some channel through which they might reach and
devour the prisoners.

By some secret telegraphy a crowd had soon gathered.
One by one, the "byes" dropped down from the village,
and to each in turn Jem had to tell all he knew about the
mermen. Then commenced a running fire of chaff from
every quarter.

"Where are yere banjoes, gintlemin? Ye might as
well spind the Sunday pleasantly, for the sorra a wan o'
ye will get off before night."

"Start 'Way down the Suwanee River,' Jem, and
we'll give 'em a chorus,"

" You're Jem Deady, I suppose," said one of the
bailiffs. " Well, Deady, remember you're a marked
mon. I gut yer cherickter last night from a gentleman
as the greatest ruffian amongst all the ruffians of Kilronan—— "

" Yerra, man, ye're takin' lave of yer sinses. Is't
Jem Deady? Jem Deady, the biggest *omadhaun* in the
village."

" Jem Deady, the greatest *gommal*[1] that ever lived.'

" Jem Deady, that doesn't know his right hand from
his left."

" Jem Deady, who doesn't know enough to come in
out of the wet."

" Jem Deady, the innocent, that isn't waned from his
mother ayet."

During all these compliments Jem smoked placidly.
I had forgotten one of the most serious duties of a novelist—the description of Jem's toilette. I had forgotten
to say that a black pilot coat with velvet collar, red silk
handkerchief, etc., was a veritable Nessus shirt to Jem.
So passionately fond of work was he, and so high an idea
had he conceived of the sacredness and nobleness of
work, that integuments savouring of Sabbath indolence
were particularly intolerable to him. He moved about
stiffly in them, was glad to shake them off, and resume
his white, lime-stained, patched, and torn, but oh! such
luxuriously easy garments of every-day life. Then I regret to have to record an act of supreme vanity, that
might be pardonable or venial in a young lady going to a
ball or coming out in her first concert, but was simply
shocking in a middle-aged man going out to Mass on a
Sunday morning. Jem Deady actually *powdered his
face*! I do not say that it was violet powder or that he
used a puff. His methods were more primitive and more
successful. He went to a pot where lime was seething,
or rather had been seething. He took up the thick lumps

[1]A half-idiot.

and crushed them into dust. He made his face as white as if he were going to play the king in Macbeth, and Banquo's ghost was arising; and he turned his glossy locks into a cadaverous and premature grayness, and Bess didn't like it. She wanted to see him only one Sunday in " his best shuit "; but Jem, unkind fellow, would not grant her that gratification.

Where was I? Oh, yes!

Jem, nothing loth, " ruz " the " Suwanee River," and accompanying himself on an imaginary banjo, drew tears from all eyes by singing, with mingled pathos and regret :—

> " All the world am sad and dreary
> Eberywhere I roam;
> Oh! darkies, how my heart grows weary,
> Far from the old folks at home."

Then commenced a fresh cross-fire of chaff.

" The gintlemin in the orchaystra will now favour the company wit' a song."

Suddenly one young rascal shouted out :—

" Begor, perhaps it's badin' ye were goin'. Don't ye know the rigulations of the coast? If ye were caught takin' off even yere hats here without puttin' on a badin' dress, ye'd be dragged before the Mayor and Lord Lieutenant of Kilronan, and get six weeks' paynal servitude."

Then suddenly a bright idea seemed to dawn on these scamps. There was a good deal of whispering, and nodding, and pointing; and at last Jem Deady stepped forward, and in a voice full of awe and sorrow he said :—

" Wan of the byes is thinkin' that maybe ye're the same strange gintlemin that are on a visit with the priest for the last three days, and who were dacent enough to shtand ' dhrinks all round ' last night at Mrs. Haley's. 'Pon the vartue of yere oath, are ye? "

" We are. Und dom fools we made of ourselves."

" Now, aisy, aisy," said Jem. " Ye don't know us as yet; but sure wan good turn desarves another."

" Ye appear to be a dacent sort of fellow," said one of the bailiffs. " Now, look here. If ye get us 'ut of thus, we'll gev ye a pun' note, and as much dhrink as ye can bear."

Here there was a cheer.

" The tide goes down at four o'clock," said Jem, " and thin for eight minits there is a dhry passage across the rocks. Thin ye must run for yere lives, and we'll be here to help ye. But how the divil did ye get there? We never saw but a goat there afore."

" That's a matter for the Queen's Bench, my fine fellow. God help those who brought us here! "

" Amen! " cried all devoutly, lifting their ragged hats. Then they departed to make the needful preparation. After they had half mounted the declivity, one was sent back.

" The gintlemin who are going to resky ye," he said, " wants to know if ye have any conscientious objection to be brought over on the Sabbath; or wud ye rather remain where ye are till Monday? "

He was answered with an oath, and went away sadly. He was scandalized by such profanity. " Sich language on a Sunday mornin', glory be to God! What is the world comin' to? "

Four o'clock came, and the entire village of Kilronan turned out to the rescue. There were at least one thousand spectators of the interesting proceedings, and each individual of the thousand had a remark to make, a suggestion to offer, or a joke to deliver at the unhappy prisoners. And all was done under an affectation of sympathy that was deeply touching. Two constables kept order, but appeared to enjoy the fun. Now, in any other country but Ireland, and perhaps, indeed, we may also except Spain and France and Itaiy, a simple thing is done in a simple, unostentatious manner. That does not suit the genius of our people, which tries to throw around the simplest matter all the pomp and circumstance of a great event, and in the evolution thereof every man, wo-

man, and child is supposed to have a personal interest.
and a special and direct calling to order and arrange and
bring the whole proceedings to perfection.   Now, you
would say, what could be simpler than to fling a rope to
the prisoners and let them walk across on the dry rocks?
That's your ignorance and your contempt for details; for
no Alpine guides, about to cross the crevasses of a dangerous glacier, with a nervous and timid following of
tourists, ever made half the preparations that Jem Deady
and his followers made on this occasion.   Two stout
fishermen, carrying a strong cable, clambered down the
cliff, and crossed the narrow ledge of rock, now wet with
seaweed and slippery.   They might have gone down,
with perfect ease, the goat-path, sanded and gravelled,
by which the bailiffs were carried the night before; but
this would not be value for a pound and the copious liba-
tions that were to follow. They then tied the cable around
the bailiffs and around themselves, and proceeded on
their perilous journey.   With infinite care they stepped
on rock and seaweed, shouting hoarse warnings to their
mates; but all their warnings were not sufficient to prevent the bailiffs from slipping and floundering in the deep
sea-water pools left by the receding tide.   Somehow the
rope would jerk, or a fisherman would slip, and down
all would come together.   Meanwhile hoarse shouts
echoed from the gallery of spectators above.

" Pull aft there, Bill."

" Let her head stand steady to the cliff."

" Port your helm, you lubber; don't you see where
you're standing for? "

" Ease her, ease her, Tim!   Now let her for'ard."
And so, with shouts, and orders, and a fair sprinkling of
profane adjurations, the rescuers and the rescued were
hauled up the roughest side of the cliff, until the black
visages of the bailiffs were visible.   Then there was a
pause, and many a sympathetic word for the "poor min."

" Where did they come from, at all? "

" No one knows.   They're poor shipwrecked fur-
riners."

" Have they any talk? "

" Very little, except to curse."

" Poor min! and I suppose they're all drowned wet."

Whilst the rescuing party halted, and wiped the per-
spiration from their brows, one said, half apologetically:

" I am axed by these gintlemin to tell ye—ahem! that
there's a rule in this village that no credit is given, from
the price of an ounce of tay to a pound of tobakky. An'
if ye'd be so plasin' as to remimber that poun' note ye
promised, an' if it is convanient and contagious to ye,
perhaps—— "

One of the bailiffs fumbled at his pockets in his critical condition, and making a round ball of the note, he
flung it up the cliff side with a gesture of disgust. Jem
Deady took up the missive, opened it calmly, studied
the numbers, and put it in his pocket.

" Now, byes, a long pull, a sthrong pull, and a pull
thegither! "

And in an instant the bailiffs were sprawling on the
green turf.   Such cheers, such congratulations, such
slapping on the back, such hip! hip! hurrahs! were never
heard before. Then the procession formed and passed
on to the village; and to the melodious strains of " God
Save Ireland! " the bailiffs were conducted to Father
Letheby's house. Lizzie, half crying, half laughing with
delight for having escaped arrest and capital punishment,
prepared dinner with alacrity; and then a great hush
fell on the village—the hush of conjecture and surmise.
Would the bailiffs remain or depart? Would they recognize the deep hatred of the villagers under all the chaff
and fun, or would they take it as a huge joke? The same
questioning agitated their own minds; but they decided
to go for two reasons, viz., (1) that, fresh from the conflict, they could give a more lurid description of their adventure, and obtain larger compensation; and (2) that
whilst Jem Deady was scraping, with no gentle hand,

the oil and lampblack from their faces, that he had placed there the evening before, he told them, confidentially, to put a hundred miles between themselves and the villagers that night, if they did not care to leave their measures for a coffin. And so, at six o'clock a car was hired, and amidst a farewell volley of sarcastic cheers and uncomplimentary epithets, they drove to catch the night-mail to Dublin. Father Letheby promptly took possession, and found nothing wrong, except the odour of some stale tobacco smoke.

Next day was All Souls', and it was with whitened lips, and with disappointment writ in every one of his fine features, that he came up after Mass to ask had I received any letter. Alas, no! He had pinned his faith, in his own generous, child-like way, to Alice's prophecy, and the Holy Souls had failed him. I went down to see Alice. She looked at me inquiringly.

" No letter, and no reprieve," I said. " You false prophetess, you child of Mahomet, what did you mean by deceiving us? "

She was crying softly.

" Nevertheless," she said at length, " it will come true. The Holy Souls will never fail him. The day is not past, nor the morrow."

Oh, woman, great is thy faith!

Yet it was a melancholy day, a day of conjecture and fear, a day of sad misgivings and sadder forebodings; and all through the weary hours the poor priest wore more than ever the aspect of a hunted fugitive.

Next morning the cloud lifted at last. He rushed up to my house, before he had touched his breakfast, and, fluttering one letter in the air, he proffered the other.

" There's the bishop's seal," he cried. " I was afraid to open it. Will you do it for me? "

I did, cutting the edges open with all reverence, as became the purple seal, and then I read :—

BISHOP'S HOUSE, All Souls' Day, 187-

I nodded my head. Alice was right.

MY DEAR FATHER LETHEBY :—

" What? " he cried, jumping up, and coming behind my chair to read over my shoulder.

I have just appointed Father Feely to the pastoral charge of Athlacca, vacated by the death of Canon Jones; and I hereby appoint you to the administratorship of my cathedral and mensal priest here. In doing so, I am departing somewhat from the usual custom, seeing that you have been but one year in the diocese; but in making this appointment, I desire to mark my recognition of the zeal and energy you have manifested since your advent to Kilronan. I have no doubt whatever but that you will bring increased zeal to the discharge of your larger duties here. Come over, if possible, for the Saturday confessions here, and you will remain with me until you make your own arrangements about your room at the presbytery.
I am, my dear Father Letheby,
Yours in Christ,

_____

" I never doubted the bishop," I said, when I had read that splendid letter a second time. " His Lordship knows how to distinguish between the accidents of a priestly life and the essentials of the priestly character. You have another letter, I believe? "
" Yes," he replied, as if he were moonstruck; " a clear receipt from the Loughboro' Factory Co. for the entire amount."
" Then Alice was right. God bless the Holy Souls! —though I'm not sure if that's the right expression."
There never was such uproar in Kilronan before. The news sped like wildfire. The village turned out *en masse*. Father Letheby had to stand such a cross-fire of blessings and questions and prayers, that we decided he had better clear out on Thursday. Besides, there was an invitation from Father Duff to meet a lot of the brethren at an *agape* at his house on Thursday night, when Father

Letheby would be *en route*. God bless me! I thought that evening we'd never get the little mare under way. The people thronged round the little trap, kissed the young curate's hand, kissed the lapels of his coat, demanded his blessing a hundred times, fondled the mare and patted her head, until at last, slowly, as a glacier pushing its moraine before it, we wedged our way through a struggling mass of humanity.

" God be wid you, a hundred times! "

" And may His Blessed Mother purtect you! "

" And may your journey thry wid you! "

" Yerra, the bishop, 'oman, could not get on widout him. That's the raison! "

" Will we iver see ye agin, yer reverence? "

Then a deputation of the " Holy Terrors " came forward to ask him let his name remain as their honorary president.

" We'll never see a man again to lift a ball like yer reverence."

" No, nor ye'll niver see the man agin that cud rise a song like him! " said Jem Deady.

Father Letheby had gone down in the afternoon to see Alice. Alice had heard, and Alice was crying with lonely grief. He took up her small white hand.

" Alice," he said, " I came to thank you, my child, for all that you have done for me. Your prayers, your tears, but, above all, your noble example of endurance under suffering, have been an ineffable source of strength to me. I have wavered where you stood firm under the cross—— "

" Oh, Father, don't, don't! " sobbed the poor girl.

" I must," he said; " I must tell you that your courage and constancy have shamed and strengthened me a hundredfold. And now you must pray for me. I dare say I have yet further trials before me; for I seem to be one of those who shall have no peace without the cross. But I need strength, and that you will procure for me."

" Father, Father! " said the poor girl, " it is you that

have helped me. Where would I be to-day if you had not shown me the Crucified behind the cross?"

He laid in her outstretched hand a beautiful prayer-book; and thus they parted, as two souls should part, knowing that an invisible link in the Heart of Christ held them still together.

The parting with Bittra was less painful. He promised often to run over and remain at the "Great House," where he had seen some strange things. Nor did he forget his would-be benefactress, Nell Cassidy. He found time to be kind to all.

What a dinner was that at Father Duff's! Was there ever before such a tumult of gladness, such Alleluias of resurrection, such hip! hip! hurrahs! such grand and noble speeches? The brave fellows had joined hands, and dragged the beaten hero from the battlefield, and set the laurels on his head. Then they all wanted to become my curates, for " Kilronan spells promotion now, you know." But I was too wise to make promises. As we were parting for the night, I heard Father Letheby say to Duff:—

" I am under everlasting obligations to you. But you shall have that boat money the moment it comes from the Insurance Office. And those sewing-machines are lying idle over there; they may be of use to you here."

" All right! Send them over, and we'll give you a clear receipt. Look here, Letheby, it's I who am under obligations to you. I had a lot of these dirty shekels accumulated since I was in Australia; and I'm ashamed to say it, I had three figures to my credit down there at the National Bank. If I died in that state, 'twould be awful. Now I have a fairly easy conscience, thanks again to you!"

When I reached my room that ev—morning, I was shocked and startled to find the hour hand of my watch pointing steadily to two A.M. I rubbed my eyes. Impossible! I held the watch to my ear. It beat rhythmically. I shook my head. Then, as I sat down in a com-

fortable armchair, I held a long debate with myself as to
whether it was my night prayers or my morning prayers I
should say. I compromised with my conscience, and said
them both together under one formula. But when I lay
down to rest, but not to sleep, the wheels began to re-
volve rapidly. I thought of a hundred brilliant things
which I could have said at the dinner table, but didn't.
Such coruscations of wit, such splendid periods, were
never heard before. Then my conscience began to trouble
me. Two A.M.! two A.M.! two A.M.! I tried back through
all my philosophers for an apology. Horace, my old
friend, came back from the shades of Orcus.

> " Dulce est desipere in loco,"

said he. Thank you, Flaccus! You were always ready :

> " Quandoque bonus dormitat Homerus,"

he cried, as he vanished into the shades. Then came
Ovid, laurel-crowned, and began to sing :—

> " Somne, quies rerum, placidissime somne deorum! "

But I dismissed him promptly. Then Seneca hobbled
in, old usurer as he was, and said :—

> " Commodis omnium læteris, movearis incommodis."

" Good man! " I cried; " that's just me! "
Then came dear, gentle St. Paul, with the look on his
face as when he pleaded for the slave :—

> " Rejoice with them that rejoice, and weep with them that
> weep! "

Lastly, came my own Kempensis, who shook his head
gravely at me, and said :—

> " A merry evening makes a sad morning! "

I like à Kempis; but indeed, and indeed, and indeed
again, Thomas, you are sometimes a little too personal
in your remarks,

CHAPTER XXXI

FAREWELL

THOMAS À KEMPIS was right in saying that next morning would be a sad one—not on account of previous merriment; but, as I drove home alone, the separation from Father Letheby affected me keenly. He had, to use a homely phrase, grown into my heart. Analysing my own feelings, as I jogged along the country road, I found that it was not his attractive and polished manner, nor his splendid abilities, nor his sociability that had impressed me, but his open, manly character, for ever bending to the weak, and scorning everything dishonourable. It was quite true that he " wore the white flower of a blameless life "; but that is expected and found in every priest; it was something else—his manliness, his truth, that made him

> " —my own ideal knight,
> Who reverenced his conscience as his king,
> Whose glory was, redressing human wrong;
> Who spake no slander, no, nor listened to it.
> . . . . .
> . . . We have lost him; he is gone;
> We know him now; all narrow jealousies
> Are silent; and we see him as he moved,
> How modest, kindly, all-accomplished, wise,
> With what sublime repression of himself,
> And in what limits, and how tenderly! "

My poor boy! my poor boy! I thought he would be over me in my last hour to hear my last confession, and place the sacred oils on my old limbs, and compose me decently for my grave; but it was not to be. *Vale, vale longum vale* !

There was a letter from the bishop, and a large brown parcel before me when I reached my home. I opened the letter first. It ran thus:—

My dear Father Dan:—The prebendary stall, vacated by the death of the late Canon Jones, I now have much pleasure in offering for your acceptance. I suppose, if the *to prepon* always had force in this world, you would have been canon for the last twenty or thirty years; but at least it is my privilege now to make compensation; and I sincerely hope I may have the benefit of your wise counsel in the meetings of the Cathedral Chapter. It will also give you a chance of seeing sometimes your young friend, whom I have so suddenly removed; and this will weigh with you in accepting an honour which, if it has come tardily, may it be your privilege to wear for many years.

I am, my dear Father Dan,
Yours in Christ,

_____

" Kind, my Lord, always kind and thoughtful," I murmured.

Then I cut the strings of the parcel. It contained the rochet, mozzetta, and biretta of a canon, and was a present from some excellent Franciscan nuns, to whom I had been formerly chaplain, and who were charitable enough not to have forgotten me. So there they were at last, the dream of half a lifetime. God help us! what children we are! Old and young, it's all the same. I suppose that is why God so loves us.

I took up the dainty purpled and ermined mozzetta. It was soft, and beautiful, and fluffy. I could fold the entire rochet in the palms of my hands, the lace-work was so fine and exquisite. I put them down with a sigh. My mind was fully made up.

Hannah came in and took in the situation at a glance.

" Did he give 'em to ye at last? "

" He did, Hannah. How do you like them? "

" 'Twas time for him! Lor', they're beautiful! "

" Hannah," I said, " have you any camphor or lavender in the house? "

She looked at me suspiciously.

" I have," she said. " What for? Aren't you going to wear them? "

" They are not intended to form the every-day walking-suit of a country parish priest," I replied. " They must be carefully put by for the present."

I took my hat and strolled down to see Alice. After telling her all the news, and Father Letheby's triumphs, I said:—

" The bishop wants me to change my name, too! "

" *You* are not going? " she said in alarm.

" No; but his Lordship thinks I have been called Father Dan long enough; he wants me now to be known as the Very Rev. Canon Hanrahan."

" It's like as if you were going away to a strange country," she said.

" Do you think the people will take kindly to it? " I said.

" No! no! no! " she cried, shaking her head; " you will be Father Dan and Daddy Dan to the end."

" So be it! " I replied.

I returned home, and just before dinner I penned two letters—one to my good nuns, thanking them for their kindness and generosity; the other to the bishop, thanking his Lordship *ex imo corde* also, but declining the honour. I was too old, *et detur digniori*. Then I got my camphor and lavender, and laid the fragrant powder between the folds of the mozzetta. And then I took a sheet of paper and wrote:—

To the
Very Reverend Edward Canon Letheby, B.A., P.P.,
a gift from the grave
of his old friend and pastor,
the Rev. Daniel Hanrahan, P.P.,
more affectionately and familiarly known as
" Daddy Dan."

Then the old temptation came back to wind up with a lecture or quotation. I ransacked all my classics, and met with many a wise and pithy saying, but not one pleased me. I was about to give up the search in despair, when, taking up a certain book, my eye caught a familiar red pencil-mark. " Eureka! " I cried, and I wrote in large letters, beneath the above : —

> " Amico, Io vivendo cercava conforto
> Nel Monte Parnasso;
> Tu, meglio consigliato, cercalo
> Nel Calvario."

I placed this last testament in the folds of the lace, tied the parcel carefully, carefully put it away, and, after the untasted dinner had been removed, I lowered the lamp-flame, and sat, God only knows how lonely! as I had sat twelve months before, in my armchair, listening for the patter of the horse's hoofs, and the knock at the door, and the sounds of alighting, that were to mark the advent of

MY NEW CURATE.

MORE MERCIER BESTSELLERS

The Walk of a Queen

The Weldons of Tibradden

Annie M. P. Smithson

Annie M. P. Smithson (1873-1948) was the most successful of all Irish romantic novelists. The twenty-two books she wrote were all bestsellers.

In *The Walk of a Queen* the scene is set in Dublin during the War of Independence and it is a gripping story of passion and intrigue which holds the reader's interest from start to finish.

The Weldons of Tibradden follows the fortunes of three generations of the Weldon family beginning in the 1870s and ending in 1935. It is a fascinating story of success, courage, love and betrayal.

****

The Farm by Lough Gur

Mary Carbery

The English born Mary Toulmin came to Ireland and fell in love with
Lord Carbery of Castlefreke, County Cork and his Irish background.
She learned the Irish customs and traditions and wrote about her
adopted heritage. In *The Farm by Lough Gur* she records the
memoirs of an old woman who spent her youth on a nineteenth century Irish farm.

This is the true story of a family who lived on a farm by Lough Gur,
the Enchanted Lake, in County Limerick. Their home, shut away
from the turmoil of politics, secure from apprehension of unemploy-
ment and want, was a world in itself. The master with his men, the
mistress with her maids worked in happy unity. The four little girls,
growing up in this contented atmosphere, dreamed of saints and
fairies. They lived in a rare world where the piper in the chimney
corner piped jigs and country dances; the wandering fiddler played
Mozart while the spinning-woman whirled her wheel; the old
dancing master in knee breeches and velvet coat chasseed and
pirouetted in his buckle shoes. Of course they had real problems and
ambitions but their literal and dream world fused into a lovely background of growing, learning and loving.

The story is also a picture of manners and customs in a place so
remote that religion had still to reckon with pagan survivals, where
a fairy-doctor cured the landlord's bewitched cows, and a banshee
comforted the dying with the music of harp and flutes.

* * * * * * * * * *

Folktales of the Irish Countryside

Kevin Danaher

Nowadays there is a whole generation growing up who cannot remember a time when there was no television; and whose parents cannot remember a time when there was no radio and cinema. It is not, therefore, surprising that many of them wonder what people in country places found to do with their time in the winters of long ago. People may blink in astonishment when reminded of the fact that the night was often too short for those past generations of country people, whose own entertainment with singing, music, dancing, cards, indoor games, and storytelling spanned the evenings and into morning light.

Kevin Danaher remembers forty of the stories that enlivened those past days. Some are stories told by members of his own family; others he took down in his own countryside from the last of the traditional storytellers. Included are stories of giants, of ghosts, of wondrous deeds, queer happenings, of the fairies and the great kings of Ireland who had beautiful daughters and many problems.

A homely, heartwarming collection of tales that spring naturally from the heart of the Irish countryside.

* * * * * *

Stories for Preachers

James A. Feehan

Part of the challenge facing the preacher today is getting the message across Sunday after Sunday. Only too often he faces a television saturated congregation which seems either unwilling or unable to listen to him. If he doesn't actually hear the click of the switch-off, then one glance at the glazed looks in the pews should convince him that the pulpit may well be losing the battle with the box.

Stories for Preachers is written from a conviction that the massive boredom in our churches today stems from the fact that the average Sunday worshipper is incapable of sustained listening for more than a few minutes. If it can't be said in six to seven minutes it can't be got across at all. The short homily calls for long and painstaking preparation and needs to be illuminated by apt and imaginative illustrations.

Christ taught and preached in stories. His stories were from real life; stories about farmers and fishermen, weddings and wakes, self-righteous humbugs and prodigal sons. The preacher today is faced with the challenge of bringing the reality of Christ to a people bewildered by the fantasies of the media.

Stories for Preachers is an attempt to meet this challenge through the storytelling process. Its aim is to assist the preacher in proclaiming the 'old, old story' and in the process perhaps sow the seeds from which his own creative thoughts will develop.